These Boots Were Made For
Made For
STOMPING

Julie Kenner
Jade Lee
Marianne Mancusi

LOVE SPELL NEW YORK CITY

LOVE SPELL®

April 2008

Published by

Dorchester Publishing Co., Inc.
200 Madison Avenue
New York, NY 10016

ISBN 10: 0-505-52760-X
ISBN 13: 978-0-505-52760-8

Visit us on the web at www.dorchesterpub.com.

THESE BOOTS WERE MADE FOR STOMPING

USA TODAY BESTSELLER
JULIE KENNER

"Kenner [has a] flair for dialogue and eccentric character-izations."

—*Publishers Weekly*

"Ms. Kenner doesn't need mystical powers…to command the love and adoration of her followers. She's earned that the old-fashioned way—with unmistakable talent and a wonderful imagination."

—*Reader to Reader Reviews*

USA TODAY BESTSELLER
JADE LEE

"Make room on your shelf for Lee next to Thea Devine, Robin Schone and Cheryl St. John."

—*RT BOOKreviews*

"Lee's deft eroticism hasn't lost any of its power…[her] star continues to burn bright."

—*Booklist* on *Burning Tigress*

EMMY AWARD WINNER
MARIANNE MANCUSI

"A sparkling debut…a nice twist on the modern girl's search for prince charming."

—*Publishers Weekly* on *A Connecticut Fashionista in King Arthur's Court*

"Mancusi's witty, tongue-in-cheek remarks and sprightly dialogue make for a joy ride of a read."

—*RT BOOKreviews* on *What, No Roses?*

These Boots Were Made For
STOMPING

TABLE OF CONTENTS

Julie Kenner

A Step in
the Right Direction

To Catherine & Isabella,
my two little supergirls.

Nikko:

Council Intelligence reports that adverse activity is currently being undertaken in the New York area by mortal Council archenemy Rex Ruthless, in part through the use of recently pilfered patented Council technology allowing the user to dis- and reintegrate at will locally, as well as teleport to certain preselected destinations in either an integrated or disintegrated state.

As you are aware, all tools, devices, inventions and other paraphernalia invented and/or acquired by Protectors (including but not limited to those Protectors with the particular power of inventive ability) remains Council property, and any Protector found to have facilitated the removal of such technology to Outcast or non-Protector entities will be severely reprimanded.

Your immediate assistance with regard to the capture of Ruthless (and his cohorts, to the extent discoverable) as well as the return of said technology, is hereby requested, and you are required to report to the Manhattan Field Office immediately for further briefing and instruction.

Form 89-C(2)(a), on file with the Mortal-Protector Liaison Office (MLO), indicates that you have already been issued the following Council-controlled items (to the extent such list is incorrect, please immediately submit Form 29-B(2)(a) in triplicate with all necessary corrections):

> Propulsion cloak, model E-10 (expert model);
> and
> standard issue cellular phone (speed dial included) with full Web access, direct communication to Council headquarters, laser pulse capability, and Always-On Deception Detector® with text-message result display

Upon your arrival at the Manhattan Field Office, you will be issued a Mission Essentials Kit, including all standard mission equipment. To the extent such equipment is utilized during the course of your mission, please file in triplicate (by no later than the fifteenth day of the first month after completion of your mission) Form 827A(4)(b) with the MLO. Return all unused equipment to Council headquarters.

We look forward to your prompt arrival at the Field Office. Excuses for late arrivals will not be tolerated.

As a side note with regard to your particular circumstances, please be reminded that you remain on probation for previous indiscretions. Additional lapses in judgment requiring intervention from MLO specialists will not be tolerated.

Thank you for your attention to this matter, and have a great day!

Sincerely,

Phelonium Prigg
Phelonium Prigg
Assistant to Zephron, High Elder
PP:jbk

CHAPTER ONE

"Come on, Ruthless," whispered Nikko, peering down at the street through his Council-issued binocs from the observation deck of the Empire State Building. "Come on, you scum-sucker. Show yourself."

Three months. Three long, dull, hideous months he'd been forced into this assignment. Dragged away from his Colorado mountain retreat and shoved into the bright lights and endless noise of the big city he'd been forced out of five years ago. And why? To catch Rex Ruthless: a conniving madman that no one else could manage to get their hands on, a madman who'd just about managed to piece together complicated technology capable of actually shrinking New York City—Manhattan and all the other boroughs—to an infinitesimal fraction of its actual size. So small, in fact, that the landmass would fit inside a snow globe. Which, naturally, was exactly where Ruthless intended to stick the island if the Powers That Be didn't meet his demands.

Not that any of those Powers yet knew about the threat. It had only been through Nikko's long-standing underworld contacts that he'd learned what Ruthless was up to. More, he'd learned that Ruthless still needed one more component before his contraption was operational.

Nikko's original mission to retrieve the stolen Council equipment had immediately been upgraded, and now he was in charge of stopping Ruthless altogether by whatever means necessary. And, of course, that meant preventing Ruthless from getting his hands on that final component.

What that component was, though—about that, Nikko had no clue. His sources could say only that it focused energy, but considering that the Learning Annex courses advertised the same, although in a more metaphysical sense, the clue was hardly earth-shattering.

Equally troubling was the fact that, though Ruthless was purely mortal, he was enough of an inventor that he could hold his own in a fight. Worse, he'd recently stolen a device invented by little Davie Murphy, a prepubescent Halfling genius. The device, about the size of a billfold, let Ruthless disintegrate and reintegrate things at will, *and* also teleport himself to a preselected destination. A pretty cool invention when you got right down to it, though there were those in the Council who dissed the thing simply because it was invented by a Halfling—and a child at that. Personally, Nikko didn't care. So what if a Halfling had one mortal parent? They still had Protector blood, were still descended from the Greek and Roman gods (who, of course, weren't really mythological beings at all, though mortals from Homer to Edith Hamilton had done a great job weaving a fabulous cover story).

Of course, being a full-blooded Protector—complete with all the standard powers like speed, strength and agility, and even individualized powers like his own ability to melt weapons—didn't make life all sunshine and roses. Nikko had learned *that* the hard way after his one tiny little mistake had left him ostracized, censured, and essentially abandoned to his Colorado cabin. The Venerate

Council of Protectors—the ruling body for all with
Protector blood—had doled out the punishment, and
Nikko had accepted it. Now, they'd called him back, os-
tensibly to give him a second chance at becoming an ac-
tive member of the Protector community again. Nikko,
however, was certain there was an ulterior motive. Like,
maybe, the fact that Ruthless's shrinking device *might* be
considered a weapon. And, if so, then Nikko *might* be able
to use his powers to melt it.

He doubted that the definition of "weapon" applied,
though. More than that, since the thing wasn't finished, it
was still technically harmless. Which meant his particular
power was useless against it. And *that* meant he was stuck
in a regular mission, trying to track down a bad guy who
was trying to acquire a bit of contraband. He felt like a cop
participating in a sting. Or at least what he assumed a cop
would feel like. Nikko tended to watch a lot of police dra-
mas in his Colorado retreat.

At first he'd been excited about the assignment. But
after months of chasing bogus leads, he was just plain
frustrated. It was bad enough that he didn't have solid information. What made it worse was that with the stolen
teleportation device, Ruthless could bounce all over creation, and unless Nikko's information was beyond solid,
catching him was next to impossible.

So far, Nikko's intelligence was decidedly mushy.

And each and every day that passed, Nikko cursed the
unknown idiot who hadn't protected Davie's teleportation
invention with the care it deserved, probably assuming
that a half mortal, half Protector kid couldn't invent anything either useful or dangerous.

What was that old saying about never assuming anything?

Not that Nikko could waste time with might-have-beens,

he thought as he focused the binocs on the sidewalk below; Davie's device had been stolen long before he'd been sucked into the game. Now he needed to find Ruthless's lair, destroy or secure Ruthless's technology, and then secure the man himself. All of which was made a heck of a lot harder by the villain's fascination with dis- and reintegrating himself all over the city.

Not to mention the fact that Nikko couldn't simply grab the man. No, that would be too easy. Instead, the Council had made clear (and he had to reluctantly agree that the mandate made sense) that the shrinking device was the first priority. Because while Ruthless might be the brains of his operation, he had a lot of automaton followers, any of whom would be happy to step up to the plate, flip a switch, and win one for the Gipper.

All of it boiled down to one simple reality: Nikko was stuck in New York until he got a lead on the location of Ruthless's lair, and so instead of being a quick in-and-out mission, this assignment had turned into a scavenger hunt. And *that*, frankly, was making him even grumpier than the constant stares and finger-pointings on those days when he bothered to walk down the city streets rather than traveling by stealthed propulsion cloak.

You would think he'd be used to it by now, every time some nine-year-old pointed and squealed, "Wow! Look! That guy looks just like the Silver Streak!" Nikko wanted to rewind his life by five years, two months and fourteen days. Before he'd made the mistake of jumping off this very observation deck.

On that fateful day Reed Mystory (a pen name if ever Nikko heard one) had seen him and found comic book inspiration . . . in Nikko. The truly annoying mortal Reed had taken what he'd seen, including Nikko's appearance, right down to the battle scar that ran across his left eyebrow and caused it to permanently quirk up, and turned it all—looks and powers—into an instantly popular comic book character. And that wildly popular first issue had not only immortalized Nikko in ways other than the standard Protector longevity but also directly resulted in Nikko getting put on probationary status.

Because, while a Protector leaping off a tall building without an invisibility cloak in front of a crowd of mortals might be overlooked so long as the Mortal-Protector Liaison Office could concoct a reasonable cover story, if one of the crowd members happened to be a comic book writer . . .

Unfortunately for Nikko, the Council frowned on that kind of publicity. As he'd heard innumerable times during his many administrative hearings, the role of the MLO was to cover up Protector activity, a task made exponentially more difficult when every corner newsstand was essentially advertising Protector exploits.

He really hadn't stood a chance.

And now that two movies had come out to huge box office success, he figured he'd lost whatever chance he might have had for appeal.

In truth, he didn't much mind. He'd been happy to leave the city. Happy to have the chance to relax. He'd been on the go for years, bringing down some of the baddest of the bad. And three months ago he'd been *this* close to figuring out not only *how* to fly-fish but also *why* mortals bothered. Then the Council called him back in for this sorry assignment.

Sometimes, he thought, life really wasn't fair.

Right now, though, it turned a tiny bit fairer. Because who should step into his field of vision but the man himself, Rex Ruthless, surrounded by a flock of cronies, practically genuflecting before him.

"I have so got you," Nikko whispered, pulling his propulsion cloak out of his mission supply bag. Flying over the streets of Manhattan might be verboten, but he'd convinced the Council that this mission justified the use of one of the experimental propulsion cloaks—the new model with both the invisibility feature *and* jet propulsion *and* built-in radar and night vision goggles. All he had to do was get the dang invisibility component working, then swoop down and follow Ruthless to his lair; neither Ruthless nor the folks treading the early morning Manhattan streets would be the wiser.

Since his entire plan hinged on the invisibility feature functioning, naturally it failed.

"Hopping Hades," he muttered under his breath, even as the elevator leading up to the observation deck dinged. He checked his watch and silently cursed again. The invisibility feature had functioned fine two hours ago when he'd flown up here before the deck's official opening time. Why had his four-point-three seconds of good luck run out right then, with the public arriving *and* the cloak malfunctioning? Honestly, you'd think the Fates had it in for him.

He pulled his cloak off and turned it over, hoping he could diagnose the problem before whoever was getting off the elevator noticed him or, worse, before Ruthless slipped into a limousine and Nikko lost track of him. No such luck. Not only was a limo pulling up to the curb right that very minute, but a preadolescent male voice behind Nikko screeched, "Mom! Mom! Look at that guy! It's the Silver Streak! I know it, Mom! Check out his scar! I know it, I know it!"

"Eddie," a woman whispered, her soft voice carrying on the wind, "that poor man probably gets compared to that character all the time. Don't go bothering him. He's probably sick to death of it."

"But it *is* him, Mom! I'm sure of it."

"Eddie," she repeated, her voice this time stern.

And though Nikko would have preferred to sit there innocuously, silently proving the mom right, he knew he didn't have that option. Ruthless was already in the limo, and it was poised to pull away from the curb as soon as traffic cleared. He'd spent three weeks chasing the lead that had allowed him to track Ruthless to this location, and he wasn't about to lose the villain now. Who knew when he'd have such good intelligence again?

The limo accelerated, its front bumper nudging into traffic. *Hopping Hades.* He had only seconds to make a decision. Leap off the building and he could follow the limo easily with the propulsion cloak, but with the invisibility feature broken, Eddie would see him flying and undoubtedly spread the word. More than that, the deck was now filling, and some of these folks had video cameras. No hiding his antics from the Council. He'd be plastered all over blogs and YouTube within hours.

Do nothing, though, and Ruthless would get away. For all Nikko knew, the monster was mere hours from finishing his device, which meant that by nightfall, the whole island of Manhattan could be the size of a Saltine.

Honestly, it was a no-brainer, he decided; and he stood up, whipped the cloak around his shoulders, then bent at the knees and shot up into the sky, the power of the cloak thrumming through his body as he twisted to start his descent to the street.

And then, just because he was feeling a little devious, he paused over little Eddie and fired off a single Silver Streak salute to the gaping, gawking child.

If he was going down, he might as well go down big.

CHAPTER TWO

"You're still here?"

The voice came from above, and Lydia Carmichael tilted her head up, her gaze following a path of comic book pages she'd taped to the interior wall of her teensy cubicle until she found herself looking into a pair of smugly superior dusky brown eyes.

"If you'd quit wasting all your time reading that trash, you'd get your work done fast enough to get out of here at a normal hour," Darla Dingbat sniped. Okay, so her name wasn't actually Dingbat, but if there were justice in the world, it would be.

Lydia opened her mouth to tell Darla to: a) mind her own business, and b) get a freaking clue. It just so happened that Lydia had finished every scrap of work in her cubicle *plus* reviewed her neighbor Jason's expense report over three hours ago. She was still in the office for the sole, limited and highly irritating reason that her boss, the infinitely obnoxious Martin Stout, insisted he wanted to talk to her about a cost-benefit analysis she'd turned in before lunch.

He, however, was chatting on the phone in his office, oblivious to the fact that it was well after five and he was wasting her time. And she, Lydia, was sitting in her tiny blue cloth–framed prison cell, seething, her irritation kept at bay only with massive doses of *X-Men*, Season 8 of *Buffy the Vampire Slayer*, a few classic *Wonder Womans*, and, of course, her entire collection of *Silver Streak* comics. Because when she was in a really pissy mood, about the only thing that calmed her down was losing herself in the fantasy of . . . well, losing herself in the dark, sexy, slightly bad-boy arms of the Silver Streak, with his sexy scar and his superpowers. In addition to the standard superhero fare, the Silver Streak could melt weapons. In the comics, he was also always melting women's hearts.

That, of course, really was a fantasy. As much as Lydia might dream of the perfect man—sweet, funny, strong, capable and, yes, a superhero (it was fantasy, after all)—it wasn't as if she'd ever land such a guy. Even if she tripped over him on the street, she'd probably manage little more than a mumble and a shy attempt at communication. Was it any wonder she liked to lose herself in comic book fantasies where she could be a hero, too? Saving the world even while saving herself at the same time?

Not that Lydia relayed any of this to Darla. Instead, she said, "Yeah. You're right. Whatever," then dipped her head back down, her cheeks burning merely from the effort of that tiny bit of defiance.

Get a backbone, Carmichael.

Lydia scowled, ignoring the voice in her head that sounded remarkably like her best friend Amy's familiar drone. Amy repeatedly told Lydia she needed to stand up for herself. For that matter, Amy also repeatedly told Lydia she needed to get up her nerve to talk to a man. Any man. What Amy failed to ever do was give Lydia a clue how she was supposed to manage either of those things.

"Have a *nice* evening," Darla said, the sneer in her voice matching the one on her face. Then she turned sharply and sashayed down the corridor, balancing on her designer shoes, swinging her designer bag, and looking for all the world like a woman who always got exactly what she wanted. In other words, the antithesis of Lydia.

It's not so bad, Lydia thought. *Who'd want to be like Darla, anyway?*

But a tiny voice inside her head answered up: *Me*.

Okay, so the truth was, she didn't want to *be* Darla (because, you know, what a bee-yatch), but there were certain Darla-esque qualities it would be nice to acquire. Like, oh, the ability to talk to someone without turning all shades of purple.

She went back to her comic books, even burning through the stash of fanfic Silver Streak novellas she'd found on eBay, while she waited for Mr. Stout. Nothing.

What she needed to do was get up, march down the hall and firmly and resolutely tell Mr. Stout that she was waiting. What she did was pull up her Internet browser, pop over to eBay, and start searching for good deals on vintage comics.

Typical.

Her whole life—or at least since she'd been five—she's turned to comic books when she couldn't quite get up the nerve to face real life. Comics soothed her. More than that, they spoke to her. Comics were a window to another world. A world that was happening all around, if only people would wake up and pay attention.

Or maybe the superheroes needed to just stop hiding.

She frowned, remembering that summer right before she'd turned six. Her parents hadn't believed her when she'd told them what she'd seen, and when the newspapers printed a perfectly reasonable explanation for how the baby had survived being tossed out of a moving limousine, that had been the end of it. Everyone had assumed that Lydia had a vivid imagination rather than really good eyesight. But even now Lydia could remember the spectacle that had played out before her. How the warm, thick air had felt across her face as she'd stood on the sidewalk in Times Square, stared goggle-eyed at—

Thud, thump!

She sat bold upright, her memories vanishing in a poof. Footsteps. Finally, there were footsteps, and she sat up straighter, anticipating Mr. Stout's bellow, calling her back into his office.

It didn't come.

She scowled at the side of her cubicle, checking out the pink kitty clock with the ticktock tail. Already past seven o'clock. *Damn.*

She frowned, then slumped down in her seat and started throwing Velcro darts at the side of her cubicle. Then she stopped, realizing that maybe—just maybe—Mr. Stout had shot off an e-mail asking her to pop down to his office and—*finally*—go over those reports she'd spent the last two days hammering out.

She pulled up her e-mail and skimmed through the incoming messages. Nothing. She clicked over to the junk mail folder in case the computer thought Mr. Stout was spam. Nothing.

She considered walking down to his office and telling him that she was supposed to meet Amy for dinner, and even if she left right this very minute she'd still be late. And *that*, frankly, would suck. Because after two years of trying for a baby, Amy and Cash had finally managed to get pregnant, and exactly five months and twenty-seven days ago, Lydia's goddaughter Chenda had been born.

Lydia wanted to tell Mr. Stout what a big deal this dinner was, because Amy so rarely went anywhere without Chenda these days. Lydia was craving girl night with her best friend, and Mr. Stout's tardiness was completely messing it up. She needed to get off her butt, march down to his office, and tell him exactly that.

Except, she didn't. No surprise there. Just the idea of telling Mr. Stout—or any boss—to get a move on was enough to give her heart palpitations. Actually *doing* it? Um, no thank you very much.

No, no, no. She had to start getting a little backbone. How painful could it be? It wasn't like he was going to fire her on the spot. All she had to do was push back the chair, stand up, walk out of the cubicle, march down the hall, knock on Mr. Stout's office, and then—

What?

She frowned, considering. Asking him what the holdup was wouldn't work. No way. Even if she could manage to grow some backbone in the next five minutes, that was really too ballsy to hope for.

But, maybe, possibly, perhaps she could poke her head in the door and say she heard something and had he called her? That would be good, right? And even if he said no, surely it would remind him that she'd been sitting out there waiting for him for one hour and fifty-seven minutes. She could do that. Right? *Right.*

Lydia took a deep breath, pushed back her chair, stepped out of her cubicle, and ran smack into Martin Stout.

"Oh!"

"Carmichael," he said, his caterpillar eyebrows wiggling as his brow furrowed. He glanced down at his watch. "What are you doing here at this hour?"

"I . . . um . . . I . . ."

"Gotta get more efficient there, Carmichael. You see anybody else here now?"

"No, sir," she squeaked.

"They got their work done and went home. That's the

point, young lady. Gotta learn to balance work and life."
He gave her a friendly pat on the shoulder.

"But . . ." She froze, the words trapped in her throat.

"Well, speak up," he said. "I'm late for drinks."

She drew in a breath. "The cost-benefit analysis sir. I
thought—"

"That's exactly my point," he said. "That should be on
my desk. Get it to me in the morning, and we'll overlook
that it's late this once."

"But—"

He lifted a finger, then cocked it. "You finish and lock
up," he said. "Get that report in, and this conversation
stays in the past. *Capiche?*"

She swallowed, her mouth working, but nothing coming out.

Say something, she shouted in her head. *The report's done.
It's been done and on your desk for half the day. I've been waiting in this stupid cubicle for hours to talk to you about it because
you told me to.*

The words didn't come. And as she stood there, her
mouth hanging open and her tongue tied in a knot, Martin
Stout walked down the hall, pushed the button for the elevator, and disappeared.

Damn.

"Tell me you're kidding," Amy said, tapping a perfectly
manicured nail on the tabletop. "You have *got* to be kidding."

Lydia took a long draw on her piña colada, managing to
finish off half the glass in one suck. Other than that,
though, she ignored the question.

"Honestly, Lyd, do I have to tie you down and shove a
steel bar up your butt?"

"Excuse me?"

"Dude! To give you some backbone."

"That is positively gross," Lydia protested. "A steel bar?"

Amy waved the words away. "Got your attention, didn't it? That's what you need, my friend. A great big wake-up call. You need something to happen where you *have* to stand up for yourself."

"I think that happened two hours ago," Lydia said, thinking of the debacle with Mr. Stout. "And in case you weren't paying attention, I blew it."

"*See?*" Amy said, inexplicably. "That's what I'm talking about?"

"What?"

"Just now. That tone that you took with me right this very second. You were standing up for yourself."

"Well, sure. You said—"

"My point," Amy said with a haughty wave of her hand, "is that you're perfectly capable of standing up for yourself. You simply don't do it when it counts."

"Okay. So?"

"So, why not? Why stand up to me and not Mr. Stout?"

"Um, because I know you? And because Mr. Stout is my boss and could fire me, or tell me I'm an idiot and suck at my job. Or demote me to the mail room or something."

"But do you really think he would? I mean, *do* you suck at your job?"

"No," Lydia said automatically. Because she didn't. She simply never had the guts to tell Mr. Stout as much.

"Exactly," Amy said, leaning back in her seat and crossing her arms over her chest in a case-closed sort of manner.

Lydia shook her head, clueless. "And your point is?"

"Confidence," Amy said. "We need to find something that's going to make you as self-confident around Mr. Stout as you are around me. Or, hell, even twenty-five percent as confident. I mean, honey, you don't have anywhere to go but up."

True enough. "But how?"

"A talisman. A token. Something that you can have on you to remind you that you're a competent, successful woman who has the right to stand up for herself and—surprise, surprise—actually knows how to do it, even if you forget half the time."

"A talisman will do all that?" Lydia quipped. "What are you thinking of? A voodoo doll? I poke pins in my confidence centers and figure that will be good enough?"

"We could try that," Amy said, her lips pursing in concentration. "But maybe something less complicated at first. Take me. I've got my Scooby-Doo underwear."

"Well, yeah," Lydia said, remembering how her best friend had—ever since high school—worn Scooby-Doo panties whenever she had a big test, presentation, date—anything important. "But I don't like Scooby-Doo."

"Heretic," Amy said. "And I'm not thinking that for you, anyway. No, I think you need something a teensy bit more than underwear." She tapped her index finger against pursed lips as her eyes skimmed over Lydia. "Yeah," she said, in the kind of voice that always made Lydia very, very nervous. "Definitely a little bit more."

"I don't look like me," Lydia protested, looking in the mirror at the face staring back at her. It was a pretty face—no, a stunning face—but certainly not a familiar one.

"Don't be stupid," Amy said. "It *is* you. So of course it looks like you. It's just you with eyeliner, shadow, blush, powder, and some lip gloss. If you'd ever once bothered to step into Sephora . . ." She trailed off, clearly deeply offended by Lydia's failure to bend to the power of the cosmetics gurus.

"It's not that I don't appreciate it," Lydia said. "But I don't think it's really doing the trick." She pursed her lips at her reflection, waiting for that little *oomph* of confidence. *Nada.*

"Not even with the hair?" Amy asked, sounding so disappointed that Lydia had to rush to reassure her.

"No, no," she said. "The hair is great. Love the hair. But, well, do you really think highlights are my thing?" She tilted her head, admiring the way the golden streaks seemed to shimmer against the tawny brown that a few hours earlier had seemed so plain. Okay, yes. So maybe it really did look good. But still—

"It's not like hair is going to do it for me," Lydia insisted. "That's just not who I am. Besides, is a makeover really a talisman? I thought you said I needed a talisman."

"Patience, grasshopper," Amy said. "That's the last step. And lucky you, we've already reached the penultimate step in my plan to completely rehabilitate you. Clothes."

Lydia looked around dubiously. "We're in my apartment."

"Yup," Amy said. "Because, as luck would have it, your clothes don't suck."

"Thanks. I think."

"Honestly. Come here," Amy said, and Lydia dutifully followed her to the closet, where Amy began pulling out the jeans, shirts and jackets that Lydia collected during her thrift, floor sample, and bargain-shopping excursions. Yes, she might still be on the low rung of the salary ladder (with no way to climb it, if Mr. Stout kept ignoring her) but at least she looked cute down there at the bottom.

"This," Amy said, holding up a pair of black hip-hugger jeans, a low-cut pink shirt with a baby blue lace camisole underneath, and a silver chain-link belt. "Absolutely darling."

"Can't do it," Lydia said, asserting herself just for practice. "No shoes. I haven't got anything in my closet that I like with jeans. Especially not with black jeans."

"I said penultimate, didn't I?" Amy reminded her. "You've hit on the final step. Footwear. The perfect shoe. And not only the perfect shoe," she added, leading Lydia into her living room and parking her in front of her computer. "But shoes that can make your dreams come true."

"Been nipping into my Kahlua stash?" Lydia asked.

"I'm serious," Amy said. She leaned over and put her fingers on the keyboard, then typed, www.hiheelia.com. Immediately a colorful, funky Web page came up, filled with images of shoes, a lot of nice-sounding language and the ultimate promise that a purchase from the site would "get a girl exactly what she needs and wants."

"Um, okaaaaaaay," Lydia said. "And you want me to what?"

"I want you to order shoes," Amy said. "That's all. Just shoes."

"But what about all this stuff about a magical journey?" she asked, waving her hand vaguely at the Web page. "And your heart's desire?"

"That *is* your heart's desire, isn't it?" Amy asked. "To be bolder? More confident?"

"Well, yeah. But I thought maybe I'd take a night class or something. Purchasing footwear from some supposed goddess named Shoestra wasn't exactly what I had in mind. How did you find the site, anyway?"

"In the bathroom."

"Excuse me?"

"It's true," Amy said, defensively. "Or at least that's where the woman found me."

"What woman?"

"I was at lunch with some of the girls from work, and we

were talking about babies and stuff, and I was going into one of my pity-fests since I couldn't get pregnant. And there was this fabulous-looking woman at the next table over, and I had the feeling she'd been listening to our whole conversation. It was freaky."

"And so, what? She threatened to kill you?"

"Sort of."

"*Amy*. Tell. Now."

Amy lifted an imperious eyebrow, making it clear that she was telling the story her way or not at all. "I went to the restroom, and I was sitting there and someone knocked on the stall wall, and then this hand came under. I thought they needed toilet paper, you know? But I looked down, and they were handing *me* toilet paper."

"Um, why?"

"That's what I wondered, and good thing I didn't just use it, right? Because there was a note scribbled on it. And it had the web address and some flowery language about achieving your heart's desire."

"And you *believed* it?"

"No," Amy said. "Actually, I flushed it. But, well, the note ended with an instruction to pass the site address on to someone else who might need it. And the more I thought about it, the more I thought it sounded sincere, and so—"

"And so you thought you'd sucker *me* into the potty site. Great."

Amy frowned, looking thoroughly dejected. "I thought you would have trusted me a little bit more. You're the one always wanting to believe in the supernatural."

"It's superheroes, not the supernatural. And of course I trust you," Lydia said. "But . . . oh. Did you imply—"

Amy shrugged. "After I left the restaurant I decided I was curious. So I logged on." Another shrug. "Shoestra might have had a little something to do with Chendra's arrival."

Lydia's eyes opened wide. She'd never once expected practical, no-nonsense Amy would have put her faith in something as dicey as the Web site of some so-called goddess. A *shoe* goddess of all things!

Still, there was no denying little Chendra. The tiny tot made her presence known every time Lydia came to visit. And wasn't there something to be said for pop psychology? If you believed something, then couldn't you subconsciously make it come true?

Could she believe?

Mentally, she rolled her eyes. No way, no how. But she *could* order a pair of shoes to make her friend happy.

Maybe she could find a pair of shoes on the site that completed her cute new outfit. That was about all she could hope for, really, because she knew damn good and well that no shoe would give her the backbone to stand up to Mr. Stout. *That*, frankly, would require a whole lot more than magic. That would require a whole new Lydia.

And things like that . . . Well, things like that simply didn't happen to ordinary girls from Brooklyn.

CHAPTER THREE

"Let me guess," Nikko said. "You're sending me back to Colorado. Kicking me off the Council. Making me Outcast."

Zephron, the Protectors' white-haired High Elder, smiled indulgently. "Perhaps we can keep that eventuality at bay for a bit longer, eh?"

Nikko slumped in his chair. "It was too much to hope for," he said, drawing a chuckle from the older man.

"Do you truly wish to remain on probation? You do not want to prove yourself and earn back your full Protector rank?"

"Considering I took a flying leap from the Empire State Building in full view of half of Manhattan, I'm thinking that's not a realistic possibility."

"That was an unfortunate circumstance. Certainly we have all appeared to mortals in moments of dire need."

"Have we?"

Zephron shrugged off the question. "Fortunately, the MLO team assigned to the incident has concocted a wonderful cover story. Something involving a circus and an IMAX film, I believe."

"Still a moot point," Nikko said. "Only way I'm getting off probation is to bring down Rex, and I'm beginning to think that's not possible. The man's slippery. If I didn't know better, I'd think he was an Outcast, not a mortal."

"He's mortal," Zephron confirmed, his piercing gaze aimed right at Nikko's face. "But I'm sorry to tell you that you're not too far from the mark."

"What are you—Oh." Nikko pondered the suggestion, running through all the ramifications and not liking how they added up. Not liking it at all. "You're saying he has help? From an Outcast?"

"Not an Outcast," Zephron said, his expression infinitely sad. "From someone within the Council."

"Mother of Zeus!" Nikko said, rising to his feet. "Who? I swear I'll nail the bastard to the wall."

Zephron chuckled, indicating with his hand that Nikko should sit down again. "Your loyalty is to be commended," he said. "Especially considering you've made it no secret that you aren't exactly a Council cheerleader these days."

Nikko shrugged. The truth was, he loved his Colorado retreat. But lately he'd missed the action, the sense of being involved in something big. Something important.

And, yes, there was another factor working on him, too, pushing him to abandon his reclusiveness, to make amends for past mistakes and fight his way back into action: as much as he hated to admit it, he was lonely. He missed his Protector friends. And he damn sure missed Protector women. Sure, there were girls in Colorado, but he'd found none he could really talk to. Not that he'd had a great dating record among his own kind, but at least they shared a common ground.

If anything, the one thing hanging out alone in his beautiful Colorado retreat had taught him, it was that the place was significantly less beautiful without someone to share it with.

All interesting ruminations, he supposed, but hardly of

concern to Zephron at the moment. Nikko took a breath and met the elder's eyes. "I'm a Protector, plain and simple," he finally said. "It was my decision that got me in trouble, and it's going to be my hard work that gets me out of it. *If* I can get out of it. If Ruthless has inside help—"

"The help has been located, apprehended, and appropriately punished," Zephron said, his expression hard. "Of that, I assure you."

"Good," Nikko said.

"I agree," Zephon replied. "But it is good in more ways than one," he said, tossing Nikko a significant look.

Nikko caught it with a grin. "You have information," he said.

"Two pieces of intelligence, actually. Used properly, both should serve you well. Act recklessly, however, and the window of opportunity will not only slam shut, it will be painted and nailed closed."

"Got it," Nikko said, feeling more than a little chastened.

Zephron laughed. "I would give the same speech to anyone. Perhaps you are too touchy about your current situation, and that touchiness is your Achilles' heel? Achilles is, I believe, an ancestor?"

"Very far removed," Nikko said. More directly, Nikko was descended from Nike, the goddess of victory, though lately he'd felt less than victorious on all counts. If Zephron had an "in," Nikko was all over it.

"The difficulty lies in locating Ruthless's lair," Zephron reiterated. "As you know, we have stumbled at every turn, which drove our frustration level exceptionally high, especially prior to learning that he obtained the assistance of one of our own."

"Yeah," Nikko agreed. "That burns."

"Indeed. At any rate, the information we now have sheds light on the problem. His lair, you see, is mobile. More, he has devised a system whereby he never travels directly there. Instead, he disintegrates, then that disembodied form reintegrates at the current location. Tracking him, you see, often ends in nothing more than a wild-goose chase."

"That one I was beginning to learn the hard way," Nikko admitted.

His recent failure had been the direct result of a faulty invisibility module coupled with Ruthless's stolen escape tactic and a mole who had revealed to Ruthless that he was being watched. All in all, a losing situation. Nikko had known it at the time, of course, but he'd decided to take the risk. Who knew when he'd get another solid lead on Ruthless's whereabouts? It just hadn't ended well.

"I screwed up, and I know it. And I'm glad to hear there's a bit of good news hidden somewhere in this mess. Anytime you want to share it, you feel free."

"Patience," Zephron said, his eyes twinkling as he held up a finger. "It is our belief that Ruthless is becoming desperate to locate the final component of the shrinking device he is constructing. So desperate, in fact, that he will soon be resorting to drastic measures."

"Such as?"

"Such as threatening to kill a Protector if his terms aren't meant."

"Cold."

"Indeed," Zephron said. "Though not entirely unexpected. There is a reason, after all, that he is the bad guy and we are not."

"Fair enough," Nikko remarked, leaning back in his chair and kicking his feet up on Zephron's desk. The corner of the Elder's mouth turned down, but he didn't say anything. Nikko hid a grin. Years ago, he'd been among Zephron's favorites. Nice to know some things hadn't changed.

"It occurs to me," the Elder continued, "that we can use this desperation to our advantage by handing him a Protector. A victim whom he can use as a bargaining chip— or, at least, a victim that he believes can be used as such. Someone he will take back to his lair, seemingly conquered. And once there—"

"He can storm the castle and take the place down from the inside," Nikko finished.

"That is the idea," Zephron said. "We can equip you with a tracking device that is undetectable prior to activation. We will set the device so that the process of reintegration activates it. Once you are in the lair, the signal will be transmitted, and we can be there almost instantaneously."

"Great plan unless he kills me in transit," Nikko said.

"We shall hope that doesn't happen."

"Yeah," Nikko said. "We shall."

"You are in agreement, then?"

Nikko nodded. "It's the best lead so far. But how do I get captured if I can't get close to him?"

"Simple," Zephron said with a smile. "You will be in the right place at the right time. And, of course, you're going to have to lose a fight. Can you do that?"

"It'll be tough," Nikko said, deadpan. "But I think I can manage."

On Tuesday, Lydia talked herself out of wearing the new outfit Amy had put together for her. The shoes were supposed to arrive at her office on Wednesday morning by priority shipment, and so she held off, wanting to wow the folks on the fifth floor with her keen fashion sense. Or, rather, *Amy's* keen fashion sense.

At ten of six, though, Lydia was wishing she'd tried the outfit after all. For that matter, she was wishing she had the shoes. Forget the goddess factor, at that point she would have been happy with a placebo effect. Anything to help her stand up to Darla and her cronies, all of whom had heard that she'd been given a second chance by Mr. Stout.

"Poor Lydia," Darla had said. "Maybe next time you'll get your work in on time. And don't forget about the eight a.m. meeting tomorrow. After turning in your work late, I can't see Mr. Stout keeping you on if you blow off a meeting, too." She pressed her fingertips to her lips and made kiss-kiss noises. "Just trying to be helpful, Lydia," she added, her white teeth gleaming like wet sugar.

Bitch.

But Lydia had only stood there, seething, knowing damn well that she'd turned her work in early, but too chicken to tell Darla to take a flying leap. More than that, *she'd* actually arranged the details for tomorrow's meeting, so it was hardly likely she'd miss it. But Darla couldn't miss an opportunity to stick in the knife and turn.

"You're a wimp," Lydia told herself as she marched down the crowded city sidewalk to catch the train to her tiny apartment. One of a thousand girls trying to make it in Gotham, Metropolis, the Big Bad City.

And then—in case she thought the day couldn't get any worse—she stumbled on a subway grate and the heel on her ancient black pump snapped. She fell forward, skinning her knee and eliciting the kind of curse words that she always swore to her mother she didn't know.

Naturally, she hadn't thought to shove a pair of flip-flops into her tote bag, and so she had to stumble home on one good shoe, her face burning as construction workers, commuters, and other pedestrians turned to watch her, a few snickering about her predicament. Since that got old quickly, she took a shortcut down an alley, where a few scary guys in leather jackets, pants and lots of tattoos ogled her, making colorful (though completely unappealing) suggestions as to ways they could entertain her sexually. *Ick.* And rather unnerving, too.

She hurried on, head down, as the shouted comments got bolder and more graphic. She clenched her fists, wishing she had the courage to stand up to them, but knowing she'd be stupid to do so even if she were ballsy enough. Those guys were scum, and they wouldn't exactly back off if she decided to stick up for herself. More than likely, they'd decide to make her their girlfriend. All of them. In turn.

She swallowed, then hurried faster, her hand in her purse so that maybe—just maybe—they'd think she was armed and leave her alone.

By the time she hobbled off the train a few blocks from her apartment, Lydia was more or less wishing she'd taken the easy way out and crawled under a rock. She climbed the stairs of the front stoop of her converted brownstone apartment, then slipped the key in the front door. She checked her mail—nothing—then hurried up three flights of stairs to her apartment. There was a box sitting in front of her door, and she looked at it curiously. She wasn't expecting anything except the shoes, and they weren't scheduled to arrive at her office until the next morning. Plus, all packages were supposed to be left downstairs.

The package was indeed about the size of a shoebox, and relatively light. She shook it, then checked out the wrapping. No clues there. The thing was wrapped in brown paper and twine, like an old-fashioned parcel. And although there was a return address, it only listed a PO box in Queens.

Weird.

Still, a present was a present, and Lydia wasn't about to turn away this one. Especially not on a day when she could use a pick-me-up. She took the box into her apartment, peeled off the wrapping, and found an honest-to-goodness shoebox, albeit one covered in shiny gold foil. Taped to the outside was a notecard, and Lydia opened that first.

> We thought you could
> use this early . . .
> With love,
> all of us at Hiheelia

Okaaaaay.

That was a little bizarre, because how on earth could they change their courier service like that? Then again, Lydia thought, maybe the policy was to ship early with this little note simply so gullible buyers would believe in all that magical hocus-pocus stuff. Pretty handy PR tool, when you got right down to it.

Still, she wasn't inclined to look a gift shoe in the mouth. Especially not a shoe as fabulous as the one she'd picked out online last night.

Carefully, she opened the box, then peered beneath the gold foil inside. Probably an optical illusion from the way the light hit the wrapping, but when she first glanced into the box, it almost seemed as if the shoes glowed.

Get a grip, Lydia.

She was beginning to sound like Amy. And as much as she loved her best friend, Lydia really, really, *really* didn't believe that nonsense about a magical Web site that delivered magical shoes that brought you your heart's desire.

A nice idea, but she lived in the real world, thank you very much. And in the real world, shoes kept your feet protected, looked hot, and cost a fortune. And that was pretty much that.

At the moment, it was the looking-hot aspect that interested Lydia the most, and she pulled the top the rest of the way off the box and gasped in excitement as she saw the soft, supple black leather of the ankle-high lace-up boots she'd picked out last night.

Lydia picked the left one out of the box where it was nestled in tissue paper, the smooth leather cool to her fingers. She kicked off her hideous pumps and slipped the boot on, feeling the way the arch cupped her foot and the leather hugged the shape of her toes.

It laced up the side, the golden cablelike thread hooking through silver eyelets. She laced the left, then slipped on the right and repeated the procedure. Amy might have her quirks, but she was most definitely a good friend, because while these shoes might not make Lydia want to go out and kick serious butt, they really did make her feel . . . well . . . *special*.

She stood up and walked around the apartment, surprised at how comfortable they were, considering the two-inch heels. She did a few little pirouettes, laughed like a loon, then headed to the couch, where she kicked back and watched the Tuesday-night lineup. Maybe not the most exciting night of her life, but at least she was being boring in really cool shoes.

When the time came to pack it in and get to bed early—so that she could be refreshed and ready for the meeting Darla had so kindly reminded her of—Lydia left the shoes right beside her bed. Ready to slip on the second she woke up.

The weird thing was, she woke up with the shoes *on* her feet: a little fact that came to Lydia's attention when the shrill ringing of the telephone woke her. She leapt out of bed, landing awkwardly on the heels.

Not that she had time to wonder about her toes' midnight migration into her shoes; the caller ID identified her office, and she snatched up the phone and uttered a breathless hello.

"Lydia? It's Joanie," announced Mr. Stout's secretary.

"Looks like we'll have an extra ten heads at the meeting this morning. Can you swing by a bakery on your way in and pick up a couple of dozen doughnuts?"

"Sure," Lydia said, eyeing the clock and mentally adjusting how fast she had to get out the door. No problem. She could do this.

She had to take the shoes off to shower, and weirdly, she actually felt a little bit of a letdown as she stripped them off her feet. "I'm coming right back to you," she assured them, leaving the shoes tucked under the foot of the bed. She felt a little silly talking to her footwear, but since she was alone in her apartment, what did it matter?

Showered and clean, Lydia slid into the outfit Amy had picked out for her and slipped on her fabulous new boots. A nice little electrical charge zipped through her and—yeah—she felt different. More spunky.

Pretty damn cool.

The bakery on the corner was her absolute favorite, so she grabbed two dozen mixed doughnuts even though she would have to schlep the boxes all the way into the city, her business tote slung over one shoulder and two boxes in a Twin's Bakery bag clutched tight in her other hand. With extreme willpower, she managed to not eat the doughnuts during the train ride, and she was feeling supremely smug by the time she was a single block from the office with seventeen minutes to spare. Oh, yes! No way was she getting any grief from Darla today. This was a major brownie-point day in the making.

That's when she heard the scream.

Lydia froze. Her feet didn't, though, and suddenly Lydia found herself racing pell-mell into a dark, scary alley, with absolutely no idea what she'd find there. Or, more important, what she'd do once she found it.

* * *

It was the scream that caught Nikko's attention, and damned if he didn't try to ignore it.

The sound had come from the west, at least a couple of blocks over from where he was perched, biding his time until that late that night, when Ruthless was supposed to show up in the alley behind a particularly seedy gentlemen's club. According to the Council's new intelligence source—aka, the rat-fink who'd leaked information and technology to Ruthless—Ruthless had received a tip from a psychic (honestly!) that the single source of his still-missing component part would be at the club near the cocktail hour. At the moment, Nikko was insanely early from the anticipated rendezvous, but he didn't trust the source at all. Better to come early and stay late. Because this was one assignment he wasn't taking any chances on.

Still, though . . .

A woman had screamed.

He shifted a bit on the fire escape, the repaired invisibility cloak weighing heavy on his shoulders. True, people got mugged every day out there in the big, bad world, and Protectors couldn't be all places at all times. Sometimes, you had to make sacrifices for the greater good. And preventing New York from shrinking to a size he could shove in his pocket would seem to fall into that category.

Still, though . . .

A woman *had* screamed. And that was one thing that Nikko couldn't ignore, no matter how much he might tell himself he should.

"Whhhooooooooaaaaaa!"

Without even thinking about it, Lydia found herself racing into the alley, her discombobulated body aimed straight toward a greasy-haired fiend with wild eyes and a gun pointed right at a teenage girl's face.

Lydia tried desperately to head in the other direction. To make her feet turn around and run to find the police. Because only a fool would jump in front of a hopped-up mugger, and although Lydia was a lot of things, she was absolutely not a fool.

Or, maybe she was. Because even as she screamed, "No, no, *noooooooo*," her feet propelled her forward. The mugger looked up, apparently misinterpreting her words as a message for him, rather than a plea to her feet.

Still, the surprise worked in her favor. The victim ducked, and Lydia's feet went flying. She kicked out hard, managing to catch the bad guy in the chin and send his head spinning. He tumbled backward, and she gave a shout to the girl: "*Run.*"

The girl didn't waste any time, hightailing it out of there with her school logo–emblazoned backpack smacking against her.

Great for the girl, not so great for Lydia. Especially considering how the thug had decided to turn his attention on her.

"You little *bitch*," he snarled, clambering to his feet and swinging the gun around at her.

Lydia opened her mouth, but only a squeak came out. Still, her feet managed to rise to the occasion—literally. One foot snapped up, knocking the gun out of the mugger's hand even as the rest of her body cringed, wanting nothing more than to crawl under a Dumpster and hide.

Mostly, anyway. A tiny little part of her thought that this kick-ass thing was pretty darn cool.

Not, however, cool enough that she wanted to stick around and watch her feet get her killed. *Nothing* was that cool, and she tried to turn around and race out of the alley before the creep either grabbed her or his gun.

No such luck. Instead, her feet pulled her forward against

her will, and she knew—somehow she just *knew*—that she was going to end up kicking this guy in the face again.

Which would have been great if she was, oh, qualified to go around kicking the crap out of people, but her? Lydia Carmichael? No, no, no.

She'd been way, way, *way* too lucky so far. If she didn't get out of here—and right now—something was going to go horribly wrong and she'd end up dead. Or worse.

Although her feet were moving forward, her mind and the rest of Lydia's body beat a swift retreat. She reached out, grabbing the iron bar of a nearby fire escape and putting a big old kibosh on the overeager-feet thing.

Unfortunately, that meant she also put a big old kibosh on her balance, and she jerked backward, her whole body in shock from the internal fight between her feet and her sense of self-preservation.

That's when she noticed that the guy had retrieved his gun. Worse than that, he had it pointed straight toward her face.

Gulp!

Except it turned out it wasn't so bad after all. Because all of a sudden the gun melted into a gloppy pile of goo. Her attacker let out a yelp and jerked his gun hand back as if it were on fire, even as Lydia turned, confused, and found herself staring at an absolutely gorgeous guy who—

Oh. My. God.

Lydia couldn't believe it. She stared, blinked, then stared again.

It couldn't be! It simply couldn't be happening. And yet it was.

She'd been rescued by the Silver Streak!

CHAPTER FOUR

"Are you okay?" Nikko asked, handily apprehending the gunman even while blatantly staring at the stunning—and obviously stunned—woman. Her face, so innocent and guileless, was contorted in surprise, and her deep blue eyes reflected both shock and relief.

She'd been falling, her body in the oddest contortion he'd ever seen, almost as if she was trying to run forward even as she ran away. And he shoved his captive to the ground so that he could zip sideways and hook his arm around her waist, pulling him close to him, the warm softness of her body wreaking havoc on his senses in a way he hadn't experienced in a very, very long time.

Mentally, he shook his head. Yes, he missed having a woman in his life, but he'd been focusing on this mission too long if the simple press of a woman against him distracted him so much.

Not a mere woman, a voice in his head argued. *She is anything but.*

Maybe so, but now wasn't the time. He turned sharply, the girl still in his arms, and pointed an accusing finger at the cretin on the ground who was even then struggling to get up. "I don't think so," he said, and the gunman sank back down, trembling, his eyes darting between Nikko and the girl.

"*You*," the girl whispered, her brow furrowing to form an adorable vee above her nose.

"I heard your scream," he said. "I'm sorry I didn't get here faster."

"I . . . that's okay. I—well, she's safe now, right?"

He cocked his head. "She?"

"The girl. The girl I was trying to rescue. Or . . ." she added, her brow furrowing into thoughtful lines. "Or, at least, I think that was what I was doing."

"I didn't see another girl," he said, wondering if perhaps she was a tiny bit hysterical.

For some reason, that made her smile. "Then I did it. I really did it." She met his eyes, hers flashing with amazement and pride. "I haven't got a clue how I did it, but I saved her!" She smiled up at him, a dimple furrowing her left cheek. "And then *you* swooped down and saved *me*. It was amazing—"

"Honestly, it was nothing."

"Me," she continued without missing a beat, "rescued by an honest-to-goodness superhero. Rescued by the Silver Streak. What an amazing day."

It had been, Nikko thought. Until she said those two little words, it really had been.

Right away, Lydia knew she'd said the wrong thing.

"I'm sorry," she sputtered. "I . . . I'm just so grateful and—" Amazed. Awed.

In lust.

"Don't worry about it," he said, but the words lacked the warmth she'd heard only seconds before, and as he turned to bind the wrists of their captive, all she could think was that she desperately wanted to run and hide. Her feet, however, stood firmly rooted to the spot. The same feet that only moments ago had been dead-set on running.

Traitors.

Except, of course, they weren't. For that matter, her feet had the right idea. Because deep down, under that oh-so-familiar-Lydia layer of scared, all she wanted in the world was to stay there. Near him. Soaking him up, absorbing the essence of him. This man. Whoever he was.

Because he couldn't really be the Silver Streak, could he? Sure, he'd seemed to swoop out of nowhere, but she had been a little preoccupied

And, true, the gun had melted, which was rather out of the ordinary.

And, yes, he did look exactly-freaking-like her comic book fantasy.

But, really, what did that mean?

Most likely the irritation she heard in his voice stemmed from the fact that dozens of women told him on a daily basis that he looked like the Silver Streak. Would she like to be told she looked like Wonder Woman?

She frowned. Okay, bad example. But still—

Still, she told herself firmly, superheroes do exist. *You know it. Even if no one believed you.*

She'd been standing with her mother, holding her hand tight as they prepared to cross the street. That was when the limo had zoomed by and a baby of all things had been tossed out of the sunroof. Lydia had seen it quite clearly, though she'd later learned that most passersby had been focusing on the naked woman trying to crawl out of the front window.

Weird.

Weirder still was the man who'd swooped from the sky and rescued the baby—just *swooped.* And he didn't even grab the baby, not at first. Instead, he'd levitated it up into his arms, looked in Lydia's direction with a twinkle in his eye, then soared away, up over the rooftops.

Lydia had told her mother what she'd seen, and had been scolded for making up stories. When she was older, she'd pulled newspaper reports and discovered that the child had been rescued in a high-speed gangster chase through the use of amazing SWAT technology.

Yeah, right.

It had been a superhero—even if she was the only one who realized it. And here was another one, standing right in front of her. Amazing.

"Are you okay?" he asked.

She blinked, forcing herself out of her mental meanderings. "Yeah. Um. Yes." Her feet no longer seemed compelled to run her life, and she'd survived a mugging and so, yes, by all the standards of polite society she was, in fact, okay.

"I need to get him to the authorities, and then I need to get back to . . . well, I need to get back to a project I was handling before I heard your scream."

"It wasn't my—never mind." Really, not important.

"Can you get home okay?" he asked, reaching down to grasp her hand and pull her up. She gasped, the touch of his hand against hers affecting her like a million volts. Or at least the way a million volts would feel if it didn't kill you immediately.

Honestly, her mind was turning to mush, and it was all this guy's fault. This sinfully gorgeous, hunk of a male specimen *hero*, who'd saved her life and—she blinked. Did he say *home*?

She shook her head, reality crashing down around her in the form of an eight a.m. meeting for which she was now very, very late. "I'm not going home," she said, scrambling to her feet, Darla's warning not to be late ringing in her ears.

"Oh, damn!" she cried, looking at her watch. "It's already forty past."

She bit her lip and searched frantically for the doughnuts, but she knew it was futile.

Because unless her new shoes could turn back time, she was screwed. And somehow, Lydia knew that that was simply too much to hope for.

"But the *guy*, Lydia," Amy wailed, almost spilling her merlot. "I had to get a babysitter and everything. You can't dangle a carrot like that and then not tell me. What about the *guy*?"

"The guy?" Lydia repeated, taking a long sip of her Cosmopolitan. "I tell you that my shoes are turning me into some sort of crime-fighter. And," she added, counting it out on her fingers, "that I got *fired*, and all you want to know about is the guy?"

"You said he was a superhero. You said he was the spitting image of the Silver Streak."

"Yes, yes, yes," Lydia said in a rush, because she'd already decided that she was an idiot for stupidly hurrying away. Considering there were umpty-bazillion people in Manhattan, the odds of ever seeing the guy again were slim, and no way was she getting her hopes up. Better to pretend the encounter was no big deal and push it firmly out of her mind. Except maybe, possibly late at night with a glass of wine, a bubble bath, and appropriately dim lighting.

Not that she was going to admit that to Amy. Not without another Cosmo, anyway.

"So?" Amy pressed. "The guy looked like the Silver Streak, your major crush for the last two years because— as we have conclusively established on innumerable occasions—you are a twelve-year-old girl at heart. Though why you'd want to date a superhero is beyond me."

Lydia's eyebrows went up. "You're kidding, right?"

"Oh, sure, strength and prowess is all good and fine. But

he'd be running off to fix some other girl's problems all the time."

Lydia forced herself not to smile. "Exactly why *my* fantasy is for a superhero with a domestic side. Strong and sexy, but nurturing, too. The kind of guy who'd fix me a romantic candlelight dinner and not have it catered. Or breakfast in bed other than Frosted Flakes."

"That man doesn't exist," Amy said with a mischievous grin. "I got the last model."

"Congratulations," Lydia said, lifting her Cosmo in a toast. "Guess you're buying this round."

Amy laughed, but didn't drop the ball. "Tell me!"

Lydia sighed, clinging to her forget-about-him plan by her fingernails. "You're missing the whole point. He was a superhero—*and so was I.*"

Amy, however, seemed less than impressed. "Told ya, didn't I?"

"That I was going to be able to kick serious butt if I bought these shoes? And that the shoes would be calling the shots?" Lydia asked, kicking her feet up into the air and drawing a few stares from the other bar patrons. "Um, no. I don't think those words actually left your mouth."

Amy lifted a shoulder. "Maybe you just weren't listening."

Frustrated, Lydia leaned forward and banged her head on the table three times. When she was near to concussing herself, she looked up at her friend's amused expression. "You know you're hopeless, right?"

"I'm deaf to everything you have to say until you tell me about the guy."

"And I'm not telling you about the guy," Lydia said, "until you have appropriately consoled me over the fact that Stout fired my sorry butt."

"Okay," Amy said, looking contrite. "The guy will hold. Tell me what happened."

"Total unfairness is what happened," Lydia said. "And nobody—*nobody*—bothered to consider the fact that maybe I was out there trying to make the world a better place. Honestly, Good Samaritans have a hell of a time these days."

"The story, Lyd," Amy said, apparently not caring about the plight of the Samaritans.

"It all started with the guy," Lydia began. "Or, actually, it started before the guy. But it *really* started when I sat on the doughnuts."

Amy's face squished up as she bit back a laugh. To her credit, she managed to keep it at bay. Lydia took that as an invitation to continue, and launched herself full-blown into the story of her humiliation, publicly rendered in front of the entire staff. Absolutely mortifying at the time. Now, after three Cosmopolitans and with one more on the way—she signaled the waitress to make sure—she was beginning to find the hidden humor. It was waaaaaaaay down there, hiding under the lemon twist, swimming in a puddle of alcohol-laced cranberry juice, and shouting dire predictions of one whopper of a hangover in the morning.

Lydia ignored her inner responsibility and continued to sip. She'd met the guy of her dreams, lost the guy of her dreams, and gotten fired, all within a two-hour time frame. She deserved a bender.

"I was already late," she said, "so I couldn't stop to get more doughnuts. So not only did I race into the conference room a full forty minutes late, but everyone was staring at me because they had assumed I was running late because I was waiting for the snacks—like I'd stand in line at a bakery instead of getting to a meeting on time."

"So what happened?" Amy pressed, twirling her hand as if that would make the story come faster.

"I stood there. Except, I didn't. I *wanted* to stand there, all cowering-like in the doorway. But my feet had a mind of their own and they marched me to my seat. So now I was standing by my chair instead of by the doorway."

"You sat down, right?"

"Nope," Lydia said. "I was going to, but Mr. Stout called me back to the door. And even though my feet didn't seem really keen on going, I managed to get moving in that direction." The whole feet thing was rather bizarre, actually, and Lydia wasn't sure she liked it. Ever since she first put the shoes on, the shoes seemed to be leading the show.

"He totally read me the riot act for not getting to work on time, for not turning in the report on time, and for forgetting a simple task like the snacks."

"But you did turn the report in on time," her loyal best friend replied, suitably indignant.

"And I tried to tell him that," Lydia said. "I had this whole long spiel about how the report had been on his desk for hours yesterday, and that he was the one who'd made me stay late even though I'd done all my work, and that it was completely unfair of him to assume that I'd blown off getting doughnuts when, in fact, I'd been saving a girl from being mugged."

"No way! You go, girl!"

"No, no," Lydia rushed to correct. "I said I *tried*. It was all there in my head, but I couldn't quite get it past my lips."

"Lydia!"

"Well, I tried."

"You're telling me you raced into an alley to fight a guy with a gun, but you couldn't tell Mr. Stout to go jump in a lake?"

"Pretty much," Lydia said miserably.

"So then what?"

"Then he had me sit back down, I went through the whole stupid meeting, went back to my desk and finished two projects, and, as I was shutting down my computer, Mr. Stout came by and fired me."

"No way."

"Way," Lydia said.

"And you *still* didn't say anything?"

Lydia shook her head, looking down at the floor. "I'd taken off my shoes and was kind of sitting there relaxing, you know? And I couldn't open my mouth. He fired me and I just sat there and took it. I even thanked him." The memory washed over her, making her shudder.

"You didn't!"

"I totally did. I'm such a dweeb."

"You are not. You rescued that girl. That has to count for something."

Lydia cocked her head and crossed her arms over her chest, leaning back in her chair as she examined her friend. "Yeah, it counts for the fact that I have good taste in shoes." She pointed at the things. "*These* guys did it. Not me."

"*Phhhbtt*," Amy retorted, calling on her cunning intellect to draw up that snappy comeback. "Shoes can't make something out of nothing. It's in there." She leaned across the table and tapped Lydia on the chest. "It's in you."

"Maybe," Lydia said, but her heart wasn't in it.

"So, what are you going to do? For a job, I mean?"

Lydia frowned, because that little problem had crossed her mind, too. "I'm not entirely sure," she admitted.

"Maybe the Silver Streak can find you a job," Amy suggested.

"I doubt it," Lydia said. "I don't even know where to find him, and—"

"I was joking," Amy said. "That was my subtle ploy to lead you into telling me about him."

And so Lydia did. Everything from the way she'd found the girl in the alley, to how Silver had shown up, looking all sexy and competent, to the electric tingle she'd felt when he'd touched her hand.

"Sparks?" Amy asked. "There were really sparks? Oh, my God, Lyd. I'm practically swooning."

"Well, I thought there were sparks," Lydia said. "I'm not so sure about him. And since I haven't a clue how to find him, I guess it doesn't much matter." How stupid had she been, rushing off to work when her fantasy man was right there? And for what? To get fired?

Idiot, idiot, idiot!

"Maybe if you go back to that alley . . ." Amy suggested.

Lydia shook her head, not wanting to get her hopes up. "Let's get real. The guy's a freakin' superhero. What's he going to want with me?"

Amy looked pointedly down at Lydia's feet.

"No way," Lydia protested. "That's not real. I'm just me. No superhero here," she said, spreading her arms.

"Well, I think you should go for it. He's your fantasy guy, Lydia. What harm is there in trying to snag him? I mean, come on. A guy who can fly and beat up thugs has to be pretty darn good in be—"

"Amy!" Lydia protested, feigning shock.

"Well, it's true," Amy pouted.

"And it's moot," Lydia said. "Don't know how to find him. Case closed. The end. Over and out."

Amy just scowled.

"Let's focus on getting me a new job," Lydia said, taking a sip of the fresh Cosmo the waitress put in front of her—her fourth. "That's productive, right?"

"Productive," Amy agreed. "But not fun."

In the end, Lydia decided it wasn't that productive, either. They batted ideas around, but considering the level of Cosmopolitan in Lydia's blood and the level of merlot in Amy's, they didn't get very far.

The best Amy came up with was Lydia standing at a major intersection and having her shoes kick the snot out of surly-looking passersby. All with an open guitar case, of course, to collect the coins thrown in by other amused pedestrians.

"Can you *please* be serious," Lydia begged, though she had to admit the idea made her laugh—the thought that she could not only stand out in public like that, but actually beat somebody up. Maybe she could start with Mr. Stout.

"Probably better to print out a million copies of your résumé and deliver it all over town," Amy admitted. "Not as interesting, but at least you'd have benefits."

By the time they finished drinking and planning Lydia's future, it was near midnight, and Lydia had quite the buzz. "Wanna split a cab home?" Amy asked, stumbling a little.

"No thanks," Lydia said. "I think I'll walk." Her heels were at least twice as high as Amy's—and she'd had twice as much to drink—but she felt remarkably sure-footed. Light-headed and giggly, but totally sure-footed. More than that, she had a feeling the cool October breeze would feel great on her alcohol-flushed face.

"You're sure you'll be okay?" Amy asked, but Lydia just raised an eyebrow. "Right. The shoes. Okay. But Lydia . . . be careful."

"I will," Lydia assured her, then saw her friend safely into a cab. After that, she turned and started walking uptown toward the subway station that would whisk her away to her empty, boyfriendless apartment, now being paid for out of her savings since she was a jobless loser.

Oh, hell. Maybe she should have shared a cab with Amy. Her friend at least would have propped her up when her confidence started to fail.

"Fat lot of good you guys are doing," she said to her shoes. "What good does it do to beat up muggers if I lose the only job I've had since college?"

The shoes didn't answer (which was probably a good thing) and Lydia continued to stumble forward, her thoughts a collage of bills, thugs, gorgeous superheroes, résumés, hunky tawny-haired men, Cosmopolitans, and, yes, the Silver Streak.

Not that she was obsessed with him or anything. It wasn't as if she hadn't thought of anything else all day. She had. She'd thought about her job. And losing her job. And telling Amy about losing her job. And she'd thought about Cosmopolitans and hanging out with Amy.

And, yes, she'd thought about the guy. But not in an overly obsessive way. It wasn't as if even now she could hear his voice, low and sultry and slightly dangerous as if delivered on the wind from Mount Olympus or something, because he was certainly gorgeous enough to have descended from the ancient Greek gods.

"You think . . . defeated me . . . never . . . not . . . life-time . . . impossible."

Wait. What?

The voice wasn't in her head, it was in her ears. On the street. *Just around the corner.*

She turned and raced in that direction, her heart stopping at the sight before her—a black-haired man dressed all in red, his hand tight around the throat of Lydia's beloved Silver Streak—or Silver Streak look-alike—who looked like he was about to pass out.

She didn't stop to evaluate, but instead ran forward, her feet leading the way.

"Let him go!" she screamed, then launched herself at the man in red. Her whole body hit his arm, and Silver was jostled free, falling back with the oddest expression on his face. Undoubtedly gratitude.

She didn't stop to chitchat, though. His attacker was

turning to flee. "Oh, no, you don't," she said, running after him, even as Silver leaped to his feet.

Lydia focused on her foe, attacking him with a solid kick to the face, but he surprised her by grabbing her heel and forcing her to flip backward in the air, resulting in a stomach-churning aerial somersault from which—miracle of miracles—she landed on both feet, knees bent to absorb the impact of the jump.

Those few seconds in the air, however, were enough. As she gasped and trembled, Red fired off a little salute, then disappeared, his body glowing like a billion charged particles of Captain Kirk going through the transporter one too many times.

"He's gone," she said, not quite able to believe her eyes.

"He's gone, all right," Silver said, his voice cutting as sharp as a knife. "Do you have any idea who that was? Any idea at all how many man-hours I put into planning this?"

She blinked at him, the world tilting a little as five Cosmopolitans sloshed around in her bloodstream. "I . . . What?"

"He's gone, the mission's blown, and I'd have to say it's all your fault."

CHAPTER FIVE

"My fault?" Lydia repeated, her excitement at seeing Silver again starting to fizzle away. "My *fault?*" The world was spinning, but whether from his words or from her previous Cosmopolitans, she didn't know. "How the heck is it *my* fault he got away? I *saved* you."

"You screwed me," Silver said, his eyes flashing. "I had it under control."

"Look, Silver. I don't know—"

"Dammit," he said. "I *knew* it. I *knew* that was what you thought."

She blinked, her entire defense crumbling around her. "Um, sorry?"

"I am *not* the Silver Streak," he said, with way more force than she thought the situation warranted. "Sorry to shatter your illusions, but—"

"Whoa there, dude," Lydia said, holding up her hands in defense before he could launch into a tirade. "I didn't say you were. But you didn't bother to throw an introduction in when you were screaming at me, now, did you?"

She put her hands on her hips and cocked her head, then almost fell over sideways. Either the shoes, her surprising new gumption, or the alcohol was getting to her, because it certainly couldn't be the guy. Gorgeous though he might be, she was beginning to think that maybe looks weren't everything. She'd saved his butt, and he wasn't even being nice to her! What was up with that?

She drew in another breath, all set to lay into him all over again, but he beat her to the punch. His face relaxed, the tight jaw loosened, then actually curved up into a sexy smile—the kind that shows a dimple and a sense of humor.

"Nikko," he said, holding out his hand. "And you are? Other than trouble, I mean."

"Lydia," she said. "Lydia Carmichael."

"Well, Lydia Carmichael, you want to tell me how long you've officially been a Protector? And why you didn't tell me when we met earlier today? Because I think I can document about twenty-seven breaches of protocol here."

"Protector?" she echoed, even as he leaned in to sniff her breath.

"Cosmopolitans," he said, so close she could feel his hot breath on her face. "Don't you know drinking on the job isn't allowed?"

"Try *after* the job," she griped. "I got fired this afternoon. And thank you *so* much for making my evening that much more special."

"Fired," he repeated, the tone of his voice making her feel even more like a loser. "You want to tell me why?"

She hung her head, her eyes going to her shoes, and that maneuver inexplicably gave her a boost of confidence. "A ridiculous misunderstanding," she said, looking up to face him. "But it all went back to this morning. I ended up being late, and then everything just spiraled downward from there."

"Dammit to Hades," he said. "Did *I* do that?"

"Huh?" She stared at him, baffled.

"Did I accidentally interfere with a mission? This morning, when I thought you were in trouble?"

"Oh, yeah," she said. "I—"

"Sorry," he said, taking a step back and holding up his hands, looking so contrite that she decided maybe it was best not to correct his mistaken impression. After all, he'd started out supremely pissed, and now he seemed to be warming up to her.

"Trust me," he continued, "I know what it's like to come under the Council gun for something that isn't entirely your fault."

"You do?" she asked, wondering what the heck the Council was.

He nodded but didn't elaborate. "Okay, back to square one. You got fired today?"

"Pretty much," she said.

"And how long have you been a Protector?"

She shook her head slightly, trying to keep up. The man certainly did change topics quickly. Or maybe her fuzzy brain simply wasn't processing fast enough. "Um."

"Were you on a mission this morning, or weren't you? Surely that wasn't your first."

"Oh!" she said, finally getting it. He thought she was a superhero, too. That must be what Protector meant. And the only reason he'd think that was because she'd been kicking butt. And the only reason she'd done *that* was because of the shoes.

Did he know something she didn't? Like, maybe the shoes came with instructions and an assignment? If so, she'd clearly missed it.

Her head pounded, the alcohol pulling out the big guns now and blasting away inside of her skull, reminding her loudly and painfully of why she rarely drank.

"Right," she finally said. "Yes. My first."

"A Halfling, then. Just passed your tests?"

"I—" She couldn't think with the hammering in her head.

"And then you went out drinking, got your powers all mucked up, got cocky, and stepped in and tossed a giant monkey wrench into my operation. Honestly, *what* is the Council teaching you newbies?"

"*Nothing*," Lydia wailed, all the stress of the day falling right on her shoulders. Because she'd wanted so desperately to help. She'd thought she was helping. And now this gorgeous stranger—whom she'd at first thought maybe she had a teeny-tiny hint of a spark with (*that* was obviously only happening in Lydia Delusion-Land!)—was standing here berating her. "Nobody taught me anything. I got the shoes, I got the power, and everything just went wonky!"

"So, you're a brand-new Protector *and* you got fired today?"

"Pretty much," she said, though she didn't see what one had to do with the other, unless it was the fact that she'd been a total loser-girl with Mr. Stout. She *really* should have had the gumption to tell him off. But even with the shoes on, she'd kept stupidly silent.

She opened her mouth to tell Nikko all that, but then shut it again the moment she got a glimpse of his face. *Sympathy.* And something even softer. Something that made her insides melt and made her crave his touch. *This* was the man she'd fantasized about, and when he reached for her in a sympathetic hug, she moved into his arms without thinking.

This was the man she'd spent long nights fantasizing about, and she wasn't sure if it was the cocktails, the guy, or a pending electrical storm, but the air around her seemed to shimmer, looking exactly like it had when Red had up and disappeared so very abruptly.

"I'm sorry," he said. "That has to be hell, getting in so much trouble on your very first day."

"It wasn't fun," she admitted. She leaned back, then tilted her head up to look him in the eyes. "But I have to say it's getting better," she added, her voice low, sultry and definitely inviting.

Whoa. Had she actually said that? She'd never come on to a man in her life. Never even considered being so bold, and yet here she was, and so far at least, the ground hadn't fallen out from under her.

She didn't know if it was the shoes or the man or the alcohol that had loosened her inhibitions—not to mention her tongue—but she had to admit she liked it. And from the spark of interest reflected in those deep gray eyes, she had to think that maybe he liked it, too.

"I'm sorry if I seemed harsh earlier," he said. "They've got me working a killer mission, and the key to our brilliant plan just disappeared in a puff."

That, she realized, was his polite way of reminding her that she'd screwed up royally. Obviously she had a lot to learn about this Protector thing. Hopefully the manual wasn't too long, because she intended to read it cover to cover tonight.

He shifted, and she felt the press of his long, lean legs against her, and the caress of his hand along her back. Immediately she decided to ditch reading the manual. He'd pulled her to him in sympathy, but if she was reading the signs right, there was a subtle shift in the tenor of his touch.

He smiled at her, warm and dreamy, and she said a silent prayer that it really was interest she saw in the depths of his eyes, and not an alcohol-induced hallucination. "Will you accept my apology?"

She nodded, her knees feeling a little weak from the way he was watching her so intently. "I . . . I think I better get home." She swallowed, then pressed on boldly, surprising herself, and yet at the same time somehow feeling more like herself than she ever had before. "Would you come with me?"

The corner of his mouth curved up. "You live near here?"

She shook her head. "Brooklyn," she said. "I was on my way to the train when—"

"You're not in any condition to walk," he said.

"Unless you have a pumpkin you're planning on turning into a carriage, I haven't got a choice." She frowned, remembering with crystal clarity exactly why a taxi was out of the question. *Fired.* She couldn't freaking believe it.

"I think I can do you one better than a pumpkin," he said, even as he pulled her close and held her tight around the waist. And then, without any warning at all, he shot upward, leaving the ground far below. Lydia trembled in his arms, thinking that a day that had started out like crap was seriously looking up.

Lydia Carmichael.

Somehow, it seemed like the perfect name. She'd been on his mind since he'd rescued her that morning—or, rather, since he thought he'd rescued her. Now that he knew she was a Protector, her earlier protestations made sense. *She'd* rescued a girl who'd screamed, and he'd somehow interfered in her follow-up. True, she'd looked to be in trouble, what with the gun in her face, but that could have been a ruse. Much like the one she'd inadvertently interrupted only moments ago.

Already, he forgave her that. There was, quite simply, something about this woman. Something that made his heart beat a little faster and his Protector instincts fire. He wanted to gather her up, to keep her safe. Apparently he'd been lonelier than he realized.

Empirically, the girl was trouble: a new Protector, obviously clueless, she'd gotten in the way of one of the biggest stings of his career and one of the most important operations in Council history.

And yet, here he was, feeling all warm and fuzzy toward her. *Libido*, he reminded himself. Not real, just lust.

Still, he thought, as her soft body clung to him and the lights of the city twinkled beneath them, it was the sweetest kind of trouble. And if she'd set him back a week or two on his mission—well, sometimes payment could be delicious, too.

Lydia was floating in the night sky, the stars as background and her head as light as a feather. Best of all, she was in her dream man's arms.

True, he'd been a teensy bit grumpy at first—not exactly sweeping her off her feet—but the reality was that he'd been as confused about her as she was about herself. Now, he'd both warmed up to her and was warming her up, because she'd never felt safer or more heated than she did at that particular moment with her arms tight around him, his body hard against hers, and the world whizzing by below.

He shifted then, and her stomach rose all the way into her throat, then did a hard nosedive into her toes as he started a descent over her neighborhood. Had she told him where she lived? She tried to mentally push rewind, realized her brain was basically mush, but had a vague memory of him asking for details and her describing her apartment through an alcohol-and-lust-induced haze.

"Did I get it right?" he asked, setting them down gently on the fire escape.

"Wow," she said, which pretty much took all of her effort. "Um, yeah."

"Wait here," he said. Then he shot off into the sky while she stayed behind, looking stupidly up toward the stars.

Less than a minute later, he was inside her apartment and pulling the window open. "How did you—? Never mind." She decided against asking.

"I like your place," he said, and she smiled wryly.

"I'm thinking I need to have the locks checked and an alarm system installed. You got in far too easily."

"Now you're thinking like a mortal," he said. "You've passed your test, right? You're a Protector now." He tapped his head. "I'm full-blooded, so I've grown up with it, but eventually you're going to have to simply accept that the way things work for Protectors aren't always the way things work for mortals."

"Believe me," she said dryly, "I'm figuring that out."

She headed across her apartment and pulled a bottle of water from her tiny refrigerator, then offered one to him. "So what exactly were you doing that I messed up? I'm sorry about that," she added quickly, her cheeks heating.

He hesitated, and she felt her blush deepen. "I guess I shouldn't be asking you those kinds of questions, right? For all you know, I'm working for the bad guys."

"For the record," he said, "I don't believe that. But you're right about my needing to be careful. Hopefully you'll never be on probation. Trust me when I say you have to watch yourself every step of the way."

"That's okay," she said. "I get it." For that matter, she really did understand. She'd read enough complicated comic book plots to give her some idea of what she'd stumbled onto. "I thought you were trying to take that guy down, but that he'd somehow turned the tables on you. But it was all a ruse, and you'd planned on getting caught all along so that you could find his secret lair where he's hatching his evil plot." She waggled her eyebrows, then crossed her arms over her chest and looked up at him. "So, how'd I do?"

He didn't answer, but his lopsided grin was enough to tell her she was right on the mark.

She licked her thumb and smashed it on her hip, then made a sizzling noise. "Am I good, or what?"

"I have a feeling you're very, very good."

She nodded her head, feeling bold, smug, and a little bit sexy. "Touché." She moved to the couch and patted the cushion next to her, inviting him to join her. "So riddle me this, Batman. If this mission is so important, how come you're here with me? My sparkling personality? Sexy legs? Keen fashion sense?" She blinked, a little amazed at her own gumption. Whatever happened to shy Lydia?

Apparently, she'd been kicked to the curb. And that, frankly, was just fine with the new model.

"I sent in a report while we were in the air."

"Right," she said, remembering the PDA he'd typed a message on as she'd been gawking at the ground below them. "So, they answered already?"

"Not yet. I'm waiting for new intelligence. That lead was the best we'd had in months, and with zero hour drawing closer—"

"In other words, I blew it big-time."

"You did," he said, "but you didn't know. And if it comes down to a Council investigation, I'll be sure to let them know that."

"Thanks," she said, but her brow furrowed, wondering how the heck she'd gotten drawn into a whole world of rules and regulations simply by ordering a pair of shoes. Somehow, that didn't seem fair.

What *did* seem fair—or, if not fair, at least fabulously fortuitous—was that for the time being at least, she got the guy. This wonderful guy was spending time with *her*. Waiting in her apartment until he got his marching orders. And, frankly, he seemed perfectly on-board with that plan.

She tilted her head, watching him and drinking in the wonderful curve of his jaw, the sculptured lines of his body, and the intensity of his gaze. What was he thinking, she wondered. Because *she* was thinking that she wanted him.

More than that, she was thinking about actually telling him that she wanted him. Which, honestly, wasn't the kind of thing that Lydia Carmichael did.

She wasn't entirely sure who she was turning into, but part of her liked the new Lydia. Liked the confidence and directness. Liked the idea that if Mr. Stout had fired her now, she would have had the cojones to stand up to him. Liked that she seemed to be growing stronger from the inside out.

That was what part of her thought.

The other part was scared to death.

The other part couldn't quite get the words out.

Her feet were more than willing to move, however, and before she had the chance to think about it—before she could be scared or shy or anything else that screamed old-school Lydia—she'd moved toward him, pressing her body against his and hooking her arms around his neck. She didn't speak, because the words wouldn't come. But the truth was, she didn't need words to ask for what she wanted. No, because what she wanted was him. His hands. His mouth. Every single, solid, sexy inch of him.

Boldly she drew him closer, her eyes locked on his. No surprise or shock reflected back at her; instead, she saw only her own need mirrored in those azure depths. A need as deep as an ocean, and a pull as strong as the tide.

She took his mouth with hers, feeling bold and crazy and more than a little drunk. Only, not from alcohol. No, this inebriation was of a purely sensual variety. She wanted more and, so help her, she told him so.

"What's that?" he asked, his whisper warm and sensual and teasing. "I'm not quite sure I heard you."

"You," she said, taking a quick nip of his ear. "I want more. I want you," she added, more boldly than she'd ever spoken. "I want all of you."

"Sweetheart," he said, as his hands slipped under the back of her shirt, "I think that's the best thing I've heard all day."

Sweet shockwaves rushed through her, tumbling down to her toes and bubbling right back up again, like carbonated electricity. She felt fizzy and floaty and more turned-on than she could ever remember being. She'd dated men before, of course. Even slept with them. But she'd never felt this way. Never had a man's touch so thoroughly fire her senses. It was as if everything in her life had disappeared except for *this* man and *this* moment. Right here, right now, and the warmth of his caresses.

With a low moan, she again lifted her mouth to his, desperate to taste him. His hands slipped down, fingers dipping beneath the waistband of her jeans and edging under her panties even as his tongue tempted and teased.

He tasted salty and male and a bit like dark chocolate. *Candy,* she thought. Decadent and sinful, but at least this candy wasn't fattening. She could have as much as she wanted, and then go right back for seconds.

Boldly she pulled away from his lips, ignoring his soft growl of protest as his lips moved to her hairline, then teased the top of her ear. She tried to concentrate on what she was doing, which was attacking his shirt. A black T-shirt made of some unusual material, she could only assume it was an honest-to-goodness superhero garment. But despite her lifelong fascination with comic books and superheroes, right then, she really didn't care. All she wanted was to have that thing off him. To touch his chest and feel his skin against hers.

With fingers trembling from desire rather than fear— was this really her?—she reached down and grabbed the bottom of the shirt, then pulled it over his head and stole a kiss as he smiled at her.

"I was thinking that very thing," he said, his hands

leaving their soft perch on her backside, riding up and taking her own shirt with them.

The cool air in her apartment brushed her overheated bare skin, and she shivered, goose bumps rising on her arms and belly. She drew in a breath, her whole body trembling with desire.

"You're beautiful," he whispered, and she shivered more, unable to form words; every effort was called on to help her breathe.

He reached out, his fingers twining in her hair. The soft strokes were long and sensual, but not where she wanted him. She wanted him to feel her heat, to know just how much he was driving her nuts. She wanted it, and she knew that to have it, she was going to have to ask. To tell him. To show him what she wanted and how she wanted it, and so help her, that wasn't the kind of thing she'd ever—ever—been able to do before.

With every other man in her life—and now they seemed like a large gray blur behind her—she'd laid back, letting the man take the lead and never once saying what she wanted, what she needed.

Today, though—

Today, she took his hands in hers and moved them down, cupping his palms over her breasts, nearly melting when his sensuous moan drifted over her, firing her libido and making her wet and silky and so very ready.

"Touch me," she demanded, delighting in both the man and her own unfamiliar boldness. She was like a new woman, herself and yet more, and it felt so good.

She wanted him to make her feel even better, and even though it wasn't the kind of thing that the old Lydia did, this Lydia reached for the button on his tight, black jeans. She fumbled a little, but managed to open it, and then reached down to find the prize inside.

He smiled at her, slow and sultry, and she knew that she was doing the right thing. That anything would be the right thing with this man.

And as he closed his mouth over hers, real thought escaped her, and she lost herself in a sea of sensuality and heat and sweet sensations.

His body seemed to dance over hers, until every tiny hair follicle seemed charged with energy, and her body thrummed so tight that any touch would send her over the edge.

It wasn't *any* touch she wanted, though. She wanted him inside her, hard and deep, and then fast and wild. Any way and every way, and, so help her, she wasn't afraid to ask.

"Whatever the lady wants," he said, and for the next few hours, he proved that he was a man of his word. He was a painter, and she was his canvas, and over and over he painted such amazing bursts of light and color that she could hardly breathe, hardly move, and she certainly couldn't think.

"I think I'll be the first person to die of complete and utter satisfaction," she said sleepily, her head resting on her pillow.

Nikko lay beside her, his hand stroking the hair around her ear. "Don't tell me you're tired," he teased.

"Never," she said, though her body was limp as a noodle and her eyes drooped. She wanted to stay awake. Wanted to never sleep, if sleep meant missing out on any moment with this man. If by closing her eyes and resting she wouldn't feel his caresses or know the heat his fingers generated against his skin.

But it didn't matter. The sun was coming up and her eyelids were falling down. And as Lydia drifted off, safe and secure in Nikko's arms, a tiny smile touched her lips.

Stamina, she realized, was yet another perk of making love with a superhero.

CHAPTER SIX

Nikko thought that she was even more beautiful asleep, and he would have been content to lie there for hours beside her, watching her dewy lips and the slow rise and fall of her chest.

That, of course, was impractical. Instead, he pressed a soft kiss to her cheek, then went off to explore her kitchen. Not badly stocked, actually, and he took his time, figuring that she could use the sleep. They had, after all, stayed up late.

Cooking had always been his favorite way to relax and, in fact, his house in the mountains had a fabulous kitchen. There was something relaxing and engaging about the process. Edible chemistry. And when he hit upon the perfect combination, there was very little joy more poignant than sharing it.

In Colorado, he'd had no one to share his meals. No one he cared about, anyway. And without consciously thinking about it, he prepared a simple breakfast for Lydia with extra care, imagining what it would be like to serve her in his huge bedroom. Or, better, to take her onto the redwood deck and eat with the sky above and the trees below, suspended there with the world spread out beneath them.

It was an image that was far too appealing, frankly, and he tried to shove it away, forcing himself to instead concentrate on French toast, sausage and freshly squeezed orange juice.

He took a tray in to her and found her waking. She blinked at him, the corners of her mouth curved up; whether from happy memories or because she was glad to see him, he didn't know. Both, he hoped.

"Hey," she said.

"Hey, yourself." He slid the tray onto the bed beside her. "I thought you might want breakfast in bed."

She laughed. "Because I'm too weak to walk, thanks to you."

"I'm terribly sorry," he said, lacing his voice with false sincerity.

"I'm sorry, too," she said, seeming genuinely contrite. She propped herself up on one elbow. "About that Silver Streak thing. I never meant—"

He hushed her with a soft finger on her lips. "I overreacted. It's a sore subject with me."

"How come? I mean, I get that you'd rather not be compared to a comic book guy but—"

"I *am* the comic book guy," he said, then told her the whole sordid story. She was, in fact, the first person he'd told it to, other than the Council investigators. When he finished, he managed a grin. "When the Silver Streak appeared as a guest in an X-Men comic, the Council was more than a little miffed. And then when he got his own comic book . . . well, all Hades broke loose." He shrugged. "Let's just say it caused me all sorts of problems," he concluded, the soft skin of her shoulder so distracting under his fingertips. "You know how the Council is."

How the Council is?

"Oh, yeah, sure," she said automatically, then frowned. The truth was, she *didn't* know how the Council was, and although in the alley she'd been perfectly content to assume that the Council and the Protector thing and all the other odd little statements he'd made had related to her shoes and Shoestra and Hiheelia.com, that theory was losing credibility.

For one thing, she hadn't seen a single pair of men's shoes on the Web site. In retrospect, maybe she should have thought of that earlier. Because unless her gorgeous Silver Streak was running around in two-inch pumps, he had no business surfing to Hiheelia.com.

For another, the whole thing didn't feel quite right, not now after the alcohol haze had finally worn off and her brain was semifunctional again. *Semi* being the operative word since she was a little hungover, not to mention fuzzy from a lack of sleep about which she would never, ever complain.

Still, he thought she was someone (or, rather, something) she wasn't, and that wasn't a good way to start a relationship. And the truth was, she desperately hoped this was a relationship, or at least the beginning of one.

She took a deep breath and opened her mouth, prepared to tell him all about the shoes and the Web site, but instead, he kissed her, nodded toward the tray; then said one tiny, magic word: "Breakfast."

Lydia's stomach sprang to life, and whatever else had been in her head left, replaced by the delicious scent of the breakfast he'd fixed. For her. Wow.

She reached for the tray, her eyes on his face. Her fingers brushed the coffee cup; she pulled it toward her—and somehow managed to upset the entire delicate balance, sending the tray tumbling to the floor and the fabulous food spilling everywhere.

"Oh!" She leapt out of bed, completely mortified. "Oh, my gosh. You made it for me and I totally ruined everything!"

She felt tears prick her eyes, and she blushed furiously, wishing the shoes could turn back time.

"It's okay," he said, his smile confirming the sentiment.

"I'll make everything again," she said, feeling desperate.

He laughed, the sound warm and reassuring. "I used the last of your bread." He held out his hand. "But I'd be delighted to take you out on this fine morning."

She cocked her head. Was he seriously not mad?

His mouth quirked up as if he knew what she was thinking. "Of course, there is one downside." His eyes grazed over her naked body and made her skin tingle as if he'd trailed his fingertips over every inch of her. "It's a pity, but I think clothing is required."

"That is a pity," she said, taking a moment to boldly look him up and down before focusing on her bare feet and concentrating on *not* blushing. This new confidence was exciting, but it took a little getting used to.

After a few minutes of scrounging and peering under various bits of furniture, eventually they found their clothes. Lydia pulled her jeans and sweater back on, feeling decadent for not showering off the scent of him, then gave her hair a few strong strokes with a brush before pulling it back into a ponytail. Not the sexiest style, but from the way he was looking at her, you would have thought she was a *Sports Illustrated* swimsuit model.

"You're staring," she said.

"You're beautiful."

She laughed. "Good answer. Stare all you want."

"So, just how hungry are you?"

She cocked her head, fighting a smile. "Put it this way. I'm weak from hunger. Do you want me weak? Or do want me energized when we come back?"

"Well put," he said, tossing her one of her shoes. "Get dressed."

She caught the shoe one-handed, then frowned. Yesterday, whatever assertiveness she'd had was from the shoes. But right then, she'd bantered and joked and generally goofed around with him in a provocative way, *and she wasn't wearing the things.*

Wow.

"What?" he said, looking at her face and smiling.

She shrugged, then slipped her feet into her shoes and laced them up. "Nothing much," she said. "Only that I'm in a fabulous mood."

"That makes two of us," he said, taking her hands and pulling her into his arms.

They wandered out into the Brooklyn morning, and Lydia took him to her favorite restaurant, Maisie's, on the corner near a community park. They sat outside and talked about everything and nothing, and Lydia was absolutely certain that it was the best morning she'd ever had. Not even the din of nearby argumentative voices could put a damper on her happiness.

"Dammit, Roy," a woman said, her voice harsh and a little scared. "We're broken up! What are you doing following me?" As Lydia turned, she saw the woman, a brunette with a pale, drawn face, push back from the table. "I'm going home."

"No, you're not. We gotta talk," Roy said, reaching across the table and grabbing her arm so hard the woman winced. "Now sit down," he said, jerking her roughly back into her chair.

That did it. Lydia leapt up out of her chair and stormed across the restaurant, then pulled the guy up by the back of his collar. "I think you must have misunderstood the lady. She said she wanted to go home."

"Who the hell are you?"

Lydia smiled, feeling powerful and more than a little

righteous. "Your worst nightmare if you don't leave the girl alone."

For a moment, she thought the guy would call her on it. And, yes, she actually imagined how it would feel to smack him hard in the nose.

But he backed off, his hands lifting in a *whatever* kind of gesture. "She ain't even worth it," he said. "I got a new girl now, anyway. New job. New place. Don't need *her* at all." He glared at the girl as she shoved her chair back, lips pressed tight together and her eyes damp.

She mouthed a silent thank-you to Lydia, then grabbed her purse and ran from the restaurant.

Lydia watched her go, then turned back to Roy. "Stay away from her," she said. "Okay?"

The guy's lip lifted. "You wanna get out of my face now?"

Her fingers curved into a fist, and she was just about to thrust forward and catch him in his sanctimonious nose when she felt a hand close over hers. She turned and looked back to find Nikko holding her.

"You did a good thing, Lydia," he said. "And this one's not worth making any more effort."

Roy glared at Nikko, but sank lower in his seat, looking worn-out and pitiful.

"No," Lydia said. "He's not."

"Come on," Nikko said, paying and taking her out of the restaurant, then indulging her as she paced up and down the sidewalk in front of the park, muttering to herself.

"The nerve of some people. It's absurd. No, it's obscene! That poor girl. Oh, God," she said, looking at him. "You don't think he's going to take it out on her, do you? The fact that I embarrassed him in public?"

"It's the risk we take, doing what we do," he said, and she bit her lower lip, suddenly thinking that maybe rampant ballsiness wasn't such a great thing after all. "But, no. I think they're truly over now. More than that, I think you set a great example for her."

"Really?" she asked, starting to feel a bit hopeful. "You honestly think so?"

"Absolutely. Someone stood up for her. Valued her. I think now she'll value herself more." He met Lydia's eyes. "Don't you?"

She considered the question, thinking about her B.S. life (before shoes, that is), and tried to imagine being in that woman's place, with Roy across the table.

"Yeah," she finally said. "I think you're right. Even if she doesn't have the nerve to confront him herself, she might at least now have the nerve to say no to going out with him anymore."

"So what now?" he asked, coming closer and hooking his arms around her waist. "Your place?"

"Is yours even an option?" she asked.

He shook his head. "I've been staying at the Council's New York field office. Seemed easier than getting a hotel."

"Oh. So where's your home?"

"Colorado," he said, and she felt her heart sink a little. Colorado was far from New York. Which meant that once his mission was over, Nikko would be a long way from her.

"Oh." She licked her lips. Part of her did want to go back to the apartment, back to the bedroom and the warmth of Nikko curled up next to her, his body hard and lean and pressed close. She closed her eyes and sighed, imagining a lazy morning turning into a lazy afternoon and finally fading into a lazy night. Lazy, that is, except for a few bursts of intense aerobic activity.

Ah, heaven.

And yet at the same time, she couldn't quite bring herself to say she wanted to go back. The truth was, as much as she wanted to be with Nikko *that* way, she also craved the excitement of being with him . . . well . . . superheroly. Defeating bad guys together and all that Justice League stuff.

"You have that look," he said.

"I have a look?"

"Definitely," he said, kissing the tip of her nose. "So tell me why. What's the look for? What are you thinking?"

"I'm thinking I want to learn from the best," she said, boldly kissing him back. "I want to go do superhero stuff. And then," she added, taking his hands from around her waist and pulling them up to kiss his fingers, "*then* I want to go back home and—what do they call it?—debrief each other."

He laughed. "That may be what they call it," he acknowledged, "but I'm not sure I'm the best."

She frowned. "What are you talking about?"

He paused, then sat down at a bus stop. "I'm in town because I screwed up a while back. This is my chance to redeem myself."

"Oh." The guilt was back. "So that mission I messed up . . . You're telling me that I not only let a bad guy go, but I also messed up your chances to get back in, um, Protector good graces?"

"Pretty much."

She licked her lips. "Sorry."

He shook his head and looked at her, the smile on his lips reaching his eyes. "It's not your fault. The only one who got me in this position was me."

"What happened?" she asked, then wished she hadn't. After all, it wasn't really any of her business.

He drew in a deep breath. "I did a dumb thing. I was trying to nab a bad guy, and I blew my cover. Let mortals see me. And even though that kind of thing can usually be covered up—"

She nodded, remembering the story the newspapers had run about the baby, the limo, and a SWAT team.

"—in this case, I was seen by more than just ordinary mortals. I was seen by an artist." Nikko frowned. "Damn comic book."

"But that's one of the things I love so much about the comic," she said. "The Streak is so damn honorable."

He narrowed his eyes, looking at her. "What do you mean?"

"In all those early issues," she clarified, "he wasn't supposed to let regular people know who he was, but he did. Because otherwise, folks would have gotten hurt. He had to make a choice: follow the rules and let people get hurt, or . . ." She cut herself off with a shrug. "I think he made the right decision." She put her hand on his arm. "Sounds like you did, too. Even if it did mean you were immortalized in a comic," she added with a mischievous grin.

He made a derisive noise in his throat, but even as he did, he turned to her. "You really think so?"

"Yeah," she said softly. "I do." She stood up, then reached out her hand. "Like I said: I want to learn from the best. Teach me?"

He hesitated, then stood up. "I'm not sure who's doing the teaching here," he said. "But I think we can definitely go nail a few bad guys together." He pulled some sort of cloak out of the backpack he'd been carrying. He swooped it over his shoulders, then pulled her close, enveloping her in his strong arms. "You don't have a propulsion cloak issued to you?"

"Um, no," she said, debating whether now was the time for her confession. She looked up at the sky, remembered the way it felt to fly with him, and decided to wait a little longer. Right then, she wanted the thrill of flying with him, and the kick of doing good, of stepping into the shoes—literally—of the superhero life she'd fantasized about for so long.

"You should talk to the Council about that," he said. "Sometimes I think they do a piss-poor job of walking Halflings through procedure."

"Mmm," she said, but fortunately, he didn't mind her relative nonanswer.

"The invisibility feature is acting up, so we may not be able to— Hang on. Never mind. It's still working."

She looked down, then gasped to realize that she couldn't see her feet, her hands, any of her.

"What the . . . ?"

"Hold on," he said, his smile as bright as his eyes. And then, suddenly, they were flying, their bodies transparent against the deep blue sky, and the streets of Brooklyn spread out beneath them like a diorama.

"So, what do you do?" she asked. "Fly around looking for good deeds?"

He chuckled. "I'm usually handed specific assignments," he said, reminding her that he was on assignment right then, which meant that soon he'd have to leave her and this lovely, sensual interlude would come to a halt. "But, yeah. Since Protectors swear an oath to protect mortals, we have to step in if we see anything untoward going on."

"Right," she said. "The oath. That's exactly what the Silver Streak lives by." She peered down at the street, a morbid part of her hoping for a mugging or robbery. Or a juicy carjacking.

Nada.

In the end, they rescued a cat from a tree in stereotypical fashion, then helped a woman get her jammed front door open.

"Not exactly a superhero morning," she said to Nikko as she leaned against a maple near the woman's front door. "I never thought I'd be bummed not to see someone being mugged or harassed," she added with a laugh.

"You can't have everything," Nikko said, his dimple showing. "Besides, you—"

But he was cut off by a shrill scream as a teenager raced by, a purse banging against him as he sprinted away from a woman screaming bloody murder.

The dimple deepened into a full-fledged smile. "Go get 'em," he urged.

Lydia didn't wait for him to tell her twice, but took off after the thief, her shoes moving her at a speed she would have thought impossible yesterday. More than that, she no longer feared for her own balance. *She* was in control now. Her feet might have called the shots at first, but now it was all Lydia . . . and it felt wonderful.

In no time at all, she caught up to the guy, getting in front of him and halting him with a flat hand against his chest. "I'll take that," she said, snagging the purse back. Around them, passersby hurried over, including a beat cop. And Nikko and the victim were jogging toward her, Nikko doing his best to look very, very mortal.

"Who the hell are you?" the thief asked her.

She lifted her chin. "The Pink Streak," she said, then bit back a laugh. Okay, so maybe she understood where Nikko was coming from. Having *that* moniker stick would be no fun at all.

She passed the thief off to the officer, accepted the victim's profound thanks, then linked her arm in Nikko's and took off walking back the way she'd come.

"So how'd I do, coach?"

"High marks across the board. Speed. Agility. You got your target. You delivered him to the authorities. You were calm, controlled, and very assertive." A slow grin spread across his face. "All qualities I like in a woman."

"Is that a fact?" She took a step forward, her eyes on his and the air between them thick with electricity. "If assertive turns you on, then you should love this. Take me home," she said, clutching his collar and pulling him down so that she could whisper the rest of her invitation in the kind of language her mother had definitely not taught her.

"Yeah," he said. "I think that's a suggestion I can definitely get behind."

They took the old-fashioned way home, snuggled together in the backseat of a taxi, with roaming hands and nuzzling lips. So much, in fact, that she caught the driver peeping at them once in the rearview mirror.

But whereas old Lydia might have blushed furiously and sunk to the floorboards, this Lydia simply grinned and suggested he subscribe to cable.

Nikko rolled his eyes and pulled her close. "Newlyweds," he said, apparently more inclined to be polite.

At least, she assumed he was only being polite. Surely he wasn't thinking along those lines. Was he?

She licked her lips and leaned up against him, but turned her head to face out the window, afraid her thoughts would show on her face. Could a person know after only one night? Because Lydia thought she did. He was her fantasy come true, and when he walked into her life it was like he'd walked into a hole in her heart and filled her utterly.

Her mind was still meandering when they reached her apartment, but his soft kisses and sultry suggestions of a quick shower got her mind back on track. She gave him a quick kiss, then bent over to pull off her shoes. They were off, and she was working the button on her jeans when she heard the *bing bing* of his cell phone that apparently wasn't actually a cell phone.

He pulled it from deep in a pocket and flipped it open, then pushed a button or two. She wasn't really paying attention, but something changed—the air in the room seemed to grow colder and she couldn't help but shiver. She looked up, distracted from the act of undressing, and found him staring at her. His already familiar face seemed harsh. Harder than she'd seen it, and she shuddered a bit, not from lust this time, but from a deep, cold dread.

"Nikko?" she asked, fearing the worst. "What's wrong."

"Text message," he said, with a steely edge to his voice. He held the phone up for her to see. The screen was too far away, though, and so she shook her head, an icy chill coursing through her.

"I'm not sure I—"

"Cut the crap, Lydia," he said. "Tell me the truth and tell me now. Who in Hades are you, and how long have you been working for Ruthless?"

"What?"

She was staring at him, her mouth gaping open, her expression of surprise so sincere that he almost believed it. Almost, but not quite.

"I can't believe I didn't see through your ruse earlier. A Protector? Honestly, I've been out of the game too long."

Not that that was a legitimate excuse. The truth was, he didn't see that she was conning him because he didn't want to. He was lonely and tired of living for the mission, and when a beautiful girl appeared out of nowhere and seemed to be as attracted to him as he was to her, he fell hard and fast.

Oldest story in the book. He wasn't pathetic. He was just a typical male.

He looked at her, seeing the confusion in her eyes along with the hurt. He took a step toward her, and then stopped. *Watch it, Nikko.* She was a good one. After all, didn't Ruthless only recruit the best? Wasn't that why he'd so far been untouchable?

He forced himself to stop, to harden his heart. Because no matter how much he wanted to pull her into his arms and tell her that it was all a big misunderstanding, that wasn't the case. She wasn't a Protector, and she'd flat-out lied to him.

"Dammit, Nikko, talk to me!"

"You lied to me," he said.

Her brow furrowed as she looked from the phone to his face and back again. "No, I swear, I didn't lie."

"Do you know what this is?" he asked, thrusting the phone closer to her face.

"A phone?"

"And a lie detector. It's automatic. Analyzes every sound it picks up. Not immediately, unfortunately. But it sends a signal to Council headquarters, and a text message is returned almost instantaneously. I missed the earlier message," he said. "I was a little distracted at the time, I guess." And about *that* he was truly kicking himself, even though the distraction had been oh, so very sweet.

No. Best not to think that way. Not sweet. Devious.

"And this time?" she asked.

"This time, there were two messages: one with an update on my mission, the other reporting on the veracity of your earlier statements. When you said you were a—"

"Protector," she finished, looking at her toes. "I know. I'm sorry. But I wasn't lying. I swear."

"The phone says otherwise."

"I didn't understand." She looked up at him, tears clinging to her lashes. "I was protecting, and so I thought—" She broke off and brushed a tear from her eye, pretty much ripping him apart from the inside in the process. "It's all about the shoes, okay? I got the shoes and then suddenly I was in the thick of it, protecting that girl. And then when I heard you, I rushed in, too. And it's not like I really knew what I was doing, but I figured, well, maybe you had ordered shoes, too, and maybe you could tell me what the deal was. That's all. I swear. Do you understand? Do you believe me?"

"Shoes?" he asked, his head starting to spin.

"These shoes," she said, pointing to the boots sitting on the floor beside her. "I bought them over this Web site, and there's this shoe goddess, and—"

"Shoe goddess?"

She blinked. "I guess that sounds a little crazy, huh?"

He shook his head, just slightly. "Not as much as you might think." Considering Protectors were descended from the Greek gods, it really wasn't that unbelieveable at all.

"Well, anyway, the shoes are supposed to give you your heart's desire, and, well, I wanted self-confidence, you know? And I guess Shoestra flipped that on its ear and made me totally kick-ass, but the truth is," she continued, her words coming machine-gun fast, "I like it. It feels right. And I'm sorry if you don't believe me, but I didn't lie to you, and I only want—"

"Wait." He held up a hand, exhausted from simply watching her. "Let's take it back a notch. You're trying to tell me you're *mortal?* I've seen you in action, Lydia."

But he believed her. He really did. For one thing, his bullshit meter wasn't going off at all. For another, the text feature on his phone wasn't blipping. It should be analyzing all this, and nothing was coming back saying that she lied.

Which either meant she was telling the truth, or it meant that the response time for the Auto-Detect feature was running slow again.

Nikko was willing to bet on the truth. Lydia, he thought, was something he was more than willing to gamble on.

She, however, didn't know that yet, and as he watched, she put her hands on her hips and cocked her head, looking absolutely adorable. "Yes, I'm mortal. I told you. It's the shoes," she said. "You've seen the shoes in action." She drew in a shaky breath, then looked down at the ground. "I'm not like you. I'm not strong. I'm not really a superhero. It's all about the shoes. Without them, I'm a complete loser."

"No, you're not."

She looked up at him, her expression sad and a little hopeful. But then it changed. Her eyes widening and filling with terror.

He took a step toward her. "Lyd—?"

"Exactly, my dear," answered a new voice, the words underscored by the crash of glass. "The shoes really are the center of it all, and I realized as much when I saw you in that alley. A fortuitous moment, to be sure." He held out his hand. "And if you don't mind," said Rex Ruthless, "I'll be taking them now."

CHAPTER SEVEN

Her shoes?

The ubervillain who'd pulled a U.S.S. *Enterprise* transporter trick in the alley right before her eyes—not to mention flipping her in midair—needed her *shoes?*

Lydia had no idea why someone who seemed to ooze powers of his own would want women's shoes that upped your kick-ass factor, but she did know one thing: there was no way in hell she was letting him have them.

Those thoughts passed through her head in nanoseconds, and before she even had time to register that she *had* thought, she was rushing forward to shove her feet into her shoes, tripping over her toes in a tangle of limbs and jeans to get to them before he did.

Because he was trying!

Mere seconds after he'd spoken, he was lunging toward her shoes, with Nikko leaping on top of him. They rolled over, a mishmash of arms and legs, and then—suddenly—Nikko froze, his eyes wide with surprise.

"What did you do to him?" Lydia screamed, managing to tie the last lace and secure the boots firmly to her feet.

"It's amazing the little tricks one can manage when one has access to Council prototypes," Ruthless said, smiling thinly as he held up a small cylindrical silver contraption.

"It won't keep him frozen forever—and sadly I can't repeat the freeze once it wears off naturally—but it should be plenty of time to get those shoes and head back to my laboratory."

"You're insane," she said. "Why on earth do you want a pair of women's shoes?"

"My dear, your shoes are the component I've been searching for. The only known component of shoeidium. Very rare, and very fortunate I was in that alley to see your shoes in action. Now I have the final piece in my Miniaturizing Machine."

"Your *what*?"

His smile was pure ice. "I think you heard me."

Yeah, she thought. She was pretty sure she had. "What exactly are you planning to miniaturize?"

"Why, New York City, of course. Small enough to fit in a snow globe on my desk. The ultimate Christmas present to myself, don't you think?" He held out a hand and waggled his fingers. "Now be a good girl and pass me those shoes."

"I don't think so," she said. She might not be a real superhero like Nikko, but there was no way she was letting this thug carry out his evil plot—no matter how ridiculously comic book it might sound. And with that determination firmly in mind, she turned and started to run in the other direction.

It was a ruse, though, and when he sprinted after her, she stopped cold, then whipped around, letting those fabulous feet do their thing.

The cylinder flew out of his hand, and his head went back with a *thwack* so loud Lydia was sure his neck must have snapped. Unfortunately, though, his head was still firmly attached.

"You bi—"

"Want more?" she asked, then punched him in the nose,

surprising herself, and making her toes tingle with pride in her shoes.

"Little fool," he hissed, his voice wet and gurgly through his bloody nose. "I need only the shoes. Give them to me and you will live out your life as you are, and not smaller than a flea."

"I'm thinking no," she said, even as the air fizzled again. As she turned instinctively toward the new arrival who had teleported inside her apartment, Mr. Evil Genius, with whom she had yet to be properly introduced, dove for his little silver tube. Immediately she launched herself with an amazing *Matrix*-like kick that she'd seen only in the movies, but it was too late. He zapped her mid-leap, and she froze, her legs in an awkward, painful position as she started her frozen descent.

The new arrival caught her, thank goodness, before she landed in a stiff, painful heap. Not that the thug had her best interest at heart. No, he only wanted her shoes.

"Get them off her feet," Ruthless said with a quick glance toward the still-frozen Nikko. "And hurry. Time is working against us."

In her head, she screamed out her protests, but in her frozen state, no sound came out. Not good, and she felt her heart race inside the frozen statue of herself, the tempo increasing as the thug squatted down and started fiddling with her footwear.

Unable to bend her head to look down, she couldn't tell what was going on, but soon enough, she realized that there was a problem.

"Ain't workin'," the thug said. In front of her, the big boss's face turned an interesting shade of puce.

"Give me those shoes," he said, pointing the silver cylinder in her face. "Why can he not remove your shoes?"

He pressed a button and all of a sudden, her mouth

opened and she drew in a long gulp of air, realizing with a start how shallow her breathing had been when she was frozen.

"WHY?" he demanded, his face shifting from puce to bright red as he bellowed the question.

"I . . . I don't know," Lydia answered.

"Want me to cut her feet off?" the thug asked.

"Yes—"

"*What?*"

"No, wait," he amended. "The shoes are obviously linked to her. What if that somehow saps her power? No, we'll take her back with us. Once we are safely in the lair we can surely find a way to remove them. Even if, like Dorothy, the only way the shoes come off is if the owner is a dead little girl."

Lydia opened her mouth—not at all sure what she was going to say, but determined to give a verbal tongue-lashing even though she couldn't manage a physical one.

It didn't matter. Out came the little silver cylinder and—*phbt!*—her mouth was frozen again. Talk about irritating.

At least this time she was frozen facing Nikko. That, however, was hardly a consolation, considering they were both in deep doo-doo. Being able to see the gorgeous man who now didn't trust her wasn't exactly a reason to cheer.

Except . . .

Except there was something about his eyes. About the way they watched her, almost as if they were imploring. She focused harder, or, at least, she *thought* about focusing harder, because the truth was that as stuck as she was, she couldn't really do anything. Not even blink.

Nikko blinked.

Mentally, she gaped.

He'd *blinked.* But . . . but . . .

But he couldn't. Could he?

And that's when she remembered: the freeze ray eventually wore off. And yet there he was, still frozen stiff like a statue.

Why?

Not that she had time to ponder that mystery. The boss and his lackey had sidled up next to her.

"Get her between us," the boss said. "I want us each to have an arm, just in case she comes out of it after transit. Those damn legs are lethal."

You bet your ass they are, she thought, mentally spitting the words at him.

He pulled another device out of his pocket, the silver cylinder having disappeared. This contraption—a small, red box—had a tiny antenna on top. He let go of Lydia's arm just long enough to flip a switch, and then, if she could, she would have screamed. Because her body seemed to be dissolving from the inside out.

Beside her, the bad guys seemed fuzzy, too, as if they were also dissolving into points of light.

And just at the moment she realized what was happening to them, something hard and fast slammed into her. "Surprise," Nikko whispered in her ear, his arms and legs linked tightly to hers.

And though Lydia couldn't manage the actual movement, inside her head she smiled.

"Well, lookie-lookie," Ruthless said, his voice sounding foggy and faraway to Nikko's half unthawed ears. "We got ourselves a stowaway."

Nikko blinked, his body feeling discombobulated, apart from itself, and though he desperately wanted to look around for Lydia, he found he couldn't quite make the neurons fire properly to do that. *Teleport lag.* He'd heard about it;

now, apparently, he was experiencing it. And from what he could tell, Ruthless had already adjusted.

Not exactly the way to win the advantage, he thought, wondering if his brilliant plan to enter the lair was turning out to be not so brilliant after all.

"What should we do with 'im?" Ruthless's flunkie questioned, giving Nikko a poke in the shoulder. Nikko immediately lashed back, then winced in pain. The freeze ray had worn off, but he was still bound tight, and he'd just strained the heck out of his arm by trying to thrust his way out of a pair of Council-issued Outcast binders—cuffs strong enough to hold renegade superheroes at the peak of their power.

"Want me to kill him?" the flunkie continued, sounding perfectly thrilled by that idea.

"It's tempting," Ruthless said. "But no. If the shoes are drained of their energy when the girl dies, we may need a hostage."

"So we're really gonna off her, then?"

"Eh. I'm not going to go out of my way, but if she's killed in the machine . . . well, what can you do?"

They carried their conversation out while walking, discussing the details of their plan to hook the shoes up to the contraption—with Lydia still in them—as they exited the room. All the while, Nikko seethed and struggled, and planned his revenge.

Because nobody—*nobody*—was hurting his Lydia.

And he really needed to save New York, too.

Fortunately for New York, Lydia, and the whole free world, the grogginess from the teleportation lag wore off quickly. Not enough for Nikko to get across the room before the door slammed shut behind Ruthless, but still fast.

The downside, of course, was that he was locked in a small room, his body pressed against a concrete pillar, his wrists bound tight behind him with Protector-rated cuffs, and Lydia in danger on the far side of that door.

The good news was that the tracker embedded in his skin should have been activated during teleportation, which meant that the full weight of the Council ought to descend on this place any moment.

Then again, he'd been here for a few minutes already, and as far as he could tell, an epic battle wasn't taking place beyond those doors. Either the tracker had malfunctioned, or Ruthless's lair was somehow shielded. Either way, there was no way for him to remedy the situation with both hands tied behind his back.

Time to do something about that . . . if he could.

He looked around the room, but it was completely empty: not a single piece of furniture, not a single rivet on a wall. Simply the concrete post he was tied to, his arms thrust behind him, and his wrists bound.

The post, however, was somewhat narrow, and if he shifted a bit . . .

Yes. He could still feel it. They'd left his phone in his back pocket. All he had to do was scoot around to the left and see if he could—

Got it!

The problem, of course, was what to do with it now that he had it. Finding the buttons by feel only, he tried the communication feature first, but as he suspected, the room was shielded. The level of shielding suggested by the high-pitched response emitted from his device told Nikko that there'd be no help from the Council unless he could figure out a way to poke a hole in Ruthless's defense. And *that,* unfortunately, was a very dicey proposition without knowing the layout.

Which meant that his first priority was to find Lydia and stop the completion of the device, then get her the hell out of there. He would stay behind and try to jam whatever interference device Ruthless had installed.

In the meantime, without communication, the phone was useful only as a weapon, and he was currently running short on ammo, with only two laser powerpacks embedded in the device. He could use one to take out the column he was bound to, but that seemed a bit reckless considering he couldn't get a good look at the column to judge its density.

Better to aim the laser straight for his bonds. He might blow his hands off, true; but if luck was on his side, he'd simply blow open the binders. And at the moment, Nikko didn't see another option. Time was ticking down. Lydia was in danger. And as she'd pointed out with such insight, he was all about saving mortals.

He smiled, realizing how well she'd put his own thoughts into words, and how she'd justified and validated his decisions, even if the Council had disagreed.

Yes, she was a mortal. But she was a superhero, too. As much as he was. And right then, he was determined to save her.

He fumbled, trying to get the device in place, and almost dropping it in the process. Then he got the dangerous end lined up with the binders, tugged his other wrist as far away as humanly (well, as *Protectorly*) as possible, took a deep breath, and pressed the trigger.

A burst of heat, and he winced as pain shot across his wrists, as vibrant as a white-hot flame. But his fingers still wiggled and, more important, he could move them in front of him and look at them.

He was free!

"You've still got it, buddy," he said to himself, ignoring his aching wrist as he tightened his grip on the device and headed for the door. He said a silent plea to Zeus that it would be unlocked, because he really didn't want to waste his last laser charge busting out.

Fortunately, luck was on his side, and he found himself in a long hallway. He skulked down it, darting into a supply closet and pulling on a white lab coat. Not the best of disguises, but it would have to do. And, it turned out, not a bad choice. Because when he got to the end of the hall and stepped into the cavernous space accented by a center-piece jumble of wires, cables, tubes and pulleys, he saw that the only other people in the room were clad as he was—as out-of-place dental hygienists or CSI wannabes.

In fact, he realized as he circled the room, the only one not in a lab coat was Lydia. She was in the center of the machine, highlighted from the front by a shaft of light that came from the single glass panel in the otherwise thick, metal-domed room. The light cast odd shadows on her face, making her looked scared and frightened. Not that he blamed her.

He grabbed a clipboard from a nearby table and walked toward her, head high and with purpose in his step. He used the attached pen to bang a rhythm as he walked.

"Don't quit your day job," she said, the fire in her voice clear. "I'm thinking evil thug's flunkie is going to do you much better than percussionist."

"And here I thought I'd found my calling," he said, delighting when he saw the fire in her eyes change to a different kind of heat. She'd recognized him. And then his heart sank again when she pulled back into herself, her face turning to steel.

"So do you believe me *now?*"

"Lydia, I'm sorry. I had no idea."

She cocked her head. "You *do* believe me."

"Of course."

"Why? Because your little lie detector said so?"

"I believe *you*, Lydia. And I'm sorry I doubted you even for a second."

Her expression softened. "Yeah?"

He couldn't help his smile. "Yeah. But I'm not so sure now's the time to talk about it."

She pressed her lips together and nodded. "Right." She drew in a breath. "So you're going to rescue me, right? I mean, I'm a mortal and you're a superhero. And that's what superheroes do, right?"

There was a new harshness in her words that stung. "Lydia?"

"It's okay. I know you were only interested in me because—well, because you thought I was like you. And I know it's absurd to tell you this right now, but I'm pretty attached to this thing, and I don't think I'm getting out of here alive. So I'm going to do something I never would have done a few days ago, and that's tell you that I like you. A lot. I've probably even fallen in love with you. Or, I don't know, I think maybe I've been in love with you my whole life. But it's okay. You don't have to love me back. I get the difference between us. I'm not stupid."

"You're acting it," he said, her words flowing over him like honey. *She was falling in love with him.*

She blinked. "What?"

"There's something between us. It's not going away because you weren't born a Protector."

Surprise and hope filled her eyes, and he expected her to shout out joyously that she loved him. Instead, hesitation crowded her eyes. "There's not . . . it wouldn't . . ." She drew in a breath. "You have to know, it would never work between us. I'm not like you. I'm a fraud. Without the shoes, I'm a total wimp, and—"

"I don't care," he said firmly.

Her smile was wobbly. "Maybe you do and maybe you

don't," she said. "But I care, Nikko. I do. And I don't want you to have less of a woman than you deserve."

"I deserve you."

"You say that now, but—"

A loudspeaker crackled, and Nikko searched the area for something to throw at it. Not because that would help his mission, but because he was so damn frustrated.

"Touching, touching, touching," Ruthless's voice crackled over the speaker. "But I'm afraid you're going to be dying alone and apart. No time to make up before the end of the world as you know it. Unless perhaps you'd like me to teleport you back to Manhattan? You can live your life the size of bacteria in the snow globe on my desk. No fake snow, of course. That wouldn't be healthy for my little inhabitants."

"Do you mean that, Ruthless?" Nikko shouted.

"I—what?" Some of the confidence had left Rex's voice, replaced by confusion.

Nikko hid a smile. "I said, do you mean that?"

"Eh . . . er . . . what exactly?"

"That you'll teleport us to Manhattan? Shrink us? Let us live together forever."

"Nikko!"

"I don't care," he said to her. "I just want to be with you." He looked her in the eyes, hoping she was understanding his message. "Come on, Lydia. Toss caution to the wind and come with me."

"But—"

"She'll do it," he shouted to the room. "She'll do it because she loves me. Let her go, and she'll leave the shoes behind. That's my offer, Rex. Take it, or suffer the consequences."

A snort blasted over the loudspeaker. "You're hardly in a position to bargain."

"It's the best deal you'll get. You need her shoes, and you don't know that the machine will work with her in them. Give her freedom. Give her to me. The game is yours for the winning."

"And how do I know this isn't some trick?"

"Um, hello? I'm trapped in your lair, remember? Just me and the girl, both of us essentially helpless. And no Council to come to my rescue." He looked around to illustrate the point, his eyes falling on the dozens of technicians who'd pulled weapons out from under their lab coats and were now pointing them at him.

"It is true," Ruthless said, thoughtfully. "That ridiculous tracking device embedded in your arm won't work in here. My exterior walls have all been specially treated to block the beam emitted by your tracker."

"See? And, honestly, if you've done your homework, you should know that the Council isn't exactly number one on my favorite persons list. The chance to live my life in peace—even inside a snow globe—well, that's damned appealing." He frowned, considering. "Guess there's no chance of you shrinking some of Florida's beaches and moving them in with—never mind. The point is that you're the one with the power here."

"Actually, I believe that honor resides with your girlfriend. You may be happy to negotiate on her behalf, but I have seen no evidence that she is willing to remove the shoes."

"She will," he said, turning to look her in the eye. "Come on, Lydia. Throw caution to the wind. Hell, *throw* your insecurities to the wind. To the sky, even," he added, glancing up. "We don't need to worry about saving the world. Just ourselves," he lied. "Get rid of them and come with me. I want you with me forever. Tell me," he said, and though the words were a ploy, his heart meant every word. "Tell me you want to stay with me forever, too."

For a moment, he thought she was going to protest. That she didn't understand his ruse. She licked her lips, looking up at the largest loudspeaker. Then she nodded. "All right," she said. "Because I do want to stay with you, Nikko. I want that more than anything."

"We'll make it work," he said, meaning a life together more than the unspoken plan of escape.

"The shoes," Ruthless shouted. "Take them off."

"Unstrap my arms," she said. "And my waist so I can bend over."

"Hang on," Nikko said. "Unstrap all of her. You're teleporting us out of here, right? She doesn't give up the shoes until I see a show of good faith."

A pause and then, "Oh, all right. She's mortal, after all, and without those shoes, she's nothing. *Release her.*"

The moment Ruthless spoke the words, Lydia felt her bindings loosen. She bent over and unfastened her boots, her heart beating so loud she was sure Ruthless could hear it. Hopefully, he'd think it was because of Nikko's protestation of love and not because of their risky plan. A plan she could only hope she was interpreting right.

For that matter, she hoped that she was reading the truth in Nikko's words—that he really loved her and wanted her, and that it wasn't all a clever ploy to defeat the bad guy.

Because the truth was, no matter what she'd told him, she wanted him, too. And though they might never have forever, if she could squeeze a few more minutes out with him . . . well, surely she could store up enough to last a lifetime?

She pulled off one boot and tied that lace to the lace of the boot she still had on her left foot. Then she took the connected boots off and stood up, holding them tight.

"They're all yours," she said loudly, wondering where exactly Ruthless was. "The key to your stupid machine."

"Excellent," the voice called—was he *really* named Rex Ruthless? "Put them down in the machine well and step away."

"Right," she said, drawing in a breath. Now or never. She leaned down, pretending to place the boots, then swung back and let them fly, tossing them backward and into the air above Nikko.

Things happened in slow motion, then. He reached up with his super-duper cell phone and fired a laser blast that not only destroyed the shoes—good-bye superpowers—but also blew out the glass panel in the roof above them.

"Noooooooooo!" Ruthless cried. "You fool! You absolute fool!"

"Am I?" Nikko asked, as men in lab coats rushed to cover him with their weapons. "I destroyed the part you need and saved New York. I'm actually feeling pretty good about myself."

"Enjoy it," Ruthless said. "You'll be dead in moments, the girl soon after you."

"No!" Lydia screamed. *No more.* It was suicide, maybe, but she wasn't about to stand back and watch as those cretins harmed the man she loved. If she was going to die, she was going to do it on her terms, trying her damnedest to rescue him.

And with that thought fixed firmly in her mind, she jumped into the fray, kicking and biting and shoving and doing everything she could to get the thugs off Nikko. And, in the process, actually giving him room to maneuver, room to fight back.

Best of all, miracle of miracles, they actually seemed to be making some progress. *Some* being the operative word, because the truth was, they were outnumbered, and though she'd tried her best, without her shoes she wasn't much use in the fighting department. And Nikko, with all his powers, couldn't fight five armed thugs with Council-issued weapons designed to keep Protectors at bay.

They ended up trapped and surrounded, Nikko's hand closing over hers. "You did great," he said. "You were perfect."

"A nice thought," she countered, "but considering we're about to die, I'm thinking I didn't do so hot."

"No? You're the reason we're about to win," he said, his curious announcement explained almost immediately by the abrupt arrival of dozens of Protectors—entering from the hole in the ceiling, the main doors, through the floor. A full-fledged invasion. And as they secured the bad guys who held Nikko and Lydia at bay, he pulled her into his arms.

"Don't you need to go fight?"

"I think they've got it covered," he said. "Thanks to you." He looked up at the gaping hole above them. "Tossing the shoes so I could blast out that panel saved us. It let the tracking device signal get through to headquarters."

"And signaled the cavalry," she said, understanding. "Then, it really is over. . . ."

"It's over," he said, swinging an arm around her and pointing across the room where a team of well-armed Protectors was leading Ruthless out. "I think we both done good."

It took several hours to rid the lair of its evil bad guys and catalog all the gadgets and gizmos found in the room, and during that time, Lydia stayed firmly attached to Nikko, dreading the time when it would all be done and they would go their separate ways.

Slowly, everyone was leaving, and when Nikko stood up, she joined him, feeling the weight of loss pressing on her already. She didn't want to lose him, and yet what other choice did she have? They were from two different worlds, and no matter what he might say, she had to believe it mattered. She wasn't really a superhero, no matter how much she might wish it were so. And why would he want plain old Lydia?

"Ah, Nikko," an elderly man with white hair and a beard said, striding forward. "An excellent mission. Excellent. And you, my dear," he added, turning his attention to Lydia. "A true hero."

He bowed, then kissed her hand as Lydia fought an amused grin.

"I am so sorry about the loss of your precious shoes," he continued. "However, I believe that the Council can do more than thank you for your efforts. We can, you see, offer you a job."

Her brows lifted. "As a superhero? That's a really great offer, but I'm not sure I'm cut out—"

"I think you have proven yourself most capable," he said, looking around the room. "You did quite a bit of damage without powers just now, simply trying to free Nikko from his captors."

"Well, yeah, but I didn't actually manage," she said. "You guys had to come to our rescue."

"Mmmm," he said, as if truly considering her counterpoint. Beside her, Nikko squeezed her hand, giving her the kind of smile that suggested forever. A forever she wanted to grab on to. Honestly, though, she didn't know how.

The elderly man turned his attention to Nikko. "And what about you, young man? Now that you are off probation—congratulations, by the way—are you going to return to Colorado and avoid all Council assignments, or do you intend to get back into the thick of things?"

"I'm back," he said. "I missed it. I missed doing good.

This," he added, sweeping his hand around the room. "And even the purse snatchings and cat rescues we did together."

"Standard superhero fare," Lydia said with a grin.

"Something like that," he agreed.

"I wonder if perhaps you would like a partner?" the elderly man asked with a twinkle in his eye. Lydia did a double-take remembering another twinkling eye when she was much younger. Surely he wasn't . . .

"A partner?" Nikko responded. "Not on your life." But then she saw his hesitation as he realized that the man was looking right at her. The question was, *why* was he looking right at her?

Surely she couldn't be his part—

"Then again . . . *that*," Nikko said firmly, "I'm completely up for."

"And what about you, my dear?"

"We're right back at square one," she said. "I'm hardly qualified. And the truth is . . ." She trailed off, looking at her feet before drawing the courage to say what she truly wanted. A courage that came far faster than it would have mere days ago. "The truth is I don't want to play personal assistant or mortal sidekick. I liked having the powers, and I don't think I'd be happy working in your world without them." She pressed her lips together, not willing to go further with the statement. Because even though she couldn't *work* in that world, she did want a man from that world.

She simply wasn't sure how she could have one without the other, or if he would even want her.

"I think you misunderstood my proposition, my dear. The Council has significant technology at its disposal. You handled yourself well with your rather intriguing shoes. You can also handle our technology." Zephron frowned slightly. "Shoestra," he muttered. "I will have to look into that."

Lydia wasn't interested in the shoes at the moment. "Do you really mean it?"

"Of course. So, what do you think? Do we have a deal?"

She couldn't even nod. For that matter, she could hardly breathe. On the one hand, she'd proven to herself that she could stick up for herself, even without the shoes. That was good—great, in fact. She almost wished Darla from her old job was there, just so she could show her former nemesis up. Then again, Darla wasn't worth a second thought. And the new Lydia could be so much more with a little help from Protector technology.

Not that she needed to be more than herself.

She glanced sideways at Nikko, who was looking back at her with love in his eyes. The truth was, she *did* need a job. And what better than to sign on as Nikko's partner?

She drew in a deep breath and nodded. "I'll take it," she said, then stuck out her hand to seal the deal. "At least," she added, eyeing Nikko, "I will if you want a partner."

He answered with a familiar grin, and Lydia knew without a doubt that she'd found not only a life she loved, but the man of her dreams.

Jade Lee

Kung Fu Shoes!

Thank you Julie and Marianne for being so brilliant and sharing space with me. And thank you to Chris Keeslar for letting me use shoes instead of boots and for being so creative in the first place! As a gesture of my thanks, editor extraordinaire, I will let you have my first pair of magic shoes. Well, maybe not if they're really cool. Maybe you'll just get a fruit basket instead. Anyway . . . thank you all!

CHAPTER ONE

Michaela Becker's heart sank as she reached for *The Scarlet Letter*. Sure, she loved discussing the fate of a woman branded by passion, the issues of male-dominated religion run amok, of government repression, stoic women, and sex, sex, sex! But she doubted her classroom of sneering, giggling, or comatose high school kids were going to engage in spirited debate. At this point, she'd be thrilled if any of them had read the American classic. Even the comic book version.

Putting on her perkiest smile, she stepped out from behind her teacher desk and began the last class of the day. *Please*, she prayed, *let them listen. Let me reach someone today. If that's not possible, please let someone's hair burst into flames so I can cancel class while I put them out.*

No one listened, not even God. At best, her questions on the story received nonresponsive stares. At worst, well . . . heads in the back bobbed to "hidden" iPods while other students texted each other on their phones. And nothing burst into flames, except perhaps her dream of being an inspiring teacher.

As the period wound toward its inevitable dreary end, Michaela understood why she'd been nicknamed "Micki Mouse." She was a complete failure as a teacher. She'd wanted to revolutionize education; instead she was just another ineffective warm body standing uselessly amidst the chilling tide of teen boredom.

Maybe she should strip naked and stand on her head; that might be better than setting someone's hair on fire. A dozen other maybes filtered through her thoughts, but Micki didn't act on any of them. She *never* acted on them. Instead, she stuck to her initial plan: kill them with kindness. Surely just a little more effort on her part, a little more understanding and compassion, would do the trick.

The bell rang—thank God—but Micki wasn't done yet. There was one student whom she still hoped to reach: Lucy Varner, a smart girl with a bad boyfriend. Last year, Lucy's brother had gotten high and shot a cop. Now the boy was in jail, her single-parent mom was exhausted from working two jobs, and Lucy was at loose ends. Or she had been until she hooked up with her brother's best friend and fellow druggie. But the way she was headed . . . If only Micki could connect with the girl, maybe the child would see that she could do so much more.

"Lucy, could you wait a moment, please?"

The dark-haired girl looked up from collecting her things, and her dark eyes blinked beneath ragged bangs. Unlike some of the other girls in class, she had yet to develop a woman's curves. In truth she appeared very average for a fourteen-year-old brunette, especially in her Goodwill jeans and tee, though her skin and eyes held a hint of Mediterranean beauty. One day the girl could turn into a willowy Sophia Loren, but for the moment she was just a little kid without makeup, without confidence, and without a real friend.

"I wanted to compliment you on your short story," Micki said. "It was wonderfully written, but so sad." The piece had been about a young girl who looked for a protector in a

world that betrayed her at every turn. She found her answer in a fairy godmother who ended up getting raped and
murdered by a drug lord. Then the magic wishes turned
bad, and the heroine ended up dying of an overdose. If fic-
tion was a window to the spirit, then Lucy's soul was in dire
need of a miracle. Micki so wanted to be that miracle.
"Can you tell me a little about why you wrote it?"

Lucy said nothing.

"You know, when I was your age, I really got into Mae
West. You've probably never heard of her, but she was
beautiful, busty, and bold. She did and said things that nobody dared do, and she'll be remembered forever for it. I
desperately wanted to be her. I even used to strike a pose
and say her lines." Micki dropped a hand on her hip and
tried to look sultry. "'His mother should have thrown him
away and kept the stork.'" It was the least risqué Mae West
quote she could think of right then, but one look at Lucy
told her she should have just gone for a sexy line. The girl
was clearly bored.

Micki sighed dramatically as she straightened. "Yeah, a
complete disappointment. I would look in the mirror and
see this." She waved generally at her tiny chest and boyish
curves. "The point is that I was looking at the wrong thing.
Magic doesn't come from big boobs or a magic fairy godmother; it comes from inside. And if I had only known to
look at what I could do instead of what I couldn't . . . well,
I would have found something amazing. I just had to look
inside." She searched the girl's face, wondering if she was
getting through. "What do you think?"

Nothing. Wait! Was there a spark in the girl's eye? An
almost-comment? She'd lifted her chin and taken a breath,
but she didn't say anything. Still, there was hope. After a
long pause, Micki chose a different tack.

"How's your mother doing?" She relaxed back against

the edge of the desk. Maybe if she was on a more equal height with the girl, it would help. "She didn't make it in for parent-teacher conferences, but I could maybe meet her at Starbucks. My treat. Do you think she'd like that?"

"Lucy's mom don't like rich-people coffee," sneered a voice from the hallway. Damian Ralston, Lucy's bad boyfriend, sauntered into the classroom and wrapped his muscular arm around her shoulders.

Micki kept her smile bright, but inside she knew all hope was gone for today. An English teacher just couldn't compete with a handsome gangbanger. Sure enough, Lucy's entire demeanor shifted from anxious teen to sneering rebel. "My mom don't have time to meet you."

"Surely she has some time off," Micki pressed. "We don't have to go for coffee. I know, how about we meet at the mall? You could bring her." She glanced at Damian, and tried to think of a way to exclude him. "We'll make it a girls' night out."

Score! There was longing in Lucy's eyes. She started to straighten, even lean forward a bit, but that was as far as she got. Faster than Micki expected, Damian whipped his arm off the girl. He stretched just like a football player, bristling, and on him, those muscles looked really intimidating.

"She said she don't have time for you!"

"She *doesn't* have time," Micki corrected without thinking.

"That's what I said!" Damian shot back, stepping forward. "She don't have time—"

"Naw, that ain't what you said," cackled another voice from the hallway. Three more of Damian's gang loitered near the door, watching and commenting on every move. "She don't think you talk right. She don't think much of you at all."

"You gonna take that?" challenged one of the others.

Great. A Greek chorus of testosterone. Micki's smile was beginning to strain, but she directed all her attention to Lucy—only Lucy. "Any time you like, you just give me the word."

"The word is 'no'!" Damian growled. His arm wrapped like a vise around Lucy's shoulders, but that was nothing compared to the jeers and catcalls from the hallway. Micki couldn't even tell who they were jeering at—herself or their leader. Either way, it wasn't good. And yet, she just couldn't leave it alone.

"Do you like how he treats you, Lucy?" She took a step forward and dared to challenge Damian eye to eye—though still from a prudent five feet away. "That's not how a real man handles a woman."

Curses flew out of the boy's mouth, but his fists were faster. Micki had deluded herself into thinking that he couldn't attack her from that distance. She knew he was the local gang leader with incredible power in this inner-city school. She knew as well that he had a hair-trigger temper and issues with anyone—teacher or otherwise—who challenged his macho image. He was absolutely the wrong person to get in a pissing contest with, and yet here she was trying to take his girlfriend away. Stupid, stupid, stupid!

She barely had time to rear back from his fist. Lucy screamed, "Damian!" and then Micki's foot lost traction and she began to fall, her body tensed and her eyes slammed shut.

Her right foot reared high. It was the one that had lost traction. It flew upward—really, really high—and impacted with something solid. Micki's eyes flew open, but her leg was still moving while the rest of her body followed. Hell, she had been falling backward, but now gravity was rushing her forward, into Damian's fists.

Micki thrust out her hands to catch herself—or to block one of his blows—only she moved her hands too high. She struck Damian's jaw with the heel of her hand. His head snapped back while her other hand—the one that was trying to grab onto something, anything, to steady herself—slammed down hard on his neck. She blinked. Had her hand been straight, like in a karate chop to his neck? There wasn't time to wonder.

She scrambled to the side, her hand numb. But that was nothing compared to Damian. His momentum was carrying him forward to where she had been standing before she slipped. But now she was well out of reach, and he apparently couldn't move his arm to protect himself. Micki watched in stunned slow motion as he staggered forward to bang painfully into her desk.

If she could have spoken, she would have gasped out an apology. Something. Not because she really cared if she beat the crap out of Damian, accidentally or not, but she was trying to connect with Lucy. Giving her boyfriend a black eye was counterproductive. Getting herself beaten to a pulp by that same boyfriend and his goons wasn't all that helpful either.

She turned, thinking she had to get both herself and Lucy out of there before it got ugly, but all she managed was a too bright "C'mon, Lucy, let's go shopping!" before the room exploded into chaos.

In the hallway, the boys started hooting and pointing while simultaneously blocking the exit. Lucy was staring wide-eyed at Damian who—oh hell—was just straightening from his face-plant on the desk. His lip was fat and bloody, but there was nothing wrong with his fists or the burning anger in his eyes. Worse, he had obviously recovered from his surprise.

"Look, Damian. I'm sorry. I kinda slipped," Micki started

to say. She stood between herself and Lucy, slowly trying to back them both out of the classroom. Maybe if they pushed, they'd get through the group at the door. But Lucy wasn't cooperating.

"Damian, baby, she's not worth it. Let's just get out of here. We can go make out."

"Lucy—no!" Micki was not going to have a child trade sexual favors for her! "Lucy—"

"Is there a problem here?" A deep male voice cut into the chaos, and automatically Micki's breath eased. Looking to the doorway, she watched Damian's posse magically melt away as Joe DeLuce—school cop—stepped into the room. "Miss Becker?"

Micki smiled gratefully at the man. He was the hottest detective on the force, but a bullet in the knee took him out of the game for a while. Instead of taking light duty, he chose instead a job as the high school cop. So now all the girls—Micki included—lusted after the man from afar. All the gangbangers thought twice about causing problems on school grounds. He was a boon to the school, and at this second, the answer to Micki's prayers. "Mr. DeLuce," she said way too breathlessly.

"Damian just got his ass kicked by the Mouse," sniggered one of the retreating gang. "He should sue or something."

From his position by the desk, Damian growled—yes, growled—at his friends, but his eyes remained on Micki. The sound was so terrifyingly animal that Micki nearly squeaked in response. As it was, she could only reach out for Lucy, trying to tug the girl back from her boyfriend.

It didn't work. Lucy shrugged her off and wrapped her arms around him. "It ain't nothin', Mr. DeLuce," Lucy said. "Me and Damian here were just screwing around. I think we frightened Miss Becker, but we're real sorry."

Damian, of course, wasn't talking. He was just staring at

Micki. It was a cold stare, filled with an inhuman violence that squeezed her chest tighter than possible. Which was ridiculous. She was a grown woman. A teacher, for God's sake! She couldn't let one boy—even a large, muscular, senior—scare her like this. He didn't even have a weapon. Or not one that she could see. And yet, she couldn't speak. He was going to kill her and there was nothing, absolutely nothing, that she could do about it.

"So it's nothing, huh, Mr. Ralston?" Mr. DeLuce drawled as he moved slowly into the room. His limp was barely noticeable as he stepped between Micki and her assailant. "Hey, Damian! It's nothing, right?"

Mr. DeLuce's voice still sounded congenial, but there was an underlying threat in his tone. They were like two boxers squaring off against each other, and God help her, Micki was grateful. At that moment, she didn't care what was between her and that cold stare, she was just happy for the breather. She knew it would bother her later: she needed to be able to stand on her own against these kids. But right now she was happy to hide temporarily behind Mr. DeLuce's broad shoulders.

Lucy broke in. "Nothing at all, sir. We was just on our way to the Chem Lab," she said with false cheer. "Damian's real good with chemistry."

A lie if there ever was one. As far as Micki could tell, the boy was failing every class. Truthfully, she didn't even know why the kid kept coming to school—though she would bet her next paycheck that Mr. Gorzinsky had something to do with it. The older chem teacher had some magical way of keeping these kids in school way longer than anyone wanted them. Micki didn't know what it was, but she envied him his skills.

Especially since a simple mention of the man's subject seemed to defuse the situation. From her place a half step behind Mr. DeLuce, Micki could see Damian's face shift into a disgusted grimace. "Come on," he grunted as he started shuffling forward. "I got business that ain't with no English teacher."

Micki released a loud breath of relief, then immediately regretted it. Mr. Gorzinsky had told her to never let the kids see her sweat. That one puff of air had just told Damian she'd all but wet her pants. And a glance at the school cop confirmed her mistake. He was practically rolling his eyes.

"Move aside, boys," he said to the gang in the hallway. "It's obvious Damian needs a little help out the door." It was a jab, no doubt about it, and it had its intended effect. The boys separated, snickering all the way. Damian threw an icy glare at DeLuce, and everyone ignored Micki. Everyone except Lucy. Shooting a glance at her teacher, she tucked herself tighter into her boyfriend's side and preened.

"Damian likes me right by his side," she said. And then they were gone, the boys and Lucy swaggering down the hallway.

"Great," Micki murmured to herself. "Just frigging great."

Unfortunately, she wasn't alone in her classroom. Mr. DeLuce hadn't followed the kids out. He'd stopped at the door and now turned back to her. She glanced up, struck by his presence. As usual.

He wasn't handsome. Far from it, actually. He had a stocky build and a nose that wasn't completely straight. His jaw was square, his eyes a pleasant brown, and his skin had that roughened look that should seem scruffy but was actually kind of sexy. Nothing about Joe DeLuce was exceptional. Common stock, Micki's mother would say. And yet, when he walked into a room, everybody noticed him. He was quiet, competent, and impossible to ignore. He had Presence, and Micki couldn't help but stare.

"So what really happened here?" he asked.

She answered, because that's what you did when Joe DeLuce smiled, all friendly like that. "Nothing. I slipped and accidentally clocked him. If it weren't for you, I'd probably be a bloody mess right now."

"It's difficult for outsiders to understand how much power these gangs have. They're a law unto their own, and Damian's just recently become the new leader. He's going to be especially prickly, especially bold, or he'll lose his position. It's not the time to face off with him."

"I know." She sighed and looked at her hands, self-disgust riding her hard. "Thank you," she murmured.

"You don't sound very grateful."

She glanced up, startled because his voice was so close. He'd moved silently in front of her. Close enough to kiss, she thought. Then she blinked, startled by her disconcerting thought. She'd given up such fantasies about Joe six months ago, right after she'd seen him with Sar-ahhhh, the blonde bombshell with size DDD breasts. She'd only seen them together one time, but the sight was burned into her memory.

"Um . . . yeah. No. I mean . . ." She swallowed, forcing her thoughts—and her gaze—away from his mouth. "Thank you. Truly. I'm just sorry I needed rescuing." Then she made the mistake of looking into his eyes: soft chocolate brown and filled with sympathy. Before she even realized what was happening, her vision went wavy with tears. "I don't know what I'm doing here," she confessed. "I try so hard, but I'm not getting through to any of them. Even the good ones."

He didn't answer. His eyes widened with a brief moment of panic. "You're not going to cry, are you?"

Too late. Her lashes were already spiky with tears, and they both knew it. So rather than completely horrify the man, she bustled behind her desk to grab her purse. "Nah. I'm not the tearful type," she lied.

"Yeah. Thought not," he lied back.

She took her time gathering her things. She wanted to have herself completely under control before she faced the man again. He moved to stand on the opposite side of her desk. Out of the corner of her eye, she could see the way his pants hugged his lean hips. Even with his limp, the guy obviously kept in shape.

"Um, hey," he said, rather awkwardly. "I need caffeine. You want to go to a café or something? I know one close by."

Micki straightened slowly, forcing her gaze to travel up his trim waist, past his white shirt and broad shoulders, to finally look him in the eye. At the beginning of the year, she had fantasized about just this event. She had dreamed that he would show up in her classroom one day and casually ask her out for coffee. It would be the beginning of a beautiful romance. But then teaching became unexpectedly awful, and he became notorious for taking certain teachers out for coffee and getting them to completely re-think their lives. They even had a name for it: pity coffee.

She swallowed and found a boldness that was completely new to her. "Pity coffee, Mr. DeLuce? What if I start crying again?"

He arched a brow, obviously startled. "I thought you weren't the crying type."

She shrugged. "Maybe I lied."

He shifted his stance, his eyes lighting with humor. "And if you think coffee with you is a pity date, honey, you need to look in the mirror more. A gorgeous blonde—if anyone's getting the pity, it's me."

Micki smiled, her legs growing steadier now that she was back on familiar ground. She'd mastered flirting in middle school. And yet, she wasn't in the mood for this subtle dance of attraction, despite the chemistry she now imagined between herself and Mr. DeLuce. "Come on, Joe. We both know that *petite* blondes aren't your type." Her tiny, almost-B cups were well shaped in her Victoria's Secret bra, but they were nothing compared to the women she usually saw him with.

He looked at her, surprise sharpening his features even more. Then he slowly folded his arms across his chest, making his biceps bulge and emphasizing the breadth of his shoulders. "And what would you know about my type?"

She considered answering. What better way to get back your self-esteem than engage in a spirited flirtation with a handsome lawman? But then her gaze caught on Damian—arm wrapped around little Lucy—as he and his buddies swaggered past her classroom window. The group couldn't see her from outside; she was on the second floor and well away from the sill, but he still paused long enough to shoot her window a malevolent glare. She couldn't help it. A shiver of fear ran down her spine. Lord, she was such a weenie.

Joe's mellow voice interrupted her self-loathing. "Have you thought of taking some self-defense classes?"

"Already done," she said, without shifting her gaze from the window. "But yelling 'no!' at a friend in padding isn't the same thing as facing down an Indianapolis gang leader."

"True, that," he murmured in response.

Her gaze hopped back to him, startled by the teen slang he'd just voiced. For a moment there, she might have imagined it was one of the kids talking, albeit in a deeper, thicker, more manly voice. "Is that why you want to have coffee with me?" she challenged. "To tell me how to be stronger with the kids? How to face my fears and not let the little bastards walk all over me?" She did a fairly good imitation of Mr. Gorzinsky, who was always lecturing her on the subject.

"Would it help?"

She sighed. "Maybe." She hefted her slim Gucci purse. "Come on. I'll buy; you advise. But be warned: you're not the first person who thought he could toughen me up. Stronger men than you have failed."

He grinned, startling her with the mischievous twinkle in his eye. "I doubt that, Miss Becker. I most sincerely do."

CHAPTER TWO

Café Kopi was quiet, the music trendy, and the tables tall. Sitting on a high stool, Joe DeLuce looked distinctly out of place, and yet he seemed completely at ease sipping a mocha latte, double sweet. It was quite a disconnect for Micki, and she struggled with even looking at him. First of all, he was too big for the place. Too big for the tiny tables, too big for this intimate little space in the front corner. Hell, he looked too big for the huge picture window that backlit him with warm afternoon sun.

"Nervous?" he asked as he took a long drink.

"What? No! Not at all. Of course not." She clamped her mouth shut before she started gibbering like an idiot.

He just nodded and looked at her with his dark gaze. He knew, of course. She could look her parents straight in the eye and give a bald-faced lie: Yes, Dad, I desperately want to be a corporate lawyer. Yes, Mom, teaching is what I'll do until I can marry a future senator. And, Yes, I know the best way to work with inner-city youths is with a checkbook and an intermediary. Lying to her parents had become second nature. But with Mr. DeLuce, her insides seemed too jittery. Hell, even her feet kept twisting beneath her for no obvious reason. Her new Chinese velvet Mary Janes had felt like heaven when she put them on, but for some reason they now pinched or were too large or something. It was weird. Or maybe she was just avoiding continuing this conversation with the enigmatic school cop.

"Okay, let me have it," she said, bracing her hands around her candy apple red travel mug. "What am I doing wrong?" Then she abruptly took a gulp of coffee rather than look him in the eye.

"What makes you think you're doing anything wrong?"

She was so startled by his question that she forgot to put her mug down; she held it before her lips and stared at him over the rim. "Is this some cop technique? Answer a question with a question? Two can play that game, you know."

He smiled, and the skin around his eyes crinkled. He had a weathered look she really liked: tan and used to smiling. Awful on a woman, but on him it screamed rugged, manly stud. "No trick," he said, interrupting her lust. "Sometimes it's important to identify exactly what isn't working."

She shrugged. "That's easy; the kids don't listen to me. Which means they don't learn."

"So, that's your goal? To make them learn?"

She set her mug down and frowned. "That is my job, isn't it?"

"Nope," he said, then took a long draw from his paper cup, forcing her to wait for his explanation. "Your job is to teach English. Is that your goal?"

She rolled her eyes. How many times had she suffered this discussion: What are we really teaching, and is knowing Shakespeare truly vital to an underprivileged child? It was a fun debate in the abstract from the ivory tower. But George Washington High in Indianapolis was a long way from her masters thesis, in both time and attitude. "I'm looking for specific tips here, not an academic discourse."

His eyebrows shot up at her curt tone. She could tell that she'd surprised him, but hadn't a clue why. Then it hit her. "You didn't think I was serious, did you? You didn't think I wanted any real advice."

He shrugged, but she saw the flush of dark red hit his cheeks. "Not many people really want help. They just want to gripe, then use me as an excuse to quit." He shrugged. "That's the real story behind those 'pity coffees.'"

"So you think I'm ready to quit? That I'll resign tomorrow because it's too damn hard?"

He took a long sip of his coffee, his eyes dark and serious. "Nah," he finally admitted. "I guessed you were too stubborn to go that route. If you were going to quit, you'd do it without using me as an excuse."

She frowned.

"So, why ask me out for coffee if you didn't think I'd listen? Why even try?"

He leaned back in his chair and raised his eyebrows. "Because you're cute?"

He had nice eyebrows, she realized. Nicely arched, bushy enough to be male, but not a tree farm. Nice. And he had just said . . .

"What did you say?" she asked.

"Your ego needs me to repeat that?"

"Because I'm cute." It took a moment for her brain to process his words, but when it did, irritation cascaded through her. This was all an elaborate come-on? "I get nearly beaten to a pulp in my own classroom, and you use it to try to get with me?" Earlier in the school year, she would have been thrilled. Hell, *yesterday* she would have accepted any excuse to spend some time with him. But after today's failure with Lucy, she needed honest advice. She got to her feet, grabbing her purse as she turned for the door. "I wanted help, Mr. DeLuce, from a man the kids respect. I thought maybe you had a new perspective. Apparently, I was wrong."

"No, wait!" He made it to his feet faster than she expected. He didn't touch her, but his body was large and effectively blocked her exit from the café. It might have been intimidating, except that he looked contrite. "I didn't mean it as an insult. And I do want to help."

She folded her arms, frustration making her curt. "Not interested, okay? I got bigger problems than being dateless. And . . ." She cut off her next words. Had she just confessed her lack of a social life? God, she was *way* off today. "Let's just call this a misstep and go home, okay?"

He touched her arm. His hands were large—cop hands, work-roughened and strong—but also gentle as they hovered against her skin. "And what?"

She blinked, pretending to not understand.

"You were going to say something. 'And' something. What?"

She debated a moment about telling him the truth, but apparently there were no restraints on her tongue today. "And you're cute, too. Another time, I would be interested." She *had* been interested at the beginning of the school year, but he hadn't looked at her twice. And then she'd realized how in over her head she was as a teacher, and all other thoughts had disappeared. "I just want to get through this school year alive. Everything else is secondary."

He cocked his head to study her face. She let him for a bit, but quickly began to feel uncomfortable with his scrutiny. What did this cop see when he looked at her? Incompetent wuss? Underdeveloped waif? At last he shook his head. "No, you're not really afraid for your life. You're afraid you can't hack it as a teacher."

She opened her mouth but no sound came out. She didn't know how to respond, especially since he was absolutely right.

"You can, you know," he said. "You can be a good teacher, just not for these kids."

She swallowed, her chest too tight to breathe. In two short sentences, he had just confirmed her worst fears. She wasn't cut out to be a teacher—not to the kids who most needed her. She forced a breath into her chest, then spoke, keeping her voice low and calm. "Anyone can teach future Ivy Leaguers. I know, because I did it for five years. They teach themselves; you just have to lay out the content. It's these kids that need someone." Someone who apparently wasn't her.

He gestured to her chair. "Please sit. We can talk shop."

"I think you've said what you really think. That's about all I can handle for one day."

"But I think now I was wrong."

She almost smiled. "No, you don't. You think I'm an upper-class idealist who hasn't a clue how to handle inner-city kids." Honesty forced her to continue. "You're right about that. I just thought I could learn."

"You still can. You've just started."

"It's March, Mr. DeLuce. I think I've had enough time." She looked over his shoulder at the parking lot rather than admit this to his face. "I've taken the tough-love classes, I've done self-defense and read a library's worth of material on the subject. But my heart just isn't in the hard-line attitude. I still think that leading with the heart is the best thing any teacher can do." She shifted her gaze back to his face, challenge ringing in her voice. "You still think I can teach, what with my bleeding heart?"

He swallowed. After a moment he said, "I think you'll get disillusioned, burn out, and turn bitter. And that'd be a damn shame."

She gave him points for honesty. "Caring is never in vain," she answered. It was the motto she lived by, but by Christmas the words had begun to ring hollow. She wondered if she really believed it anymore. She'd cared. She'd tried. Nothing changed.

"Let me buy you another coffee," he urged. "Please."

She shook her head, but her lips softened at the obvious disappointment in his eyes. And then she found herself agreeing when she was sure her brain had given orders to leave.

"On two conditions," she said. "One: you buy me a brownie. I've had enough coffee for one day. And two: you tell me how you do it."

"Do what?" Wariness crept into his tone, and she could tell she'd have an uphill climb trying to get to the core of this man.

"You were shot by a kid on drugs. It's crippled you, possibly for life." She gestured at his leg. He usually masked his limp, but she knew it was there. Everyone knew it was there. "And yet you work every day in a high school without anger or bitterness. So, I want the full story, Mr. DeLuce. I will sit back down if you tell me how you keep the faith when your problems are so much bigger than a stupid little rich girl who wanted to be a teacher."

He looked at her. "Is that really how you see yourself?— as a rich girl who wanted to slum it?"

"We're talking about you here. Or I'm leaving."

They stood at a stalemate, and Micki could feel her disappointment grow. He wasn't going to open up to her, and that made her really sad. She would have enjoyed getting to know him better.

With a sigh, she turned toward the door.

"I'm buying two brownies," he grumbled. "I'm not spilling my guts without more sugar."

* * *

"It was Lucy's brother, you know." Joe watched as Micki
nearly choked on her soy latte. Soy. Who knew there were
people outside of California who drank it?

She glared at him, and he smiled at the spark in her
blue eyes. "You timed that deliberately so I'd choke."

He grinned. "Gave me an extra flash down your peekaboo
blouse."

She slapped a hand to the white linen over her cleavage.
She needn't have bothered. The tiny buttons had stayed
closed, not showing any extra skin. Then she frowned.
"This is not a peekaboo blouse!"

No, it wasn't. But that didn't stop a man from imagining.
"Not with your hand right there," he laughed.

She slowly removed her hand and peered down at her
chest. "There is no cleavage showing, Mr. DeLuce. I think
you're stalling."

She was smart, he'd give her that. And a lot tougher
than he'd initially thought. He knew better than to dismiss
someone based on looks, but she'd seemed so easy to peg. A
petite blonde with class, obviously from money, idealistic
and fresh out of graduate school. She'd cut her teacher
chops in an elite suburb of wealthy Detroit, then for some
quixotic reason decided to work with the Indianapolis
poor. He hadn't expected her to finish out the quarter,
much less the year. And, yet, she was still here, and apparently hadn't given up. But she was close.

He kept his expression congenial, but inside he grimaced. It was his unfortunate duty to push her over the
edge into running. A bleeding heart could so easily die on
this side of the tracks. "There are messed-up kids in the
wealthy part of town, you know," he said gently. "They
need you just as much as these kids."

"I know," she said, breaking off a dainty bite of brownie. "But we were talking about you."

He grimaced, adding tenacity to her list of attributes. Flirting hadn't distracted her, though he sensed she wasn't as opposed to him as she pretended. Career advice hadn't derailed her. It looked like he really would have to spill his guts. "Okay," he said as he bit off a huge chunk of triple-chocolate brownie. "So, Wayne Varner—Lucy's brother—got high one night and thought I was Satan come to claim him or something."

"Were you?"

He looked up from his brownie, surprised. "What?"

"Were you coming to claim him."

"As Satan?"

She laughed. "Did the boy have reason to feel threatened?"

"I wasn't asking him out for coffee, if that's what you're asking." Pain shot up his thigh. It wasn't real, however; it was a memory, and one he worked hard to suppress.

"Look, Mr. DeLuce. Joe. I didn't mean to—"

"Yes, you did," he snapped. "You said you wanted to know what made me tick. Well, here it is: Wayne was high that night on a new drug—a hallucinogen called Chem that's messing up kids all over Indianapolis. I was tracking a supplier and stumbled onto him. Yeah, I was gonna hassle him. Yeah, I was gonna make damn sure that he ended up in jail for dealing. And yeah, I ended up with a bullet in my knee, Wayne in jail, and still no closer to the drug connection I was looking for."

She let him sputter down into a furious silence. He glared at her, and she didn't so much as blink, just took a sip of her latte and waited in silence. In his experience, women either tried to bury him in sympathy or poke into the inner workings of a drug investigation. Micki did neither. She merely waited. He had her complete attention, though she wasn't pushing for more. And she wasn't judging him, either.

He quickly took another bite of brownie before he started respecting her strengths or something. He barely tasted the rich chocolate. Instead, he shifted his leg in a vain attempt to ease the pain there, then steeled his spine. Time to give her that little push back to her wealthy suburbs. Truth was, she'd been right about the pity coffee. He really didn't think she belonged here, though he admired her courage for trying.

"There's drugs in our school, Micki."

She rolled her eyes. "Tell me something I don't know, Joe."

"This new drug brings new money, new guns, new violence. I got shot because of it. Kids have died because of it. And frankly, you aren't equipped to either bond with these kids or handle yourself when things become violent. The kids roll over you, the adults don't respect you, and your idealism just won't be enough to keep you alive." He shook his head, wishing to hell it was different, but it wasn't. "I've been school cop here for a year now, but before I made detective, I walked this beat. And before that, I grew up three blocks from Washington High. You're not the first idealist to wander through."

"Naive, starry-eyed teacher," she said. He couldn't tell if she was mocking him or not. "God, do you really think I'm that young?"

"I think you're admirable," he said. Enough that he'd noticed her the very first moment she'd walked into the school. Beautiful, compassionate, and destined to disappear in a few months. He'd seen it dozens of times. Most were smart enough to leave before they got into serious trouble, but one in particular had left in a body bag. He'd been the detective who caught that case. He'd also been sure it was Damian's gang, but was unable to gather any evidence. That was the hell of it. Everyone else thought Damian was another surly teen on a power trip, but he knew just how dangerous the little psychopath was.

But that was tomorrow's problem. Today's task was to make sure Micki didn't wind up as another one of Damian's victims. "The truth is that you can't understand these kids. And if you can't do that, then you can't help them."

He watched the blood drain from her face, and her hand shook slightly as she raised her empty coffee mug to her lips. But she didn't leave. Instead, she set her mug down and met his eyes. Almost. "So, you were shot in the leg and then, instead of taking a desk job during the extensive rehab phase, you chose to work in the very school that spawned the problem you're trying to fight."

"Where else would I go?" he muttered.

"*You* can understand these kids." It wasn't a question. "Ergo, you can help them."

He almost laughed. "Nah, I'm not that idealistic. I'm just tracking the drugs, Miss Becker. And if I keep some kids alive while I'm at it, all the better." He dumped a packet of sugar into the dregs of his coffee. "They're our future, after all," he half-sneered.

She was silent a long time. She hadn't even finished her brownie, but her coffee was long gone. In the end, she nodded and smiled warmly at him. "Thank you, Mr. DeLuce. I appreciate your candor."

He blinked, startled. Worse, she was standing up again. "Have I just been dismissed?" he asked, his tone harsher than he intended.

"I got the impression that you were dismissing me." She lifted her chin. "Look, I know it's hard. And I know you think I belong back in the land of Richie Rich. But the truth is, I want to be here. I want to show these kids that someone cares, even if it means I get intimidated in my classroom, laughed at by other teachers and . . ." She sighed. "And I end up a bitter, old woman who tried too hard. If that's where I'm headed, so be it. But I won't re-evaluate until I start getting mean." She held his gaze for a long moment, then added, "Mean like you."

And with that, she turned and walked out.

He was on his feet and moving after her as fast as his bad leg would allow—which was decently fast—but she had no interest in talking to him and was quickly out of sight. Truthfully, he didn't blame her. He'd come on pretty strong. But it bothered him that he'd been exactly what she'd accused him of—mean—and still had not accomplished his goal. He hadn't nudged her away from anything but himself.

"Micki, wait!" He hadn't a clue what he was going to say to her, but . . . He frowned, peering at the parking lot in the cold half-light of the overcast afternoon. The lot was tiny, hemmed in on all sides by straggly bushes and tall, dirty buildings. Nothing unusual for this side of Indianapolis, but something was off. Nothing he could see. A sound? He only heard cars. Smell? Coffee, exhaust, and . . . cologne? A fancy kind, favored by some rich folks. Rich folks plus Damian Ralston, hell-spawn of Washington High.

Where had Micki gone? She'd turned left and then . . . There! She was walking down an alleyway to her car, and sure enough, there was Damian cutting in behind her. And where one reprobate went, the others were sure to follow.

She didn't notice, of course. The woman had no survival skills. Joe quickly considered his options. Normally, he'd just charge up and warn the gang off. He might even be able to do it hard enough to keep Damian and his crew off her for the rest of the school year. But that would only give

Micki a false sense of security. Eventually she'd challenge the wrong gangbanger and end up dead. He had to give her a good scare. And what better way to do that than by letting Damian and his gang at her? Not for long. Just long enough to make her appropriately terrified. Meanwhile, Joe was here to make sure it didn't get out of hand.

He followed about seven steps behind, slipping behind cars and generally feeling like an idiot. He wasn't low profile enough to be really hidden, and not out in the open enough to be acting normally. He stopped at the corner of the building, hugging the brick wall as he crouched behind a bush. Micki had almost made it to her car—a ridiculously chipper yellow Beetle—when Damian stepped around to confront her. She jumped, obviously startled. Her shoulders tightened and she shied backward but there was nowhere for her to go. She butted up against a delivery truck.

Joe couldn't hear what was said, though he tried. The group's body language told him exactly what he expected: Damian was being threatening, Micki was scared, especially as a couple more thugs slid around from the other side of the truck. None of them looked out of control—not even Micki—so there really wasn't any danger to her. Damian was just trying to scare the teacher who had embarrassed him. It was something gang leaders did. And yet . . .

He couldn't do it. He couldn't watch this happen, even if it was the best thing for Micki in the long run. He pushed out of his crouch and stomped up to Damian. "You got a special interest here, Mr. Ralston?"

Micki visibly relaxed, and Joe felt a brief surge of male pride that his presence could reassure her. But Damian turned, a shit-eating grin on his face. That was never good. "I knew you were around here somewhere. Joey wouldn't let a fine woman like Miss Mouse wander alone." Then the bastard reached out to touch Micki's face.

He only made it halfway. "Touch her, Damian, and I'll kill you." Joe spoke the words quietly, but everyone froze at his tone. Even he was startled by the vehemence in his voice.

Damian smirked, but he drew his hand back. "Got a thing going here, Joey?"

Joe raised his eyebrows and tried to stare Damian down. It didn't work. Damian was hopped up on something, but it didn't seem like drugs. No, this kid got off on something entirely different: power, pain, maybe even blood. Whatever it was, Joe didn't want Micki right in the middle of it.

"You're pushing it, Mr. Ralston. Be on your way."

"Aw, no, I ain't." Damian lounged back on his heels, the smirk back. "I came here specifically to see you."

"Then you got no business with Miss Becker." He glanced at Micki. "Go on. Get in your car."

Her eyes widened, but predictably she shook her head. She wasn't leaving him. Joe grimaced. Very soon now, he was going to have to explain to her the difference between being a help in a fight and a liability. Meanwhile, Damian gestured to his friends. "I found someone, Joe. Someone who says he belongs to you."

Joe frowned, but Micki gasped in shock. From behind the truck, another couple of punks dragged out a boy beaten to a pulp. Stevie Crames—a kid who had come to Joe once to warn that Damian was power-mad and going to get someone killed. Joe's breath squeezed tight as he quickly scanned the kid. Stevie was conscious—which meant he was alive—but all that blood!

Joe started to move around Damian, but Micki got there first, wrapping her arms around the kid. "What have you done?" she cried. "Oh my God!"

The thugs released Stevie to Micki, who staggered under his sudden weight.

"Call 911," Joe said. His voice was tight, the guilt threatening to eat him alive. The boy was beaten up, but not dying. In truth, he looked like he was conscious and pissed off. Good. He wasn't as bad as he first looked, which meant Joe's priority was to get control of this situation. A quick scan told Joe he faced one gun—on Damian—and four knives. Not good odds, given his bad knee and two civilians who needed protection.

"Found him over there," Damian continued, waving vaguely toward the school. "Said he's been talking with you, Joe, and some people don't like that much."

Joe narrowed his eyes and put on his best confused frown. "Who is it?"

"It's Stevie Crames," Micki said from around her cell phone.

Joe blinked and stared. "I haven't been talking to Stevie Crames!" he lied. Then he stepped up to Damian, not needing to fake his fury. "You beat up a kid for no damn reason! Jesus, Damian, what the hell is wrong with you?"

Damian lifted his hands, his grin still in place. "I don't know what you're talking about, Joey. We jes' found him, right, boys?"

Right on cue, the other kids' heads bobbed up and down. "That's right! We just found him!" They spoke with so much enthusiasm that Joe knew they were terrified. Which meant that Damian really had gone off the deep end. That happened sometimes: a kid got delusions of grandeur and made all sorts of bizarre mistakes. The problem was keeping the innocents out of the crossfire while a gang leader self-destructed. Innocents like Micki, and Stevie, who had just lifted his head. He was down on one knee, but struggling with Micki's support to make it to his feet. "I told you," he growled to Damian. "I ain't talked to nobody."

"What kind of leader are you?" Joe pressed. "Were you bored and just decided to beat up one of your followers?" He let his gaze wander to the other boys. "Damn, I'd be scared just hanging around a psycho like you. No telling who you'll turn on next."

It was a calculated risk. Stirring the pot when outnumbered five to one wasn't the safest move, but anything he could do to erode Damian's power base was a good thing. And from the way a couple of the boys shuffled their feet, he had scored.

"Nice try, Joey," Damian sneered, "but I got reliable information. Stevie's been blabbing."

Joe put all his sincerity into his voice. "Not to me, he hasn't."

Doubt flashed briefly in Damian's eyes. It was a split second of hesitation, but that was all that was needed. Not for Joe, who was busy trying to think of the next thing to say; as much as he wanted to smash his fist right through the gang leader's face, it was best to defuse the situation. He never guessed that Stevie would roar suddenly to life.

With a strangled bellow, the kid flew out of Micki's arms and straight at the gang leader. Joe tried to intercept. The last thing he needed was more of Stevie's blood on his conscience. But the kid was too fast. The best Joe could do was lunge for Damian's gun as the gangster tried to quick-draw. He didn't get a hand on the gun, but he managed to grip Damian's forearm. A shot rang out, but it went wide; then all three of them—Damian, Stevie, and Joe—tumbled to the ground in a heap.

Stevie was on top, his fists flailing as he tried to bash in Damian's face. Joe was struggling to gain control of the gun, which was waving every which way. Damian was screaming, "Get him off me! Get him—"

Joe had enough focus to see the other thugs draw their

knives. Shit. Then he saw Micki leap forward as well. Double shit. He needed to get that gun! Almost . . .

Stevie must have seen the gun. Pretty amazing with all the blood flying, but he managed a backhanded blow that struck both Joe's fingers and Damian's forearm at the same time. The strike was fast and wild. Joe's fingers went numb, Damian's arm snapped back and the gun flew out of his hand.

Joe twisted as fast as he could. The gun clattered against a tree and dropped near one of the gangsters. No way could he get there first, but Joe still tried. He rolled toward it, reaching as far as he could. He missed by a mile as one of the boys—Bobby McCoy—picked up the weapon. Worse, the kid obviously knew how to handle it. He gripped it like an expert and was bringing it to bear on Stevie.

"No!" screamed Micki, her voice cutting through the air like a whip.

"Don't do it, Bobby!" Joe called, his voice as loud and authoritative as possible. It wasn't going to work; Bobby had too much adrenaline in him. His eyes were wide and his leader was still getting pummeled. The best Joe could do was throw himself forward and pray. He was already shoving himself upright, his bad knee screaming all the way, when a black blur rushed past.

That's all he saw at first—a black blur—as Micki kicked the gun away. It took Joe a moment to realize he'd seen her feet, and her sensible black shoes, leap forward in a perfect kung fu kick. He blinked, but didn't have time to gape. The other boys were entering the fray, and Stevie was tiring. His blows were less wild, his screams more like gasps. In a moment, Damian was going to flip the boy over and start killing him.

No, there was no time. Joe managed to shift his weight enough to stop one gangster, but the other two were already drawing their knives.

"Don't be stupid!" he bellowed, and was gratified to see them hesitate.

Which was when the tornado hit. Micki flew in between him and the nearest boy, drawing her arm down on the gangster's forearm hard enough to break it. Joe was sure he heard a snap. He heard a muffled, "Oh! Sorry!" from her; then she moved on. And it all happened before the kid even managed a scream.

"Micki—," Joe began, but she wasn't listening. Running past him, she leapt into a perfect karate lunge, leg extended as she flew over Damian and Stevie and caught the next kid square in the chest.

"No! No!" she cried. "This isn't right!"

The kid fell backward with an *oomph*, but Micki wasn't done yet. Still in the air, one foot planted in the boy's chest, she backflipped and clocked the last kid in the face.

"Oh my!" she cried. "That's not what I meant! Are you all right?"

The first kid was falling. His butt hit the ground, then his head, landing hard enough that Joe could feel the impact a full seven feet away. The other kid simply spun and went down.

Joe managed to gasp while Micki landed like a cat on all fours. Her eyes were huge. "Oh my God! Oh my God!" she gasped, sounding exactly like a woman in hysterics. But then she sprang forward. She struck Stevie gently on his side. How she managed to control her motions so well was beyond incredible, but the boy didn't even grunt. He toppled off Damian to land with a groan on his back, right in front of Joe.

When Micki dropped again, she was eye-level with a furious Damian. His nose was bleeding and his eyes were swelling shut, but his fist looked huge as it slammed forward right toward her face. She caught it neatly in her palm. The impact sounded like a splat of a rotten tomato, and then she spun her wrist, twisting Damian's hand. He went down with a scream.

Micki pulled back and looked Joe in the eye. All around, the gangbangers were screaming in pain. Well, not the one who had been knocked unconscious.

"How . . . ? What . . . ?" Joe sputtered, unable to form a coherent thought.

Micki blinked, and he saw the tears that had formed in her eyes. Her lip trembled. "I don't believe in violence!" she whispered. He took a step forward, but she abruptly tensed. Faster than he thought possible, she slipped forward, picked up the gun and neatly dropped it into his hands. But she didn't stop moving. She kept running, right by him, and within seconds she had disappeared down the street.

CHAPTER THREE

Micki sat in a tree. Actually, she was perched on a branch like a bird. On a branch that she normally would have called a twig, but the thought that it was the only thing between herself and a three-story plunge to her death made her revise the term. And she was not breathless.

That was what was really occupying her thoughts right now. She wasn't panicking at the possible plunge to her death. She wasn't obsessing on the recent knife fight, or that she had run for miles only to climb an oak and then start running through the treetops. She hadn't even climbed as a kid; now she was running through them?

She resolutely slammed the door closed on those thoughts. She would not think about anything involving knives or broken bones or blood or trees. Nothing. Because if she did, she would hyperventilate, then probably pass out, which would then mean a three-story drop to her death.

Ergo, she was not thinking about what she'd just done. She was thinking about the fact that she was not winded. Sure, she could prance through an aerobics class with the best of them. She could even do an hour and a half step-class marathon without passing out from lack of oxygen. But she had been running—running!—and climbing through trees for hours.

She'd left the café at four. It was now dark. She'd run the whole time and she wasn't winded. She wasn't even breathing hard. And her legs did not feel like Jell-O.

Time to panic.

A noise rumbled beneath her: a car driving into her apartment complex parking lot, its headlights bright on the blacktop. She peered down at it. It was hard to see, but she was pretty sure it was her car. Even in the dark, her bright-yellow Beetle was hard to miss. She liked to think of it as her own little sun bug that she could always find in a parking lot.

She began to climb down to see better. She frowned for a moment to look at what she was doing—her foot on another tiny twig, her body sliding sinuously through branches she wasn't even sure were there. But at that exact moment, her hair snagged, her hand slipped dangerously, and something dug painfully into her hip.

Bad thoughts! Bad brain! She'd already realized that whenever she focused on the incredible things she was doing, she immediately lost all skill. Not a big problem when she was running; that had happened a couple hours before. She had realized she was running faster than she'd ever run before in her life, and she immediately stumbled on a curb. But as she gasped about the curb, she'd neatly swung up into the tree. From that moment on, she'd decided not to think about what she was doing.

Tripping over a curb was one thing; tumbling three stories to the hard pavement was something else entirely. Therefore, she closed her mind to anything but seeing her happy little sun bug, and proceeded painlessly down the tree. Not to the ground. She wasn't prepared to meet the world yet. So she descended about a story and twisted to look at her car.

Who was driving it? Well, she knew the answer. After all, she'd left her purse, her car, and her cell in the café parking lot. There was only one person who would drive her car back to her. One person who had seen what she had done. One person who was damn sure going to ask questions she couldn't answer. Hell, right now she was too afraid to even consider them.

There he was. Even knowing it was Joe DeLuce, she still wasn't prepared for the sight of him unfolding his large body from her little bug. He moved slowly, but with a tension that she could feel all the way up here. He grabbed her little Gucci purse from the passenger seat, dangling it like something smelly between two fingers, and turned to look at her apartment building.

When he turned toward the back door, Micki got a look at his face. Rugged, handsome as always—yes. But this time he was angry. Like a bulldog that had just scented the man or woman who had stolen his dinner. His jaw was thrust forward, his eyes were narrowed as he looked at the upper stories, and he rolled his shoulders just like some of the teen boys did when they were anticipating a fight. It was a threatening gesture, it was primal, and it reminded her more than anything that he was not her friend.

In short, it scared her spitless, which was why it was so very bad that she slipped on the branch right then.

Instead of screaming, she simply surrendered to the inevitable. Obviously, her newfound whatever couldn't last forever. Clearly fate had decided to return her to normal at the worst possible moment, and she was going to fall to her death at Joe DeLuce's feet.

Except, she did nothing of the kind. The moment she relaxed into her coming demise, her body took over. She fell, but only far enough to grab the branch with her hands. Then she swung her legs up and around, releasing at just the right moment. Her body arced through the air and she landed in a perfect crouch on a neighboring tree.

Micki looked down. She was now level with the second floor of her apartment building and perched right over the back door. Joe was taking his time crossing the parking lot, looking at his surroundings the way a cop would: gauging distances, checking out shadows—even glancing up in the trees. Micki swallowed.

The desperate urge to talk to someone surged through her. It was ridiculous. She did not want to talk to anyone right then. Not until she understood what was going on. But she had been sitting in trees for the last hour at least, and had gotten no closer to an answer. Obviously, she wasn't figuring anything out by herself. She had to work this out with someone who had perspective, logic, and a clear head.

But Joe? No! She wanted a sense of normalcy, of her world returning to something that made sense. Talking to Joe would be the opposite of that. The absolute opposite.

She dropped down to a lower branch. It wasn't a graceful movement; the tree was wet and her shoes were not designed for climbing—the last few hours notwithstanding. She struggled a bit and got slapped in the face by leaves covered in something black and slimy.

"Yuck!" Had she said that aloud? Moron! Sure enough, when she dared glance down, Joe was looking right up at her.

"Hello, Miss Becker," he drawled. His expression had turned congenial, almost warm, but Micki couldn't forget the predatory look of a moment before. "I brought your car back."

She nodded, unable to speak.

"Perhaps you could come down from there? We can have a little chat."

She shook her head. It was a childish movement similar to one she'd made in grade school when she'd been caught sneaking M&Ms from her best friend's lunch.

"Micki, we really need to talk."

His voice was gentle, and she so wanted to trust it. But he was going to ask her questions she couldn't answer. She didn't know what was happening to her. She didn't know how she could have done those things she couldn't allow herself to think about. She didn't know, and all she wanted was to climb into bed and have someone else solve all her problems for her.

Tears threatened, and she closed her eyes. She did not want to feel sorry for herself, and yet everything—the fear, the confusion, the wonder—was so overwhelming.

"Stevie's fine," he said. "Bloody, but not as bad as you might think. Not even a broken bone, which is kinda miraculous when you think about it."

"The others?" she asked, her voice a whispered croak.

"Ah, well, the others weren't so lucky. Damian's got a black eye and assorted bruises. No tears from me, though Lucy was wailing about it."

Micki opened her eyes enough to peek down. Joe was watching her closely, and she rapidly shut them again. Moronic, really. Like he couldn't see her if she closed her eyes? But the truth was, she didn't have a prayer of dealing with life if she looked directly at him. He was just too much to handle right then. And yet, perversely, this normal conversation was exactly what she needed to ground herself in reality. Even if that ground was a tree branch.

"What about the others?" she pressed, forcing herself to hear the truth. One sound had pursued her more than others, one memory followed as she ran through the trees: the sound and feel of Vince's arm snapping. It had been unmistakable and sickening.

Joe shrugged, his voice as casual as if they were discussing brands of coffee. "Toby's got a welt but no concussion. Same for the other two."

"Vince?"

"Broken arm. Snapped clean." He took a breath, then switched to a more professional tone. "He's fine, Micki, but we've booked them all for assault. My friend Larry is the detective on the case, so we've got a little time, but you need to make a statement."

She nodded. It was hard to refuse him when he spoke with such authority. She dropped to a lower branch. It swayed alarmingly beneath her, and she heard him gasp, dropping her purse into the mud to lurch beneath her.

"Be careful!" he called.

She stilled, knowing better than to question her absolute balance on the branch. The minute she let doubts into her brain, other things crowded in. Then she'd be back in panic attack mode, and she'd never come down again. Or she'd slip off the branch and go splat on the asphalt.

"Micki, you're giving me a heart attack here. I'm not a young man, you know. Just come down."

She looked at the ground. It wasn't that far a leap, and yet it still looked too scary. "Joe, I can't. I can't think right now. I can't—"

"Take off your shoes."

She blinked. "What?"

"Your shoes." He pointed at her brand-new Mary Janes. "I don't know how you've been climbing trees in them, but you've got no traction. Take them off and toss them to me."

She frowned. "Why?"

"Then you can grab hold of the trunk and put your toes on that branch there." He pointed to a large vee perfect for bare feet. "There's another toehold here. And I'll help you the rest of the way down."

It made sense. In this whole wacky day, this one thing made sense. And truly, it was kind of nice to let him tell her what to do. So she dropped onto her bottom on the branch and toed off her shoes.

Then she toppled right out of the tree.

She had enough time to squeak in alarm, helicopter her arms in a vain attempt to stabilize herself, and then she fell backward so that her knees caught on the branch and saved her from splattering her brains on the ground.

Joe dove forward and barely managed to catch her head and shoulders before she brained herself against the tree trunk.

"Actually," he drawled, "I said you should use the toe-hold *over there*."

"Er . . . yeah. This was faster." With luck, he would think the heat in her face was because she was hanging upside down. "Um . . . do you think you could help me?"

She didn't need to ask. He was already gently supporting her as she maneuvered her legs. Her skirt ripped with an ominous sound, and the remaining tatters slid all the way up her hips. Oh hell. And she'd chosen to wear a thong today.

As quickly as possible, she dragged her legs off the branch, scraping her calves painfully, to tumble right into his arms. She didn't dare look at his face. Even if he hadn't seen the thong, his hands had certainly slid over her bottom as he helped her to her feet. He didn't say a thing, and in a few moments, when she was finally standing on her own stocking feet, she glanced at him and froze.

She had expected a knowing smirk, a half-sleazy flirtation that would make her embarrassed and a little excited. What she saw instead was a coolly assessing gaze. He now knew what she wore and was filing it away in his brain, yet another characteristic to be weighed and judged.

And yet, there was more. A new sexual awareness lay beneath that dark assessment, a call of man to woman that stiffened her spine and made her stronger. She smiled and felt like an animal baring her teeth when cornered. He looked at her like a predator, and she straightened to her full height and arched an eyebrow back at him. *Bring it on, big boy*, was the response her body made. Just like Mae West, she was wondrously bold and bossy.

And yet, never in her entire life had she ever responded in such a way to a man. She was soft and feminine. She never challenged a man so boldly. It just wasn't how she operated. And yet, as she stood there in ripped panty hose, she tilted her head up, held his gaze, and waited.

His nostrils flared. In the background, the wind picked up, a truck rumbled down the street, and somewhere a dog barked. But between the two of them, there existed a crackling silence. When he spoke, his words were so low as to be more felt than heard.

"You're not what I thought," he said.

"Good." She didn't have to say the rest. They both knew he'd long since dismissed her as a bleeding-heart failure. That's what they'd been discussing at the café. And right then and there, the memories flooded back. Their conversation in the café. Damian by her car. Poor Stevie. The attack and her . . . And what she'd done. Running. Trees. And now?

Panic surged through her body, making her heart race and her hands shake. Her fight-or-flight reflex kicked in. Given that the only person to fight was Joe, she chose flight. Swooping down, she grabbed her shoes and purse from the ground. Her keys were there, too, and within seconds she'd managed to open the door to her apartment complex and fly inside. He followed.

She didn't want to wait for the elevator, so she took the stairs, getting winded by the first landing. He remained beside her every step of the way—even with his bad leg—and he wasn't breathing hard at all. By the fourth floor she was gasping but determined. And her feet were freezing. She fumbled her apartment door keys, but managed to push inside. He went with her, flipping on the light as she headed straight for her bedroom.

Ingrained politeness made her throw a "Make yourself at home" invitation over her shoulder. Confusion made those words sound surly. Then she ran into her bedroom, shut the door, and burst into tears.

She was crying. Joe dropped his head against the wall and listened with horror to Micki's big, gasping sobs. They tore at his insides. He could go in there; he didn't think she'd locked the door. And even if she had, the flimsy catch would break open easily. But once inside, what would he do?

He went into her kitchen. It was neat and girly, just like he'd expected. Flowery canisters of coffee and tea on the counter right next to a porcelain gingerbread house for cookies—empty. In her refrigerator, she had orange juice, yogurt, and tofu burgers. Plus all the mixing for a first-class salad. Yippee.

But she was still a woman, and so he looked in the freezer for her comfort food. Score! Ben & Jerry's Cherry Garcia, frozen cookies, frozen brownies—a treasure trove hidden among Lean Cuisines. He grabbed the ice cream. A quick search revealed utensils with fake crystal handles in rainbow colors. He grabbed a spoon and headed for the bedroom.

He knocked. "Micki?" No answer. "Micki, I'm coming in. And I've brought ice cream."

He opened the door and peered inside. She was curled up on the bed, her knees to her chest, and she'd buried her head in her pillow. Her blond hair curled every which way, easily obscuring her face, but her legs were exposed all the way to her hips.

God, she was gorgeous. He knew he shouldn't be thinking that. There were plenty of mysteries surrounding this woman and he had no wish to get distracted by her body. But what a soft and beautiful body it was. Petite. Shapely. Like a porcelain doll, only alive and strong. He'd never have guessed that she could kick the crap out of gangsters. Who knew there was such power in those legs? That she wore a thong made his dick thicken with interest, and . . . and this was way out of line. In Siberia, out of line.

"Come on, Micki. We've got to talk. You've got to give a statement. And the ice cream is starting to melt all over your floor." The last part was a lie; he'd just taken it out of the freezer. But no woman could stand to see ice cream go to waste. Certainly not one this neat.

She took a deep breath. He didn't hear it, but watched her back lift and lower in the shadows.

He reached over and turned on the bedside lamp, then blinked as the room was abruptly thrown into rich forest greens and golds. The lamp shade was a remarkable stained-glass forest, with a golden pathway that wound around the shade. Beneath the lamp was a circle of clear light that shone directly on Micki's face as she emerged from her pillow. On the walls, though, was the projected forest scene. The creamy white was transformed into something magical.

"Wow, that's some lamp," he said, as she pushed her hair out of her eyes and reached for the ice cream.

"Ann Arbor art fair," she murmured. "Mom and I go every year." She took the spoon from his hand, then looked down at the pint container. "Bowl?"

"Hmm?" He'd been considering the smooth curve of her bra. No lace, just smooth silk cupping golden skin as revealed by her undone blouse.

"Never mind," she said, and popped off the top. She carefully set the lid down on her bedside table, then dug straight into the container. "And quit looking at my boobs. You can't see anything."

"I'm seeing more than I usually do."

Without looking up, she tugged sharply on the bottom of her blouse. The edges immediately straightened, covering the view. "Thank you for the ice cream," she said. "Now go away. I've had a hard day."

"No."

She shot him a glare. "I'll give you a statement tomorrow. I promise."

"No."

Her glare turned defiant as she took a big bite of ice cream. When she'd finally swallowed, she huffed. "I don't have your answers today. Sorry, but I don't. Try again tomorrow."

This time he didn't bother saying no; he just sat down on her bed and looked at her. Her skin was still blotchy from crying, her lips were swollen as if she'd been biting them to hold back her sobs, and her eyes were red and ugly. All in all, she was not a woman who looked beautiful when she cried, but still, his insides melted.

"I don't want to push you, Micki. Honest, I don't, but I need some answers." He folded his arms across his chest and tried to remember he was a tough cop. "How did you get your martial arts skills, and why are you hiding them?"

She blinked at him and didn't answer. He thought she was about to for a moment, but then she took in another big bite of ice cream.

"Are you undercover? A narc?"

Her eyes widened, and she slowly shook her head.

"It's okay, you know. I'm a cop. Professional courtesy and all. I just wish your department had told my department."

He paused. "You're really good, you know. I would never have made you as anything but a glass-tower liberal."

She stiffened, squaring her shoulders and glaring at him. Finally, she pulled the spoon out of her mouth and whispered, "I am."

He leaned forward to hear better. This was the only explanation, and yet it didn't sit right. She just didn't feel like a cop—narc, fed, or otherwise. "You are," he said anyway, his voice flat.

She nodded and her voice gained strength. "I am a . . . a glass-tower liberal. Bleeding heart and all."

"And a narc."

She shook her head.

"Fed?"

Again, the slow denial.

"How did you kick those kids' asses? Micki, you spun in the air and backflipped and roundhouse kicked."

"No, I didn't," she said in a tiny, tiny voice.

"Yes, Micki, you did."

She buried her spoon in the ice cream and didn't answer. He reached out to grab her hand before she could shove another bite into her mouth.

"Micki, talk to me. I'm a good guy, remember?"

She swallowed and raised her gaze to look at him through the shadow of her bangs. "I don't know."

He stiffened. "Of course I'm a good guy."

"I don't freaking know how I did it!" she snapped, her voice growing shriller as she continued. "I suck at athletics. I've never taken a martial arts class in my life. I've never even climbed a tree, much less run through them. And I don't freaking ever hit a freaking child! I don't believe in it!"

Joe stared at Micki, trying to figure her out. She certainly seemed sincere. And sincerely freaked out. But skills like this didn't appear out of thin air. Something was up with her, and he wasn't leaving until he figured it out.

"So, what's the black belt in?" he asked casually. "Jujitsu? kung fu? Monkey voodoo? Come on, what's the style called?"

She glared at him, then twisted her spoon in the ice cream. "It's okay," she said after taking another bite. "I wouldn't believe me, either." She swallowed, her gaze on the nearly empty pint. "Maybe it was adrenaline. I mean, I've never been attacked by a gang before."

To his annoyance, it didn't sound like she believed herself. He tried a different angle. "It's not unfeminine or anything. You're really, really good. In fact, it's pretty sexy even, knowing you could probably kick my ass if you wanted to."

She looked up at him, her nose crinkling in horror. "God, you're hitting on me because I have freaky kung fu powers! What the hell is wrong with just me?"

He stiffened at the slight. Not because he was insulted—much—but because the soft approach wasn't getting him anywhere. Maybe she was the kind of woman who needed to be insulted to get a spark. "What, you too hoity-toity to like a cop?"

She blinked, startled enough to halt with her spoon halfway to her mouth. "What? No!"

"But I insulted you by thinking a woman black belt is hot?"

"I never said that! You're twisting my words—"

"You're the one who's twisted, lady. I'm here trying to help, getting you ice cream, bringing your car home. Now you're too good for me?"

"Stop it! Just stop it!" She barely missed kicking him as she shot out of bed. "You're being awful!"

Progress. She was on her feet now, stomping to the kitchen. The little lost girl was gone beneath a surge of fury. He followed her, still pushing. "What? Don't you like it that I think you're sexy as hell? That I've got a boner the size of Detroit for you, right now? Does that upset you?"

She whirled around and nearly upended a vase of flowers on the breakfast bar that separated her kitchen from her living room. "No, it doesn't upset me!" she bellowed. "A few months ago, I would have been thrilled to death if you paid any attention to me at all. Anything but pity, that is."

He spread his arms wide. "Well, here I am. Hot to trot for you. Come and get me, girly-girl. This isn't pity."

"I am not a girly-girl!" she snapped, her eyes tearing up. She threw her empty pint carton in the garbage and then hurled the spoon into the sink. Both missed by a mile. The spoon clattered against the wall, leaving an ice-cream smear on the pale yellow. "Just stop it!" she said again. "You're being horrible."

He crowded tight to her shoulder, close enough to smell her sweat as it mixed with the scent of some very expensive shampoo—vanilla and gardenia—and his arousal really did get the size of Detroit.

"You're a liar," he said. "A liar and a fraud, hiding behind tight skirts and expensive shampoo. What kind of car do you really drive? No one actually drives a yellow Beetle," he scoffed. He grabbed her elbow and whipped her around. "Who are you really?"

She jerked her arm back, to no effect. His grip held tight. Her face twisted into a grimace as she banged her free hand against his chest. "Let me go!"

In terms of a punch, hers had the force of a two-year-old. She had no leverage. Even her hips were at the wrong angle, so that her feet got tangled up beneath her. He began slowly backing her up against the breakfast bar.

"You want me to let go? Make me." He pushed his groin hard against her.

"Stop it!" she gasped. "Just stop it!" Her head was almost level with the too-perky daisies on the counter. She tried to punch him again, but he was relentless.

This had started out as a game to make her reveal her fighting skills, but with his body pressed tight against her soft curves, his mind temporarily shorted out. A primal need to own this woman flared inside him, and he quickly trapped her against the counter, his hips thrust against her belly. His head dropped to her neck, and he inhaled deeply, loving the musky scent there. He heard her breath catch, and felt her shudder against him. He rubbed his cheek against hers, glorying at the soft slide of her skin.

"Stop," she whispered, anguish in her tone.

"I'm going to kiss you," he said. "Unless you stop me. I'm going to kiss you right now." He ground his hips forward again, the pleasure burning through his blood and pushing him farther.

He took her mouth. He thrust his tongue inside and touched every part of her. His hands slid down her sides. She was slender, but wow, her curves were perfect. Her breasts fit his hands, and he squeezed. Her mouth had come alive, fighting with him, tasting him, touching him, but he gave her little opportunity. This wasn't about sharing; this was about domination.

He slid his hands off her breasts to her hips. He pinned her, holding her tight as he moved against her. Geez, she was so tiny, and yet everything about her screamed woman. *His* woman. He wanted her naked.

He grabbed hold of her blouse. The silly white buttons had been driving him crazy all day. He ripped it open with one jerk. She gasped, and he could see her belly tremble. Better yet, he could feel it where he still ground into her. Hell, he was pressed so deep against her, he knew every ripple of her abdominal muscles.

"Oh . . ." she moaned. Or maybe it was "no." It was hard to hear over the roar of his blood.

"Stop me," he said. "Stop me now."

She pushed at his chest. Her tiny hands planted on his chest and shoved. She had leverage, she had power, but not enough. Not nearly enough to keep him from popping the clasp of her bra from behind and burying his face in her glorious breasts.

Why wasn't she defending herself? One karate chop to the back of his neck and he'd be too dizzy to stand. One slam to his instep and he'd be walking on his knees. Her hands were free. She could grab his ears and pull him right off her. Instead, she just pushed ineffectively at his shoulders while he took a ripe nipple into his mouth.

It was tight and firm, and he suckled until she gasped. Then he rolled his tongue around it before nipping lightly. She had stopped pushing at his chest. She had stopped fighting altogether, and that more than anything filtered through his mind. Could she want this? Could she really want to have sex with him?

His body screamed *yes!* But his mind couldn't handle the conflicting thoughts. He'd expected her to flatten him five minutes ago. He'd left himself wide open. Anyone who could fight like she had this afternoon could drop him in seconds.

He looked up into her face. Her lips were swollen from his kiss, her breath was coming in rapid gasps, but her eyes were wide with shock. And she was crying. There were distinct trails of moisture on her cheeks. But he was sure there was passion in her eyes. An unmistakable hunger.

"Do you want this?" he asked. Despite his noblest intentions, he couldn't stop himself from grinding against her again. It just felt too damn good. "Micki, do you want me to keep going?"

"N-no?" A *yes* if he'd ever heard one.

"Stop me. Yank on my hair. Slam my instep. Put your hand through my nose."

She remained absolutely still.

"Need me to show you how?" he offered.

She nodded.

He slowly lifted her arm until the palm of her hand was level with his face. "Now jerk it across your chest. You'll break my nose."

"But I don't want to break your nose."

Green light! Green light! screamed his dick. He gritted his teeth. He had to stand up. He had to get some distance. Taking a deep breath, he began to maneuver away from her. His groin did one last glorious push into her as he sought new balance.

Bam! Her palm hit his cheek, and his head snapped back. The blow wasn't hard enough to throw him off her, but his vision blurred and his eyes watered. Thankfully, she'd hit his cheekbone, not his nose, or he'd be bleeding all over her floor.

"I was stepping back!" he groused.

"You were not!" she snapped. Then she peered at him. "Wow, you're swelling. That really works."

He tried to glare at her, but he couldn't see well enough yet. Meanwhile, facts began lining up in his brain. Except for the bizarre fight this afternoon, she'd acted exactly to type. His inner Neanderthal noticed that her nipples were still tight, her skin flushed, and her lips had that moist, dome look. His brain noticed that she was anxious, peering at his face and muttering something about ice.

"What?" he asked.

"Back up. Let me get you some ice."

Did she really think he had blood anywhere but in his cock? Or that he could walk upright? Apparently so, because she shoved at his shoulders. He spun sideways and promptly ran into her stupid daisies. The vase toppled and shattered on her linoleum floor.

"Shit!" she snapped. "This day just gets better and better."

"Sorry," he mumbled. "I'll clean it up." He needed something mundane and physical to do. Pushing around the corner, he heard the crunch of glass shards beneath his shoes. She was halfway to the freezer—presumably to get him ice—when he noticed that she was barefoot. At some point, she'd obviously stripped out of her ruined panty hose.

"Don't move!" he snapped. "There's glass everywhere!"

She sighed and pointed to the inch that separated the refrigerator from the counter. A broom and a Swiffer rested neatly in the crack. "Just grab me that—"

"Don't move!" he repeated more forcefully. "I'll get your shoes. Then I'll sweep." He was starting to move more easily now, though his mood had rapidly gone south. He grabbed her sensible black shoes—the kind that little girls wore—and watched as she slipped them onto her feet. Thirty seconds later, he cursed as he realized he'd been staring at her dainty feet disappear into the silly Chinese shoes. They were velvet black with a bright red Chinese character embroidered on the top, and her pretty toes with their bright pink nail polish had slipped so easily inside.

And then—rather abruptly—everything got really strange.

CHAPTER FOUR

Micki tottered uncertainly as she slipped on her shoes. She so wanted to be a stronger woman, a capable woman. Someone who was respected by her students, who exuded grace and skill. Someone who could clean up a kitchen, kick butt against gang members and then still have the skills—and attitude—to jump this hunky cop without double-thinking everything. She sighed. She was only herself, and yet—

She was herself jumping off the refrigerator, grabbing the broom and swirling the glass into a tight little pile. She kicked the dustpan with her foot, flipping it into the air, then caught it one-handed. Swooping down, she pushed all the glass into the pan, then did an elegant ballet leap across the room. The glass shards dropped into the wastebasket, then she tossed/spun the broom back to its place in the inch between refrigerator and counter. Last—but definitely not least—she gave Joe a flirty little wink before sashaying back to the bedroom. She didn't stop until she was stretched out on the bed, her body arrayed in a sexy, sideways lounge. She didn't come back to herself until she felt her own hand at her blouse, making sure it was open to her navel and showed everything. At that point she simply froze in place, one hand on her stomach, while Joe slowly entered her bedroom.

She raised her gaze to meet his. He looked startled, aroused, and extremely wary as he stopped just inside the doorway.

"I'm possessed," she whispered. "By the spirit of Jet Li and . . . and . . ." She looked down at her open shirt. "And Vampira."

"Don't people have to be dead before they can possess you?" he asked.

"Fine!" she snapped. "I'm possessed by some kung fu Mae West!" She abruptly closed her blouse.

He frowned. "That's your explanation? You're possessed?"

She blinked, startled and ashamed by the tears returning to her eyes. "Yeah, I guess it is. You got a better idea?" She looked at him, praying he did. "And don't go with secret undercover fed or anything," she added. "You know as well as I do that's not true."

He frowned as he moved slowly into the room. "I like it a lot better than possessed." He settled slowly onto the base of her bed. "You've never done *any* martial arts before?"

"Not even kick-boxing."

"Huh." That was it, the sum total of his response. And Micki was hard-pressed not to lose it completely. He must have seen how close to the edge she was, because he abruptly scooted closer on the bed and said, "Okay, okay. I believe you. Not a fed."

"Feds too tough to cry?" she taunted, for really no reason at all.

"Let's just say you don't give off the cop vibe." He touched her arm. The stroke was tentative, but she felt it all the way through her spine. "So, let's go through this step by step. Have you ever . . . um . . ."

"Run across treetops before? Pivot-turned off my refrigerator? No."

He nodded. "When did this start?"

"The fight this afternoon."

"What about when I came into your classroom? You said you fell, but you managed to get Damian's face. Was that a—"

"I kicked him. A solid roundhouse to the face. I thought it was a lucky accident at the time, but . . ."

"Now you think you might have gone all ninja on him." She nodded.

"So, what changed between yesterday and today?"

She threw up her hands. "Nothing! Nothing at all. Same bagel and coffee this morning, same drive to school, same everything." Then her gaze dropped to her overstuffed wastepaper basket. An empty shoebox teetered half in, half out. "Well, new shoes, but that doesn't count."

"No, that doesn't count," he agreed. "Unless you think the shoes are possessed."

He said it as a joke, but then again she didn't think he was taking any of this very seriously. She, on the other hand, knew for a fact that she did not have secret kung fu skills of her own. Ergo, *something* was possessed with superpowers. Shoes made as much sense as anything else.

She scrambled off the bed to pull out the empty shoebox. "I ordered them from some Web site. Here it is: www.hiheelia.com. It promises shoes that will give and get a girl exactly what she needs."

"You don't seriously think it's the shoes, do you?" He folded his arms across his chest and his tone was uber-ironic.

Resolutely ignoring him, Micki turned her attention to her shoes. They were black, Chinese-style Mary Janes. Not that exciting. And yet . . . She toed them off, watching

GET UP TO
4 FREE BOOKS!

You can have the best romance delivered to your door for less than what you'd pay in a bookstore or online. Sign up for one of our book clubs today, and we'll send you **FREE* BOOKS** just for trying it out...**with no obligation to buy, ever!**

HISTORICAL ROMANCE BOOK CLUB

Travel from the Scottish Highlands to the American West, the decadent ballrooms of Regency England to Viking ships. Your shipments will include authors such as CONNIE MASON, CASSIE EDWARDS, LYNSAY SANDS, LEIGH GREENWOOD, and many, many more.

LOVE SPELL BOOK CLUB

Bring a little magic into your life with the romances of Love Spell—fun contemporaries, paranormals, time-travels, futuristics, and more. Your shipments will include authors such as KATIE MACALISTER, SUSAN GRANT, NINA BANGS, SANDRA HILL, and more.

As a book club member you also receive the following special benefits:

- **30% OFF** all orders through our website & telecenter!
  (Plus, you still get 1 book FREE for every 5 books you buy!)
- **Exclusive access to special discounts!**
- **Convenient home delivery and 10 days to return any books you don't want to keep.**

There is no minimum number of books to buy, and you may cancel membership at any time. See back to sign up!

*Please include $2.00 for shipping and handling.

YES! ☐

Sign me up for the **Historical Romance Book Club** and send my TWO FREE BOOKS! If I choose to stay in the club, I will pay only $8.50* each month, a savings of $5.48!

YES! ☐

Sign me up for the **Love Spell Book Club** and send my TWO FREE BOOKS! If I choose to stay in the club, I will pay only $8.50* each month, a savings of $5.48!

NAME: _____

ADDRESS: _____

_____

TELEPHONE: _____

E-MAIL: _____

☐ **I WANT TO PAY BY CREDIT CARD.**

☐ VISA   ☐ MasterCard   ☐ DISCOVER

ACCOUNT #: _____

EXPIRATION DATE: _____

SIGNATURE: _____

Send this card along with $2.00 shipping & handling for each club you wish to join, to:

**Romance Book Clubs
1 Mechanic Street
Norwalk, CT 06850-3431**

Or fax (must include credit card information!) to: 610.995.9274.
You can also sign up online at www.dorchesterpub.com.

*Plus $2.00 for shipping. Offer open to residents of the U.S. and Canada only.
Canadian residents please call 1.800.481.9191 for pricing information.
If under 18, a parent or guardian must sign. Terms, prices and conditions subject to change. Subscription subject to acceptance. Dorchester Publishing reserves the right to reject any order or cancel any subscription.

JOIN NOW!

them drop to the floor with a slight *pfft*—as if power evaporated off her skin the minute she slipped them off. Then again, that might have been her overactive imagination.

Whatever. She squared her shoulders. "Punch me."

"What?"

"Punch me. Right in the face. My plan is to block it, then . . . uh . . . slam my other arm straight for your nose, and then knee you in—"

"We don't need to go that far, do we?" His tone continued to be mocking, but he stood up from the bed. Apparently, he intended to humor her.

"Okay, no groin kicks. But I swear to you, I'll fight back for all I'm worth."

He nodded and threw the punch. It was a slow punch, obviously halfhearted. She met it with her palm extended—*smack*—but she couldn't stop his forward momentum, and she certainly wasn't braced for how very big he was. He drove her shoulder backward to bang painfully against the wall. As for the cool arm-block move—she'd forgotten to do it. Within a half second, she was pressed flat against the wall, Joe's large hot body tight against her. She couldn't even raise her knee. His legs trapped hers quite nicely.

She swallowed and looked in his eyes. His honey-brown irises were dark, and his breath heated her lips.

"This wasn't what I planned," she said, her voice ten times huskier than she'd intended.

He arched a brow. "You sure?"

She nodded, though only by a fraction of an inch. She didn't dare move or she'd be kissing him. Hell, her lips were tingling from the desire, but she wasn't going to go there. Because she wasn't Mae West and she wasn't that bold. No matter how much she liked his weight against her.

"Ease off," she said, pushing uselessly against the solid wall of his chest. "Let me put on the shoes." She was able to stretch the toes of her left foot to drag one shoe closer. A couple more seconds, and she would be able to slip it on.

Meanwhile, Joe wasn't moving. If anything, he was dipping his face closer. "This doesn't work, you know, unless you really fight. Unless you're really in danger. You could be faking—*umph!*"

With one shoe on, she suddenly discovered a zillion ways to escape. Whereas before he had been an unmoving wall of muscle, now he was a man with vulnerabilities. She let one hand slip down, and she abruptly dug a single, pointy finger into his side. He squirmed, resisting mightily, but it gave her the inch she needed to wiggle away. She simply slipped down, rolled her hips around him—managing to tease him with her breasts in a strangely erotic move—and then elbowed his back hard enough to slam him into the wall. Then she whipped around, leaned into his back, and pressed her groin hard against his behind.

"One shoe on, Joey, and I'm more than a match for you." Her voice was taunting and frankly sexual. She'd never been so overt in her life, but she suddenly liked it. Or she did until he shoved backward.

He'd caught her off guard and, worse, her balance was on her bare foot. Apparently, her bare foot didn't have the same skill as the one with the magic shoe. She slipped and fell backward. Magic foot still managed to kick out and nail him in the thigh, but there wasn't enough force in the move and she dropped to the floor.

He spun and began stalking forward, his eyes dark with intent, but also with an electric kind of hunger. He was aroused and willing to fight for domination. So was she. And yet, the thoughts were so unlike her, she knew it wasn't her. "It's the shoes!" she cried. "Joe! Put one on. You'll see! It's the shoe!"

He halted, looking down at her covered left foot. Then his gaze slipped to the abandoned right shoe. "It won't fit me."

"Maybe if you hold it. Put it on your hand."

He arched a brow at her, but she simply echoed the look right back at him. "I can feel the difference," she said with total honesty. "My left foot has balance and power. My right . . ." She waved at her other foot. "It's just . . . normal." She twisted a bit on her bottom so that her feet squared up with her nightstand. She kicked out with her bare foot. It connected awkwardly with the old oak leg, then slid sideways off it, scraping the ball of her foot in the process. "Wow, that hurt," she groused.

"Well, of course—"

Her other foot shot out. The outside ridge of shoe and foot snapped the oak leg clean in two. She hadn't even been thinking about kicking, and *wham*, the nightstand was broken. "It's the shoe!"

He frowned at her, obviously unconvinced. But then he shrugged and picked up the black Mary Jane. He turned it over and over, inspecting it from all sides. It really was a simple design. Rubber sole. Black velvet. The Chinese character embroidered on top was done in a rich bright red. She wore "kindness" on her left foot. He was slipping "love" onto his right hand. And yes, it looked really silly, but her heart kinda melted when he looked at her, a shoe on his hand.

"Well?" She straightened to stand before him.

"Well, what? It's a shoe. On my hand."

"You don't feel any different?"

He shrugged. "I feel stupid. Why? Do you feel different with them on?"

She concentrated on her feet. A little bit of energy seemed to tingle up her left leg, but she thought it was because the shoe fit really well. "Good shoes always give me a bit of a lift."

He started to roll his eyes but froze at her grimace.

"Yeah, I'm a girl. I like shoes," she said.

"So hit me, *girl*," he taunted, spreading his hands, one shoe-clad, wide in the air. "Hit me like you mean it."

Wham. She did. She didn't even think about it, and *bam*, her arm was flying out toward his face. He blocked it with his shoed hand. Then they were kung fu fighting just like in the movies. It was just arms at the moment: Punch, block, double punch, double block, jab. It was too fast for her to follow even as she was doing it. She saw his eyes widen in shock, and yet neither of them stopped. It was as if they couldn't.

Then she cut under his punch, spinning to grab hold of his upper arm and throw him across the room. He countered by wrapping his arm around her belly—but that was a critical mistake. It knocked the shoe off his hand. Meanwhile, she was too committed to the throw to stop. She bent and catapulted him to her bed, but with his arm wrapped around her belly, she flew through the air right along with him. They ended up flipping over, landing with a thud, Joe on his back, her on top.

But without the shoe, he didn't have the dexterity she did. Plus, he might have been a bit winded from her full weight dropping on his admittedly wide and muscular chest. She let her mind dwell on that—his large, studly body beneath her—because otherwise she'd be thinking about her next move, and that was certainly the way to disaster. The magic only seemed to work if she let it take its own course.

So, she concentrated on how she'd love to get Joe nicely naked beneath her as her body flipped around to land hard on his hips. Then she leaned down to pin his arms, but he obviously wasn't completely vulnerable—even without the magic shoe on his hand. He muscled her over onto her back. She might have gained super ninja powers, but she couldn't defy the laws of physics. He had at least fifty pounds on her and she couldn't stop their momentum.

But she could wriggle beneath him. And she did have amazing flexibility and abdominal strength as she kicked out at the back of his head. He reared back but didn't let go. She used his backward momentum to pull herself upright and neatly flip him over. Except, he didn't have the flexibility to land on his back with his legs under him. She was sure she heard his knee snap—well, pop at least—and she immediately slid to the side, off him.

"Are you all right?" she gasped.

He was straightening, slowly, and so she reached out, gently supporting him as he came back up to his knees. Then he looked at her, his eyes dark, his breath fast.

"That is the coolest thing ever!" He sounded like an eight-year-old boy. He leaned over and grabbed the shoe, popping it back onto his hand. "Let's go again."

She grinned. "Don't you think your knee has had enough?"

He frowned at his leg, then gingerly maneuvered off the bed and tested his knee. He slowly lunged forward, then again faster. Deeper. Twisting. "It hasn't felt this good in years!"

Micki bit her lip. "But what about when the shoe comes off?"

He paused a moment, slowly straightening to stand in front of her. "I don't care. God, you don't know what it's like to be suddenly whole again! To be strong and . . ." He shook his head. "I don't care. This is too cool!" Then he frowned. "What about the neighbors? We're going to get noisy."

Yesterday, she would have worried, but today she had magical shoes that let her live out her bold and brassy fantasy with her perfect man. She grinned. "Let them suffer. Tonight, it's my turn to play."

He matched her grin. "And I do have some pull with the authorities. Professional courtesy between officers." Then he lunged at her. She hadn't been prepared, but that didn't seem to matter. She leapt backward and he crashed on the bed. But he arched his back and flipped his feet over himself in a move that he probably could never, ever have completed normally without major surgery. But he did it, and she was so stunned that she slowed to stare.

Was this really possible? Apparently so, because he was once again facing her, a grin making him look so much younger. "Ready?"

His joy was infectious. And exciting. She could see his pants were tented, and had a moment's double take at his size. The shoes couldn't possibly be . . .

"Micki? I'm coming for you, and I'm not stopping."

She looked into his eyes, all too aware that her nipples had pebbled and her thighs were trembling and wet. They both knew where this was going. It didn't matter how it started, they were headed for bed.

She smiled, and her tongue slipped out to wet her lower lip. His gaze riveted there, and his nostrils flared. "Micki," he began, her name a low growl.

In her best Mae West voice she said, "Bring it on, big boy."

He lunged, she parried, and they fought. Against the wall, on her dresser, over the bed, actually on the wall as she ran around the room, then out the bedroom door. It rapidly became clear that he was the better fighter. Whereas she had super kung fu powers, that didn't make her a smart fighter. He, on the other hand, had equal skills, more body mass, and an awareness of fighting techniques.

It also became clear that his objective wasn't to pin her, but to undress her. She lost her blouse over the dresser. He ripped her skirt in half as she ran into the main living room. Her bra disappeared during a half nelson, but her panties remained firmly in place.

Meanwhile, he managed to quickly divest himself of his shirt and pants without ever once losing the shoe on his hand. Pretty amazing, actually, given how she would take those moments to pummel him. Knee kicks, face punches, roundhouse whatevers. She went at him with them all. He parried one-handed or simply took the blows with a grunt. And soon, he was completely naked.

Then he grabbed her around the middle. She had been halfway through a leap over the couch, but he caught her and slammed her against the wall. She twisted, taking the impact on her shoulder so that she could roll to the other shoulder, then right out of his grip. But he was prepared.

He spun with her, then toppled them both down to the floor. She gasped in surprise, but his grin was triumphant. And then he kissed her. He pushed his mouth against hers and invaded in one swift motion. She arched against him, allowing their fight to continue with teeth and tongues. Here, too, he was the victor, owning her by touching every part of her mouth despite her best efforts.

And yet she had the distinct feeling he was getting as branded as she. She was nipping and taking and thrusting into him almost as much as he into her.

He lifted up a bit, taking his weight on his shoed hand, while the other roved all over her body. Face, collar, breast. Oh, he spent a masterful time on her breasts and nipples. She gasped, shifting her arms to tweak his chest. He pulled back enough to grin at her. Her legs were already spread wide to cradle him. He was thrusting hard against her wet panties, but the fabric still kept them apart.

"What you going to do now, big boy?" she taunted.

He stretched above her head, his body weight enough—for the moment—to keep her pinned. She was too breathless and aching to fight him just then. But in a moment . . .

Zzzip.

She looked up. "What did you just do?" She asked the question, but the answer was obvious. "You handcuffed me to my couch?" Her right wrist was held fast.

He grinned. "That's not a handcuff," he answered as he slid back down her body. "That's the plastic thingie."

She yanked hard against the thin strip of plastic zipped tight around her wrist and the couch. All she got was a red mark on her arm. The couch didn't even wobble. "Plastic thingie?" she taunted. "Is that a cop term?"

"Yup. Very technical." And then he bit lightly down on her nipple, sending a lightning bolt straight through her brain.

When he lifted his head, she bared her teeth at him. She knew how she looked—nearly naked with one arm stretched above her head. She looked and felt gloriously wanton. "We still got a problem, big—"

"You gotta stop with that awful 'big boy' stuff."

She arched a brow back at him.

"Call me Joe," he said. "I want to hear you scream my name when you come."

"One plastic thingie does not make a screaming orgasm . . . big boy," she teased.

He smiled, slow and predatory. "A challenge if I ever heard one."

She was going to say something. Something really clever, but he returned to her nipple. The way he rolled it in his mouth, then bit down with just the right tension. . . . She closed her eyes and let the lightning roar through her.

While she was still trembling from that, he began kissing down her side. She felt his body move. And though he kept at least one arm pinning her down, his weight was shifting, rotating, as his teeth grazed the underside of her breast, her side, and her hip.

She opened her eyes. "What are—?"

He took hold of the side of her panties with his teeth and began pulling them down her leg. It was the most erotic sight she'd ever seen. His teeth, sharp and white, pulling at the thin cotton thong. But most of all, it was the look in his eyes. As she lifted up enough to see him, she met his gaze. Dark and possessive, yes, but with a hint of mischief. He wanted her in the most primal way possible, yet that twinkle in his eyes made it seem so human.

She knew it was the shoes that were making them both this deeply sexual. She'd certainly never been so bold on her own. But that sparkle told her that it was him and her enjoying each other. No mystical compulsion or taint— simply them, having adult fun.

She lifted her hips to help him slide the last of her clothing off. He dragged the thong all the way down her thighs and off her feet. Then he began kissing and licking his way back up on the inside of her legs.

She had one free hand, and so she made good use of it. His hips were beside her, his large penis within reach. She began caressing it, stroking the velvety tip, sliding up the dark thick rod and then cupping his taut sac. He growled deep in his throat as he nudged her knees apart.

She allowed him to, because she was doing a little shift of her own. Her head went to the inside of his knee, nudging him farther open. And then her tongue began an exploration of her own. He tasted hot and salty. He smelled of musk. And he *was* going to submit to her.

It took very little leverage to topple him to his side. But as he fell, he took her with him. She felt him knock the shoe off his hand as he gripped both of her thighs. And then he spread her and took her into his mouth just as she was drawing him inside her.

His tongue was wicked as he licked her. Every inch got his loving attention. And when he pressed a thick thumb inside her, she began bucking. She couldn't stop herself. God, she wanted this so badly.

She wasn't ignoring him as she sucked and licked for all she was worth, but all too soon, she couldn't concentrate. His hips began to move, picking up his rhythm as he plunged fingers inside her. She held on as best she could, pleasuring him while his tongue began to stroke the center of all her sensation.

She felt his belly tense, knew his buttocks tightened, and then he abruptly pulled away. She didn't have the angle to stop him. "Wait," she gasped.

"Not until you scream my name," he said. Then he applied himself with a vengeance. She made futile attempts to draw him back, but there was no power left in her body. It was all centered where he was stroking with long pulls of his tongue.

She tried to resist. She tried to maintain some semblance of control. But every stroke of his tongue seemed to pull her mind from her body. Pleasure built beneath his mouth. It grew and expanded, taking her belly and spine with it. And then, he sucked. One long pull and her brain became engulfed in wave after explosive wave.

She screamed. She probably screamed his name, but didn't even know. Bliss!

Eons later, she opened her eyes. Her arm had just flopped free of the couch as she lay completely boneless on the floor. Forcing her eyes open, she watched Joe easily set the heavy couch off to the side.

She smiled. Or rather, she kept smiling, even as her gaze fastened on his erection. "Did I scream your name?" she asked.

He settled beside her with a grin. "Yes."

She reached out idly to stroke his thigh, her strength returning with amazing speed. She pushed her hand higher up his body. "Got any condoms?"

He shook his head with a sigh.

"No problem," she said, slowly levering up on her knees, then abruptly shoving him backward. "I think there's still something we can figure out."

"It's going to take a lot for me to scream your name," he warned.

"I want my full name, big boy. Michaela."

He arched a brow in challenge.

Leaning down, she made a long, slow sweep of her tongue. "But you don't have to scream it," she added. "Begging is just fine."

CHAPTER FIVE

Morning came too early. Nevertheless, Joe dutifully opened his eyes only to see a white eyelet ruffle from a pillowcase that was not his own. Memories brought a smile, and his returning senses gave him her smell on her sheets and the sound of humming from her shower.

Clearly, she was one of those early risers. He grinned. Today he was prepared to forgive such unnatural behavior. He climbed out of bed and began his morning routine of exercises. He was stiffer than usual—a lot stiffer—but he didn't mind one bit as he started working the aches out. He finished a set of deep squats, then dropped to the floor to begin his push-ups.

That's when he saw it: one black shoe. It was the one he'd worn on his hand, the one with the Chinese character for love stitched in red on the top.

He wasn't a man who accepted magic in his world. Not even the normal heart-fluttering, stars-in-the-eyes love kind. He'd long since categorized that as lust and chemistry causing a brain aneurysm or something. But last night had proved him wrong—on both counts. What had happened with Micki hadn't been just lust. Maybe not love, but certainly more than simple lust. And as for the sudden kung fu power? He had no answer, so he started doing his push-ups instead, glaring at the simple black velvet shoe all the while.

He was only halfway through his routine when she came out of the bathroom. He glanced up and was immediately distracted enough to blow off the rest of his workout. Pink skin barely covered by a towel, sparkling blue eyes, a shimmering fall of freshly blow-dried hair, and best of all, moist lips curving upward in a shy smile.

"Now that's a sight to wake a man," he said.

She blushed all the way down to her towel. "Good morning, Joe," she said. Her tone was breathless and anxious, but she was smiling. He was smiling. And he was getting harder by the second.

Then her phone went off: a steady cascade of tones that sounded more like an alarm than a ringtone. She gasped and dashed to her dresser, her naked legs passing almost within touching distance. She grabbed her phone and thumbed it off.

"That's the alarm," she said breathlessly. "I have to leave for school in ten minutes."

He frowned, wondered what time it was, then immediately decided he didn't care. "Take the day off. Call in sick."

She shook her head. "It's too late."

"No, it's—"

"I don't *want* to." She looked up long enough to meet his gaze. "I want to go to work today."

He understood the underlying message, at least in part. She wasn't a woman who did one-night stands, and so this morning after left her feeling awkward and embarrassed. He could sympathize. And if it were just that, then he would happily let her run off to school where she could think and talk and do whatever women did when they were deciding about a relationship.

But it wasn't just about them. "We have to talk about those shoes," he said.

She swallowed, then squared her shoulders. Her smile had long since faded, and now she looked determined as she stepped past him and quietly slipped one on. "We're not going to discuss it. They're mine. I don't know if they're possessed or what, but they're mine. I'm not giving them up."

He slowly stood to his full height, not caring that he was completely naked and aroused. "I never said I wanted them."

She lifted her chin. "Yes, you did. Last night. You said—"

"That they were cool. And they are. And they're also . . . magical." He almost choked on the word, but he got it out. "You don't know anything about them except what they let you do. Don't you think we should study them a bit first before you use them any more?" He used the word "we" deliberately. For better or worse, he was involved in this . . . magic. No way was he going to let her pursue this alone. "They could be dangerous."

She leaned down and buckled the shoe on, and the view of her nicely rounded tush distracted him more than he wanted. "They don't feel dangerous," she said.

"Not every dangerous thing does."

She straightened, looking a little silly dressed in a towel and one shoe. And yet, he was never further from laughing in his entire life. "Listen to me, Joe, because I don't know if I can say it twice. I like you. I always have, from the very beginning. Last night was . . ." Her face softened into a dreamy smile. "It was the best. But we both know that it's not me you like."

He frowned, working hard to think of the best way through her female logic. He decided to simply go for brutal honesty. "We're talking about the shoes, not us."

"But it is us, too. I've noticed you from the beginning, but you've always gone for the . . ." She waved her hands in front of her breasts. "For *other* types. You dismissed me by the end of the first day."

Actually, within the first five minutes, but he wasn't going to tell her that. "I noticed you," he countered. "I just thought you had your hands full."

"I did. I do," she agreed with a sigh. "And these shoes are one more complication. But see, that's my point. If it weren't for the kung fu powers, you would never have noticed me. You wouldn't be here. And I would never have . . ." She blushed and looked away.

He stepped forward, but didn't dare touch her. The way she looked right then, she would probably bolt. "You wouldn't have what?"

"Seduced you."

He felt his shoulders stiffen. "You think last night . . ." How to phrase this? "You think what we did last night was because of those shoes?" He took a step forward. "Micki, we weren't wearing those shoes for most of it."

She lifted her chin. "But we were at the beginning. At the start."

"So?"

She threw up her hands. "So, nothing! So, I'm not a slut. I don't seduce men like that—"

"I never said you were!"

"But you'd never go to bed with me unless something made you."

He blinked, wondering for a moment if she was serious. Obviously she was. "That's total bullshit! Of course I would!" Skittish be damned; he was across the room and grabbing her arms before she could run. "You can't seriously believe that I wouldn't—"

"Well, of course you would. If I were just a stranger or something. But I'm a coworker."

He stared at her, feeling the insult all the way to his bones. "You honestly think I sleep with anything with tits?"

She nodded, though her eyes were obviously big with fear. "Big ones! Who you don't work with!"

"That's ridiculous!" he exploded.

"That's what I'm saying! This whole thing is ridiculous. It wasn't real!"

"It sure as hell was!" He was gripping her arms too tight. He knew it, but he couldn't stop himself. She obviously thought he was some awful player.

He abruptly released her, stomping away to grab his clothing. "Micki, you obviously don't know me at all."

She didn't answer at first. She was silent so long that he had to glance over his shoulder to see her standing still in her towel, her face as white as her eyelet pillowcase. "That's what I've been trying to say," she finally whispered. "We don't really know each other at all." She glanced down at her feet. "It was all fake."

Then she abruptly turned and grabbed some clothes out of her dresser. He tried to think of something to say. There had to be words to make her see reason. But he couldn't find them. Truthfully, some tiny piece of him did wonder if last night's amazing sexual explorations had been shoe-induced. So he remained silent as she gathered up the last of her clothes and ducked into the bathroom. The last thing he saw her do was brush the hair out of her face. Except, of course, he knew it wasn't really hair but tears.

With an abrupt curse, he stomped out of the room, threw on his clothes, and then just kept going. Thankfully, he didn't live that far away, and the run would do him good.

* * *

The roses arrived during fourth period. Micki had time to smile, bury her nose in the blooms, and then glance at the card. Three words, no signature: *It was real.* From Joe, of course. And a lie if there ever was one. So, blinking away the tears, she returned her attention to her class.

She saw him at lunch, but ducked away. He followed, of course, and almost had her in her classroom. But then his radio went off—disturbance in the cafeteria—and he had to go. He left with a muttered curse, but not before he sent her a look that practically screamed determination.

During fifth hour, he sent one of her students to her classroom with a sealed note. It read: *Dinner tonight.* The boy who delivered it stood in the classroom door fidgeting. When she asked why, he simply shrugged and said, "Mr. DeLuce said you'd have an answer."

Micki's heart beat triple-time, but she held back her *yesyesyesyesyes!* In the end she used her most professional voice as she said, "Mr. DeLuce was incorrect. You may go now."

During sixth hour, another note read: *Don't make me arrest you.*

Then during seventh hour: *I can't wait until dinner. Coffee right after school.*

Then, finally, during last hour, a single sheet of notebook paper arrived. On it was one word: *Please.*

She ignored them all. Sure, she'd started looking at every student who walked into her room, hoping to see another note. Yes, she'd gotten a thrill deep down inside when a note did magically appear. But most of all, she'd started to feel cornered.

Clearly, Joe was not a man to back off when he set his sights on something . . . or someone. He'd been right when he said that she was in over her head at school. She was.

Add in magical shoes and a handsome cop, and she just wanted to hide under her bed.

But she couldn't do that. She had a job and kids to teach. Most especially, she had a young girl—Lucy—to talk some sense into. And she had to do it fast before Damian destroyed her.

The final bell rang. Just like yesterday, kids scrambled out of their seats and headed for the door. Just like yesterday, Micki smiled at them but focused on her target. "Lucy, could we talk for a moment, please?"

The girl nodded, reluctantly, but remained, though her gaze kept wandering anxiously to the classroom door where yesterday Damian had appeared and ruined everything. So, Micki grabbed her purse. "I need some air. Let's step outside and talk."

She didn't even let the girl stop by her locker. She was too afraid that Damian would show up. Instead, she steered the girl through the busy teachers' lounge, then beyond to the employee parking lot and a cozy alcove between the Dumpster and a rather stately-looking elm. There were a couple of folding chairs set up beneath the tree, and Micki gestured to Lucy to take a seat.

"Um, I gotta get home, Miss Becker."

"No, we gotta talk, Lucy. About Damian."

The girl's eyes widened, and her head started shaking back and forth. "Miss Becker, you don't know nothing 'bout—"

"Come on, Lucy." She took a deep breath and decided to go for broke. She just didn't have the time or patience for subtlety. "You're a smart girl. A really smart girl. I can easily see you going to college. You could have such a bright future. God, Lucy, you have no idea how really talented you are."

Lucy's chin lifted, and her mouth dropped open in surprise. Micki could tell that the girl hadn't expected that. And worse, she certainly hadn't ever heard it before.

"That ain't possible for me," she whispered. "It just ain't."

"Of course it is. And I could help you. There are foundations, scholarships, opportunities for kids like you—especially if a teacher really takes an interest. I could sponsor you, make recommendations. You could have a great future." Micki reached out and touched the girl's hands. Lucy did not pull away. Progress. Micki decided to push it a bit further.

"But none of that is possible if you get in trouble. One arrest, one bad choice, and it will all disappear, and I won't be able to change that. That's the reality of the world. There just aren't a lot of second chances."

The girl looked down at their hands. "You're talking about Damian," she mumbled.

Micki nodded, knowing it was now or never. "Why are you with that boy? He beats up people. He runs a gang. God only knows what else he's doing, but you can be damn sure it's illegal and dangerous. You can't afford to get caught up in what he's doing."

Lucy looked up, but not at Micki. Her gaze traveled out beyond the parking lot to God only knew where. "He was my brother's best friend," she whispered.

"And didn't he get your brother addicted? I mean, I don't know about you, but I might blame Damian for what happened with your brother. The drugs, shooting Joe . . ." Micki's voice wavered on those last words. "I mean, shooting Mr. DeLuce." She leaned forward. "I want to understand, Lucy. Please tell me the good things about that boy. Tell me what you see in him."

Lucy just shook her head. "He likes me because I'm good at chemistry. I understand a lot of stuff. Mr. Gorzinsky's even given me a college text to study."

Yay for Mr. Gorzinsky. "But that doesn't explain why you like Damian."

Lucy just kept shaking her head—a slow movement of denial. And then, finally, she whispered. "You don't understand."

"Probably not," Micki admitted. "But I'm trying to."

The girl abruptly spun back to Micki, her eyes huge, her words intense. "It's different for you. You're rich. You don't know how hard it is for a girl like me." She swallowed, and tears shimmered in her eyes. "I'm scared all the time. I'm not like you!" Lucy gripped Micki hard. "I saw you. You knocked the knives out of their hands. You kicked Damian in the face! You hide it, but you got skills. I don't have anything!"

Micki almost laughed out loud. The girl thought she was some great kung fu fighter or something. "Oh, Lucy, if you only knew. I'm just as terrified as you. Probably more. I'm nothing special. Honest. All I can do is try—every day—to help."

"Bullshit!" Lucy snapped. "I've seen 'em." Her voice dropped a little lower. "And Damian's seen 'em too. He's pretty pissed."

Great. She'd ticked off a teenage gang lord. "I'll deal with Damian. I have a plan for him," she lied. "I'm just concerned about keeping you out of the crossfire. Lucy, you have to break up with the boy."

Lucy angled her head. "Is it you and Mr. DeLuce? You two got a plan?"

No way was Micki going into what was happening between her and Joe, regarding Damian or anything else. "We're talking about you."

"You gonna bust Damian? You got something on him?"

"Lucy—"

"I hafta know!"

Micki stared at the girl. Lucy was nearing panic. Her eyes were wide, her voice shrill, and her hands were tightening into claws.

"You need to calm down, sweetie. You have to let things happen on their own."

"You don't understand, Miss Becker!" the girl wailed. "He's dangerous! You could be hurt!"

Micki frowned, trying to follow Lucy's thoughts. "You're afraid for me? That I'm going to get hurt?"

"You ain't from here, Miss Becker. You don't know."

Wow. Now she had kids like Lucy trying to protect her. Did everyone think she was a complete incompetent? "I thought you said I was protected. That I had amazing skills and all. And now you're worried for me?" She dropped backward against the chair. "Lucy, what's going on?"

But Lucy wasn't talking. She just kept shaking her head. After a minute of that, she finally murmured, "The world is all fucked up."

Micki sighed. "No argument there, kiddo, but there's good stuff, too. There's magic and . . ." And really sweet cops. "And people who care about you."

"There ain't no magic, Miss Becker. No justice neither. If there were, then my brother wouldn't be in jail. It'd be the asshole what shot that crap into his arms."

Someone had made her brother shoot up? Obviously Lucy was in denial, but now wasn't the time to work that angle. "There *is* wonder in this world," Micki repeated. "You have to know that." She put her whole heart into her words because she believed them. And because she'd come to this school to deliver exactly that message. "There are people who care and who will help you. I'm here. Joe—Mr. DeLuce is here. There are lots of teachers who will help."

"Like Mr. Gorzinsky?" It didn't sound like a compliment.

"Yeah, like Mr. Gorzinsky. He gave you the college chem text, didn't he?"

But Lucy wasn't buying it. "He's just like all the rest."

This conversation was going nowhere. Like so many of her discussions with the kids, it just went around in circles, with Micki offering hope and the kids set in the belief that there was nothing. Micki needed something different, something shocking enough to break Lucy out of the cycle of bitterness; something magical.

"Life can be different, Lucy," she began. "It can have surprises that you'd never expect. I got a very special surprise just yesterday."

Lucy screwed up her nose. "You pregnant or something?"

"No!" The word came out more forceful than Micki intended, mostly because she was trying to cover the unexpected pang of longing. Wouldn't a little baby Joe be adorable? "Um . . . no, Lucy, I'm not pregnant. And I wouldn't do that without getting married anyway. It's just too hard to raise a baby alone."

"Hollar that," Lucy murmured.

"My surprise was much more . . . different." She was about to say magical, but honestly, a baby would be pretty magical all on its own. Especially if it was a boy with dark Italian eyes. Rather than dwell on that thought, Micki abruptly popped off her shoes. "Here," she said offering the velvet Mary Janes to Lucy. "Put them on."

"Your shoes? Whatever for?"

"So you can see how magical the world can be sometimes. That sometimes life has the most unexpected turns."

The girl picked up the shoes by the tiny black straps. "No offense, Miss Becker, but these ain't really my style."

"I'm sure they aren't. But these shoes aren't about style." She abruptly leaned down and tugged at the ties of Lucy's grubby sneakers. "Come on, Lucy. It'll just take a second." Fortunately, Lucy's feet were about the right size.

It took a little more coaxing, but the girl finally gave in. She pushed off her sneakers and buckled the Mary Janes on. Then she turned and plopped her hands on her hips and said, "So?"

Micki smiled, anticipating the moment when Lucy's teen attitude was wiped away by amazement. "So sweetie, jump. Kick. Or punch something."

"You been drinking, Miss Becker?"

Micki let her head sag. "Just do it, Lucy."

The girl shrugged, then threw her hand forward in a punch. She was aiming at Micki's shoulder, but what Micki got instead was a rapid pummel of rabbit hits that knocked her out of her chair.

"Oh my God!" Lucy cried.

Micki would have smiled at the look of astonishment on the girl's face, but she was too busy dealing with her own soon-to-be black-and-blue arm.

"Oh my God, Miss Becker!" Lucy cried again.

"I'm all right. I'm all right," Micki said, slowly rolling to her feet.

"But . . . oh my God!"

Finally, Micki got to face the girl and grin. "Pretty amazing, huh? I don't have any secret ninja powers, Lucy. It's all the shoes. They're magic or something. Go ahead. Try and kick something."

Lucy spun and extended her right leg at her own chair. The thing shot across the tiny stretch of grass to bang hard against the brick wall.

Micki narrowed her eyes at the crumpled metal. "I think you broke it."

"Oh my God!"

"Yeah, that's pretty much what I said yesterday. Over and over while I was running through the trees."

Lucy stared at her. "You ran through the trees? Wait a minute—you did! I saw you! Not through the trees, but like the wind." Her eyes widened even farther. "And all those things you did—the kicks, the punches . . ."

"All the shoes. I haven't ever even taken a class. They just did it for me."

"You think I could do that? Run through trees and kick stuff?"

"In those shoes, I think Annette Sticklan could do it." She'd named the most unathletic girl in school. "Come to think of it, I am Annette Sticklan, athletics-wise. I never played a sport, never really did anything physical, and you saw what I could do."

Micki kept talking, but Lucy wasn't listening. She was too busy performing chops and kicks and roundhouses on the elm.

"Hey, go easy on that tree!" Bark was flying, and the poor thing was shuddering under the impact of Lucy's blows. If the trunk weren't larger than two kids around, Micki doubted it could have held up.

Lucy fell back a bit, not even breathing hard. "This is . . . This is . . ." Apparently there wasn't an adjective cool enough to describe the experience.

"I know," Micki said with a grin. "It's amazing."

Lucy grinned back, and her eyes sparkled with a delight that Micki hadn't ever seen in them before. Her entire soul seemed to shine through her eyes, bright and beautiful and so happy. "I don't feel afraid in these shoes. They're . . . like . . . like God!"

"They're just shoes, Lucy. Magic shoes, yes, but they won't change your life." At least Micki hoped not. "And they won't stop a bullet or an arrest warrant. They're . . ."

Micki's voice trailed away. Lucy's thoughts were obviously far away. She was squatting down and then, with a look of intense concentration, she leapt upward. The first jump took her up into the elm branches at least a story up. She landed with a light plop, then dropped into a squat, perching just like Micki had done last night.

"I stayed like that for an hour, I think," Micki said. "It was so easy, but so . . ." She shook her head. "It was too much." Adults just didn't accept the magical as well as kids.

"Wow." Lucy looked out over the parking lot, the school, maybe as far as the freeway. "Wow."

"Yeah." Cool as it was seeing Lucy's face shine like that, it was time to get back to message. "So, you believe me now? You believe that cool things can happen? That there's magic and hope and . . ."

Lucy leapt up to a higher branch, then another. Then from there, she easily cleared the distance to the school roof. Moments later, she ran like the wind across the school and well out of sight. Micki stood frozen, her hands on her hips.

"Lucy?" she called. "Lucy, come back. I don't know the limits of what they can do." She waited even longer, a bad feeling growing in her gut. "Lucy? Lucy, come back!"

Micki stepped over to the parking lot to get a better angle on the roof. Nothing. Then she went farther back. Then into the street. Still nothing. Eventually, Micki walked entirely around the building, hoping that what she feared wasn't true. Except, it was.

Lucy had just stolen her magical shoes.

CHAPTER SIX

Most of the building had emptied by the time Micki gave up waiting for Lucy's return. She trudged wearily through the quiet halls, barefoot, her mind a relative blank. Sure, she had thoughts, but most of them involved too much of an emotional charge for her to even attempt to sort them out. So she walked mindlessly toward her classroom and prayed that sometime soon a brain cell would fire and she would suddenly have a plan.

"Bloody hell! Stupid, bloody moron!" Mr. Gorzinsky's voice echoed loudly down the hallway. In truth, this wasn't unusual. He was extremely volatile for a man in his sixties, and given to pretentious curse words. What struck Micki as unusual were the added sounds of Joe's voice.

Again, Micki moved without thought. At the moment, Joe's voice was more real to her than anything else. Maybe he would have a plan.

But what she saw from the door of the chemistry lab stopped her cold. Mr. Gorzinsky, white hair flying every which way, leaned heavily against the front lab table as he clearly tried to contain his emotions. Joe stood just inside the door, his arms folded across his solid body. He had his back to Micki, but she could tell that he was calm, relaxed, and not in the least bit sympathetic to Mr. Gorzinsky's aging heart. Didn't Joe see that the poor man was risking a heart attack?

Micki rushed into the room, neatly sidestepping Joe. "Mr. Gorzinsky! What happened?"

The chemistry teacher's head snapped up. His hair continued to fly wildly around his face, but his eyes were clear and direct as they pinned her with laser-point intensity. "Sam. Sam Wheaton died this morning. Drug overdose."

"Oh no!" she gasped, her mind slipping through the faces of the children. Sam was a junior and not one of her kids, an underprivileged boy who abruptly started doing better in school when he hit chemistry last year. "He was doing better! Wasn't he one of your Advanced Chem students?"

"Drugs don't care what your grades are," Joe commented from behind her. "And this drug kills extra easy."

Mr. Gorzinsky grunted, then dropped down onto a stool. "Stupid, stupid boy."

Micki couldn't agree more, but it wasn't helpful to say. Instead, she turned to Joe. "Which one? Which drug was it?"

"They call it 'Chem,'" answered Mr. Gorzinsky with a snort. "Nothing flashy like 'ecstasy' or anything like that. Just Chem."

"And it's killing them," continued Joe.

Mr. Gorzinsky shook his head. "Just the stupid ones." He abruptly straightened. "Maybe it's for the best. Maybe this is evolution in action. The dumb kids die. The smart ones survive."

Micki grabbed the older man's hands. "You don't really mean that!"

He turned, looking at her with eyes that seemed to reflect decades of teaching the underprivileged. "Bleeding hearts don't last long here," he said. "Toughen up or leave. These children don't understand your brand of kindness."

She straightened. "Kindness is never lost on anyone."

He snorted. "It's the carrot or the stick with them. And the carrot has to be immediate and obvious."

She sighed, the sound coming from her toes. This was familiar ground between the two of them. More than any teacher here, Mr. Gorzinsky got results. She respected that. But she hated his obnoxious, superior, evolution-in-action attitude. Especially as he rarely wasted an opportunity to sneer at her.

"Go back to the suburbs, Micki Mouse. You don't belong here." Then his gaze softened. "You just weren't raised for this jungle."

She shuddered, and Micki fought the tears. But then she felt Joe's touch across her shoulders. His hand was large, his warmth seductive, and without even thinking about it, she leaned into him.

"I'm glad you're retiring, Mr. Gorzinsky," he said with an angry rumble. "It's definitely time."

The chemistry teacher shot him a dour look, then apparently thought better of saying whatever was on his mind. Instead, he reached down to gather his things, muttering to himself the whole time. Micki couldn't hear exactly what he said, but it sounded like his retirement plans in the Bahamas.

Joe guided her to the door, gently urging her back toward her own classroom. "Don't let him get to you," he murmured in her ear. "He's old and bitter and—"

"Wrong?" She stopped and looked Joe in the eye. "Do you think Mr. Gorzinsky is wrong in what he said?"

Joe fidgeted. His shoulders tightened, and he fixed his gaze over her shoulder at a bulletin board. "It doesn't really matter what I think," he finally said. "What do you think?"

"That you're both full of shit." She abruptly spun on her heel and walked away. But in the privacy of her own head, she cursed herself for a fool. She believed in kindness. She believed in giving of herself until some child somewhere responded. Unless, of course, they were right. That the children she should be teaching were in the wealthy sub-urbs. In which case . . .

"He bribes the kids, you know." Joe's voice stopped her cold in her tracks.

"What?"

"Mr. Gorzinsky. He pays them in cash. To finish their homework or do well on a test."

She turned to look him in the eye. "How can he afford that? I mean, doesn't he have an ex-wife or something? He bitches enough about paying alimony."

Joe closed the distance between them. "I talked to her. He hasn't paid alimony in years. She says he uses that money to bribe the kids. And since they need the money more than she does, she's cool with it."

Micki frowned. "I thought she hated him."

Joe shrugged. "That's Gorzinsky's story. She seemed rather sweet to me, and very forgiving. Said they split up because he spent all his time at school or in their basement lab preparing the next week's experiments."

Micki frowned, trying to process that information. "That's his secret? That's how he gets these kids to work so hard for him? He pays them?"

"Yup."

"That's some carrot."

"Yup."

"Wonder what his stick is."

"Chores and stuff at his home or here. The chem lab gets pretty disgusting."

She glanced back down the hallway to where Mr. Gorzinsky was locking up his classroom, then striding away. "But how does he get the kids to do that? I mean, who would go do chem clean-up just for failing a test?"

Joe turned with her, watching Mr. Gorzinsky round the corner into the stairwell. "If you want the cash later—"

"And what teen doesn't?"

"—then you do the chore. And do better on each test."

She frowned, already thinking of her trust fund, of how much she could afford to give. But then she grimaced. That wasn't the way. She could empty her bank account and still not get anywhere. And, there was something else that Mr. G had over her, something else that made the kids respect him.

She grimaced. "The kids are afraid of him. Flat-out afraid, and so they respond better to his bribes." She wasn't built that way. She just didn't inspire fear.

"What happened to your shoes?" Joe asked.

Micki blinked. She'd almost forgotten that she was standing in her now destroyed panty hose. "I took them off. They were pinching my feet."

"You're a terrible liar, you know."

She looked up at him, shame heating her face. "They're gone. Lucy took them."

He blinked at her. He blinked again, and his chin shot forward. Then his eyes widened into horror. "She'll give them to Damian! Geez, Micki, do you know what he could do with those shoes? Oh my God . . ." He shuddered— actually shuddered—as he thought about it.

She felt her belly sink even deeper than her toes. "Maybe she won't. Lucy's a smart kid."

"She's dating Damian! She's a teenage girl dating a drug dealer. Oh geez, how the hell did she find out about those shoes?"

Micki hunched her shoulders. "I . . . uh . . . I told her."

Joe's gaze felt piercing, even though she wasn't looking at his face. His silence was even worse.

"I let her try them on. And then she . . . well . . ."

"She took off with them." His voice was excruciatingly dry.

"Yes."

"God."

Micki dared to peek up at his face. He looked angry and frustrated, but within moments his expression shifted to resigned. Then he shifted his gaze to meet hers. "I'm starved. You up for Italian food?"

She reeled from his abrupt shift. "But . . . but what about . . ." She gestured helplessly to her feet.

"What about them? It's not like I can call the police department and say be on the lookout for Damian in velvety black Mary Janes because they give him super ninja powers. Larry would fall off his chair laughing."

"True," she said with a nod. "And on the upside, I doubt they would fit on his feet. I really can't see him walking around with them on his hands."

Joe's expression lightened. "He does have a reputation to maintain." He took a deep breath. "Okay, that gives me at least a day while Lucy convinces him to try it." He smiled. "Plenty of time for dinner."

Micki shifted uncomfortably, grimacing as she felt her panty hose snag. Seconds later, a run shot up her ankle. "Joe . . ." she began.

"Micki, you don't have the shoes anymore, do you?"

Her gaze jerked back to his face. "No. I told you—"

"They're far away from you. Aren't influencing you in any way, right?"

"Lucy has them. I told you—"

He arched a brow in the sexiest smirk she'd ever seen. "So, don't you think it's time we found out if we like each other completely outside of the shoe influence?"

She swallowed, unable to keep her insides from melting into a gooey little puddle. "Are you sure you want to?"

His smile turned both hungry and mischievous at the same time. It was a really good look. "Ohhhh yeah," he drawled. "I'm definitely interested."

She felt her cheeks heat, and abruptly spun on her heel. "Then let's stop by my home first. I need to get some new shoes."

They never made it to the restaurant. Joe started talking about how he admired her spirit and her willingness to try new things. Stupid little compliments, but they worked because he seemed to mean them from his heart. It was the most natural thing in the world to kiss him in thanks for his words. And once kissing, well . . .

Apparently, Joe had stopped by a drugstore on his run home this morning, and he had a brand-new box of condoms in his pocket.

Hours and hours of ecstatic heavy breathing later, Micki rolled over onto her side and pressed tiny nibbles into his jaw. "Well, I guess I can safely say we have chemistry," she drawled.

"Chemistry, physics, and I think a healthy dose of poetry," he murmured back, his eyes still closed. But he still managed to move his lips to meet hers.

Micki smiled. She couldn't agree more. Instead of the wild tumble lovefest of last night, they had enjoyed long leisurely kisses that progressed to tender excitement. Today had been as perfect in its sweetness as yesterday had been in its fantasy fulfillment. Who knew she had such passionate range?

They continued to exchange tiny nips until his stomach growled. Micki laughed. "You promised me Italian food. So . . . will pizza do?"

"Mmmmm," he said against her jaw. "I think I love you."

It wasn't meant as a serious statement. It was just a joke about liking a woman who would accept sex and pizza rather than a fancy Italian meal. But Micki's heart froze nonetheless. And when she stiffened, so did he.

He pulled back, his eyes widening in horror at what he'd just said. "I—," he began.

"No worries, Joe," she said at the same moment. Her heart was beating triple-time. "What's your favorite pizza?"

"I didn't mean it like it sounded—"

"I know, Joe. It's fine," she said as she pushed out of bed. She couldn't look at him. Not because he looked so panicked, but because she had no right to be so devastated. Sure they'd known each other for the whole school year, but they'd only just begun talking yesterday. She didn't even know how she felt about him. No way could she expect him to have figured his own feelings out.

"But I'm not sure I don't mean it," he continued. "I mean, it's just too soon. I really want to get to know you more. I really like what we do together."

She glanced back at him, her eyebrows arched. "Joe, it's okay. I liked it, too."

He flushed a deeper red, one that really made his skin look rugged. "Well, yes, I liked that. I like it a lot. But I mean, I like being with you."

She didn't think she could bear to hear any more. Those three words could not be said casually between lovers. Not to her. So she leaned forward and pressed her finger against his mouth. She would keep the tone light even though it killed her.

"Joe, focus here. What kind of pizza do you like?"

He lifted her finger off his mouth and gently spread her hand before he pressed a long, tender kiss into her palm. It was a small gesture, but so sweet her eyes teared up. "I love whatever pizza you want. I'll eat anything, even if it's vegetarian."

She grinned. "Pepperoni and sausage?"

His eyes sparkled. "Now I really do—"

"Don't, Joe," she whispered. "Don't joke about it. I'm in a vulnerable place here, and I think I could easily fall in love with you." Maybe she already had. "So don't tease me if you're going to turn around in a week or a month and start parading around some big-boobed wonder."

He straightened, his face shifting into harder lines. "We're going to have to talk about this obsession you have with breasts. Believe me when I say that I like yours just fine." He reached to stroke her left one, lifting its tiny weight almost reverently. His touch was so perfect that she arched her back to give him better access.

His lips descended. Soon he was stroking her nipple with his tongue, and she was gripping his shoulders as the strength left her legs.

"Show me that you want me, Joe. Just me. No shoes, no kung fu power—even if I'm a bleeding-heart liberal who can't make it in Indianapolis. Show me that you—"

Her words were cut off with a gasp as he flipped her onto her back. She was at the edge of the bed, her legs dangling off the side, and he was abruptly standing between her knees.

"Look at me, Micki," he ordered.

She had been looking at him. She had been watching the dark intensity of his eyes.

"No," he said. "Look here."

She lifted her head to see his large and thick erection standing proudly between her thighs. His hands were shaking as he ripped open another condom and slid it on.

"This is our third time today, Micki. Three times. I have never, ever been able to do that. Not with any blonde bombshell. Not even when I was a kid." He dropped forward so that his arms framed her shoulders, and they were almost nose to nose. "I want *you*, Micki Becker."

He thrust himself hard inside her. A single shove and

she arched at the cascading shivers he created—delight that came as much from the intensity of his gaze as the power of his strokes down below.

"You, Micki Becker, with your bleeding heart." He thrust again. "With your perfect breasts." Another thrust. "And your stubborn, stubborn personality."

She wrapped her legs around him and began to tighten, pulling him into her in time with his movements.

"God, I want you, Micki," he growled. Then he slipped his hand between them and pushed his thick thumb against her. It was all she needed to fly. Her orgasm ripped through her, drenching every cell of her body in pleasure. He slammed against her once more, then shuddered help-lessly inside her, his own explosion as powerful as hers.

And only then did she touch ecstasy. Not from the waves of delight that still rolled through her. Not from the wonderful feel of Joe inside her. But in the abrupt and star-tling revelation that she loved him.

It made no sense. What did she know about the man ex-cept that he was kind, he cared about the kids, and he tried to protect her? That he had brought her car back to her, that he'd loved it when she sparred with him, and that even though he didn't like her teaching style he'd never undermined or berated her? He'd even stopped by her class-room on a regular basis to make sure she was okay. Not much of a foundation for love. But apparently, her heart didn't care. He was a great guy, and he wanted her. At least for the moment.

She was in love. And at that moment, the feeling was wonderful. She smiled as he collapsed beside her. She loved him. She would enjoy that—and pray she kept his interest—until the end of the school year. And then she would regretfully kiss him good-bye.

Yes, she abruptly decided, he was a great guy, and he was

also right. She didn't belong here. Which meant at the end of the school year, she'd go back home to Detroit and try again at a less challenging school.

They woke when a cell phone rang. It wasn't Micki's phone, but in the middle of the night, she wasn't paying that much attention. It was on the nightstand by her head, and so she grabbed it and answered. "'Lo?"

"Mr. DeLuce?"

"Uh-nuh." Then Micki frowned. She recognized that voice. "Lucy?"

"Miss Becker?"

Joe rolled over, his eyes barely open, but his voice strong. "Was that my phone?"

"Here," Micki said as she passed it over. "It's Lucy."

"Lucy? Lucy!" He sat up as he tucked the phone next to his ear. "What is it?"

Micki turned to look at the alarm clock by her bed. It read 1:27. In the morning. What could Lucy want with Joe now? Suddenly the man rolled out of bed and started grabbing his clothes. He found a sock first and pulled it on.

"No, Lucy, you wait for me. It's too—Lucy! I'm coming right now."

Micki was moving as well, pulling on clothes and tossing Joe his at the same time.

"Tell me everything you know," he ordered into the phone while pulling on his pants. "You're sure? What about—No! Wait! Lucy!" He pulled the cell away from his ear and cursed.

"What's going on? Is she okay?"

"Maybe. I don't know. Hell." He pulled on his dress shirt. "I gotta go."

"Not without me, you're not." She finished tying the bow on her gym shoes, then grabbed her purse. "I'm going."

He shook his head. "It's too—"

"Dangerous. Yeah, whatever. I'm going."

He grimaced as he pulled on his other sock. She stood in front of him and tried to sound tougher than she felt. "Look, I'll do whatever you say. I'll stay down, stay in the car. I'm not stupid. But I'm strong enough to help you even without kung fu shoes. You know I am."

"Micki—"

"I'm going."

"Micki!"

"What?"

He tossed her his car keys. "You drive while I call for backup."

CHAPTER SEVEN

"Where are we going?" Micki demanded as she backed Joe's SUV out of her apartment complex parking lot. Joe didn't answer. He had her cell phone to his ear—his was on his lap in case Lucy called back—and he was fiddling with another electronic device that she couldn't quite see.

A second later, he plopped the thing on the dash and she heard a soothing electronic voice speak: *"Turn left in five hundred feet."*

"A GPS! Cool!" That's why he had insisted they take his car. Plus, his car certainly had more muscle than her little sunshine Beetle. "But where is it taking us?"

"Hello! Hello, Larry? It's Joe. I got a situation . . ."

Ding, ding. "Turn left now. Then in two miles, take ramp right."

"Yeah, yeah," Micki murmured at the machine. "But where are we going?" She accelerated too fast down the street. "Don't you have a police light or something?"

Joe rolled his eyes at her. "I'm a school cop, not SWAT."

Guess that meant no.

Ding ding. "Take ramp right."

Micki overplayed the wheel and they swerved, prompting curses out of both of them. But within moments they were on the freeway and zipping down the far left lane.

"*Continue for three miles, then take ramp left.*"

"Yeah, yeah. But where . . ." Micki remembered her brother's GPS. This wasn't the same make or model, but they ought to be similar. She leaned forward and started pushing buttons. It was quite a feat given that she was driving a zillion miles an hour, but thankfully, the freeway was fairly empty.

Finally, she found it. She brought up a list of turns until she arrived at her destination: an address she was sure she'd seen before. Then she swerved to avoid a teen on a cell who was going almost as fast as she was. She winced because of the bad example she was setting, but then had to focus on getting over for her exit.

Ding, ding. "*Take ramp right now, then turn left.*"

"I know, I know," she muttered. She made it—barely—then snaked through a residential area that looked solidly middle class. "I know this place . . ." she murmured again.

Meanwhile, Joe snapped her cell shut and pulled out his gun, checking it. She didn't know anything about guns except what she'd seen on TV, but just the knowledge that he had one—apparently in perfect working order—made her feel . . . well, she wasn't sure how it made her feel. Good, she decided. Scared, but good.

"How'd Lucy know your phone number?" she asked.

He shoved the gun in the back of his pants, just like they did on TV. "I give it to all the kids. I'm there for them if they ever need a cop. Yeah, they laugh at me and the crank calls suck, but a few of them keep it. Just in case."

She smiled. Of course he did. He was just that kind of guy.

"*Drive for 0.8 miles, then arrive at destination.*"

"That's Mr. Gorzinsky's minivan!" she cried, peering ahead through the darkness.

Joe cut in, "Pull over here. I'll walk the rest."

"That's how I know the address," Micki continued as she pulled over. "I had to drive him home one day when he got the flu. . . ."

A dark form dropped from the branches of a huge oak tree. One moment, Micki was busy parking, the next a black figure landed, *thump*, right beside the SUV. Micki bit back a scream, belatedly recognizing the tiny figure of Lucy in dark jeans and a black tee. Then Micki cut the engine and slammed open the car door. "Lucy, what the—"

"Shhhh!" That came from both Lucy in front and Joe from the other side.

Micki buttoned her lip, but it wasn't easy. She had way too many questions. Fortunately, one of them was answered as she looked down at Lucy's feet. Yup. The two red Chinese characters for love and kindness showed clearly in the darkness. They might even be glowing.

"You took too long!" Lucy hissed to Joe.

"We got here as soon as we could. There's cops on the way—"

"No time! We gotta catch him red-handed!"

"Calm down—" Joe began.

"Who's in there?" asked Micki, unable to keep her mouth shut.

"Damian and his crew. They're loading up the truck now," snapped Lucy as she peered around the hedge. Sure enough, there was a truck in the driveway. Mr. Gorzinsky's minivan was on the street.

"Ladies," Joe snapped back, "settle down! We can just get the truck. It's okay."

"You gotta get Mr. Gorzinsky!" Lucy shot back. "He's the one done all of this!"

Micki felt her brain finally catch a clue. Damian and his crew were loading up drugs into a van. Drugs that were somehow hidden in Mr. Gorzinsky's home. Wait, why would they be in Mr. G's house? Unless . . . "Mr. Gorzinsky's manufacturing the drugs?" she exclaimed in a half yelp.

"Shhhh!" hissed Joe, while Lucy gave her a "duh" look.

"But . . ." She bit her lip rather than speak, but . . . Mr. Gorzinsky?

"You don't believe me!" Lucy snapped.

"I believe you," Joe pressed. "I've been watching him for a while, trying to get enough evidence to shut down the whole operation. And if we just wait—"

Too late. Lucy sprinted off at a run. And with the magic shoes on her feet, there wasn't much hope of catching her.

Micki tried anyway. With Joe's limp, Micki was their only hope of getting the girl, so with a half-muffled "Lucy!" she took off down the street after her. At which point, she heard Joe curse—something to the effect of "Girls!"—then his uneven footfalls pounded after her.

Lucy slipped in and out of shadows like a ninja. Even knowing exactly where the girl was, Micki had a hard time seeing her. She felt like a lumbering ox as she chased—on tippy toes in an attempt at silence around Damian's van and into the backyard.

It was a normal enough backyard, complete with a privacy fence to block out the sight of rocks and weeds. Or, of course, it could shield neighbors from seeing teenage boys carrying shoebox-sized plastic bins up the stairway from the basement.

Micki shrank back against the house as one of Damian's gang climbed up the outdoor stairs from the basement. He was bobbing and weaving his head in time with whatever was coming over his headphones. Micki watched him load two storage bins into the truck, then turn around and bob back down.

Okay, so Lucy was right. The boys were loading something

suspicious into a van. From Mr. Gorzinsky. Fine. Micki could accept that. A chem teacher was poisoning the very kids he was teaching. But where was the girl?

"They're almost done!" whispered Lucy from right behind Micki.

Micki almost screamed, but stifled it into a squeak. "Yeah," she gasped when her heartbeat settled from terrified into panicked. She reached for the girl. "Let's go. We can't be seen—"

"No!" Lucy said, executing a perfect chop to Micki's wrist. "We've got to get Mr. G with his drugs. It's his fault about everything!"

"Trust in the police," Micki urged. Her numb fingers couldn't hold Lucy back, but maybe her words could.

Not a chance. "I'll delay them as long as I can," Lucy whispered. "They can't catch me with these shoes!" Then the girl started skipping—yes, skipping—straight down the stairwell.

"Lu—" Micki gave up; the girl was gone. She turned, looking for Joe. She knew he was around here somewhere, but all she could see was shadows. She listened for the sound of car engines. Lots of cars. Squad cars with sirens all rushing here to save Lucy.

Nothing. Where was Joe?

She turned and went *oomph* right into a male chest. Unfortunately, while it was a solid chest, it didn't smell good at all. She looked up.

Damian.

Joe cursed as he watched Micki being shoved down the basement steps by that psycho punk Damian. Great. Two innocent civilians deep in the middle of bad guy central. Worse, it was two civilians with delusions of grandeur. Micki was bad enough with her noble belief that kindness would win the day, but Lucy had those damn shoes on. He knew from experience just how heady that magic kung fu could be. The kid probably thought she was impervious to bullets.

Whipping out his cell phone, he connected to Larry.

"We're coming! We're coming!" said his friend by way of greeting.

"Change of plans. Got two innocent females in the mix," Joe grumbled. And didn't just saying that send icy chills down his spine. "I'm going in now to do what I can."

"You sure that's a good idea?"

"I don't see a better option. I can't leave them in there alone. One's a kid. And the other . . ." *Is the woman I love.* Joe froze as that last thought filtered through his brain. It wasn't a real thought. It couldn't be. It certainly wasn't the truth . . . was it?

It was. He knew it was the truth. But he really couldn't deal with that right then because he'd freak out completely. The woman he loved in the middle of a drug bust? Not possible. Not something he could even remotely contemplate. Ergo, he was not in love.

He slipped his phone—with the line still open—into his belt. Not perfectly stable, but it would give Larry some idea of what was going on. At least he'd hear if gunshots started going off.

Then Joe grabbed his gun and slipped around the house to the front door. Even that little delay burned through his gut, but he had to think clearly here. Stealth was his best option. The front door was locked—naturally—but not difficult. A little judicious lock-picking, and he was inside without a problem.

He made out the shadows of a plush recliner, expensive take-out cartons, and a big-screen TV. Beyond that, he skirted through vintage bachelor decor, complete with dirty dishes in the sink and discarded beer bottles—imported. He quickly found the door to the basement. It was closed but not locked, so he eased it open and slipped downstairs.

"Miss Becker, this is a difficult conundrum."

Gorzinsky, sounding smug. Who used words like "conundrum" except when trying to be an ass? Joe risked a peek around the corner.

Crap. Five bad guys plus the girls. And this time, Joe saw guns. No way could he take out all five before an ugly firefight began.

Then, even worse, he watched as Damian—busted-up face and all—grinned and draped his arm across Micki's shoulders. He clearly couldn't wait to beat the crap out of her or worse. Lucy was beside him, wheedling as only a teenage girl could.

"It ain't her fault, Damian. She must have followed me. Just let her go. She don't know nothing."

"Shut up, Luce!" Damian said as he backhanded the girl. Micki was moving in a second, shoving at Damian's side and trying to dive for the girl.

She got nowhere. Damian tightened his arm around her throat, and she was pulled up short, gasping and kicking for all she was worth.

"This is what a leader does, Miss Mouse," he taunted as he began to squeeze the life out of her. "Ain't so mighty now, huh?"

Joe had his weapon up and took aim, ready to kill the boy, but Gorzinsky intervened first. "Not here, you idiot! You can't kill her here!"

Meanwhile, Micki slammed her foot down on Damian's instep. The boy howled and released her enough that she fell onto her knees. "Can't kill me!" she gasped. Then she looked up, a fierce anger in her eyes. "You *can't* kill me, Gorzinsky," she hissed.

The chem teacher raised his eyebrows. Joe didn't even have an angle on the guy's face, but he knew Gorzinsky's supercilious look from just the tone of voice. "My goodness, the mouse speaks." Pause. "Or was it squeaks?"

Micki rolled her eyes. It was a great move, reminiscent of every snotty teen on the planet, bringing out just the right attitude of disdain from Gorzinsky. Then, before Damian could do more than draw back his fist, Micki spun around.

"Don't tempt me," she hissed. "You know what I can do. I'll kill you if you like, but I'd rather have a discussion here with the brains of this outfit." She gestured at Gorzinsky. Clearly, it was a bluff. Since she wasn't wearing the shoes, Micki had no skills whatsoever. But Damian didn't know that. And he was intimidated enough to pause.

"The mouse has teeth," drawled Gorzinsky. "Too bad teeth don't do anything against a gun." And just like that, all the bad guys—chem teacher included—drew their weapons.

Micki blanched, but her voice remained strong. "Go wait in my car, Lucy. This is between the adults."

The girl gasped and started to object in a purely instinctive reaction to Micki's authoritative tone. It might have worked on a different crowd, but not this one. Lucy rose from a half crouch but stood her ground.

"I been in on this from way early," the child said softly. "It's you who needs to go."

"It's you who needs to *die*," Damian said as he aimed his gun at her temple.

Micki glared at the kids—all of them—but didn't argue. Instead, she rounded on Gorzinsky and stepped right up to his gun. "Put that thing away. You look ridiculous." To her credit, her voice barely quavered. "So, you're making drugs for the kids to sell. That's your big carrot and how you get them into the chem lab. Good idea, in a really twisted way." She lifted her chin. "I want in."

Gorzinsky blinked. So did Joe. It was a good try, and it might have worked if it wasn't coming out of Micki's mouth. She just didn't have the feel of someone who would sell out for cash. That was one of the things he loved about her.

Then she had to go and push it. "It's either let me in or shoot me," she snapped. "And we both know that all that blood could be problematic. Not to mention disposing of the body, yadda yadda. It's just not worth the effort."

"Hmmm," drawled Gorzinsky. "You have a point. Except, like every liberal arts major on the planet, you just don't have a logical mind. I have a third option." He looked at Damian. "Shoot her up, then dump her in the usual place."

"No!" That was Lucy, launching herself forward with her magic shoes. She was on the table, kicking Gorzinsky's gun aside. Good move, except it clattered to the wall right next to Tommy Wilson, who stooped to grab it. Two down—sort of. Joe doubted he would get a better chance.

He jumped the last few steps and landed in a crouch, calling out in his most authoritative voice, "Stop! Police!"

One kid dropped his gun, but Damian didn't. "Bitch!" he screamed, and aimed his gun at Lucy, who was still on the table. There was no choice. Joe had no doubt that Damian was about to kill her.

Joe pulled the trigger.

Lucy screamed as Damian collapsed, even as she did a spinning flip to the floor. Micki dove forward, grabbing the girl and tucking her body around the small teen. Joe barely had time to register the move as he was diving to the iffy cover of the lab table. Bullets ricocheted around the room.

Fortunately for him, the bad guys were kids, too inexperienced to handle a firefight with calm. Their shots were wild, and their bodies stayed exposed. Joe crawled under the table as fast as he could. He took aim and fired. Once. Twice.

Not bad. They went down, and he was pretty sure he hadn't killed them. Thirty seconds later, Larry and three other officers burst in—two from the back, two from the stairs. They barked something official. Joe hadn't a clue what. He couldn't make out a thing over Lucy's screams. And he most especially didn't hear a peep out of Micki.

Had she been hit? Was she dead?

"No," he whispered as he started crawling over. "Nononononono."

"It's all right. We're okay. You're okay. Don't worry. I'm here."

He didn't even hear the words at first. They were a kind of low, soothing murmur beneath Lucy's wails. But once he caught the steady vibration, he fixated on it like a lifeline.

"Lucy, take a breath. That's good. Inhale."

Micki was alive. She was trying to settle Lucy down. He pushed the little girl aside and wrapped his woman tight to his chest. "Mickimickimicki."

"Umph!" That was all the protest she gave as she tightened her arms around him.

"Marry me," he said into her ear. "Right now. We'll find a judge. I know where one lives."

He felt her freeze in his arms. Then she pulled back. He only let her go about an inch, but it was far enough for him to see her eyes as she scanned him from head to shoulder. It was as far as he would allow her to move. "Did you get hit?" she asked.

"What? No. I'm fine. Are you fine?" He had already scanned her entire body twice, but maybe he had missed something.

"I'm fine. And Lucy's . . ." She glanced to the side where the girl was staring at them with wide eyes. "Lucy's fine, too. She's stopped screaming. And she's breathing now, right, honey?"

"Everything all right there?" Larry cut in from above them.

"Yes, Officer, I think we're good. Thank you."

"That's not an officer, that's Larry," Joe cut in. Then he turned to his friend. "Larry, we need a judge. Right away."

Larry's gaze sharpened. "For a warrant?"

"A marriage license," Joe answered, his mind churning fiercely.

"I think he hit his head," said Micki as she ran her fingers through his hair.

Joe pushed her hands away. "I did not hit my head!" he snapped. "Oh God, did *you?*"

"I'm fine," she answered again, but he was running his hands through her hair just to make sure. "Joe—"

"I've never been so scared in my whole life," Joe snapped. He took a breath rather than relive the last few minutes. "We're getting married, and that's that."

Micki was silent for a moment. He opened his mouth to argue further, but she pressed her fingers to his lips. It stopped the words cold—not because he couldn't speak around her hand, but because he was lost in the feel of her two dainty fingers hot against his lips. One little mistake, and she could be dead right now.

"Micki," he groaned, but she was looking at Larry.

"I think a paramedic ought to check him out."

"But—" Unfortunately, Larry seemed to agree. He leaned down and lifted Joe up by the arm. Meanwhile, Joe was nearly sputtering on adrenaline-fueled outrage. "I just said I love you, and you think I need a paramedic!"

"Actually, buddy, you never said you loved her."

"I damn well did! I—"

"Joe!" Micki straightened. She kept an arm around Lucy, who wasn't screaming anymore, but was still obviously in shock. "We'll talk more later. I swear. Right now, we've got children to handle."

Joe blinked, feeling both foolish and stupid at that moment. He'd just shot three kids, and he was more concerned about marrying his girlfriend than their lives?

He glanced around him. Gorzinsky was being led out in handcuffs, as was the one who'd bent down to recover the chem teacher's gun. Both were completely unscathed. The two he'd shot at the end were bleeding and complaining to the cops who were giving them first aid. They'd live. If the sound of sirens was any indication, there were ambulances on the way.

Finally, he let his gaze travel to Damian. No way was that kid alive. He'd known it before he looked, but he forced himself to see anyway. Two shots to the chest—one from Joe, one from one of his own gangbangers. Yup, very dead.

"The paperwork is going to be hell," he murmured. Not the most PC thing to say, but he couldn't regret the shooting. Damian had been about to kill Lucy. And he sure as hell was going to kill Micki.

"I'm glad he's dead." Lucy's voice was high and thin, but still strong. Her gaze slid to Joe. "I only dated him to find out where the drugs came from. He only dated me because I know about chemistry. He wanted me to make the drugs for him, but I had to get proof on Mr. Gorzinsky."

"No, you didn't, honey," Micki said as she stroked Lucy's hair out of her face. "That's what the police do. Your job was to be a kid."

But Lucy wasn't listening. She was toeing off her magic shoes. "That's why I took your shoes, Miss Becker. I never thought you'd follow me in here."

"Amen to that," muttered Joe. "And don't you ever do that again!"

Micki wasn't even listening. She stopped Lucy with a quick squeeze. "Keep them on, Lucy. I think you need them more than I do."

"What?" gasped the girl.

"What!" bellowed Joe. "She can't—"

"She can," interrupted Micki firmly. "Keep them, sweetie. I won't need them back home in Michigan."

"What!" bellowed Joe again. "I can't move to Michigan!"

Micki looked up, but not at Joe. Instead, her eyes trained on Larry. "Lucy's been incredibly brave, but I think she's about done in for tonight. Can she stay with me, and I'll bring her in for a statement tomorrow?"

"Take the kid, Larry," Joe interrupted, his patience completely exhausted. "Take her away, right now."

"Joe!" Micki exclaimed, but he didn't give her a chance. "Just give me a minute, please. Just a damn minute with the woman I love, okay?" He didn't know if he was talking to Larry or Micki, but it didn't matter so long as everybody left him alone with her. Just for a single minute. And until they could find a judge.

Larry snorted, then wrapped an arm around Lucy, who was still shaking. "Come on, kiddo. Let's get out of this basement." And while Lucy was slipping her shoes back on, Larry took a moment to smile at Micki. "For what it's worth, ma'am, I think he really does love you. I've never seen him this rattled before. Not even when he got shot."

"Getting shot is easy," grumbled Joe. "Damn stupid, but

easy. It's watching someone you love get shot—that's hard. Life-changing kind of hard."

Beside them, Larry sighed. "That's as romantic as he gets, ma'am. If that's okay with you, then I think you ought to say yes and marry him."

"I don't need your help!" Joe snapped.

"Yeah, buddy, you do. You proposed to a woman in the middle of a drug lab right after—"

"Yeah, yeah. Get out of here."

Larry looked like he was going to argue, but after a glare from Joe, he shrugged and buttoned his lip. A moment later, he and Lucy were climbing the stairs.

The basement was still overflowing with paramedics for the boys. Soon there would be the M.E. for Damian, and a host of other people doing their jobs. But for this second, it was just Micki and him in their little corner of Mr. Gorzinsky's drug lab.

He didn't give her a moment to think. "You can't go to Michigan, Micki. My life is here. And you can't give up your job. You're too good at it."

"Joe, you don't know if you love me for real. You love—"

"If you wave at your boobs again, I'm going to lose it. Micki, let me explain something. I'm not attracted to big boobs. I'm attracted to strong women. Sarah, the blonde bombshell you keep referring to, is a triathlete and an ADA. She can reduce a lying witness to infancy and look fabulous while doing it. And Marjorie, the second bombshell you saw me with, is a firefighter. No shit. A firefighter with a nose for arson like you wouldn't believe. She's smarter than any PhD, and she can flop a two hundred-pound man over her shoulder without breaking a sweat."

"Okay—"

"Listen to me!" He held her arms, afraid that if he let go

she would disappear back to Michigan. "I like strong women. I love you."

She shook her head. "I gave those shoes to Lucy. She needs them way more than I do—"

"I don't give a damn about the shoes! Micki, you are the strongest women I've ever met. Tonight, you faced down a drug-dealing gang without any damn magic shoes. You were terrified, and yet you kept your head and even made a good stab at fooling that ass Gorzinsky."

"It didn't work."

He shrugged. "Yeah, well, that's why you're not a cop. Micki, you're a teacher. And a damn good one."

"You think I'm a terrible teacher!"

"I think you're a naive one. But with my help, you'll be so amazing—damn it, you already are amazing! And I love you! It's not adrenaline, it's not any magic whatevers, it's not even the trauma of seeing you in the middle of a firefight. It's because I love you. And I want to marry you. So please—"

"Oh, for crying out loud!" bellowed Larry from the stairwell. "Get on one knee, ya moron!"

Joe shot an angry look up the stairs. Apparently neither Larry nor Lucy had really left. But Joe went down anyway. In fact, he went on both knees, letting his grip slide to Micki's hands. "I love you, Micki Becker. Will you please marry me?"

She didn't answer. She was studying his face, her eyes misting up . . . with love? Could it be?

"Yes," she finally whispered.

Larry and Lucy cheered from the stairwell. Joe blinked, then abruptly wrapped Micki in his arms. His knees wouldn't lift him up.

"I love you, too," Micki said against his ear. It was the greatest moment of his life. In fact, he had a full two minutes of absolute joy before he remembered something else.

"Uh . . . we're not going to Michigan, are we? I mean, I could possibly get a job, but—"

"I guess . . . well, I guess I haven't explored all the possibilities available for me here in Indianapolis. Besides," she said as she helped him stand, "Lucy's here. How am I going to borrow the shoes every now and then if I'm not in the area?"

His heart—and his groin—lifted at the thought. "You mean, we could maybe borrow the shoes. Like one night a week?"

She glanced over her shoulder at Lucy, who nodded. "That, or go back to that Web site."

He grinned. "God, you are the greatest woman alive!"

She wrapped her arms around him and kissed him soundly. "I love you, too . . . big boy."

MARIANNE MANCUSI

Karma Kitty
Goes to Comic Con

To fellow Rebel of Romance Liz Maverick.
May this year's "costumes" give us superpowers, too.

CHAPTER ONE

"Whoa. Have you ever seen so many people in one place that wasn't Disney World in your entire life?" Hailey Hills asked, stepping through the hallowed doors of the Jacob K. Javits Center, home of the 2008 New York Comic Con. She scanned the room, her eyes taking in the myriad colors, lights and sounds. To her left, Captain America stuffed foam muscles into his latex shirt. An Elvis Stormtrooper crooned to a bevy of bikini-clad Princess Leias on an elevated stage. And Captain Kirk challenged Captain Picard to a *World of Warcraft* duel over at the Blizzard booth down the aisle.

Comic Con. Geek heaven. She was finally here.

Her artist, Thomas Carol, shook his bleached blond head. "No way, José," he said, his voice filled with appropriate awe. "This place is more colorful than a parade in P-Town. I can't believe we're actually here." He turned to her, his eyes sparkling (and not just from the glitter he'd applied in the cab). "Squee!" he cried, grabbing Hailey's hands in his and jumping up and down.

"Squee, indeed," Hailey said with a laugh. This was the day she'd been waiting for her entire career. She shuffled her heavy bag to rest better on her shoulder. "Come on, let's find our booth and get situated for our signing."

Thomas consulted his map. "According to this, we're in 2134." He looked up at the numbered banners flying high above them. "Which is approximately the other side of the universe," he added. "We'd better start hoofing it."

They weaved their way through the crowd, trying to stay focused on their destination and not be sucked into the exciting displays flanking their path. After all, they weren't here as spectators. They'd been asked by their publisher, Straylight Comics, to do a signing of the latest issue of *Karma Kitty*. Straylight was a smaller publisher, and only asked a few of its authors and artists to sign each year, so it was a huge honor for Hailey and Thomas and their little comic-book-that-could to be amongst the chosen ones. And they planned to make the most of the opportunity.

"I wonder if Collin's here," Hailey mused, half to herself, as she ducked under a fierce lightsaber duel between Luke Skywalker and a somewhat potbellied Darth Vader, who'd obviously taken Yoda's "Size matters not" mantra to heart when hitting the old Mos Eisley Cantina on Tatooine for a few brews.

Thomas rolled his glittery eyes. "Girlfriend, please do not tell me you're planning to spend the best weekend of your life moaning over Mr. Hollywood. I simply will not be able to take it and will be forced to commit hari-kiri with some savage sword stolen off a hunky Conan cosplayer. And you know how I hate having to borrow my suicide weapons."

"I'm not!" she protested, feeling her face heat. "Please. I couldn't care less if he's here or not. Honestly. I was just making casual conversation to pass the time during our million-mile march to Straylight's booth. If you like, I could go back to chatting mindlessly about the weather. Would that topic be approved by the thought police?"

They pushed past a seven-foot-tall caveman robot. "You're at Comic Con!" Thomas cried. "The best you can come up with is ex-boyfriend extrapolating or whether it's going to rain tonight? That is sad, Hailey. Truly sad."

She sighed. Thomas had a point. She should be over-joyed to finally be here. It was an opportunity of a life-time and one she'd waited years for. A chance to promote her beloved Karma Kitty, meet fans face-to-face, and get her serious geek on with like-minded folk.

And yet, despite all of this, all she'd been able to do for the last few weeks was create wild scenarios in her head about running into Collin Robinson and what she'd say to him if she did.

Collin Robinson. College boyfriend and former love of her life.

They'd met in Film 101. Him, a straitlaced corn-fed Midwesterner. She, a hippie-dippie artist from San Fran. And yet they'd hit it off right away when they both burst out laughing during the final scene of *Citizen Kane* as they realized Rosebud (SPOILER ALERT!) was just some stu-pid sled. He'd asked her out for coffee, she'd said yes, and the rest was history.

A year later they'd started sketching out ideas for the original Karma Kitty. Hailey would write the stories of the superhero cat and Collin would draw the pictures. She'd found him to be an amazing artist—totally self-taught—who'd really helped her vision come to life. They'd spent hours working on the first issue, staying up late every night and ordering pizza as they drew and wrote. Hailey couldn't remember a time before or since that she'd been so happy. It seemed, up until their wedding day, that everything would have a happily ever after.

Until two things happened.

The first was Karma Kitty's rejection for publication. The second, well, we'll get to that in a minute.

Collin and Hailey had finished the first issue of their

comic book and had been sending it out to publishers. Problem was, while every publisher under the sun seemed to praise Hailey's writing and storylines, they always, in the next breath, criticized Collin's art.

Hailey never understood why. To her, Collin's Karma Kitty was beautiful—exactly how the character should look. But for some reason, his style was not going over well with the publishers. And let's just say their rejections were not going over so well with Collin. He started becoming more and more discouraged by the whole thing, and though he put on a brave front, Hailey could tell he felt like he was bringing her down. Finally, one day he'd told her he was done drawing and ready to get a real job; she needed to find herself a new artist. She tearfully begged him to reconsider—Karma Kitty was nothing without him—but he'd made up his mind. He signed over his rights to the comic to her and never drew again. Not even a doodle. Which was really sad, because he had loved it so much and was really, really good, no matter what those stupid publishers thought.

But Hailey hired a new artist and they were still in love and still going to get married.

Until the Hailey Curse kicked back in.

You see, while at first glance Hailey Hills seemed your typically normal free-spirit twenty-something, the more time you spent with her (and Collin spent quite a bit, seeing as they were in love and all) the more you started to realize there was something odd about her experiences. Weird things happened to Hailey. Really weird things. You know that "friend of a friend" they always mention in urban legends? Well, that was Hailey.

Sometimes she'd see dead people. Other times animals would talk to her. She'd once spotted a blind albino alligator down a NYC drain. The cactus she'd brought back from Mexico really had been filled with spiders. And on the same trip, she'd adopted a big rat she'd thought was a dog. (He ran away from home, sadly.) She'd even once found a piece of chocolate that looked just like the Virgin Mary. (Problem was, before she could alert the media and become rich beyond her wildest dreams, the hot sun melted it into a more Jabba the Huttlike shape—which, oddly enough, still ended up fetching $14.95 on eBay.)

The problem was, these things only seemed to happen when she was by herself. And when she tried to explain them to people later, she often had a hard time getting anyone to believe her. In fact, no one, except maybe her mother, bought any of it at all. And since Hailey's mother was currently whittling away the remainder of her life in a locked psychiatric ward after one day waking up in a bathtub with a stolen kidney and a note suggesting she not move and call 911, she honestly didn't make the best character reference.

Some would dismiss Hailey as crazy, others called her a flake, while still others would decide she was flat-out lying in order to make excuses for her aforementioned flaky behavior. That was Collin's deal, anyway. Mostly because every time something weird happened, it ended up interrupting something he'd planned for them. And when she'd show up, hours late, blaming the ghost who'd begged her to help him avenge his death, Collin just assumed she couldn't admit she'd forgotten, got tied up, or just simply hadn't wanted to go to the event in question in the first place. And no convincing on her part would get him to change his mind.

In a way, Hailey didn't blame the guy. If the weird things didn't always happen to her, she probably wouldn't believe in them, either. For example, she'd never forget the time Collin's dog, Skippy the Schnauzer, informed her there was buried treasure in Central Park. Excited, she'd dragged Collin to the location in question to help her dig. Which would have been fine, had it not been Superbowl Sunday—the Superbowl Sunday where the Patriots eked out a win over Collin's beloved Rams in one of the biggest upsets of all time, to be exact. Collin accused her of being jealous of his sports addiction. Worse, the only treasure they found after digging in the supposed spot was an old can of hash. (Though to Skippy's credit, to him this might very well have been the Holy Grail.)

So for Collin's sake, she tried to reverse the curse. When Elvis called out to her from the Frozen Foods section of Stop & Shop, she pretended she didn't hear him. (Even though she'd been sorely tempted to suggest the Lean Cuisine over the triple-pepperoni pizza he'd tossed into his cart.) And when Bigfoot attempted to kidnap her on her trek through the Appalachian Mountains, she'd had her Taser ready.

But on her wedding day, she'd been distracted, and naturally let her guard down. So when the kitty cat meowed that it was stuck in a tree, she'd walked out of the house to rescue it. An obvious trap, of course, and soon she found herself spinning away from Earth in a flying saucer, minutes before the ceremony. She was greeted by catlike aliens and informed she'd been chosen to star in their new reality show, *Who Wants to Live with an Earthling?* When she got back to Earth three weeks later, $52,000,000 Catonian dollars richer (not that you could buy much with Catonian dollars, save kitty litter and catnip), Collin had been nowhere to be found.

After some intense Googling, she learned he'd moved to LA by himself—just as they'd once planned to do together. She'd dialed him up and tried to explain the whole alien reality show thingie, but as you might guess, she didn't get much past the initial abduction part before he cut her off. He told her if she didn't want to marry him, she should have just told him so, instead of making him stand up there at the altar like a loser, while his friends and family shot him pitying glances from the groom's side of the church. (And let's just say her vegan-dieting, goat-milking, harvest co-op-shopping family whooping it up after they realized Hailey must have come to her senses and damned the misogynistic tradition that Collin had intended to trap her under didn't go over that well either. Nor did PETA-member-in-good-standing Uncle Earnest's *Free the Doves* campaign or AA-member-in-very-poor-standing Aunt Edna's *Free the Vodka* one.)

He loved her, he said. But he just couldn't take it anymore. He needed someone reliable. Someone who was there for him, not stuck on Mars.

She tried to argue that they had been light-years and light-years from Mars, but he was in no mood to listen. Finally, she gave up, realizing it was a lost cause. And maybe it was for the best anyway. How could she agree to spend the rest of her life with a man who refused to believe her?

That was five years ago, and though she'd forced herself to go on a string of disastrous first dates, she'd never met anyone who could live up to Collin. She thought about him all the time and Googled him on a daily (okay, sometimes hourly) basis. Their breakup certainly hadn't hurt him career-wise. In no time at all he'd become one of Hollywood's top producers, with a special knack for developing movies based on comic books. Everyone and their fanboy brother was in love with him, if one believed LiveJournal blogs. They linked him to movie stars and waxed poetic about his life of red wine and red carpets.

It should have been her life. He should have been her guy. If only that stupid alien-abduction reality show hadn't happened at the worst possible time. If she ever ran into Executive Producer Fluffy McGee again, they'd have some words, for sure. ("Bad Kitty," came to mind. The other words would be unprintable in the more polite publications.)

"Hey, let's go throw on our costumes," Thomas suggested, nodding toward the bathroom sign at the back of the convention hall. She'd hired Thomas after Collin quit and he ended up working out quite well—though Hailey would always be partial to Collin's sketches. Karma Kitty sold to Straylight soon afterward, and they'd been working on the comic ever since.

Hailey nodded, pushing thoughts of Collin to the back of her mind. "Good idea."

Wanting to make a good impression on their publisher and their fans, she and Thomas had created their own custom costumes, based on characters from Karma Kitty. Hailey, of course, was dressing as Karma Kitty herself, with a short plaid skirt, white button-down shirt, schoolgirl tie, and glittery thigh-highs. She had clip-on cat ears and tail to complete the outfit.

After much protest, Thomas had agreed to go as Big Kitty, the evil cat pimp. He'd original wanted to play Fifi, the frisky, flirty sidekick, but Hailey had ultimately vetoed the idea, saying she didn't think even Comic Con was ready for a six-foot, three-hundred-pound bikini-and-fishnet-clad drag queen walking around. (Though now that she was actually here, she realized that perhaps Thomas may not have even gotten a second glance. Still, at least hers wouldn't be the only eyes bleeding, which was always a plus.)

She entered the bathroom stall and started peeling off her street clothes, replacing each item with its kitty-wear counterpart. Once outfitted, she pinned the ears to her head and the tail to her skirt. Then she reached into her bag for the pièce de résistance—the boots.

They were golden-colored, lacing up to just below her knees, exactly the type of shoes her feline heroine wore when fighting crime. Of course, while the real Karma Kitty could effortlessly kick ass wearing five-inch platform soles, Hailey would be lucky if she could walk in them to booth 2134 without breaking an ankle.

Still, she thought, as she pulled the first boot out of its box, they were absolutely perfect. She'd so have to thank her Aunt Dottie for the Web link. Usually overbearing, matchmaking Aunt Dottie never forwarded anything to Hailey except Match.com and eHarmony profiles. Then, out of the blue one day, she'd sent Hailey a link to a Web site called Hiheelia.com, suggesting she peruse the footwear ASAP. The site was actually pretty odd—not surprising, considering it came referred by Aunt Dottie—and had a lot of mumbo jumbo about the power of shoes. In fact, Hailey had been about to close out the site altogether when suddenly she spotted THE boots. It was almost uncanny how exactly they looked like Karma Kitty's. As if the site had read her mind and produced the footwear from her imagination.

Which, once upon a time, wouldn't have seemed too unusual to Hailey. But she'd turned over a new leaf and abandoned the weirdness, so she decided to just deem it a coincidence.

She sat down on the toilet and slid on boot #1, praying it'd fit. The pair had arrived by airmail yesterday—some weird foreign postage stamped on the box—and she hadn't had a chance to try them on yet.

But lucky for her, the boot slipped onto her foot as if it were a glass slipper and she Cinderella incarnate. She reached down and slid on the other boot—also a perfect fit.

She stood up, ready to go show Thomas her outfit, when a sudden dizziness came over her. She had to brace herself against the bathroom stall walls, so as not to fall and hit her head on the toilet. A tingle tickled her stomach, flushing her skin and prickling at her fingers and toes. She felt panic rise to her throat as her heart picked up its pace and butterflies in her stomach swarmed the remains of the Starbucks cheese Danish she'd consumed back at the airport.

She sat down again, closing her eyes and sucking in a breath, trying to regain her composure.

"Hello? Hailey? Are you in here?" She could hear Thomas enter the ladies' room, unconcerned, as always, about the gender requirement. He banged on the stall door. "You do realize that *I'm* the queen, right? Therefore I should be the one that spends way too much time getting ready, not you."

"One second," she cried, exhaling the breath. She unzipped her boots and kicked them off her feet. No way was she going to walk to the booth in those when she was feeling faint. She'd put them back on when she got there. She unlocked the door and swung it open.

"Are you okay?" Thomas asked, squinting at her. She giggled. It was hard to take him seriously in his purple faux-fur pimp daddy suit. "You look weird."

"Hello, pot, I'm kettle," she quipped, already feeling a bit better. She grabbed the boots off the floor and slid on her flip-flops.

"Seriously, Hail, you look really pale."

"Yeah, I felt really weird there for a moment," she admitted. "Like, dizzy and faint."

"Maybe you're dying," Thomas said helpfully.

She rolled her eyes. "Thanks."

"Or, more likely, maybe you're nervous about seeing Collin," he added, with a sly wink.

She groaned, realizing that made a lot of sense. Stupid Collin. Stupid, stupid Collin. It was so not fair that he retained the power to make her weak in the knees (literally) after so many years, with his deep, soulful, chocolate eyes, and hair so black it was almost blue. She could picture him now—dressed to the nines, his full mouth quirked into one of his amused smiles, shaking his head at one of her antics. He used to tell her no one made him laugh like she did.

She sighed. Wonder who was making him laugh now?

"You're probably right," she said, grabbing all her bags and following Thomas out of the bathroom. "I'm just stressed. But I'm fine."

"You're more than fine, sister. You're fab," Thomas proclaimed, putting an arm around her shoulder. She smiled. Thank goodness for good friends.

"We're both fab," she agreed. "Uberfab, in fact. Now let's go sell us some comic books."

CHAPTER TWO

"Welcome!" exclaimed the hook-nosed woman with gold-rimmed glasses who stood behind booth 2134. She held out her Olive Oyl–length arms in greeting. "I'm so glad you were able to come by."

Hailey glanced over at Thomas, who shrugged in response. Of course they were "able to come by"—they had a signing in less than an hour! And who was this woman, anyway? With her graying hair pulled back into a severe bun and her suit jacket buttoned up to her neck, she looked like she belonged at a bankers' banquet rather than a comic-book convention. Was she a den mother, perhaps, hired by Straylight to keep the booth seats warm while the editors got their geek on around the Comic Con floor?

"Thanks," Hailey said, hesitantly. "Is this where—"

"Yes! Of course. You're at the right place: your home for all things Karma Kitty. It's so great to see fans here. Real fans! The signing will begin in"—she glanced at her watch—"less than an hour. You're welcome to stay. The artists aren't here yet, but they're expected soon."

Thomas burst out laughing. Hailey shook her head, realizing the mistake. "Oh," she said. "We're not fans."

The woman raised a skeptical eyebrow, eyeing their attire. "I see," she said, losing a level of perkiness.

"No, you don't understand. We're the creators," Hailey clarified. "I'm Hailey Hills, the writer, and this is Thomas Carol, my artist. The masterminds behind *Karma Kitty*."

"You're . . ." the woman started, trailing off as she stared at them as if in disbelief. "You're . . . oh, my. Well, I'm so sorry for the mistake. I didn't recognize you in those . . . those . . ." She scrunched up her face with obvious distaste. "Those costumes," she finished, spitting out the word *costume* as if it were poison she was desperately trying to expel. She sniffed, then stuck out a hand. "I'm Martha Hannah, the publisher. You can call me Mrs. Hannah."

Hailey took the cold, bony paw, trying not to let her mouth drop open in shock. *This* was their publisher? Where were the black-rimmed-glasses-wearing geeks who'd skip lunch to check their *World of Warcraft* auctions? Or at least throw down a few rounds of *Magic: The Gathering*? Mrs. Hannah looked as if she'd prefer a compelling game of bridge at the local country club.

Don't judge someone on their appearance, she scolded herself. Mrs. Hannah, despite her outfit, could be a huge fan and advocate of the comic book world. And she did publish and distribute *Karma Kitty*. So obviously she had good taste.

"So, what do you think of the costumes?" Thomas asked, pumping Mrs. Hannah's hand eagerly. "Pretty badass, huh? I made mine myself. I'm Big Kitty."

"Indeed you are," Mrs. Hannah said, yanking her hand away and brushing it against her gray flannel suit.

"And I'm Karma Kitty," Hailey added, enthusiasm extinguishing at a rapid rate. This was so not how she'd envisioned this meeting at all. She'd expected to walk up to the booth to a spattering of "oohs" and "aahs"—maybe even a little clapping—for their creative attire. Instead,

Mrs. Hannah looked like she wanted to send them to the principal's office.

"I see." Mrs. Hannah pursed her thin lips, then glanced at her watch. "Well, you're scheduled to sign in less than an hour, so I suggest you start getting changed."

Hailey and Thomas exchanged puzzled glances. "Changed?" Hailey inquired.

"Into your normal clothes," Mrs. Hannah said slowly, as if speaking to dim-witted children. "What you're going to wear for the signing."

"But we're going to wear—"

"That?" She gave them a horrified once-over. "Certainly not."

"But . . . but we're dressed like our characters."

"Yes, I see. That is quite obvious. But we simply can't allow you to represent our company dressed like you are. This kind of thing just won't fly here at Comic Con."

An amputee with a machine gun for a leg picked that moment to limp by, followed by a trio of Batmen—'60s TV series, Tim Burton, and Dark Knight varieties.

"How can you say that?" Hailey demanded. "Look around you. Half the people here are in costume."

Mrs. Hannah shrugged. "They're fans. It's fine for fans to dress up. But as artists—you should be above this sort of thing. I've spent fifty years trying to legitimize comic books to an industry that considers them nothing but child's play. The last thing I need is a couple of my artists to foil years of hard work with a single fashion faux pas."

Hailey's heart sank. All that hard work creating her costume—for nothing. All the money she'd spent on her amazing shoes—wasted.

"Come on, lady," Thomas whined. "We're just having a little fun. We're not going to bring down the whole comic-book industry just by a little dress-up."

"Maybe. Maybe not. But I own Straylight Comics, and if you want to sign at my booth, which I paid for, you will do so in respectable attire."

"Yeah? Well, I say you can take your respectable attire and—"

"Okay, okay!" Hailey interrupted Thomas before he said something he'd regret. After all, this *was* their publisher. The person who signed the checks and distributed their work. Even if they didn't agree with her—even if they thought she was insane—they had little choice but to respect her wishes. After all, she'd paid for them to come to Comic Con in the first place. "We'll just hit the bathroom and be back in a few."

Mrs. Hannah nodded, looking smug. Hailey noticed Thomas opening his mouth again, so she grabbed him by his purple velour sleeve and dragged him away.

"Come on, Big Kitty," she quipped. "Retract the claws, please, please."

Thomas grunted, but allowed her to drag him away. "So unfair," he grumbled, once out of earshot. "How'd we pick such a lame-ass publisher, anyway? Legitimizing comic books, my ass. Comic books aren't meant to be legitimate. They're books with freaking pictures! We're not publishing Shakespeare, people!"

"Hush!" Hailey scolded. "People here will kick your ass for saying shit like that."

"They can try!"

"Oh grow up, Thomas," she said, feeling rather old all of a sudden. "Mrs. Hannah means well. She wants people to take the books more seriously. So we can get wider distribution in bigger bookstores. Get the mainstream audience to pay attention. It makes sense in many ways."

"She wants us to sell out, in other words," Thomas interjected.

"You can call it that, but will you really complain when the big paychecks start rolling in?"

"Please. What about Hiro Kim? He's the best-selling comic artist in the world—Hollywood's been begging him to sell his movie rights to his pirate series for years. And he's said time and time again he'll never, ever do it." Thomas held out his hands. "You think he's busy collecting welfare because he takes a moral high ground?"

Hailey sighed. "It's not like I don't see your point. I'm just saying there are different ways to look at it. Anyway, it's not like I'm not as disappointed as you are. You know how long I spent on this outfit?"

"Well, maybe we can wear them after the signing," Thomas suggested. "We can be our own fangirls."

Hailey smiled. "Exactly. And then we can . . ." She trailed off, her voice getting stuck in her throat as her eyes fell on the one person she'd been searching for/trying to avoid.

Collin.

He wasn't exactly hard to miss. Standing tall on a raised platform in the middle of what had to be the biggest booth at Comic Con: Darken Pictures, the film company he worked for. He was lecturing a gathered crowd of scantily clad elf girls while a swirling animated screen lit up the stage behind him.

"Hailey? You okay? You're suddenly white as a—Ohhh!" Thomas followed her glance and put two and two together. "It's the Hollywood Hunk, eh?"

Hailey bit her lower lip, her traitorous body trying to step forward and retreat all at the same time. Her legs were mud and her eyes refused to look away, drinking in the tall, lanky figure on stage. His fitted Darken Pictures tee nicely showcased his pecs and trim stomach while his black jeans hugged his narrow waist and thighs. She remembered all too well running her hands up and down that body, sans clothes, once upon a time, exploring the hard planes of muscle beneath. She remembered the pleasure she felt from touching him. From him touching her back.

She shook her head. That time was past. And while he was still unbearably sexy on the outside, he was also probably still as pig-headed on the inside as well. And sure, sexy was good for a romp in the sack or two, but when it came to committing to a person for the rest of your life, Hailey wanted more than that. She wanted a guy who would believe her. No matter what.

"So you gonna go say hi?" Thomas asked, nudging her in the arm and yanking her back to the present.

"No way," she said. "Absolutely no way." She turned to leave, finally getting her Jell-O–like legs under some sort of control. "We'd better get to the bathroom, quickly, so we can change in time for the signing."

"Too late, kitty kat," Thomas replied, his voice ripe with amusement. "You've been spotted."

She glanced back and cringed as she realized she was indeed the target of Collin's steady, piercing gaze. He caught her eyes with his and, as if by some kind of magic cosmic ray, refused to let go.

"Hailey!" she heard him cry. "Hailey Hills!"

"I'll meet you at the signing, lover girl." Thomas chuckled, before ducking out of sight.

Collin couldn't believe it. Absolutely couldn't believe it. Hailey Hills. His Hailey Hills was standing there in the middle of Comic Con, not ten feet away from him. Forgetting he was in the middle of a Q&A, he leapt off the stage, pushing past all the annoying bimbos who had been asking moments before whether or not he thought Paris Hilton would make a good Catwoman. He could hear his assistant call after him, her voice high with distress, but he ignored her. Hailey Hills was now nine feet from his grasp and he wasn't going to let her get away.

"Hailey!" he cried again, pushing through the crowd. She stared at him dully, as if with little recognition. She did remember him, didn't she? They were only engaged to be married once, after all . . .

He caught up to her and stopped, panting from his effort. He took her in, raking his gaze from her flip-flopped feet, up her shapely legs—sheathed in glittery lycra—to her micro-mini and schoolgirl button-down shirt. She was carrying ridiculously high golden boots and wore little cat ears on her head.

His body responded as his eyes involuntarily returned to the inch of bare skin located at the spot where the thigh-highs ended and her skirt began. God, she looked good. Way too good. It was all he could do to stop himself from pinning her against a post and lifting her skirt to see if she'd started wearing panties or still went commando. He imagined himself running his hands up her creamy white thighs, higher and higher until he reached . . .

He shook his head. This was not the time or place for this kind of thing. Still, it'd been an awful long time since he'd felt this way about a woman, and part of him was relieved to feel his sex drive kick back into gear. It'd been a while, for sure.

"Hi, Collin," Hailey said breezily, as if it wasn't the oddest thing in the world to run into him in the middle of Comic Con. "What's up?"

He stared at her, his usually quick mind—the one that got him big Hollywood deals on a daily basis—locking up like a steel drum and refusing him the ability to form a complete sentence. "Y-you . . ." he stammered, raking a hand through his hair. "You . . . Are you dressed as a cat?"

If there had been awards given out at Comic Con for

saying lame things, he would have won the grand prize for sure. Of course she was dressed up like a cat. She was Karma Kitty—their creation. Collin had been following her successes on her blog for the last five years. She'd come a long way from the crazy hippie-dippie girl he'd fallen in love with back at school. She was a successful comic book writer with a cult following that would likely only get bigger as time went on.

"I'm supposed to be Karma Kitty," she said, her cheeks coloring as she glanced down at her feet. She still had the light dusting of freckles powdering her nose. Collin remembered his favorite lazy Sunday morning activity—curling up in bed with her, kissing each and every one.

"Yeah, right, of course," he said, struggling to redeem himself. "I've been reading it. It's really great."

Her sexy, black-rimmed eyes widened at this. "You've been reading the comics?"

Now it was his turn to blush. The last thing he wanted was for her to know how hung up he'd been—how hung up he still was—on her. The girl had ditched him at the altar. Humiliated him in front of his family and friends. He remembered standing up there, wearing his ridiculous penguin suit, waiting and waiting and waiting. Hearing the guests on the bride's side snicker. His mother sob. How long had he actually stood there before he realized she wasn't going to show up?

Anger replaced lust in his gut. "So," he said. "Get abducted by any aliens lately?"

Her face darkened. He'd struck a nerve. Well, good. She deserved to feel guilty after what she had done. Making up some stupid excuse as to why she hadn't shown up on that day. If she hadn't felt she was ready for marriage, if she wasn't sure about moving to LA, she could have just told him. He'd have understood. But no, she'd all runaway-brided him, making him worry for weeks before she finally showed up out of nowhere, expecting him to just believe her crazy tale and forgive her.

Her face fell and he felt himself soften. He hadn't chased after her to yell at her, after all. And he *was* happy to see her, even under the circumstances. It'd been too long. "Sorry," he amended. "I didn't mean . . ."

"No, it's okay," she said, recovering quickly. She threw him a big Hailey grin. "But no aliens. No voices. No . . . well, no weirdness at all. I've shut it all out of my life. Turned over a new leaf. All that."

"That's great," he said, an inane hope rising inside him. Stupid. He shoved it back down. No need to get all school-boy over her again, waste all those years of therapy. They were two separate people who lived two separate lives on two separate coasts. They'd shared something once, but it was long over. Heck, he barely knew her anymore, and it was best to keep it that way. "I'm glad you're doing so well," he added, stiffly.

"You, too!" she replied with her typical bouncy enthusiasm. "You're so famous now. It's awesome. Hell, you even have groupies." She pointed behind him and he groaned to realize the bimbos in his audience must have followed him over. They stood, huddled a few feet away, giggling and whispering furiously. One held up her camera phone to take a picture. He could almost see the PerezHilton.com mention now: DARKEN PRODUCER CUDDLES UP TO KARMA KITTY. MEOW!

Oh well, maybe it would be free press for Hailey's comic. He'd be okay with that. She deserved to do well. She'd obviously worked so hard.

He turned back to Hailey, rolling his eyes for emphasis. "Oh yeah," he said, allowing his voice to drip with sarcasm. Didn't want her to think he bought into all the Hollywood hype. "I'm a real kingpin."

She giggled, then shuffled her feet, looking up at him with those big bedroom eyes of hers. The ones that would never fail to make him weak in the knees. God, this was awkward. If only he could get her somewhere alone. To talk, that was. Nothing else. Well, maybe nothing else. Have to see how the talk went, first. Would she agree to meet him later? Or would she turn him down flat? Could he take the rejection if she did?

Collin squeezed his hands into fists and summoned up all the courage inside of him. *Just ask her,* he willed himself. *It's not a big deal. Be a man, for chrissakes.*

She spoke before he could. "So, uh, I've got to go . . . get changed," she said, blushing a bit. "I have a signing in a few minutes over at my publisher's booth. We're giving away two hundred copies of *Karma Kitty* volume one and then selling the newer issues." Her face brightened as she started talking about her work.

"Cool." He felt his insides warm at her enthusiasm. Despite all they'd been through, he wanted nothing more than for her to succeed. Hell, how many issues of *Karma Kitty* had he ordered over the years in an effort to raise her sales ranking? Hundreds, he'd guess. Of course, those copies were put to good use—he'd bring them over to the pediatric cancer ward of his local hospital. The kids' faces lit up each time he arrived with a new issue. They were Hailey's biggest fans. If only he could tell her about them without sounding like a pathetic loser who'd been unable to let go when she ditched him.

His eyes involuntarily fell back to her outfit. "Um, why are you changing, though? You look very Karma Kitty–esque now."

She laughed. "I know, right? But my publisher totally vetoed the costume. She said it wasn't professional."

Professional wasn't the word he'd use, either. Delicious,

maybe. Sinful, perhaps. Lust-inspiring, for sure. He swallowed hard as his brain launched into a full-on instant replay of one of the many nights they'd spent together, wrapped in a delightful tangle of naked limbs. Light sweat sparkling off her freckled skin as she moaned for him—even begged for him. Running his hands over every inch of her, touching, tasting, making her tingle. Then making her scream.

Maybe it would be better for her to change. After all, he didn't really relish the idea of other men coming over to ogle her.

Yes, he decided. She should change for the signing. Then wear the outfit again tonight.

Just for him.

So he could rip it off her.

Get a grip, Collin. She's never going to end up at your hotel room if you can't even get up the courage to ask her to dinner.

"Would you like to go out to dinner?" he blurted, necessity being the mother of getting over yourself.

Her eyes widened, giving him another jolt in the groin. God, those eyes of hers. Pale blue, framed by the longest lashes. He remembered her softly brushing those lashes against his cheek over and over again. *Butterfly kisses*, she'd called them, giggling. More lazy Sunday memories.

"Um," she said. "Um."

Something inside of him died. "Never mind," he said quickly, seeking out a shred of dignity. "You're busy, I'm sure. It was just a . . . never mind."

"I'd love to," she blurted, looking almost as surprised at her answer as he was.

"Great," he said, allowing himself to smile. He realized he was shaking. "Meet me at Blue Fin at eight?"

"Perfect. See you there." She flashed him a grin and gave a small wave before turning and sashaying down the aisle, her kitty tail lazily swinging back and forth as she walked.

He groaned, glancing at his watch. Nine hours. Nine hours before he could see her again.

He gave her one last glance. If, that was, she didn't get sidetracked by the Loch Ness Monster or something.

Hailey raced to the bathroom, dodging superheroes, robots, and Klingons while trying not to trip on her flip-flops. She was going to be so late for the signing! Still, the massive amounts of adrenaline currently thrumming through her veins made it nearly impossible to be regretful about the fact.

Collin had asked her to dinner. She was going to dinner with Collin. She and he would sit down at a table and order food and drinks. And they'd talk. They'd *have to* talk! And when they did she could swear that her life was normal now. No St. Peter-shaped cheese Danishes. No alien abductions. Nothing to stop them rekindling the old flame.

And oh that flame! She was still feeling a bit moist just thinking about his piercing gaze on her. The way his eyes roved her body, as if she were a tasty dessert and he'd been eating nothing but salad for years. He wanted her. She was sure of it. Maybe they'd even end by hooking up after dinner.

She shook her head. Hooking up was all well and good, but she needed to be thinking bigger picture here. This was her chance to convince him she'd changed. That she was now a completely normal girl with a completely normal life.

She glanced at her watch. Funny, she'd once been so excited about being at Comic Con. Now she couldn't wait for it to end and dinner to begin.

Their signing went extremely well. Lots of fans came out of the woodwork, gushing about how much they loved the comics. A lot of newbies showed up, too, eager to be introduced into Karma Kitty's world. Some fans had dressed up, though none of their outfits were as cool as the ones Hailey and Thomas had stuffed under their chairs. If only they'd been allowed to wear them!

They signed until their hands ached. Then they signed some more. By the end of the two hours, Hailey was sure she'd developed a severe case of carpal tunnel. But she was happy. The hand pain was worth it.

"You both were great. Thank you for doing the signing," Mrs. Hannah said when it was over, extending her hand to each of them and looking genuinely pleased. Evidently she had gotten over the costume thing when the cash register started heating up.

Thomas hadn't, of course, and brought it up again as soon as they were out of earshot of the Straylight booth. From the annoyed look on his face, Hailey realized she should be grateful he waited that long.

"Such a waste," he griped. "I can't believe we work for those wankers."

"I know," she consoled. "It sucks. But we have to remember, they're the ones who send the checks. So while we're on their time, there's not much we can do." Still, it was uber disappointing. Seeing so many of her fans show up in Karma Kitty knockoffs and feeling like a total poseur wearing ratty jeans and a T-shirt to sign their comic books. At least if she'd known they'd be forced to change she could have brought something halfway cool to wear.

The convention hall was beginning to empty out, with everyone running off to this party or that. The movie folks gathered at scene-y restaurants while the true geeks headed back to their hotel rooms to drool over their new limited-edition collectible action figures. Hailey glanced at her watch. She had an hour and a half before she had to meet up with Collin at the restaurant. She turned to Thomas, quirking her lips up in a grin.

"Let's go change into them now," she suggested. "We can wander around and check out all the booths."

"But no one will see us," Thomas whined. "Everyone's leaving."

"Exactly. Then we won't be shaming our publisher with our unprofessional behavior. And, as a bonus, we can check out all the exhibits without having to deal with any crowds."

Thomas pondered this. "Well," he said, not sounding entirely overjoyed. "I guess it's better than nothing."

"Just for a half hour," she added. "Then I've got to go meet with . . . someone."

"Someone? Someone?" Thomas asked, immediately glomming on to this choice nugget, forgetting he was supposed to be sulking. "Has Miss Karma Kitty been holding out on pimp Big Kitty?" He wagged a scolding finger at her. "Could she be actually planning to hook up with Mr. Hollywood himself?"

Hailey felt her face burn. "Well, maybe," she said, looking down at her feet. "I was going to tell you before, but we were all busy with the signing and stuff."

"Ooh, you are a bad kitty. Bad, bad kitty."

She giggled. "Would you want it any other way?"

"Oh, of course not. But word to the wise, darling? Do not go getting your heart broken on me, okay? You need to promise you'll keep things casual."

"Yes, Dad."

"Don't you 'yes, dad' me. You know I'm right. You two broke up for a reason, after all. Not that I know this reason, mind you, since you are such a terrible friend and never broke down and told me—even after that time I bought you ten vodka martinis trying to get you to spill."

"Hang on, that was an open bar!"

"Well, whatever. Point is, there is a reason you two are not together now and you need to go into this remembering that."

"I will," Hailey said, realizing he had a point. "Though, things are different now." After all, she'd closed herself off to the weirdness that used to dominate her life. She was a normal girl now. One who lived a normal life. And she never saw anything that wasn't—

Out of the corner of her eye she saw a fully-clad ninja darting down an aisle.

She shook her head. This was Comic Con. There were bound to be ninjas and pirates and other such oddities wandering the convention hall. Just fans dressed in costumes, not anything weird she needed to concern herself with. She was normal. Life was normal. And there was going to be no weirdness to mess up her and Collin's impending reconciliation.

"Time's a-wasting," she said to Thomas. "Let's get changed."

They headed into the adjoining men's and women's bathrooms and she pulled her costume out of the shopping bag. Hopefully this time she'd be okay to walk around in the boots. After all, they really made the outfit and were hella expensive. She wanted to get at least a little use out of them. So, after donning skirt, shirt and thigh-highs, she pulled the first boot onto her foot and zipped it over her calf.

A bolt of lightning struck her square in the face.

Okay, it wasn't literally a bolt of lightning, but it sure felt like one, slamming into her full force and shoving her backward. Nausea swam into her stomach, and her arms and legs tingled with electricity.

She sucked in a breath, trying to regain her composure.

What was wrong? Was she having a panic attack? Was she that stressed about meeting Collin tonight?

Wanting to get out of the stall as quickly as possible—before she passed out or something equally embarrassing—she grabbed the second boot, slipped it on and zipped it up.

As quickly as the dizzy, sick feeling came, it faded, replaced by the most thrilling sense of euphoria, hitting her like a tidal wave. As she pushed open the stall door she felt all-powerful. Triumphant. Ready to take on the world.

Um, weird.

She stuffed her old clothes into the bag and headed out of the ladies' room. She found Thomas already out there, wearing his purple velour tracksuit. The convention hall was almost completely empty now, save for a few janitor types making the rounds.

"Whoa," Thomas said, giving her the once-over. "You didn't tell me you were going to do that. Way to go all out, girl. I feel totally inferior in this piece of crap."

She cocked her head in confusion. "What are you talking about?"

He gestured to her head. "Duh. The ears thing. And your tail. How'd you do that?"

She stared at him, racking her brain to figure out what on earth he was talking about. "You mean my headband?" She reached up to pat her head, recoiled when she touched what felt like real fur. What the hell was going on here?

She shoved open the bathroom door and ran inside to check herself out in the mirror. A moment later she was staring at her reflection in disbelief.

Somehow, some way, she had turned into Karma Kitty. Like, for real.

The ears that had once been a headband were now growing out of her skull, replacing her normal everyday human ears, which seemed to have somehow disappeared.

And the tail she remembered gluing to her skirt was now literally growing out of her butt.

She groaned. So much for the no-weirdness thing. And just in time for dinner with Collin, too. How was she going to explain this one? Would he believe her about the alien thing if she showed up to dinner as a humanoid cat? More likely he'd run screaming in the other direction and never talk to her again.

Of all times for this to happen, this had to be the worst. Five years of avoiding weirdness and then slamming head-first into it right before her rendezvous with her ex. She walked back out into the convention hall, her feet feeling like lead. Thomas was checking out a Superman display.

"You know," he said, not bothering to look back at her, "Superman was really pretty hot. But I mean, Lois Lane? Come on. Total beard, if you ask me. No way that chick ever got a glimpse of what he was packing in those tights of his."

"Um, Thomas?"

"Now Batman, on the other hand, I'd say he was edging out of the closet. Always hanging with his boy toy Robin. Though, of course, they must have had some kind of arrangement, right? Maybe what happens in the Batcave stays in the Batcave?"

"Thomas! Listen to me!" she demanded. "Something's happened! I've turned into Karma Kitty!"

"Uh, yeah, that was the idea, right?" Thomas said, still distracted by the Man of Steel.

She balled her hands into fists. "No, I mean, I'm really her," she said, trying to explain. Wishing he'd just turn around and give her his full attention. "I put on the costume and the"—she looked down at her golden feet—"and the boots," she added. "And now I've changed."

Thomas sighed loudly and turned away from the exhibit. He put his hands on his hips and threw her an exasperated look. It was one to which she was very accustomed. One she used to see more often than not on Collin's face when she'd try to explain why she was late for whatever she was late for.

"I know it sounds crazy," she said, "but it's true."

"Yeah? Prove it."

"Prove it?"

"Sure. Show me some tricks," Thomas instructed. "If you're really Karma Kitty you should have Karma Kitty powers, right?"

Would she? She wasn't sure of anything at this point. "Um, maybe?"

"Great." Thomas was obviously enjoying this. "So go ahead. Do a backflip."

"Thomas, you know I can barely touch my toes. There's no way I can do a backflip."

Thomas shrugged. "Well, there you have it, then. You haven't magically changed into your comic book character," he comforted. "Because everyone knows Karma Kitty can easily do backflips."

Hailey narrowed her eyes at him. Fine. If he was going to be like that . . . She drew in a breath. Here went nothing. She launched herself backward, bracing herself for a boatload of pain.

Instead, she flew effortlessly backward. In fact, not only did she achieve a before-now-impossible backflip, she managed five of them. In a row. The last one with no hands.

"Oh my God," she cried, righting herself. "I just . . . Wow!"

Now she had Thomas's full attention. "Okay, not bad," he said.

"Not bad? If this were the Olympics I'd have beat out the gold-medal girl."

Thomas shook his head. "Uh, no. You'd have lost way

too many points on form." He pointed up to a neighboring booth's scaffolding. "Climb up there," he said. "And jump."

"Um, hello? Karma Kitty can't fly."

"Maybe not. But she certainly lands on her feet."

"Next time you're going to suggest killing me to see if I have nine lives," she grumbled as she made her way over to the platform.

"Hey, you're the one claiming to be your comic character," he said, holding up his hands.

"I'm not insured for this kind of thing," she muttered as she climbed up the King Kong display. Soon she and Fay Wray were hanging on for dear life. "Ready?"

"Go, go, Karma Kitty, go!" Thomas cheered.

She took in a breath, then leapt—landing perfectly on her feet moments later.

"How is this happening?" she wailed after Thomas finished wooting for her. The weirdness was obviously back with a vengeance. Just as she'd finally settled down to normalcy. Just as she'd finally had a chance to win the love of her life back.

"You got me." Thomas shrugged. "When did it all start? And how come it didn't happen last time you put on the outfit?"

She puzzled it all for a second or two, then the lightbulb went on over her head. "The boots!" she cried.

"The boots?"

"I wasn't wearing them before, remember? And the second I put them on, I started to feel weird. That has to be it."

"Why would the boots give you the power to become Karma Kitty?"

"I have no idea. But it's got to be them." She reached down to unzip them and kick them off. "I got them off this

weird Web site, hiheelia.com. It promised me inner power.
I thought it meant some bullshit chi or something."

Sure enough, the second the boots left her feet, she felt
the power draining out of her. She reached up and patted
her head. Ears were once again clip-on. And thankfully
her tail was again safely attached only to her skirt.

"Okay, do a backflip now," Thomas suggested.

She threw herself backward, but only succeeded in landing on her back, sprawled out on the floor.

"You're serious?" he asked. "You're not playing around?"

She stared down at the boots. "No," she said. "There's
something about these boots."

Thomas's face lit up like a kid's on Christmas. "Ooh,
ooh! I want to try!"

She shook her head. "No way. They're not your size.
And besides, they're mine." Now that she knew she could
avoid the weirdness just by yanking off the shoes she felt a
little better about things. At least she wouldn't have to explain cat ears and a tail to Collin.

Thomas, on the other hand, looked sulky. "No fair, you
got magic boots and I'm stuck with a purple velour tracksuit."

Hailey ignored him, slipping the boots back on her feet
and feeling the power surge through her once again. "So
amazing," she murmured. "So cool."

Thomas opened his mouth, probably to spew forth more
jealousy, but before he got any words out, a thirty-something
Asian guy zoomed up to them, running as fast as his legs
could carry him. He saw them a split second too late and
tripped over Hailey while trying to brake. He went flying
into the Mr. Toast booth, sending stuffed bacon and eggs
everywhere.

"Arrr!" he cried, scrambling to his feet. It was then that
Hailey realized he was dressed as a pirate.

"Are you okay?" she asked, standing up, herself. "You should really look where—"

His white face and frightened eyes cut short her rebuke. She looked down the aisle in the direction he'd come. "What are you running from?" she asked. "Is someone chasing you?"

The man jabbered at her in a language she didn't understand, repeatedly gesturing behind him. She saw nothing at first; then, to her surprise, she spotted a group of five ninjas heading toward them at full speed.

"Uh," Thomas said, squinting at the approaching wall o'armed Japanese dudes. "Are they after *you*, man? 'Cause to tell you the truth, we're not really interested in some weird role-playing crap."

He yammered at them in Japanese once again. The ninjas were getting closer. They were also brandishing swords that didn't look fake. The man dove behind Hailey, trying to hide.

Hailey gulped as she watched the approaching army. "I think I'm going to have to fight them," she said.

"What?" Thomas cried. "Are you insane?"

"No. But I'm Karma Kitty," she said slowly, not sure where the swelling courage inside of her was coming from. "And, strangely enough, I feel compelled to save the day."

"Oh my God." Thomas shook his head in disbelief. "This is so fucked up."

CHAPTER THREE

Hailey braced herself for the oncoming fighters, bending her knees, holding out her hands. Her boots pulsed gold, as if excited about the pending assault—just like Karma Kitty's would. It was bizarre. It was unreal. It was impossible. But bizarre, unreal, and impossible was something Hailey was used to.

The first ninja let out a chilling cry and dove toward her, launching into a kick aimed at her stomach. Just before contact, she swiped at him with her arm, blocking the kick and effortlessly sending him twirling into the air and a cardboard Teenage Mutant Ninja Turtle.

Woo-hoo! Score one for Karma Kitty! Who knew she was so strong?

The second ninja stepped forward, jabbing at her throat with a fist. She leapt back, dodging his blow by launching into a half-back-handspring. Once her hands hit the ground, instead of completing the move, she shot forward again, slamming her heels into his clavicle. He collapsed and she tumbled on top of him, then rolled off and readied herself for the next guy.

This ninja, seeing how easily a random chick incapacitated his friends, decided to draw his katana from the sheath tied to his side. The blade flashed under the fluorescent

lights as he waved it in front of his face and squinted men-
acingly at her. She grinned back, then dropped to the
ground and swept her foot out and around, tripping him
where he stood. He went flying into the first guy, knocking a
stack of comic books on his head. Hailey slammed her heel
into his stomach and he bellowed in pain.

Last guy. He stood at a distance, then reached into his
hand and pulled out a shuriken—a Japanese throwing star.
He flipped it like a Frisbee and sent it spinning in her
direction. She leapt into the air—very *Crouching Tiger,
Hidden Dragon*—and the star ended up only skimming the
heel of her boot before lodging itself in Superman's plastic
chest, just below the S.

Hailey fluttered back to the ground and started after the
guy. But he and his buddies had evidently had enough of
Karma Kitty. They took off down the aisle, as fast as their
ninja legs would carry them.

"Phew," Hailey said, brushing off her skirt. "That was
close." She turned back to her friend and the Asian guy.
They were both staring at her, mouths open, eyes wide, ex-
pressions freaked out beyond belief. She suddenly felt self-
conscious. "Uh, you can stop looking at me any time now."

"Oh. My. God," Thomas marveled. "I've never seen
anything like that in my entire life. They all came at you
at once."

"No, they didn't. They came one after another. Just like
in those dumb kung fu movies."

"Maybe to you, Neo, but we mere mortals just watched
you take on five guys at one time. You had them all down
in five seconds flat."

"Wow. It sure didn't feel like that." She rubbed her forehead. "I hope I didn't hurt them too badly."

"Dude, they're bad guys, remember? You should have
killed them."

"Um, yeah, except there's that whole pesky lifetime in jail, maybe the death penalty thing to consider," she reminded him. "It's not like we're in a real-life comic book here."

"It certainly feels like it, though." Thomas looked down at her shoes. "I so need to get a pair of those in my size FedEx'd to me for tomorrow. What was that Web site again?"

The pirate Asian guy cleared his throat. In the excitement, Hailey had forgotten about him. He bowed to her, a deep respectful bow from his waist, then retreated down the aisle, almost as fast as the ninjas had, but in the other direction.

"I wonder why they were after him," Hailey mused as she watched him go. "Some kind of 'ninjas are way cooler than pirates' game?"

"*Pirates* are way cooler than *ninjas*, FYI," Thomas corrected. "But no, I doubt it. Those guys looked really serious. And Hiro looked really scared."

"Hiro?"

"And you call yourself a comic book fan?" Thomas scolded. "Did you really not recognize Hiro Kim, Japan's premier manga artist? We were talking about him earlier, remember? He does that pirate manga called *Shadow Booty Clan.*"

"That guy wrote *Shadow Booty Clan?*" Hailey cried. "That's, like, the most best-selling comic of all time."

"Duh. The latest volume even hit the *New York Times* best-seller list."

"So why would a boatload of ninjas be chasing down Hiro Kim in the middle of Comic Con?"

"Beats me."

Hailey suddenly remembered the shuriken the ninja had chucked at her. She walked over to Superman and yanked it out of his stomach. She realized it wasn't a real throwing

star at all, but a toy one, made of black plastic. On the back
it said BOOTH 4294, MEIYOSERAPH AGENCY.

"Weird," she mused, turning the star around in her
hand. "We should check this out. Maybe it's a clue."

"Um, hello? You're trying to solve the Case of the
Weirdo Ninja Fight now? How about figuring out why
you've suddenly morphed into your comic-book cat first?"

"We've already solved the cat thing."

"By attributing it to magic shoes? Oh yeah, you're a regular Nancy Drew."

"Veronica Mars, actually. So what do you say we go
check out the booth?" She glanced at her watch. "Oh wait.
Shit. I'm totally late to go meet Collin."

"Just tell Mr. Hollywood you got stuck battling a herd of
ninjas. I'm sure he'll understand."

Hailey cringed. "No. That's the problem. He won't. In
fact, that's exactly the type of thing he just won't understand. The kind of thing I wanted to avoid trying to explain to him ever again. After all, he still hasn't gotten
over my alien abduction." Whoops. She hadn't meant to
say that out loud.

"What a closed-minded fool." Thomas fanned himself.

Hailey gritted her teeth. "I'm serious," she said. She
looked at her watch again. "Crap! I have to get changed. I
can't go looking like Karma Kitty." She kicked off her boots
and ran to the bathroom, quickly discarding the costume
for street clothes. Her muscles ached and her brain felt like
mush. Being a superhero evidently took a lot out of a girl.

She exited the bathroom, bags in hand, and handed
them to Thomas.

"Wow, that was faster than Superman in a phone
booth," Thomas observed. "Though not half as sexy." He
ran a hand down the Man of Steel's plastic bicep for
emphasis.

"Um, yeah. So, I'll catch you later. And don't you dare put on the shoes," Hailey said, calling over her shoulder as she dashed down the aisle.

"Wow. If they looked up 'selfish friend' in the dictionary, they'd find a big fat picture of you."

"I hope they photographed my good side."

It took her a good forty-five minutes to hail a cab outside of Comic Con. By the time she got to the restaurant, she was over an hour late. As her cab pulled up to a red light, she saw Collin, across the intersection, exit the restaurant, hail a cab and get in.

No! This could not be happening! "Follow that cab!" she cried in desperation, waving a finger at the vehicle. If only she'd remembered to get his cell phone number when she had the chance.

"What do you think this is, a fuckin' movie?" the Queens-born driver asked, taking a precious moment from his very important cell phone convo to address her. "I ain't running a red light for you, baby."

"Please!" she begged, watching as Collin's cab pulled out into the street.

A man banged on the cab window. "Are you getting out or not?" the driver demanded. "I ain't got all night, you know. Some of us have to make a living."

Hailey sighed and reluctantly left the cab. She walked into the restaurant and up to the maitre-d'. He informed her that Collin had been waiting for an hour and finally just left. Sorry, no message. The man gave her a disapproving look.

It's was the ninjas' fault! she wanted to shout at him, but she knew it would do no good.

If only she could find Collin. Explain what had happened. *Explain?* a voice inside of her jeered. *Explain what? That you turned into your comic-book character and fought a platoon of ninjas with your bare hands to save a pirate manga artist from certain death?*

Okay, maybe not that. But she could give him some kind of excuse. A rational one. Like, she had been held up at her signing. Or her publisher had scheduled a last-minute meeting she just couldn't miss. Something, anything to convince him that she hadn't meant to stand him up.

So you'd lie to him? the inner voice jeered. *Is that really the right foot on which to resume the relationship?*

It wasn't, of course. In fact, it was pretty close to the reasons they broke up to begin with. But still, what could she do?

She hailed a new cab and instructed him to drop her off at the Comfort Inn in Hell's Kitchen at which she and Thomas were staying. When she arrived, she went straight to his room. He answered the door in bunny-footed pajamas. She was just grateful it wasn't vintage women's lingerie like the last time. After all that had happened, she didn't think she could take a three-hundred-pound Vivienne Westwood tonight.

"Didn't make it, huh?" he asked sympathetically, ushering her inside the tiny room and closing the door behind them. "Poor dear."

She flopped on the second bed, a lump forming in her throat. She tried to tell herself that she shouldn't be so disappointed, but she couldn't help it. Seeing Collin again, after all these years, had really made her realize how much she missed having him in her life. And to blow a possible second chance like that? Stupid. Truly stupid. She should have skipped the costumes. Thomas would have understood. And then she'd have gotten to the restaurant early, met him at the door. They would have wined, dined, talked, maybe even danced. Made up for lost time.

But no. She'd screwed it all up. She wouldn't be surprised if he never wanted to talk to her again.

"I saw him get into a taxi as I was pulling in," she told Thomas. "He'd waited an hour, according to the restaurant guy." She groaned. "He must think I'm a total bitch."

"Well, duh. I think that and you've never even stood me up."

She threw a pillow at him. "You're not helping."

"Sorry, sweetie. It really sucks, I know," Thomas said, looking at her with pitying eyes. "You were really looking forward to it, weren't you?"

"More than I wanted to admit," she said with a sigh. "I really love him still. Seeing him today brought back so many memories."

"Can you call him? Explain what happened?"

"I don't have his cell number. And I have no clue what hotel he's staying at." She rolled over onto her side and flipped through one of their comics. "Too bad Karma Kitty didn't have some kind of Super Smell. Then I could just throw on the boots and sniff him out."

Thomas laughed. "If only you knew you'd need it when you created her, we could have drawn it in. It'd actually be a pretty funny superpower. Would have made perfect sense, too, since all of Karma Kitty's powers have to do with cat things. And we all know how good my Fifi is at sniffing out the catnip."

Sudden inspiration smacked Hailey across the face and she jerked up in bed. "That's it!" she cried, hope surging through her. "That's totally it!"

Thomas gave her a blank look. "Er, what's it?"

"Drawing it in," she replied. "When I put on the boots, I have all the powers of Karma Kitty, right? And we control what those powers are through the artwork. What if you sketched up a few scenes where Karma Kitty is gifted with the power of Super Smell? That she can sniff out . . . bad guys or something. Then I'd put on the boots and sniff out Collin. Figure out where he's staying and go apologize."

"That is the stupidest thing I've ever heard you say. Maybe the stupidest thing I've ever heard anyone say, and I've heard a lot of stupid things in my life. Like the time George Michael claimed he was—"

"Yeah, well, before tonight you would have said me putting on magic boots, becoming Karma Kitty, and fighting a flock of ninjas was the stupidest thing you ever heard."

"Touché." Thomas considered. "But still . . ."

"Fine. I'll draw it myself, then. You'll see." She grabbed Thomas's sketchbook from off his bed and uncapped a pen.

She was no artist, but she did her best, sketching her comic cat sniffing the air. She then slipped on her boots and took a whiff. Nothing but the same old slightly dirty laundry smell the room had when she first entered. She sighed and kicked them off again.

"Oh well," she said. "I guess it was a dumb idea."

Thomas peered over her shoulder at her drawing. He scowled. "Oh my god," he exclaimed. "Of course *that's* not going to work. It doesn't even remotely resemble Karma Kitty. No offense." He huffed with annoyance. "Fine. Give me the pen."

She handed it over.

"For the record, I still think this is ridiculous," Thomas muttered as he took the sketchbook from her. "But if it's going to work, it's only going to work when drawn by a genuine Karma Kitty artist like me."

Or Collin, Hailey thought, wondering if he had taken up drawing again after they parted ways. It was such a shame when he gave up over those stupid rejections. To give up something he was so good at. Something he loved.

Hailey looked over Thomas's shoulder, watching, until he yelled at her for invading his space. So she retreated to the other bed and flipped on the television. But she couldn't concentrate on the show. She was too impatient to see if this crazy thing would actually work.

"It doesn't have to be perfect," she reminded him, after what seemed to be an inordinate amount of time to be working on a single sketch. He, of course, shot her a dirty look that told her that it most certainly did. Artists!

She lay back down on the bed and tried to be patient. Tried to focus on what she was going to tell Collin once she found him. Some kind of easy excuse. Something believable that didn't involve pirates or ninjas or her turning into a cat-woman. Would he forgive her? Would he be interested in rekindling the relationship? Maybe they'd end up getting married this time. Start a family, even.

Hang on, Hailey. First things first.

"Okay, I'm done," Thomas announced, breaking her out of her white-picket-fence dreams.

She practically dove to the other bed. "Let me see."

He held up the sketchbook, out of her reach. "No way, José. This piece of garbage is going into the trash the second you're done tracking down Mr. Hollywood. I can't afford to have it end up on DeviantArt or something. My fans would never forgive me."

"Fine, fine. As long as it works." She grabbed the boots again. "I guess I don't need the rest of the costume," she decided, yanking on the footwear. "Don't want to freak him out with cat ears and a tail. Though maybe I'll wear the skirt. He was totally eyeing it earlier."

She zipped up the boots again and once again that nauseous, tingly feeling came over her, followed by an overwhelming sense of power.

And—she sniffed—cigarette smoke?

"Thomas Mark Carol, you've been smoking!" she exclaimed, shooting him an accusing look. "You told me you quit."

Thomas scowled and opened his mouth to give some lame excuse, then his eyes widened as he realized what was happening. "It worked!" he cried, jumping off the bed and clapping his hands together in glee. "Oh my God! You have Super Smell!"

Her eyes widened as she realized he was absolutely right. She could smell the burger and fries the guy was eating in the next room. The stench of urine on the sidewalks outside. The cheesy J. Lo perfume on the desk clerk downstairs. She could smell each and every thing with a crystal clarity that was both enticing . . . and disgusting.

Thomas was back at his sketchbook, drawing furiously. A moment later he looked up. "Okay," he said, breathless with excitement. "Now shoot hundred-dollar bills from your fingers."

She stared at him. "You're kidding right?"

"Hey, the Super Smell thing worked. Figured it was worth a try."

"Fine." She held out her fingers and concentrated. Sadly, not a single penny drizzled out.

Thomas scowled. "Boo."

"Makes sense, though," she said, lowering her hands. "Karma Kitty has the same powers as a cat, only exaggerated, right? It's not like she can fly or shoot lasers or anything."

"True. Brutally disappointing, but true."

"Anyway, Super Smell works. And that's what matters."

"To you, maybe. I would have found the money-producing super claws I designed far more useful."

She rolled her eyes at him and then sniffed again, closing her eyes and concentrating on visualizing Collin. His delicious scent—Jil Sander with a mixture of aftershave—that she used to love breathing in. The smells bombarded her, fast and furious, and at first it was hard to catalog them individually.

Then she caught a whiff of something. Something distinctly Collin-like—somewhere to the northeast. "Well, I guess the best thing to do is jump in a cab and stick my nose out the window," she determined. "After all, midtown Manhattan isn't that big, right?"

Thomas shot her a doubtful look.

She sighed. If only Comic Con had been held in rural Maine. Would have made things a lot easier. "Well, here I go anyway," she said, rising to her feet. "Wish me luck!"

"Meh, you don't need luck," Thomas said, giving her the thumbs-up. "You're Karma Kitty!"

She threw him a grin, exiting the room while praying he was right.

CHAPTER FOUR

The Comfort Inn's elevator was broken, but Hailey didn't care. She skipped down the steps, practically dancing for joy. This was too cool. Too, too cool. If only she'd had superpowers back in the day when she and Collin were together. Maybe she could have kicked some alien-abductor ass and made it to the church on time. They'd be married right now. Living happily ever after.

She pushed open the front lobby door and stepped out onto West 46th Street. No use dwelling on what might have been. It was time to make the present what it should be.

The nose-out-the-cab-window thing turned out to be a lot easier than she thought it'd be, and the cab driver didn't even seem taken aback by his sniffy, indecisive passenger. Guess you got a lot weirder than that as a NYC hack, and as long as the meter ran and she didn't, it was all good for him.

Not fifteen minutes later, she asked him to stop in front of The Rock Hotel, right outside of Times Square. Collin's scent was strong here and she was positive this had to be the place. She paid and exited the cab, stuffed sack of Chinese takeout in hand. (The smell had been irresistible to her newly sensitized nose, and they *had* missed dinner, after all.)

Walking straight to the front desk, Hailey asked for Collin's room number. But the snotty clerk informed her that "due to privacy concerns" he couldn't give that information to some random girl off the street. After much pleading, he did agree to ring Collin's room, but no one answered. He suggested she come back later.

Hailey knew Collin was in the building; she could smell him clearly now. He was probably just ignoring calls or in the bathroom or something. So she headed over to the elevator, determined to sniff him out. The doors slid open a moment later, revealing a stiff, uniformed man inside. She stepped into the elevator and the man politely inquired as to what floor she'd like to go to.

"Huh?" she asked, taken aback.

"Which floor?" the man repeated, louder, as if she were foreign and thus more likely to comprehend the English language when it was spoken three decibels higher.

"Oh." This was one of those old-fashioned hotels that retained a useless elevator operator. Figured. She gave a sniff, trying to ignore the overwhelming Old Spice the man had evidently doused his body with before coming to work. "Hm."

It wasn't that she couldn't smell Collin. In fact, his scent was nearly overpowering. But all she could tell from her vantage point in the elevator was that it was somewhere, well, up. She glanced at the numbers. Ugh—fifty-eight floors.

"Floor twenty-three?" she suggested, deciding to go for something near the middle. Maybe once she was there she'd get a better sense of whether he was higher or lower. The bellhop pressed the button and the elevator chimed as the doors slid shut.

They were off.

She sniffed again, closing her eyes to concentrate on the direction of Collin's scent. Sure enough, as they rose, the smell grew stronger and stronger. Then, somewhere around the fifteenth floor, it started fading again. She glanced over at the yawning elevator operator, wondering what she should do.

The elevator dinged, announcing its arrival at floor twenty-three. The doors slid open.

"Er," she stammered, as the bellhop looked at her expectantly. "I think I meant floor . . . um . . . thirteen? Yeah. Definitely floor thirteen. Sorry about that."

The guy threw a bland smile in her direction, but something in his eyes made her realize that perhaps he was not entirely pleased by this misstep.

"What?" she asked.

"Madame, this hotel has no thirteenth floor," he explained. "Hotels rarely do. It's said to be unlucky."

She restrained from smacking her forehead in a "duh" moment. "Sorry," she said. "I meant the fourteenth floor. Silly me." Maybe she should get out and walk up and down the stairs. . . .

The operator nodded stiffly and pressed the button labeled fourteen. Once again the doors slid shut and the elevator began its descent. She watched the LCD display above the door drop in digits, sniffing each time it did, until—

"Sixteen!" she cried triumphantly. "He's on floor sixteen."

The hotel employee glowered at her. The elevator dinged and the doors slid open to the fourteenth floor, as had been directed. He made no move to push the sixteen button.

"Sixteen," she repeated, annoyed that this chump was now getting in the way of her meeting up with Collin. Why did they even have a guy operating the elevator to begin with? Surely most guests could figure out how to press the buttons themselves. . . .

The man smiled again, this time giving off a distinct, "I hate my life" look. She resisted the urge to suggest he hit Monster.com at home to look for a real job.

"Perhaps Madame would like to go down to concierge and check her room number with the staff?"

Perhaps Monsieur would like me to shove a Karma Kitty boot up his ass? "Nah, that's okay. I'm sure now. Sixteen. Definitely sixteen."

"Very well." He pressed number sixteen and away they went. A moment later, the doors slid open. "Where to now?" asked the operator, not expecting for a moment that she had indeed reached her final destination.

"Nowhere. This is it." She breathed in deeply, taking in Collin's delicious scent. Musky, dark, heavenly. "Thanks, man. Sorry about that."

"Not a problem."

Yeah, right. Feeling bad, she grabbed a few crumpled bills from her pocket and shoved them into his hand before exiting the elevator. He took them without a thank-you. Then she headed down the hall to complete her Collin-finding quest, sniffing each and every room as she passed.

At room 1623 she paused. Another sniff told her this was it. Collin's room. When she lifted her hand to bang against the door, she realized it was shaking.

"Okay, here goes nothing," she murmured and knocked.

"Just a minute!"

Panic slammed into her with the force of a ten-ton truck at the sound of Collin's voice, mixed with his heady scent. In addition to Jil Sander, he now smelled like honeysuckle and jasmine. Which could only mean—

The door swung open, revealing Collin, half naked, clad only in a towel slung low across his narrow hips. Dripping wet, obviously just out of the shower from the smell of it, beads of water clinging to chest hair.

She swallowed hard, doing all she could not to pass out with desire. Wow. Just . . . wow. She'd forgotten what an amazing body her former boyfriend had. All hard planes of muscle, encased in a smooth, olive-toned skin. No middle-aged spread for him; he had a perfect six-pack. And just enough five o'clock shadow dusting his chiseled face to make him look dangerous.

He was perfection. And suddenly Hailey felt rather lame.

"Um, hi!" she exclaimed, holding up the bag of take-out. "Hungry?"

If Collin had opened his door and found Bigfoot standing there, grinning from ear to furry ear, he couldn't have been more surprised. Hailey Hills, hovering at his hotel room door, arms full of Chinese food. His brain told him he should slam the door shut in her face, locking her out of his life forever. After all, he'd just wasted a damn hour in a very fine restaurant, waiting for her to show up for an elegant dinner for two. He'd dressed up. He'd bought roses. He'd ordered a bottle of their finest champagne. And she was a no-show. Again. Just like on their wedding day. And he'd had to endure the pitying stares all over again from the other patrons and waiters and maitre-d'. *Yes, I got stood up. I am that chump.*

And now, here she was, plastic sack of dim sum and noodles in hand, probably armed with a wild tale of why she couldn't make it to the restaurant on time, expecting that once again he would see fit to forgive her flakiness and lies.

Yes, his brain was right. He should shut the door in her face. But, of course, he didn't. The dumplings smelled good. She smelled even better. He was human, after all.

Sighing, he widened the door to allow her entrance. "Come in."

"Thanks!" she cried, sounding too eager, too cheerful. She was obviously nervous. As she entered the room, Collin realized the suite was a mess—underwear strewn on the floor, work papers everywhere. He walked over to the sofa to clear off a space. "Sorry about dinner," she said, as he set his suitcase on the floor. "I got . . . held up."

He turned to look at her, bracing himself for what would come next. The infamous Hailey Hills excuse. What would she come up with this time? He grabbed his jeans and headed for the bathroom, shutting the door behind him. "By aliens?" he asked through the door. "Bigfoot? The evil Loch Ness monster?" A bit cruel, but it couldn't have been unexpected.

"Try my evil publisher."

He opened the door, surprised. "Publisher?" he asked, peeking out at her. That certainly wasn't the answer he had been expecting.

Hailey nodded, slumping onto the couch. She was still wearing that crazy short plaid skirt she had on earlier and the gap of skin between it and her thigh-highs was making his jeans way too tight. He hoped she wouldn't be able to notice.

"Yeah," she said, staring at the coffee table, as if the copy of *Variety* held the answers to life, the universe, and everything. "She had a bunch of questions about my next issue and would not let me get away, no matter how I pleaded. I, um, actually pulled into the restaurant just as you were leaving. Tried the old 'follow that cab' trick, but the driver wasn't having it. Cabbies! I feel so stupid that I didn't get your cell phone number when we made plans. Then I could have at least let you know what was going on."

Collin let out a breath, relieved and delighted at her story. A real excuse. She had a real, legitimate, couldn't-be-helped excuse. No crazy, made-up conspiracy theory. No Marilyn Monroe ghosts or demon hunters. Just a good old-fashioned reason why a girl couldn't make it on time to a dinner with a guy she liked.

"Anyway, I rushed here as fast I could to apologize," she continued, putting her boots up on the coffee table and revealing more leg in the process. God, she was hot. How had he let her get away? "I'm so sorry for leaving you hanging. Especially since we all know I have a kind of . . . history . . . with that sort of thing." She blushed. "But I've changed. I'm a new person now. And the weird things that used to happen to me? Well, I ignore them now."

He joined her on the couch, daring to reach over and pat her thigh-high-clad knee with his hand. "It's okay," he said. "Things happen."

Hailey squirmed with delight under Collin's casual touch, wondering if he was half as turned on as she. The electricity crackled and sparked as he lingered half a second too long for an innocent pat. His fingers trailed, nails lightly scraping her thigh-high tops.

Things happen, he'd said. In other words, he totally forgave her for standing him up. She was so right to come here. *Thank you, Karma Kitty. Thank you, magic boots.*

Maybe they'd make up tonight. Maybe they'd make out, too. Maybe even . . .

Her brain chose that inopportune moment to give her a reality check. Collin only believed her because she'd out-and-out lied to him. Gave him a "reasonable" excuse. What kind of start to a reconciliation was that? Lying to get someone to believe you. Not a very good one.

Still, what was she supposed to do? Tell him the truth? That the magic boots she'd bought online had morphed her into her comic-book character, giving her the magical powers she needed to save a pirate-comic-book artist from a roving band of ninjas set on his demise? Just like the alien thing on their wedding day, he'd find it unbelievable. Sure, she could kind of prove it—do some gymnastic tricks in his hotel room or something—but then she'd come off even weirder than ever. And the last thing she wanted was for Collin to think she was weirder than he already thought.

If he really loved you, he'd love you weirdness and all, the inner voice nagged. *And he'd believe you, no matter what.*

She pushed the thought out of her brain. She was going to have sex tonight and didn't need rationality to interfere with the rare opportunity for multiple orgasms. So she'd told one little eensy-weensy lie. People told each other lies all the time. *No, that dress doesn't make you look fat. I think bald is beautiful.* No big deal.

"So, how have you been?" she asked in her brightest voice, digging into the bag of takeout and pulling out the cardboard containers. "What's LA like? Where do you live? Do you like your job?"

He held up his hands, laughing. "Whoa. One question at a time," he said, his beautiful eyes dancing in amusement. "LA is fine. Smoggy, just like they say. I live in Santa Monica, a couple blocks from the pier. Really nice place, but a hell of a commute to Studio City every day. And my job's okay. It pays the bills."

"But your job sounds so glamorous."

"It sounds that way, yeah. But it's a lot of work. A lot of meetings and asking for money. A producer isn't on the set every day, doing the actual filming. That would probably be a lot more fun."

Hailey pulled off the cardboard top of the noodles, allowing a puff of steam to escape. "Do you ever . . . draw anymore?" she asked.

He stared down at his chopsticks. "Not really," he said with a small shrug. "Not since, well, you know."

She did. She remembered the you-know like it was yesterday. The day they'd gotten their fiftieth rejection. The one that said something along the lines of "We love the concept and the storyline—come back to us once you get a better artist." The one written by Straylight Comics. He'd told her right then and there he was giving up art forever. She begged him to reconsider—said Karma Kitty was nothing without him—but he just shook his head. He was keeping her down, he told her. She could be great. She just had to let go of the dead weight—aka him.

That had been the beginning of the end for them, she realized, looking back. Collin started applying for Hollywood jobs and she had found Thomas to take over *Karma Kitty*. They were still planning to get married in a few months, but the joy had been sucked out of the relationship. The hope, plans, and dreams they shared had evaporated. And a few weeks before the wedding, when Hailey got her acceptance from Straylight for a *Karma Kitty* series, she found it nearly impossible to face Collin with the news. She'd felt guilty for her own success as it was just another dig at his failure.

He didn't say too much when she'd finally told him: Congratulations, he was happy for her, etc. But the pain clouding his eyes made it impossible for her to completely rejoice in her good fortune.

"It's too bad," she said, finding her courage now that she no longer had anything to lose. "You were a great artist."

"Not according to the comic industry."

"What do they know?" she scoffed. Then she shrugged. "I just hate to see people give up on their dreams."

He swallowed hard. "I've got new dreams now. And they're working out quite nicely." He set down his chopsticks and reached over to her knee again, this time caressing it, smoothing his hand over the nylon. "Dreams and fantasies," he added, in a husky voice.

She sucked in a breath, trying desperately to control her racing heart. He was right. What good did it do to dredge up the past? He was happy as a movie executive, and he had his hand on her thigh. This was a time when art should step aside for life.

"And what might those fantasies be?" she asked, closing her eyes and leaning forward to meet his lips with her own. She'd forgotten how good he tasted, the tang of sweet-and-sour sauce just adding to the kiss. His tongue darted out, licking her lips, coaxing her mouth open to him. She obliged and he delved in for deeper exploration, territories once charted but long forgotten.

While his mouth went to work on hers, his hand restlessly explored her inner thigh, dragging along the bare skin, hitching up her skirt. She gasped at the myriad sensations coursing through her body, her nipples hardening into small pebbles under her bra, longing for his touch. He stroked farther and farther up, finding her panties and peeling them aside to reach her soaking wet center, all the while covering her face and neck with kisses. He pressed two fingers inside of her and slid two others inside her folds to caress her most sensitive nub. She gulped as he made contact, the tingling feeling spiraling into madness as he relentlessly stroked her.

"Oh God, I've missed this," she murmured, reaching over to touch him. She felt his erection through his jeans, straining for her. It made her happy to realize how much he wanted her—as much, it seemed, as she wanted him. She straddled him, rubbing herself against the bulge. He groaned, closing his eyes and leaning his head back.

"You have no idea," he said, his voice hoarse and his breathing heavy.

But while Hailey's in-the-moment passionate part of her brain was ready and impatient to get the show on the road, a waving hand from the sensible part—way in the back recesses—kept staunchly reminding her that inserting one's diaphragm before engaging in hot and heavy action with one's ex-lover might be a decision she appreciated making sometime down the road.

So she kissed him once more on the mouth, then pressed a hand to his chest. His breaths came hot and heavy, his heart tripping a staccato beat. Yup, it was time.

"I'll be right back," she said coyly, climbing off him.

He stared at her dully—obviously his more passionate brain had taken over as well—then nodded. "Please be quick," he said, reaching out to brush her backside as she turned.

She looked back at him with a grin. "Oh, don't worry. I will be." Prancing in the direction of the bathroom, she grabbed her purse off the floor. Thank goodness she had a habit of leaving random things in her handbag—like the diaphragm, in this case. It wasn't exactly like she had planned on getting lucky during the trip.

The bathroom was immediately adjacent to the hotel-room door and, as she approached, she heard a weird noise outside. Curious, she peeked through the peephole to see what it might be.

She jumped back immediately, horrified, at what she saw.

Oh God. It couldn't be.

She peeked out again.

But it was.

There was a ninja lurking in the hallway of her ex-boyfriend's hotel. A ninja that looked very much like the ones she had battled earlier that day.

No, no, no! she cried silently. How had they found her? Did the dim-sum dude squeal? Or maybe he was one of their spies. Did ninjas even have spies?

Great. Now what was she going to do? Sure, she could probably take the guy in a fight, but then she'd have some 'splaining to do once again to Collin. About magic shoes and battling ninjas and—oh, he was going to be so pissed!

And here she'd been doing so good with her perfectly rational excuse for her earlier tardiness.

"Is something wrong, sweetie?" Collin inquired from the couch.

"Um, no. Nothing. I'll be right there." Squaring her shoulders, she determined to forget about the ninja and get back to the hot sex-with-the-ex portion of her evening. After all, how many chances did she get to win back the love of her life? She checked the door. Locked. There was no way the ninja was getting in anyway. He could hang out while she hooked up and she'd deal with him when she was done.

After doing her thing in the bathroom, she headed back to the couch, sinking down on Collin's lap, sliding her now panty-free self against him. He groaned and grabbed her hair, pulling her head back so he could nibble at her neck—one of his favorite games. She gasped in pleasure at the sensation of his teeth scraping against her sensitive skin. It felt so good. So, so good . . .

She stole a glance at the front door. Was the lock really secure? Could a mere hotel-room door really stop a ninja? After all, these guys were used to karate chopping big hunks of wood or stone. And if they did, she and Collin would be caught in a compromising and very hard to fight position. Trapped and unable to get away.

Not to mention then she'd have to tell him the truth about why a ninja had karate chopped down his front door, which would be even worse.

"Hey! Are you thirsty?" she asked, leaping off Collin's lap and scrambling to her feet.

He stared at her as if she had two heads. "Am I . . . what?"

"Thirsty."

He reached out for her hand. "Only for you, sweetness," he purred.

Cute. But rather unhelpful, given the circumstances. "Well, I'm dying of thirst. Totally parched." The excuse sounded so lame coming from her lips. But what else was she going to say? *"Hon, I'll be right back after I do battle with a ninja out in the hall."* It was excuses like that which made him break up with her in the first place.

"Um, you can check the minibar," he said, looking lost. "I mean, if you're thirsty."

Argh. Stupid minibar. "Actually, I think I need ice. I'll just run to the machine. Be right back. You, um, want some Peanut M&Ms or something while I'm by the vending machine?"

He zipped up his pants and sighed. "I'm good," he replied, looking more than a bit sour.

"Okay, cool." She glanced over at the door nervously. Had anyone tried to break through yet? How many were on the other side? "I'll be right back, okay?"

"Sure. Whatever."

He was pissed. Great. But there was no time to right things now. She'd have to do it after the ninja fight. Good thing she hadn't taken off her boots yet.

She pulled open the door and peered from left to right. Hm. No sign of the guy. She carefully crept into the hall, closing the door behind her. The thing about ninjas, she knew, was they could be very hard to spot. She took a few steps and sniffed, trying to locate them with her Super Smell. Suddenly, she got a distinctive whiff of an eel avocado roll, covered in soy sauce and topped with ginger.

Bingo.

She leapt around the corner, launching into full fighting stance. Sure enough, the ninja stood there, outside room 1612. He looked up, evidently surprised someone had been able to sneak up on him (thank you, Karma Kitty Super

Stealth), and held his hands up in a defensive pose, letting loose a string of words Hailey had no way to translate.

She charged toward him, swinging out a foot to connect with his stomach. He dodged easily and spun around, low, sweeping out a leg to trip her. Pain slammed through her ankle as his calf connected and she went sprawling through the air.

But luckily, as a rule, Karma Kitty always landed on her feet.

Hailey recovered and flipped forward, catching the ninja off guard. She jammed a fist low, connecting with his groin. He bellowed in pain, staggering backward, and she took her momentary advantage to grab a nearby vase off a hall table and whip it at his head. Flowers flew and water splashed, followed by the distinctive crash of ceramic against skull. Followed still further by the now unconscious ninja hitting the floor.

Panting for breath, Hailey poked him with her toe. Now that the rage of battle was fading she started to worry that maybe she'd hurt him too badly. She had no desire to go down for murder one, even if she could prove it was self-defense. (Which would be pretty hard to do, considering she'd landed the first blow.)

But luckily for her, the ninja groaned and sat up, rubbing his eyes. He looked up at her. She gave him a little wave, a little smile, then raised her not-so-little fists. The ninja scrambled to his feet and ran as fast as his pajama-ed legs could carry him in the other direction.

Hailey let out a sigh of relief and lowered her hands. Mission accomplished, and no serious injury done to the evil party. She now could go back to Collin's hotel room and continue where they'd left off with no more distractions.

"Where's your ice?" a fully dressed Collin asked as she

entered the room. He was flipping through TV channels with a remote, finally settling on some kind of soccer game. Hailey felt her face heat as she realized in the action of the fight, she'd totally forgotten her original fake mission. Now she was returning, disheveled, iceless, and with no explanation that would make any sense.

"Oh, well, I decided I wasn't all that thirsty after all," she replied, knowing full well how lame she sounded. Her realistic excuses were getting worse than her weird ones. She decided to give it one more try. "Just thirsty for you, baby," she added, dropping her voice to a husky tone.

Collin flipped the channel again, settling on a TBS showing of *The Shining*. He set the remote down on his lap without looking at her. Not a good sign.

"Oh, I love this movie," she tried, plopping down close to him on the couch. He shuffled to the left, putting distance between them. Great. "Um, is something wrong?" As if she needed to ask.

Collin turned to look at her for the first time since she'd reentered the room. His face was stone cold, but his eyes revealed his hurt. "Look, I'm sorry," he said. "I didn't mean to . . . well, what I mean to say is . . ." He raked a hand through his hair, obviously frustrated. "You know," he said, angrily, "if you didn't want to have sex, you could have just spoken up. You make it seem like I'm forcing you to do something you don't want."

Hailey stared at him, eyes wide, mirroring her disbelief. Was that what he thought? That she was trying to avoid sleeping with him? God, there was nothing in the world she wanted to do more.

"Collin, no!" she cried. "It's not that at all."

"Then what is it, Hailey? I'd really like to know."

And she'd really like to tell him. She slumped into the couch cushions. But admitting the whole Karma Kitty fighting ninjas out in the hotel hallway thing just didn't seem like it was going to exactly fly. He wouldn't believe her. He'd think she was lying and making excuses again. Just like before. Nothing had changed. Their relationship was still impossible.

She rose from the couch. "I've got to go," she told him.

"Fine," he replied, his voice devoid of emotion. He turned back to the TV.

Hailey took a step towards the door. "Okay, so, I'm leaving."

"Later." Obviously he wasn't interested in convincing her to stay. What a bastard. Thank God she hadn't slept with him. She gave him one more longing glance as she pulled open the hotel room door. He was still engrossed in the TV. Bastard. She wanted to slap him. But with her Karma Kitty powers, she'd probably leave too big a bruise.

You know, the kind she couldn't explain.

CHAPTER FIVE

"And then what?"

"Then I left," Hailey concluded with a shrug, sawing at her waffle with strawberries and extra whipped cream the next day at breakfast. "Went back to my hotel room, raided the minibar and passed out, surrounded by little empty bottles of booze." She shoveled waffle into her mouth, a vain attempt to use fat and calories to soak up her inner pain.

"That's a very anticlimactic story," Thomas pouted. He took a sip of the Starbucks latte he'd insisted on smuggling into the restaurant after one sip of the place's home brew the morning before. "I was hoping for fireworks. At least multiple orgasms."

"If only that stupid ninja didn't show up," she said, leaning back in her chair and letting out a sigh. "Why, oh why, do I get myself into these messes? I should have let Hiro Kim face his enemies himself instead of getting involved. What possessed me to take on a gaggle of ninjas in the first place?"

Thomas reached over to pat her hand. "Well, I thought what you did was very brave."

"Whoopdie-do." Hailey twirled her finger in the air. "Bravery, for the win and all that. Fat lot of good it'll do me. Hiro didn't even bother to thank me for putting my ass on the line. And let's face it; the guy could probably finance a small country. Shouldn't I, his kitty in shining pleather, now be entitled to a piece of that action?"

"Maybe he'll name a pirate character after you," Thomas comforted. "Besides, I'm sure he was appreciative. He just doesn't speak the language."

"Maybe . . ."

"Anyway, if you're done with your self-pity party, take a look at this." Thomas pulled out a sheaf of paper from the middle of his Comic Con program. "Someone handed it to me on the way in. According to this, Darken Pictures is scheduled to make some major announcement at ten this morning. I'm betting it's a new comic movie they're working on. Aren't you dying to know what it is?"

"No." Hailey sniffed. "Not in the least."

"Oh liar, liar, pants on fire," Thomas scolded. "You're just bitter 'cause Collin works at Darken. But come on! Don't you want to see which sad-sack comic-book artist they suckered into selling his soul to Hollywood this time around?"

She considered it. "Maybe a little. But we're standing way in the back. I so don't want Collin to think I'm stalking him or something."

"Great." Thomas glanced at his watch. "Nine thirty. We'd better head over to the convention hall if we don't want to miss it."

They paid for their breakfast and headed to the Javits Center. Once inside, they had to push through the already gathering crowd until they got to the outer limits of the large, flashy Darken Pictures booth. They needn't have worried about being spotted, Hailey realized, looking around. There were probably a thousand people milling about, waiting for the big announcement.

The folks at Darken had set up a makeshift stage at the top of the booth, and suddenly triumphant-sounding music erupted from the gigantic speakers flanking each side. Hailey watched as none other than Collin himself stepped up to the podium. She noticed, to some small satisfaction, that her ex looked exhausted and his clothes were wrinkled. Maybe he couldn't sleep last night, feeling guilty over the way he'd treated her.

Collin cleared his throat and leaned into the microphone. "Thank you all for coming," he said, and Hailey's extremely disloyal heart panged at the sound of his voice. "We at Darken Pictures are really excited to bring you some very special news. A new partnership between manga and motion picture."

"See?" Thomas poked her in the side. "I told you."

"Shhh."

"As of this morning, we will be working with the one and only Hiro Kim to develop a big-budget blockbuster film based on his amazing pirate manga series, *Shadow Booty Clan*."

Hailey's mouth dropped open. She glanced over to Thomas, realizing he was wearing a similar expression on his own face. Hiro Kim? The same Hiro Kim who swore time and time again he'd never sell out to Hollywood in a million years? The same Hiro Kim to whom Pixar once offered thirty million dollars for the rights to use his characters? He was selling out to Darken?

Something was rotten in Comic Con, that was for sure.

"What the hell?" Hailey hissed to Thomas as they watched the stage. A dazed-looking Hiro approached the podium, bowing to Collin and then listlessly shaking his hand. "What's going on here?"

Thomas shrugged, obviously as shocked as she. "I have no fucking idea," he whispered back. "But I think Hiro's going to speak."

"I happy to work with Darken," Hiro said in faltering

English. "They very good company. My manga in good . . . arms? . . . with them. Thank you."

He bowed to the audience, who erupted in cheers. Many of them had been waiting for a Hiro Kim movie their entire lives. A few diehards in the back booed and yelled "Sell-out!" but Hiro didn't seem to hear them. He just stared out into the crowd with dark, blank eyes. Finally, two security guards approached him and escorted him off the stage. Collin thanked everyone for coming by, urged them to check out the booth, then left the stage. The crowd dispersed, all abuzz with the news, many already updating their blogs with their PDAs.

"Unbelievable," Thomas murmured, still staring up at the now-vacant stage. "Hiro Kim would never sell his manga to a Hollywood studio. Never, ever, ever."

"Uh, hate to break it to you, dude, but he just did." Hailey reminded him. "Guess everyone has their price."

"Yes, but . . ." Thomas scratched his head. "Don't you think it's more than a bit odd that last night he was being chased by ninjas and now he's doing something he never ever in a million years was going to do?"

Hailey stared at him. She'd been so wrapped up in her own problems with Collin the thought hadn't occurred to her. "Oh my God, you're right!" she cried. "What if they found him again after? Maybe they work for Darken and threatened to kill him if he didn't sign away his movie rights."

It sounded kind of crazy, but the way everything else was going, that was just par for the course.

"Well, I doubt Darken Pictures employs ninjas," Thomas mused. He reached into his pocket and pulled out the shuriken from the day before. He turned the plastic star in his hands. "But these guys do." He looked up at Hailey. "The MeiyoSeraph Agency. Booth 4294. Let's go."

They headed down the aisles, focused and on a mission, ignoring all the fun diversions they passed. There would be time for browsing later; right now they had a mystery to solve: Why the world's premier manga pirate artist would suddenly give away his film rights, one night after being chased by a gang of ninjas. Seemed a bit too much to be a coincidence. Hailey felt a bit like Nancy Drew as she fingered the clue in her hand. Of course, Nancy was more of a pacifist; never once, in her hundreds of adventures, had the redheaded detective been forced to kick ninja ass.

"It should be right over here," Thomas remarked as they turned the corner. "Booth 4294."

Except there was no booth 4294. Only an empty square of carpet where a booth might have once been, sandwiched between a booth selling Pooka the Goblin Cat stuffed animals and the Voodoo Babies stall.

"Who was here at this booth?" Hailey asked the girl manning the Pooka booth. She was dressed all in black and had multiple piercings in her ears, nose, eyebrows and mouth (and who knows where else underneath her clothes!). Hailey's publisher would so not have approved.

"Um," the girl pondered, tonguing her lip ring. "I think it was some agency."

Hailey cocked her head. "Agency?"

"Yeah. You know, like, people who represent artists. They were here yesterday." She looked over to the booth and shrugged. "But when I got here this morning they were long gone."

Thomas and Hailey exchanged glances. "Do you remember if they were called MeiyoSeraph Agency?" Hailey asked hopefully.

The pierced girl thought for a moment, then shook her braided head. "Sorry, I can't remember. I was totally swamped yesterday and didn't get to chat with my neighbors much. The only reason I know they were agents was 'cause that movie producer Collin Robinson came over a bunch of times yesterday to talk to them." She fanned herself with her many-ringed hand. "God, that guy is hot."

"Oh yeah, he's steaming," Hailey muttered. Steaming mad at her, that was. Why, oh why, did everything in her life have to circle back to Collin? And what the hell did he have to do with the ninja agents? "Thanks for your help."

"Sure, no problem." The girl smacked her gum. Hailey and Thomas turned to leave. "Oh, one other thing," the girl said, calling them back. They turned around, expectant. The Goth rummaged under her booth, then held out a shiny plastic object.

A shuriken.

"I found this in the empty booth this morning," she said, pressing the plastic throwing star into Hailey's hand. "Probably from one of their ninjas."

Hailey did a double take. "Ninjas?" Now they were getting somewhere. "Are you sure?"

The girl nodded enthusiastically. "Oh, didn't I mention it?" she asked. "Some of the guys behind the booth were dressed as ninjas. I figured they must be actors, hired for whatever promotion they were doing. They looked pretty cool, though. All serious-like."

"Ninjas? Are you sure they were ninjas?" Hailey's pulse kicked up a few notches as she examined the throwing star. It was identical to the one the ninja had aimed at her head the night before.

"There's really no mistaking ninjas, is there?"

"Right. Well, thanks. You've been very helpful." Hailey and Thomas said their good-byes and hurried off.

"This is getting weirder and weirder," Hailey mused, tossing the throwing star in the air and catching it as they rushed back to the Straylight booth. Their morning signing was in less than a half hour and they were going to have to cross almost the entire floor. "Why the hell would talent agents have ninjas at their booths?"

"And why would those ninjas chase Hiro Kim after closing time?" Thomas added. "With plastic throwing stars nonetheless."

"And what does any of this have to do with Collin?"

Thomas stopped in his tracks. "Don't you see? It makes perfect sense. Yesterday, Hiro swears he hates everything Hollywood and never in a million years or for millions of dollars will he sell the rights to his pirate manga. The next day, after being chased by ninjas—belonging to a talent agent that a producer for Darken Pictures visited several times—he decides, out of the blue, to partner with said movie company. Coincidence? I think not."

"But I rescued him! The ninjas didn't get him," Hailey protested.

"Maybe they had a second round later. While you were busy attempting a *real* booty call, instead of the shadow type."

Hailey nodded enthusiastically. "Maybe Hiro's staying at the same hotel as Collin. Remember, I saw that ninja poking around there. I'd assumed he was looking for me to get revenge, but maybe he was sent to find Hiro."

"Or maybe he was looking for Collin," Thomas finished. "To tell him they'd coerced Hiro into making a deal."

Hailey shuddered. "What do you think they do to people to get them to sign? Torture? Blackmail?"

"Something bad, for sure," Thomas said. "Because there's no other way Hiro would have signed up with a production house like Darken Pictures."

Hailey's stomach rolled with realization "That means Collin's in on this somehow," she said, a sinking disappointment settling in her gut. And here she assumed he'd be one of the good guys.

Thomas put out a hand. "Hold on, don't jump to conclusions. Maybe Collin doesn't know the company's tactics. After all, heartbreaker though he may be, he doesn't exactly strike me as the type to blackmail and malign people, just to get them to sign movie deals."

Hailey considered this. "No, I guess not. But we know he visited the ninja agents during the day. And then there was a ninja outside his hotel room that night. Seems fishy to me."

"Well, I'm not saying he doesn't have dealings with them," Thomas agreed. "He's a producer; he probably deals with a ton of agents every day. But maybe he doesn't know this particular agency's methods. Who knows—maybe they offered him Hiro's movie rights on a silver platter, without giving him any clue on how they planned to acquire those rights. Any Hollywood hottie with half a brain would jump at that offer, right? It's only the deal of the century, after all."

"I guess that makes sense," Hailey mused. "I mean, as much as any of this does." She looked over at Thomas. "So, what do we do now?"

"I guess we talk to Hiro. Though he doesn't speak much English. We'll need to find someone to interpret."

"But Hiro's hanging out with the Darken people."

Thomas nodded. "Exactly." He looked at Hailey pointedly.

She shook her head. "Oh no. No, no, no. I am so not going to kiss up to Collin just to gain access to Hiro."

Thomas stopped walking and turned to her. "You'd rather let some guy lose all his life's work than go ask a favor of your ex-boyfriend? The one, may I remind you, that you were so hot and heavy on just yesterday?"

Hailey sighed. "Well, I . . ." There was no argument Thomas was going to be okay with; she might as well give in and go. And, to be fair, a certain part of her did realize, deep inside, that it would be a good excuse to talk to Collin again. "Fine," she relented. "I'll go. But first we need to motor if we're going to have our signing on time."

"Collin, my man, I don't know how you did it, but you indeed did it, and for that I am utterly grateful." Mr. Tubbs, Collin's boss and the vice president of the studio, slapped him on the back so hard Collin almost fell over.

"Well, I'm happy you're happy," he replied after regaining his balance. He threw his boss a big fake smile—the kind he'd become famous for. "I agree that Hiro's a great addition to next summer's blockbuster lineup."

"A great addition? He's the fucking headliner!" Mr. Tubbs cried. "Every studio and their decrepit old grandmother have been trying to get this guy to sell his soul to the devil for years now. But the *artiste*"—Mr. Tubbs sneered at the word—"well, he was just too high and mighty and artsy for the likes of us. Goddamn comic-book artists thinking they're freaking Michelangelo or some shit."

"Hiro's a manga artist," Collin corrected, knowing he should keep his mouth shut. "There is a difference."

"He draws silly pictures for a living—pictures with speech bubbles over the character's heads, don't he?" Mr. Tubbs scoffed. "That makes him a comic book–maker in my book." He slapped Collin on the back again. "But you, Collin, my main man, you did it. You got that bastard to finally sign on the dotted line. We've got the next goddamn *Pirates of the Caribbean* franchise on our hands and it's all thanks to you."

Collin wasn't sure how to respond. All day he'd been getting this type of congrats from the bigwigs at Darken Pictures. The president of the company had even called him up to thank him personally for bringing Hiro to Darken. He was the man of the hour. The studio savior. The one who'd won over the manga whiz kid after nearly a decade of wrangling.

So, why couldn't he be happy about it?

Two reasons came to mind. One was the weird circumstances in which it had all gone down. What people like Mr. Tubbs didn't know was that Collin hadn't even approached Hiro with an offer. He'd been handed it on a plate by the guy's people—The MeyioSeraph Agency— which Collin hadn't even heard of before today. They'd approached him out of the blue, told him they represented Hiro's movie rights, and asked him if he'd be interested in making a deal. At first Collin had laughed, thinking it was some kind of joke his coworkers had orchestrated. But as they continued to talk, he realized they were indeed serious. And they were willing and able to seal the deal.

Collin wrote up the contract then and there. Money was no object when it came to getting Hiro on the summer lineup. And now everyone was giving him huge kudos for the easiest deal of his life.

And then there was reason number two he couldn't be happy. Hailey.

He hadn't slept a wink last night, tossing and turning and thinking of their "almost" encounter and how it ended. He felt so horrible—obviously moving too fast and scaring her away. It was the last thing he'd wanted to do. But she'd looked so beautiful and she seemed really into it all—until she leapt up, ran for ice, and came back fifteen minutes later with a sheepish look on her face.

Did she think he was some kind of monster? Someone who only wanted her for her body? How could he explain to her how much she meant to him? Heck, he would have been happy just to wrap her in his arms and cuddle her all night, keeping her warm and safe and protected. He'd only gone for more because she seemed to want it. She'd instigated most of it, for God's sake.

And then she'd gotten cold feet. Just like on her wedding day. At least this time she hadn't come up with some crazy alien-abduction story to cover for it.

Just stay away from her, an inner voice lectured. *She's nothing but trouble.*

He squared his shoulders and firmed his resolve. He'd listen to that voice. He'd stop thinking about Hailey and start being happy about his huge success with Hiro. Today should be the best day of his life. And he wouldn't let her ruin it.

Mr. Tubbs punched him in the shoulder once more with feeling, and told him he'd catch him later, walking off and leaving Collin alone in the booth. He wondered what he should do with his afternoon, now that all his work was done. More than anything he just wanted to go back to his hotel room and take a nap. With Hailey cuddled up beside him, preferably. But that wasn't going to happen. In fact, likely he wouldn't run into her for the remainder of the convention. And that was for the best.

"Hey, Collin!"

Looked like "the best" wasn't in the stars. He turned to face her, masking his excitement with a stern look. No need to let her know how excited he was to see her again.

"Wasn't expecting to see you today," he said in his coolest voice. What was she up to now? Was she here to apologize for the night before? Not that she needed to apologize for not wanting to have sex, of course. He understood, under the circumstances. But the lies. The excuses. The lack of respect she showed him once again. He'd be okay with an, "I'm sorry" for that.

She blushed, dropping her gaze. Probably embarrassed

about her behavior. As well she should be, he reminded himself.

Against his better judgment, Collin's eyes took her in, giving her a thorough head-to-toe evaluation. She was dressed more conservatively then yesterday, in an adorable red schoolgirl smock with gray leggings and black Mary Jane platform shoes buckled onto her feet. He stifled a groan. The innocent outfit almost turned him on more than her much more sexy apparel of the day before, and he felt his groin respond—a part of him that didn't give two shits about apologies and remorse. Yes, while his head was tied up in knots and excuses, his cock was fired up and ready to go anytime the girl said the word.

But she won't say the word, he reminded himself. *And if you let yourself fall, she'll only make a fool out of you again.*

He realized he should say something. "Got another signing today?" he asked, trying to act cool, calm, and collected. As if the night before never happened. Maybe they could at least be friends. Or something.

"Just finished," Hailey said. "Went well, actually. There were a ton of people there. We have another one this afternoon."

An odd pride swelled inside him. He didn't know why, exactly. Not like he'd done anything for her career but hold her back a few years. Still, it made him happy to hear the excitement in her voice as she talked about her comic. She'd followed her dreams and reached the stars. He couldn't help but admire her for that.

"Cool," he said. "Maybe I'll stop by this afternoon."

Hailey nodded, looking a little impatient. She'd obviously come here with something on her mind. "So, I heard about you guys signing Hiro," she said. "That's incredible. How did you get him? From what I understood he said he'd never do a movie."

He felt his face heat. Sure, he was okay with his coworkers thinking he was God's gift. But he couldn't play superhero to Hailey. She knew him too well.

"Can you keep a secret?" he asked. She nodded, her eyes widening with anticipation. He hated to disappoint her. "Well, honestly, it just sort of fell into my lap," he admitted. "This talent agency called MeyioSeraph just showed up at my booth and offered me his stuff. At first I didn't believe them. But they had all the paperwork; all I had to do was sign." He shrugged. "Well, that and promise them ridiculous amounts of money, of course. I don't know how this agency got him to agree to do pictures, but whoever it was should get a huge bonus. The fifteen-percent commission on a deal like that is more than some third-world country's GNP."

Hailey didn't look impressed. In fact, if Collin didn't know better, he'd say she looked concerned. "Did you actually meet up with Hiro?" she asked.

"Yes. This morning. He seemed sort of out of it, actually," Collin said, remembering the strange meeting they'd had. He'd tried to put it off to the language barrier, but something in the back on his brain told him it was more than that. "He thanked me for buying his manga and said he was excited to see the film version."

"Doesn't that strike you as odd?"

It was the question he'd been asking himself all day, and she was the first person to come out and say it. "Yes," he agreed. "Really odd. The whole thing. But who knows—with these artistic types?" The second the words left his mouth he regretted them. "Well, you know w-what I mean," he stammered, blushing again under Hailey's gaze.

She waved the unintended insult off. "So, where is he now?" she asked.

"I have no idea. Probably downing lots of expensive saki.

Doesn't matter, really. We won't be dealing with him again. He signed away all his movie rights to us. If he's lucky, he'll get a ticket to the premiere, but that's about it. We'll get a screenwriter to work up a script and go from there."

Hailey finally met his eyes. "I need to see him," she said, her voice quiet and urgent.

"What?" He cocked his head. What was she getting at here? "Why the sudden interest in Hiro?" A pang of jealousy stabbed at his gut. What if she had a thing for the guy? But no, that was ridiculous. And besides, even if she did, it wasn't any of his business anymore. She'd made that clear with her quick exit last night.

"Um," she stammered. "I can't explain. I just do."

There was desperation in her voice that made him pause. Whatever this was about, she was serious. "Well, the agency's booth is 4294," Collin said, pointing in the general direction. "You could try asking them."

"I went already and tried there. The booth is gone."

Collin stared at her. "Why would the booth be gone?"

"I don't know, Collin," she said tersely. Something was really bothering her, and he couldn't figure out what. "All I know is it's not there. And I really need to find him. Do you have any idea where he could be? Maybe a contact number or something?"

Collin shook his head. "I have a contact at MeyioSeraph," he said, pulling out his Treo. He punched a few buttons then put the phone to his ear. "Hi, this is Collin Robinson," he said, after getting a "MeyioSeraph, may I help you," on the other end. "I'm wondering if I could speak to Hiro."

"Hiro is not taking any phone calls," the woman stated in a flat voice.

"My studio just paid him twenty million dollars. Surely he'll take mine."

"I'm sorry, Mr. Robinson. I'll pass the message along for you."

Collin glanced over at Hailey, who was biting her fingernails—something she only did when she was extremely nervous. He decided to try once more. "Just for a min—," he started, before the phone disconnected on him. "They hung up," he informed her.

She dropped her hand. "This is not good," she said. "Not good at all."

"What are you so worried about? He's probably just off celebrating his new fortune." He studied her closer. "Is there something you're not telling me?" he asked. "I feel like I'm missing a vital piece of the puzzle here."

Hailey sighed. Funny, that. She looked up into Collin's earnest face, his concerned eyes, and wished she could just spill it all and tell him everything—about the ninjas, about the Karma Kitty fight, every single last ridiculous thing. But she couldn't bear to see the disbelief in his eyes, the disappointment that she was once again "making up her little stories" as she did when they were together. So as much as she would have liked having Collin's help in all of this, it was better, in the end, to just go it alone.

"No," she lied, trying to sound as blasé as possible. "I was just curious to meet him, is all."

She still got the frown, the disappointment. Even without the wild story, he still didn't believe her. Though, why should he? She bit her lower lip. She wouldn't believe herself at this point either. This sucked. "I've g-got to go," she stammered, needing to get away before he saw the tears forming at the corners of her eyes. "Thanks for your help."

"Sure, um, anytime," he said, giving her a helpless look. Then he added, "Are you okay, Hailey? I mean, you're not in any trouble, are you? 'Cause if you were . . ." He trailed off, and the concern in his eyes almost broke her right then and there as a hundred nights wrapped in his warm embrace came flooding back all at once in a tidal wave of memories. The lump in her throat made her jaw quiver. If only . . .

She shook her head clear and used every ounce of her strength to walk away without looking back. It hurt, yes, but it was better in the long run. Better for both of them. She made the mistake of glancing back and saw he was still watching her. She gave him a half wave and then disappeared into the crowd, her heart breaking and rebreaking with every step.

Once a safe distance away, she punched up Thomas on her cell and instructed him to meet her at Starbucks for a latte. Thomas, who would have agreed to meet Attila the Hun if Starbucks was involved, was already there and had ordered by the time she made it through the crowd and to the coffee chain. She slipped into the chair across from him and he handed her a steaming paper cup.

"So, what did Mr. Hollywood say?" he asked.

She related all she'd found out. About MeyioSeraph Agents, Darken Pictures' involvement, and the mysterious circumstances under which the deal had been struck.

Thomas sat silently for a moment, sipping his no-whip, sugar-free vanilla, skim latte, with a thoughtful slurp, then set down the beverage and reached into his bag and whipped out his laptop.

"When in doubt, Google," he proclaimed.

She narrowed her eyes, doubting his strategy. "I hardly doubt Hiro's listed in whitepages.com. He lives in Japan, remember."

But Thomas either didn't hear her (yeah, right) or completely ignored her (much more likely) and carried on with his search. She leaned back, taking another sip of her drink, allowing him his SherlockHolmes.com moment. He was a good Internet researcher, actually. His big claim to fame was the time he met a guy at a gay bar who introduced himself as "Petey the Meaty." The two had shared a quick locking of lips on the dance floor before the clock struck twelve and Cinderfella ditched the ball without so much as a glass platform boot—never mind a phone number. The next day, a rather obsessed Thomas came up with not only the digits, but also e-mail, photos from his last drag show, his father's doctor's license, even his property records.

Which went to show you, it was never wise to piss off a professional Googler.

"Sister . . ." Thomas was muttering under his breath as he typed and scanned. "Karen Kim . . . Cleveland . . . Bingo!" He looked up with a wide grin. "I think I might have something." He pulled out his iPhone and dialed a number. "Hello?" he greeted, a minute later. "Yes, this is Tom Law, USA Today reporter. I'm doing an article on your brother Hiro and he said I should give you a call."

He gave a thumbs-up to Hailey and she smiled in return. Her partner had really missed his calling as an investigative reporter, for sure.

"What?" Thomas cried suddenly, the mischievous smirk fading from his face. "Are you sure?"

Something was wrong. Hailey held out her hands and mouthed, "What?" Thomas waved her off.

"Well, yes, I guess you would be sure. But it's just . . . well, sudden. I'm so sorry for your loss. No, no, I won't bother you again. Yes, I'll put it in the article. No problem." He pressed END and set the phone down on the table. He met Hailey's eyes, his own dead serious for the first time in forever.

"What is it?" Hailey demanded. "You're scaring me."

"Hiro's dead."

"What?" she cried. "He can't be dead. We saw him this morning onstage."

"That was this morning. According to his sister he spent the afternoon performing ritualized hara-kiri in his hotel room. The maid found him, bleeding all over the rug, just an hour ago."

"Oh my God," Hailey cried, hardly able to digest the news. "Why would he do that? After signing the deal? Do you think he was ashamed of selling out or something? Like, he regretted his decision and couldn't face his fans?" It seemed like a leap, but it was too much to be completely unrelated.

Thomas looked grim. "Or maybe it only *looked* like suicide."

"Oh my God." Hailey swallowed hard.

"Something's going on here. Something big. And all of it points to this weird ninja agency, MeyioSeraph."

"Did you Google them?"

"Yes, but all I got was message boards for some dorky *World of Warcraft* guild. There's no information on where this agency is based or who's involved or who their other clients are. Nothing. Just a 'coming soon' sign and one of those damn throwing stars as a logo."

"You really think they had something to do with Hiro's death?"

"I don't see any other possibility. We know Hiro didn't want to sell his movie rights. We saw him being chased by MeyioSeraph ninjas, then the next day he signs the deal, they clear out of Comic Con, and he winds up dead."

Hailey swallowed hard. It did seem to add up. "So, what now?" she asked.

"I'll do some research. In the meantime, you should go back to Collin and find out whatever he knows about the company itself. He must have addresses and stuff, if they've done a deal. And maybe go back to where the booth was. Maybe someone else saw them yesterday besides that clueless Goth girl. Not that ninjas stand out much here. Which I guess is what makes them the perfect weapon."

"Right. Okay." Hailey nodded, glad to have something physical to do. Especially when that something in question gave her an excuse to go see Collin again. "And we'll meet back here in an hour?"

"Make it two hours," Thomas said, checking his watch. "That's when our signing starts. We'll meet over at the Straylight booth." He turned back to his computer, then looked up again. "And Hailey?"

"Yeah?"

"Be careful," he said. "In fact, maybe you should put on the boots. You know, just in case."

"Okay. No problem. Good luck to you, too."

Hailey headed back into the convention hall and made her way straight to the Darken Pictures booth. Unfortunately, Collin was nowhere to be found. A few wandering employees said they were pretty sure he'd gone to a business lunch of some sort and wouldn't be back for at least an hour. She berated herself once again for not getting his cell phone number when she had the chance.

Nor was anyone with tons of information hanging out near the booth formerly housing MeyioSeraph. So Hailey wandered the floor, killing time before her signing, half-heartedly checking out the various booths. It should have been fun, but her thoughts were too tormented to allow her joy. Was Hiro Kim really murdered after being forced to give away his movie rights? And if he was, what could she do to make sure the ninja agents didn't strike again?

When it came time for the signing, she made her way over to the Straylight booth. Thomas hadn't arrived yet, so

she chatted awhile with Mrs. Hannah about the future of
Karma Kitty. Mrs. Hannah told her sales had been very good
and they were looking forward to a long-term relationship,
which made Hailey feel proud. No matter how messed up
the rest of her life was, at least she had her comic.

The clock struck three, time for the signing, and Thomas
still hadn't shown up. Worried, she called his cell, but voice
mail picked up after one ring.

"Mrs. Hannah," she called over to her boss. "I'm concerned about Thomas. He's not here yet."

The publisher frowned, looking down at her watch.
"Artists," she mumbled under her breath, before looking
over at Hailey. "Well, you'll just have to sign without him."

"But what if he's . . ." What, Hailey? In danger? Being
chased by ninjas? Did she want her publisher to think she
was crazy, too? After all, the woman was in complete control of the one thing in Hailey's life that was going right.
Was she going to sabotage that as well?

Hailey shook her head, clearing it of all the doubts.
Thomas was notoriously flighty and always late; he'd probably just met some cute booth boy and was too busy flirting
to realize it was time for their signing.

"Hi!" cried a skinny teen in pigtails and braces. "Can
you sign my *Karma Kitty* comic?"

"Sure!" Hailey replied, greeting her with a big smile.
She'd worry about Thomas later.

She signed and she signed and she signed and then she
signed some more. This was a lot busier than the earlier
signing—more people had arrived at the convention. Not
to mention she had a signing buddy to do half the work on
the first round. Thomas still hadn't shown up and Hailey
was getting more and more worried about him. She tried to
tell herself she was being silly—he'd probably met some

hunky superhero encased in vinyl and lost track of time—but she couldn't help thinking about the ninjas. After all, Thomas didn't have her magic shoes to help fend them off and let's just say his gym habits were a bit dodgy.

"I'll take five of each."

Hailey looked up in surprise. Collin stood above her, looking down. He was the last one in line. She stifled a shiver. "Hey," she said, keeping her voice casual. "What are you doing here?"

He looked hurt. "I told you I'd stop by," he reminded her. He grabbed a comic and handed it to her. "Of course I've already read this," he said. "But can I get an autographed copy?"

She could feel her face heat. "Oh, come on. Don't be silly." Why was he doing this? Making it so much harder not to love him.

"What? You autograph for complete strangers, but not me?"

"It's just a dumb comic. You're not going to get anything for it on eBay."

His sparkling eyes turned serious. "Come on, Hails," he scolded. "Don't demean all your work here. You've done amazingly well in such a short time." He gestured over to two giggling girls reading the comic down at the far side of the table. "You've got loyal fans, you've got multibook deals." He met her eyes. "I'm really proud of you."

Her heart panged at his words. If only things had turned out differently, she could have spent the rest of her life with this man and never looked back. And yet, they might as well be strangers now. So unfair.

"It's really noth—"

"Just take the damn compliment, Ms. Hills."

She forced a grin. "Okay. Fine. I will. And thank you. It means a lot coming from you."

He looked around the booth. "You're living the dream, Hailey. The life I always imagined for myself."

He looked so wistful, Hailey's heart went out to him. It must be so hard to have had a dream and put everything you had into making it come true—only to have it crumble and disintegrate before your very eyes. "I know your life hasn't turned out the way you hoped," she said carefully. "But Collin, you're doing amazingly well. I mean, I can't tell you how impressed I am by all you've done."

He opened his mouth. She wagged a finger at him. "Take the compliment, Mr. Robinson," she ordered.

He chuckled. "Touché." He bowed low. "Well, then thank you, Ms. Hills. That's very nice of you to say."

"However," Hailey added, "that doesn't mean I agree with your choice to give up drawing. I mean, even if you don't make it your full-time career. It's something you loved, and I'm a firm believer that no one should give up something they love." It was funny how easily the words came to her now that she knew they had no chance to be together.

Collin nodded meekly. "I know, I know," he said. "You're right. But I haven't picked up a pencil in years. I doubt I'd even remember what to do with it."

"Well, let's see then, shall we?" Hailey asked, after checking to see no one had appeared behind him. She produced a pencil and a pad of paper and pushed them across the table. "I want you to draw Karma Kitty."

"Oh, no, I couldn't—"

She pressed the pencil into his hand. "Oh, come on. You were the one who originally designed her, after all!"

"That is true . . ." Collin said. "Okay, fine, twist my arm." He got down on his knees in front of the booth to start drawing. His brow furrowed in concentration as he sketched each line. Hailey watched, pride swelling inside

of her as, inch by inch, her comic-book character came to
life on the page. Collin really was an amazing artist. It
was too bad he'd given up on his dream so long ago.
Those stupid publishers, rejecting him. They were all
fools.

"That's awesome," she commented. "I love how you do
her tail. I totally need to suggest that to Thomas."

Collin didn't look up, so immersed was he in the drawing. "Thanks," he said. "Well, maybe if we do end up making that Karma Kitty cartoon, the studio will let me work
in the art department on my days off."

Hailey started to laugh, then stopped, realizing the im-
plications of what he had said. "Wait. What do you mean,
Karma Kitty cartoon?"

This time Collin did look up. "Don't you know?" he
asked, sounding puzzled. "Your partner Thomas approached
us about it this afternoon. He was going to sell the rights
and have us create a cartoon series based on the characters.
I think it's a pretty cool idea, actually—though of course I
still need to run it by the top brass."

"Whoa, whoa, whoa!" Hailey waved her hands. "Slow
down. Thomas came to you and asked you to make a
Karma Kitty cartoon?" That didn't make any sense at all. "I
know nothing about any of this."

"Well, not him personally. He had a Straylight rep and
his agent come over."

"We don't have an agent, Collin. We do it all ourselves."

He looked at her, confused. "It was the same agency that
reps Hiro. I figured that's why you were asking about them
this morning."

"Oh my God." Hailey could feel the blood drain from
her face. "This is not good."

"What? What's wrong?"

She drew in a breath, her mind racing. Should she tell

him? He was going to think she was absolutely nuts. It might even ruin their chance to get together. But at the same time, Thomas's life might be at stake. And desperate times led to desperate measures.

"Collin, I need to tell you something. It's going to seem really crazy. Like, really, really crazy. But I need you to promise to believe me."

Collin's face didn't change, but she could imagine him thinking, *Here we go again.*

"I didn't really have a meeting with my publisher last night."

"So you lied." Collin sounded angry. "What a shock."

"Yes. But only cause I was sure you wouldn't believe me if I told the truth."

"You were kidnapped by a giant Yeti?"

"No." She refused to acknowledge the sarcasm in his voice. "I was saving Hiro Kim from a pack of ninjas."

"I see. And why, pray tell, did Hiro Kim need saving from these ninjas?"

"They work for the MeiyoSeraph Agency. And I have reason to believe that they are using violent tactics to get manga and comic book creators to sell out to Hollywood." She shrugged. "It's simple, really. Kidnap Hiro Kim and torture him until he signs away his movie rights to you guys. The agency pockets a huge fifteen percent. Then they kill the creator before he can squeal."

"Kill the creator?"

"Well, they make it look like a suicide. Hiro committed hara-kiri in his hotel room this afternoon."

Collin looked upset. "What? How do you know that?"

"Doesn't matter. The point is, these are real bad guys. And now they've got Thomas. We have to save him!"

"Hold on a second." Collin held up a hand. "Go back to the part where you were doing battle with them."

Hailey sighed. She really, really, really did not want to tell him about the Karma Kitty thing. He barely believed her about the ninjas, and that was totally plausible. Well, sort of.

"I'll tell you, but you have to promise you won't think I'm crazy," she said.

"I don't see how you're going to top the ninja conspiracy theory. But somehow I think you're about to try."

She drew in a breath and then let it spill. "I've turned into Karma Kitty."

He stared at her, silent as the grave.

"I know, I know, it sounds crazy. It IS crazy. But it's true. I can prove it."

"You can prove that you've turned into your comic-book character."

"Yes. I have all her powers. Like . . . great flexibility and the ability to land on my feet. And I can kick some serious butt. That's how I took on the swarm of ninjas all by myself. Thomas said I was like Neo in *The Matrix*. It was pretty cool." She grinned, remembering. "Anyway, it's 'cause of these shoes. She reached under the table and held up the boots. "I got them off the Internet at Hiheelia.com. When I put them on, I get Karma Kitty powers."

"I see."

Collin watched as Hailey slid her boots onto her feet, wondering why he was even there, still listening to this craziness. This was exactly why the two of them had broken up in the first place. She'd sworn she'd changed—turned over a new leaf, lived a normal life—but now, here she was again with the same old wild stories and unbelievable claims. He should just walk away now, while he still had some self-respect left. E-mail her on Monday and gently suggest some heavy-duty psychiatric meds.

"Okay," she cried, coming out from around the table, all booted up. "Here goes." She grabbed her foot with her hand and proceeded to wrap a leg around her head. "How about this?"

"What are you doing?" he asked, trying to keep his voice from sounding incredulous.

"Duh. I'm showing you my superpowers."

"Superpowers?" Collin shook his head. "You used to do that all the time when we had sex."

She dropped her foot, looking totally bummed. Great. He didn't want to hurt her feelings, but what was he supposed to do? Applaud her Super Flex? He didn't want to encourage her and her wild stories. Especially not when her latest conspiracy theory had to do with the MeiyoSeraph Agency. The last thing he wanted to do was be associated with something that had the potential to screw up the Hiro Kim deal. He could get fired. Blacklisted from Hollywood forever.

"Okay, watch this!" She waited for the aisle to clear, then proceeded to do a backflip. "Ta-dah!" she cried, looking at him for approval.

He didn't know what to say. "Congrats?"

"You don't believe me." She looked exasperated. "Well," she added, "I also have Super Smell. Thomas drew that power into the comic just last night to help me find your hotel room."

Collin didn't know whether to laugh or groan. "Wait a second. You're telling me you can just give yourself new powers by drawing them in?"

"Yup. So with Super Smell . . ." She sniffed the air. "I can determine you had pizza for lunch."

"It doesn't take Super Smell to determine that. The chef must have used three cloves of garlic on every slice."

"Fine. You give me a power then." She shoved the pad of

paper in his direction. "And then I'll demonstrate it and you'll see I'm telling the truth."

"Why don't you do it yourself?"

She cringed. "We kinda determined that only an official Karma Kitty artist can draw in powers and have them work. My stick figures just weren't cutting it."

"Of course they weren't." He let out a deep sigh and flipped to a new page. "This is so stupid," he muttered under his breath. "Okay, done." He held up the paper.

"It's blank," she said.

"Invisibility." He reached out and touched her arm. "Which you don't have, I hate to tell you."

"Right. Sorry, I should have told you." Of course she had a tidy explanation for this, too. "There are limits to her powers. They're only enhancements of things a cat could do already. So, for example, I can land on my feet or flip in the air, but things like flying and invisibility won't work. Nor will shooting dollar bills from my fingers. Trust me, Thomas tried."

"How convenient."

Hailey's face was bright red. "You know what? Forget it. I don't have to prove myself to you. If you don't believe me, then that's your problem. I've got to go rescue Thomas from that bevy of ninjas before they kill him." She stomped her foot for emphasis, so hard he felt the floor tremble. Or maybe that was just his imagination. "Give me the address."

"The address?"

"To MeyioSeraph. I need to go rescue my partner."

"No way. I'm not going to have you go charging in there and getting into trouble."

"I'll be fine. I have superpowers, remember?"

Oh, he remembered all right. "Look, how about we call the police? Send them down to investigate," he suggested, trying to appease her.

"No way. By the time they get down there, it may be too late. Now give me the address."

"I'm sorry, but I'm not going to do that. There's too much at stake."

"Fine. I don't need it anyway. I'll Super Smell my way there—just like I got to your hotel room last night."

Collin let out a frustrated breath. This was going too far. It had to end. Now. "Don't you ever get tired of playing these little games, Hailey?" he asked.

"Don't you ever get tired of being an unbelieving jerk?"

She was impossible. Simply impossible. So stubborn—once she got stuck in a lie, she'd lock onto it and never back down. The alien thing on the wedding day was one thing, but this took the cake. Superpowers because of magical shoes? Come on! Did she really think he just fell off the turnip truck?

She looked at him with her wide, sad, blue eyes. "You know, this is so not how I wanted our weekend to be," she said. "I thought maybe we'd have another chance. And I really tried to act normal, just for you. But I'm not. And I'll never be. So you have a choice. You either accept that I'm cursed with weirdness and start believing what I say or walk away now and never look back."

The quaver in her voice panged at his heart. This was it; he was going to lose her all over again. Suddenly, he wanted to do whatever it took, just to stop her from walking away. Even if that meant indulging the crazy, just for a bit. He loved her too much, he realized, to let her slip away again.

"Okay, fine," he said, reaching into his pocket. "I have an address." He read the card. "It's down by the Meatpacking District; some warehouse, probably. Why don't we go down and check it out?"

He felt safe doing this because, after all, he knew exactly

what they'd find there at MeyioSeraph headquarters. Nothing. An up-and-up agency, sans ninjas—at least, sans dangerous ones—just like the one he'd been dealing with all weekend. She'd be disappointed but relieved, and Thomas would probably be back by the time they returned to the convention center.

Sure, he'd probably get in trouble with his boss for ditching his afternoon meetings, but he was golden boy today for the Kim deal and they owed him. And if he didn't go, there was no telling what Hailey might do, charging in unchaperoned.

Her face brightened at his words, tears actually slipping down her cheeks. "So you believe me?" she asked. "You really do?"

He swallowed hard, not wanting to hurt her. "Sure," he lied. "Now let's go."

CHAPTER SIX

The address turned out to be an industrial building down by the docks. Not exactly the type of place a regular agency would hang its shingle, but maybe they were just getting started. Once they got their Hiro Kim payday, they'd be able to afford nicer digs, that was for sure.

"Okay, pull over here," Collin instructed as they cruised in front of the building. "I think this is it."

The cabdriver obliged, pressing the button to stop the meter. A receipt spit out. Hailey reached for her wallet, but Collin held out a hand to stop her. "I've got it," he said.

"Maybe we should keep the cab here," she suggested. "You know, in case we have to make a quick getaway."

"You mind hanging here for a few?" Collin asked the cabbie.

The cabbie shrugged and reactivated the meter, turning up the radio.

"Okay, guess that's a yes."

"Now, Collin, I think it's best if you wait in the car," she said, glancing over at the building. "After all, you don't have superpowers."

"No way. I'm coming in." There was no chance he was letting her run off on her own when she was in such a state.

"Okay, fine. But try not to get in the way. I don't want

you to get hurt." She popped out of the cab and started toward the warehouse. He had to sprint to catch up.

They walked into the building and into a well-lit lobby that led to a reception area with cushy chairs and a receptionist behind a large desk, filing her red painted nails. Hailey stopped short, a confused look on her face. Obviously it wasn't the scene she was expecting. She glanced back at Collin. He stepped forward.

"I'm sorry to barge in here like this," he said, sidling up to the receptionist and giving her his best smile—the one that had won him so many movie contracts the last five years. "But I'm Collin Robinson from Darken Pictures and I'm interested in talking with your client, Thomas Carol."

The secretary stifled a yawn. "No one by that name is in the building," she assured Collin after glancing down at a sign-in sheet.

"I know you guys have him!" Hailey interrupted, slamming a fist against the desk. "If you touch a hair on his head, I'll—I'll . . . I'll go Karma Kitty on all your ninjas!"

The secretary raised a perfectly arched eyebrow. "I'm sure I don't know what you're talking about," she sniffed. "Ninjas? Dear, we are a talent agency."

"Look," Collin replied, trying to smooth things over, "could we at least meet Mr. Redkin? He's the one who approached me about Thomas's television rights."

"Mr. Redkin's in a meeting."

"Fine. We'll wait."

"It's likely to be a long meeting."

"Well, then, it's a good thing you've got a nice magazine selection."

"Mr. Robinson, I'm sure if you just left your phone number . . ."

Collin led Hailey by the arm and sat her down in one of

the cushy chairs. "Could you get us some water?" he asked the receptionist.

The woman huffed, but rose from her seat to oblige them. Once she was out of earshot, Collin turned to Hailey. "What the hell do you think you're doing?" he demanded.

"They've got Thomas! They could be torturing him as we speak!"

"Hailey, I think you've been reading too many comic books. Look around you. This is a legitimate, respectable talent agency. No ninjas. No evil plans. Nothing."

"I don't expect you to believe me. You never do."

He sighed, exasperated. "That's because your ideas are always so far-fetched!"

They both fell silent. Hailey gritted her teeth as she grabbed a copy of the latest *In Style* Magazine, refusing to glance over at her doubting ex. Thomas was probably inside, right now, being brainwashed by the bad guys, and they had to sit in a waiting area for some guy in a meeting who wouldn't tell her the truth anyway.

The receptionist returned, handing Hailey and Collin bottles of water. Hailey strained her eyes to try to discover what was going on down the corridor the woman had come from. If only she had gotten that invisibility power. Then she could sneak back and see if Thomas was back there.

It was then that she remembered her Super Smell. She sucked in a breath through her nose, searching through the myriad smells for something that would signal Thomas.

A moment later, she had it.

"Toxic!" she cried triumphantly, turning to Collin. "No one but Thomas would wear that cheesy Britney Spears perfume. He's here. He's definitely here."

Collin sighed. "Can you just wait, Hailey?"

But Hailey couldn't wait. Not when her friend's life was

at stake. She bounced up from the couch and pranced over
to the receptionist. "Can I go to the bathroom?" she asked.

The woman gave her a dirty look but responded, "Down
the hall, second door to the right."

Hailey avoided Collin's questioning eyes and headed
down the hall. When she got to the bathroom, she opened
the door, then closed it again without going inside. Then
she slunk down the corridor, sniffing occasionally, to find
her friend. Thomas's smell grew stronger the farther back
she walked. Hopefully he was still okay and they hadn't
tortured him too badly yet.

She weaved through empty cubicle after empty cubicle
until she came to a dead end and a door. She sniffed. This
was it! she realized. Thomas was behind that door, she was
sure of it. Heart pounding, she wrapped her hand around
the knob and tried to turn it. Locked. Damn. If only she'd
had Karma Kitty lock-picking skills drawn in.

She froze as she heard voices approaching.

"Beth says that movie producer is outside in the lobby.
Better go see what he wants."

"The nerve of the guy, coming here."

"Right? He wasn't alone, either. Had some chick with
him. Beth said she was acting crazy and babbling about the
ninjas."

"Hang on a second. She's talking about the ninjas, blaming them? She could ruin everything!"

"Don't worry, it's not likely anyone's going to believe her."

"What about the producer? Obviously she's told him."

"Well, he can't pull out of the Hiro deal now. It's signed,
sealed and delivered."

"Thank God you pushed it through in time. Who knew
the guy was going to commit hara-kiri when he came out
of his hypnosis."

"Supposedly the note said he was too shamed for selling out to Hollywood to live. Pathetic, huh? It's just a fucking comic book."

"Artists!"

"And now we're going to have to cover up his death. After all, it's not going to look good for us once it's announced."

"Right. First things first, though. Why don't you go out to the reception area and talk to Mr. Robinson? I'll let loose the ninjas, just in case we need them."

"As if that will do much good. The ninjas you hired have been nothing but trouble this whole Comic Con. They're not stealthy, they're not organized—hell, I even caught them throwing around those plastic shuriken we gave away at the booth because they had run out of real ones."

"Annoying. I knew I never should have gone with BudgetNinjas.com."

"Totally. But we should be fine. I've got at least twenty hanging out in the back room eating sushi. Even sucky ninjas can kick ass if there's enough of them."

"And next year, I suggest we go for pirates instead. After all, everyone knows pirates are way cooler than ninjas."

The voices faded. Hailey let out a breath and stepped out from behind the cubicle. What was she going to do?

Collin glanced at his watch. Hailey hadn't come back from the bathroom yet. She'd better not be poking around and get herself arrested for trespassing. And if she did, she'd better not mention his name to the cops.

A man stepped into the lobby. Collin recognized him as Mr. Redkin, the man they'd been waiting for. He rose to greet him; they shook hands.

Mr. Redkin glanced around the room, then turned to

the receptionist. "Beth, I thought you said there was a girl with him."

"Oh," Collin said, before Beth could answer. "She went to the bathroom."

Was that a flicker of worry crossing the man's face? Mr. Redkin turned to Beth again and gave her a slight nod. She nodded back and rose from her desk, heading for the back room. Great. Probably off to inform security. He was going to kill Hailey when this was all over.

"So, is something wrong, Mr. Robinson?" asked Redkin, smiling a smile that didn't quite reach his eyes.

Collin felt his face grow red. "No, no," he assured him. "It's just . . . well, my friend who's in the bathroom . . . she's the other half of the Karma Kitty property. And I happened to mention the pending deal with her partner, and she wanted more information."

"I see. And what information is she interested in learning?"

Collin wondered what they'd say if he mentioned the ninjas. Mentioned Hailey's suspicions. Probably they'd laugh him out of the office. Still, he remembered her earnest face. She seemed to really believe it. Maybe he should at least bring it up . . .

But before he could speak, a cry cut across the room. A cry he'd know anywhere.

Hailey. She was in trouble!

Collin dove toward the hall. Mr. Redkin jumped in his path, ready to stop him. But Collin was expecting this move and had his fist ready. He popped the agent in the nose and followed it with a left-handed slam to the stomach. The agent doubled over in pain. Collin pushed by him and dashed down the corridor. He could hear Redkin laughing behind him.

"Watch out for the ninjas, Mr. Robinson."

Collin stopped short at those words. Ninjas? Hailey had been right this whole time? How could he have refused to believe her? He was a fool. An idiot. And now, because of his disbelief, she was in trouble. He had to save her!

He ran down the hall, heart slamming against his chest, praying over and over again that she would be okay. He whipped around a corner and stopped dead in his tracks as he saw the ninjas with his own two eyes, saw that they hadn't just been a promo stunt at Comic Con. There had to be twenty of them filling up the narrow hallway. Armed with katanas and throwing stars and even nunchakus. Were they all after Hailey? She didn't stand a chance.

Suddenly a whirling dervish burst from the crowd, flying into the air like no normal human should be able to do without a trampoline. Hailey. She came down kicking, knocking two of the ninjas in the head. They flailed backward, a domino effect in the narrow hallway, and managed to fell at least four of their buddies.

And Hailey wasn't done—not by a long shot, from the looks of it. She gave a loud cry and flipped backward, landed in a defensive stance. Collin shook his head, unable to believe his eyes. In addition to the ninjas, she'd obviously been telling the truth about her superpowers as well.

She was Karma Kitty. No doubt about it. He had been such a fool.

The standing ninjas lunged. There were so many of them. They fell on top of her, punching and kicking. She bravely fought them off, but even with her superpowers, Collin realized she was fading fast. She didn't have the stamina to fight them all. If only she had some kind of super energy boost that came with the package.

His next thought hit him like a ten-ton truck. He could draw it! Just like Hailey had told him she had Thomas draw Super Smell in order to help her locate his hotel room; he could give Hailey the power she needed with just a quick sketch . . .

Wait—what was he thinking? He should be calling the police. Or at least aiding her in the fight. Not that he'd be able to do much against a tribe of ninjas. But anything was more worthwhile then simply picking up a pen.

Then again, they did say it was sometimes mightier than a sword.

"Why won't you believe me?" Hailey's words echoed in his ears.

He squared his shoulders. Firmed his resolve. It was stupid. Impossible. Crazy. But he had to give it a try. She was telling the truth about the rest of it; why not this, too?

He dove into a cubicle and grabbed a pad of paper, his hands trembling as he gripped the pencil. Besides the quick sketch earlier that day, it'd been a long time since he'd drawn Karma Kitty. Could he still make the character come alive on the page and provide Hailey the powers she needed? After all, she had told him only true Karma Kitty artists could make it happen.

He didn't have time to play the doubt-in-his-art-abilities game. He started sketching, giving Karma Kitty huge muscles, retractable claws, and fangs, and a more powerful club-like tail. Then he drew a speech bubble of her saying how she'd had her blood reworked to give her ten times the strength and stamina she once had. Didn't know if that would work, but it was certainly worth a try.

He finished the drawing and signed his name. His breath came hard and heavy and his heart beat a million miles an hour. This had better work. If it didn't, Hailey would be dead. But at least she would know that for once, he believed her.

* * *

Hailey battled for breath. The ninjas were on her. She couldn't hold them off anymore. She pawed and kicked, but there were too many, and even with her powers they were too strong. She was going to die. It was all over. She thought of Collin and all the missed opportunities they'd had because of a stupid misunderstanding.

But just as she was about to give up the ghost, something happened. She suddenly felt energized, power ripping through her. Her teeth elongated, cutting into her lower lip. A tail burst from her butt, writhing with strength. Her fingernails elongated to sharp claws, and muscles burst from her skinny arms. Karma Kitty had just gotten a makeover!

She glanced around. Was Thomas somehow drawing? What great timing!

She jumped to her feet, clawing at the ninjas. She whirled around, smacking them with her tail. As one lunged at her, she bit him on the arm, digging her fangs into his flesh. (Pretty gross, but desperate times and all that!) He fell back, squealing in pain.

She bit, scratched, and tail-swatted her way through the line. A few minutes later, there wasn't a single ninja standing.

She leaned forward, hands on her knees, sucking in a breath. She'd done it: She'd beaten them all. Thanks to Super Karma Kitty. Thanks to . . .

Collin stepped into view, a pad of paper in his hands. He held it up and smiled weakly. "I uh, gave you an upgrade," he said, sounding a bit sheepish. "I guess it worked?"

She stared at him, hardly believing her ears. Collin had given her the new powers? Collin had saved her life?

She ran to him, throwing herself in his arms, careful not to scratch him with her claws. He stumbled backward. "Whoa!" he cried. "Take it easy on us mere mortals. I gave you a hell of a lot of strength there, kitty cat."

"You berieved me!" she cried, covering his face with kisses. "You rearry berieved me."

He nuzzled her back, avoiding her fangs, which she had trouble speaking around. "Yes," he whispered. "And thank God I did. I'm so sorry, Hails. I've been such a fool. And, um, you should retract those fangs. You're getting ninja blood all over me."

She giggled and complied. "Come on," she said, realizing that time for cuddling could come later. "We've got to rescue Thomas. I think he's behind a locked door down here. With my new strength I should be able to break it down."

They ran to the back of the office and stopped at the door. With a well-placed kick, Hailey burst it in. A moment later, Thomas stumbled out.

"I knew you'd save me, Karma Kitty!" he cried, giving her a big hug. "You wouldn't let those big bad ninjas take me out."

"Actually, it was Collin who saved both of us," Hailey said, looking over at Collin, who was at this point blushing bright red. "He gave Karma Kitty a little upgrade." She handed him the drawing.

"Dude, that rocks. I'm so jealous. You're a wicked talented artist."

Collin's face got even redder. "Thanks," he said. "It's been a while, but . . ."

"But you did it! And you saved us all. And now we can live happily ever after!" She stood on her tiptoes to kiss Collin on the mouth. His lips were hot and hungry and she couldn't wait to get him alone. This time without ninjas to interrupt them.

Thomas rolled his eyes. "Can we get out of the lair of danger before you two go all PDA on me, please, please?"

"Oh yeah, sure. Sorry."

They headed out into the lobby, where the secretary was helping Redkin to his feet. The two glared. "Where do you think you're going?" Redkin demanded.

"Home," Hailey said. "And sorry, but Thomas won't be signing with your agency after all," she apologized. "We will, however, be calling the police on your little operation."

Redkin lunged at her, but Collin was ready for him, stepping in smoothly and clocking him upside the head. Redkin bellowed as he went down for the count. The secretary took one look at them and turned tail.

"Nice," Hailey said with a grin once she was gone. "And here I thought I was going to have to go all Karma Kitty on them."

"Nah," Collin said, grinning sheepishly. "I may not be able to take on a congregation of ninjas, but I can handle one measly executive."

Hailey kissed him. "Very brave of you," she whispered. "My hero."

Collin kissed her back, "My heroine."

"Oh, god! Please get me to a cab!" Thomas moaned. "I'd rather face more ninjas than be witness to this disgusting public display of affection.'

They laughed and exited the office. The cab was still there, the driver half-asleep and the meter running. He didn't even give Catwoman Hailey a second glance.

Thomas grabbed the door. "Get in, lovebirds. I'll get the next one. Then you can suck face all you want and my eyes will be able to stop bleeding," he instructed.

Hailey snorted. "Thanks. I think."

"Oh, and what was that shoe Web site again?" Thomas asked, almost too casually. "I need to buy myself a pair of magic slippers!"

"Hiheelia.com," Hailey said as she got into the cab. "But behave yourself, Big Kitty. After all, we've got a big deadline coming up and that takes precedence over saving the world."

"Who said anything about saving the world?" Thomas scoffed. "I'm just looking for a tiny tomcat to call my own. Big Kitty needs love too, you know. Or at least a romp in the litterbox."

Hailey rolled her eyes. "I don't want to know. I really don't."

Collin slid into the cab behind Hailey and instructed the driver to take them to his hotel. Then he turned to her. She was sliding off her boots and her Karma Kitty features were fading to her regular beautiful self. He reached over and tucked a strand of hair behind her ear. She looked over at him, her wide innocent eyes shining with love.

"You believed me," she whispered, as if she couldn't believe it herself. "You really believed me."

"Yes," he said, holding out his arm so she could cuddle into his shoulder. "I believe you. About everything. Even that damn alien abduction. But there better not be a repeat of that. Because I want you to show up on our wedding day this time around."

She smiled sleepily, wrapping an arm around his chest. She felt so good pressed against him. Vulnerable, sweet. Hard to believe it was the girl who'd just kicked the asses of a pack of ninjas.

"Don't worry," she whispered. "I doubt there will be a second season of that reality show. It was really pretty dumb."

He cocked his head. "Reality show?" he asked.

"Yeah. I tried to tell you. They abducted me for an alien reality show: *Who Wants to Live with an Earthling?*"

He stared down at her. "*Who wants to—?*" He swallowed hard. "*Who Wants to Live With an Earthling?* Are you sure?"

She lifted her head. "Of course I'm sure. I spent weeks in that spaceship."

He started to laugh. "Oh my God," he said. "That wasn't a spaceship! That was a soundstage. Some dumb-ass reality thing that never made air because they didn't get the proper waivers from guests when they kidnapped them."

Hailey stared at him. "You mean, it wasn't really aliens?"

"Nope. Just a bunch of underpaid actors dressed as cats."

"Oh my God. And to think all this time I thought . . . Wow!"

"And to think I didn't give you a chance to explain. Oh Hailey, I'm so sorry." He cuddled closer to her. All that wasted time because of a stupid misunderstanding. He couldn't believe it.

She looked up at him. "But, um, if it really was aliens, you'd still believe me, right? From now on, no matter what the weirdness, you'll accept without question that I'm telling the truth? 'Cause I'm pretty sure there's still a lot in my life that's unexplainable."

"Hailey Hills, if you agree to be my wife, I will believe you even if you say you saw Jim Morrison buying a door at Home Depot."

"Good. Because see that guy over there? I think that might be . . ."

KATHLEEN BACUS

In need of a break from her matchmaking mother and a score of hellish blind dates, to Debra Daniels the do-it-yourself boyfriend-in-a-box kit is a gift from Above.

Fiancé at Your Fingertips: Touted as the single woman's best defense against pitying looks and speculative stares, it comes with everything the single-and-slightly-desperate woman needs to convince friends, family and coworkers that she has indeed found Mr. Right. And "Lawyer Logan" is definitely that. Tall, handsome…and fictitious. Debra is going to have an absolute blast with her faux beau—until he shows up on her doorstep, acting as if he has every right to be there and in her arms.

Fiancè at Her Fingertips

ISBN 13: 978-0-505-52734-9